PRAISE FOR TIM BLAKE NELSON

"The best, funniest, most incisive depiction of Hollywood's brute illogic since *The Player*, and the only one I can think of that so perfectly situates that illogic within the greater American power structures that have deformed us all. Tim Blake Nelson's *City of Blows* is phenomenal."

—Matthew Specktor, author of *American Dream Machine*

"A travelogue of purgatory. Brutal, but minutely rendered—a chronicle of small betrayals and vicissitudes in a ruthless world. Losers, hustlers and delusional artists, all trapped in their pretense and hollow lives; making deals with the devil at the crossroads of Tinseltown."

—Guillermo del Toro

"Tim Blake Nelson's vivid characterizations in *City of Blows* so humorously, painfully and accurately depicts the savage world of Hollywood that it is too true to be satire. Anyone in show business will recognize people they know from the headlines or from their own experiences. And most poignantly, they will recognize themselves in the Hollywood playground of damaged people who desperately seek external validation. For a show-biz outsider, this powerful, and exquisitely written novel is a cautionary, existential primer on the ego-driven workings behind an entire mega-business."

—Debbie Liebling, executive producer of *PEN15* and *South Park*

"*City of Blows* reveals the 'business of show business' for what it often truly is: a desperate, bare knuckle fight to assert identity and insist that, as Arthur Miller put it, 'Attention must be paid'.... The very best novels about the darker veins under the Hollywood dream are *Day of the Locust*, *What Makes Sammy Run* and *Play It as It Lays*.... *City of Blows* goes on the shelf right next to those classic bruisers."

—Edward Norton

"Tim Blake Nelson's *City of Blows* is a biting exposé lifting the veil on the less glitzy side of the Hollywood movie-making machine. It's bitterly funny, cruelly accurate and a compelling read."

—John Turturro

"This hard-edged debut looks at the power, savvy, and ugliness that go into making movies...Nelson is a solid writer whose dialogue is smart, pacy, and pointed...An ambitious, acerbic, entertaining take on the film business."

—*Kirkus Reviews,* Starred Review

"There's something sustaining in a story that shows how beautiful people can be just as petty—just as ugly—as the rest of us."

—*The Millions*

"This novel's depictions of Hollywood machinations are of a higher caliber than those in any other literary work that's attempted to depict that world. *City of Blows* abounds in the economy and fluidity that accompanies true authority."

—*The Brooklyn Rail*

"An unflinchingly cynical take on Hollywood's machinations and the ways in which outsized egos compromise art."

—*The Washington Post*

"*City of Blows* isn't about succeeding in Hollywood by any means necessary... Instead, it's about how easy it is to fail in Hollywood, and how you can't stop the bus without brakes from careering downhill."

—*The Bulwark*

"Nelson knowingly works in the shadow of other classic Hollywood satires. But his model is less Nathanael West's *The Day of the Locust* or Michael Tolkin's *The Player* than it is Budd Schulberg's *What Makes Sammy Run?* His trio of protagonists are ambitious Jewish outsiders working angles on finding Hollywood success and risking the loss of significant parts of themselves in doing so."

—Rain Taxi Review

"Nelson could quit his day job tomorrow. And while that would be a loss to filmgoers, the literary world would gain something in this age of branding and algorithms: an unclassifiable and unsafe writer."

—National Review

SUPER HERO

A NOVEL

TIM BLAKE NELSON

un

THE UNNAMED PRESS
LOS ANGELES, CA

AN UNNAMED PRESS BOOK

Published in North America by the Unnamed Press.

www.unnamedpress.com

Unnamed Press, and the colophon, are registered trademarks of Unnamed Media LLC.

Hardcover ISBN: 978-1-961884-62-5
EBook ISBN: 978-1-961884-63-2
LCCN: 2025945476

Cover design and typeset by Jaya Nicely

Manufactured in the United States of America

Distributed by Publishers Group West

First Edition

SUPERHERO

ORIGIN STORIES

ONE

"YOU'RE LOOKING at a man who's asking for your mercy, sir."

"Mercy, Mr. Compton?"

"I'm already in my own sort of incarceration. For a decade now. I've never hurt anyone more than myself. Even my wife, whom I've disappointed every time I've relapsed. The opportunities I've squandered. What I've put people through." The tears came easily, and not because he made a living summoning them. The sheer stupidity of his actions for someone with so much to lose merited no other response.

Like most of his episodes at the time, the trouble began relatively innocently. He'd been shooting a film at a house in the Hollywood Hills just below Mulholland. In it he played a songwriter based loosely on Kris Kristofferson. He'd lost a good fifteen pounds and grown a beard, all of which gave him the countenance and physique of Jesus on the trek to Golgotha. Yet unlike the putative son of God burdened with the means of his crucifixion, he moved with languid confidence, his muscles lean and taut from the weight loss. Much of his appeal remained, however: thick hair of the lightest brown, an impeccably proportioned face with full lips, strong bones, a cleft jaw, and fathomless blue eyes. More than one publication had called him the "face of America." There was danger in him, but also an expansive friendliness. This made him both volubly knowable and deeply mysterious. A man of impossible contradictions, ascension and utter demise perpetually at hand.

The film was set in the early seventies, and the director had chosen a suitable location for its party scene: a one story house on stilts with a pool that scooped around its edge and a deck overlooking Sunset. Extras casting had outdone themselves with a surfeit of bikini-clad women. No fewer than half a dozen of these locked eyes with him when he showed up for the camera rehearsal. He did his best to avert his famously riveting gaze.

But as the morning wore on, he simply could no longer restrain impulse. He was thirty-five years old, married for four of those, but with his ascent as an actor, the opportunities to stray had increased beyond any descriptive metric. Women in astonishing numbers just didn't seem to care. They approached him in parking lots, at restaurants, in hotel lobbies. At least half a dozen had advanced a scrap of paper with a number in the presence of his wife, most recently one who looked to be Korean American and taller than him by a good inch when they were shopping at the Grove. For the most part he resisted such entreaties, but the night before he'd partied late with a friend, and he felt the day unfolding in a carefree, reckless kind of way. No matter how desperately he wanted to give up substances, life, and the opportunities it relentlessly proffered, always seemed to intervene.

"You guys are really nice to loan us your house," he said to two twenty-somethings at the diving board. They held clear plastic tumblers primed with fiberglass cubes and tea-tinted water to connote whiskey on ice.

"Yeah," said the brunette, "we were going to charge them, but we don't need the money, and I hear the studio is struggling."

"I know," offered her companion, "they just haven't been able to monetize DVDs in the way they did VHS."

"That's actually not true, but what are you, a business major?" he asked.

"Please. Going for my master's."

"An MBA?"

"Yep."

"Fuck me. Where?"

"Pepperdine."

"What, are you, like, über-conservative?"

"No, I love Malibu."

"What's not to love?"

"Don't you have a house there? I've seen you in Carbon Canyon."

"I do, as a matter of fact. I grew up out there. On weekends, anyway."

"Yeah. Your dad was an actor."

"He was."

"Peter, we need to get you mic'd," said a voice to his left. He turned to the young second AD, a clear plastic conduit coiling tightly from her ear to the walkie at her hip. "Copy that," she said into a small rectangular piece she lifted unnecessarily to her mouth, "inviting him now."

"I go where I'm most needed," he said, smiling at the two extras. "To be continued."

Seven hours later they were at a bar in Westwood the non-MBA candidate knew about near the UCLA campus, and four hours after that he'd booked a suite for them he had the MBA pay for in cash (his) at the W hotel on Hilgard, which he entered through the kitchen. When he didn't show up for call the next morning, production learned on the news he'd been found in that same suite by police and paramedics, the result of an anonymous call from a hysterical, but memorably articulate female. The film had then shut down, perhaps indefinitely, depending on the judge's decision.

A studio lawyer sat three chairs down, beyond Peter's personal lawyer and that lawyer's second chair. Another studio attorney took notes in the first row behind her compatriot. Easily two dozen reporters, some from as far away as China and Japan, where Peter enjoyed what could only be described as rabid followings, sat toward the back, along with his then-wife Margo, his family, her family, his agent, and a claque of irrational fans, many of them in tears.

"It's like I have a knife to my own wrist," he said to the theatrically impassive judge, "and all I want to do is see as much blood as possible."

"Meaning you want to die, Mr. Compton?"

"No, the opposite."

"Then I'm not understanding."

"I want to live, but I'm addicted to the blood, so I keep slicing my own veins. It's a contradiction I can't seem to escape."

"It seems to me you need to be put in a place where you aren't allowed around any knives."

"That's exactly what I'm saying."

"I still don't think I'm understanding."

"Well, treatment, Your Honor."

"Which this court has caused to happen before, to little avail."

"I understand. Yes, I keep regressing, relapsing, hurting myself. Hurting others. No one understands this more than I do."

"Clearly that's not the case."

"I would submit to you, sir, that I do. I mean, look at me."

"That's precisely what I'm doing."

"Cameras trained on me, in this jumpsuit. Half the room filled with press. People out there sharpening their knives—"

"So to speak."

"Excuse me?"

"The aforementioned metaphorical knife to your wrist . . ."

"Right. But those knives out there I don't want cutting into me. This is the end for me, sir. The bottom. You have to understand that."

"I'm going to quote you now from the last time you appeared before this bench." The judge produced the page quickly, as if he'd anticipated the need. "'I've hit rock bottom, ma'am,' is what you said to the last sentencing judge."

"I'm aware of that, sir, but surely you'll agree—"

"I really don't like your tone."

"Of course. It's only in an effort, rhetorically, perhaps clumsily, to appeal to Your Honor's intelligence. My respect for this institution, and more importantly for how the judge has conducted himself—"

"Make your point."

"Have you read Dostoyevsky, sir?"

"I'm not discussing Russian literature with you, Mr. Compton."

"If you would just allow it, because it really illustrates what I . . . The character of Dmitri in—"

"Stop speaking. Let me repeat back to you what I take to be what you'd like the court to understand. And please don't say another word until I'm done."

"Yes, sir."

"You'd like it understood that you've hit the lowest point you can possibly go. Your career is in shambles. Your reputation is that of an addict and a laughingstock, the butt of jokes on late-night television. Your wife, who sits in this courtroom, avers she'll leave you for good if you don't straighten yourself out. You despise yourself more than anyone who's not an addict could imagine. You liken the condition to that of one with a knife to an artery desperate for the spurt of his own blood, though paradoxically he wants nothing more than to live. A seemingly impossible predicament, but one treatment, finally, will solve because you're now truly at the end of the line. You've said so before, but this time it's true, which anyone should be able to see, including, of course, me. Have I summarized accurately?"

"You have, Your Honor. In fact more lucidly than I could have."

"What I perceive is something a little different. Now everyone knows you're a very clever man, so, in light of that, I'm going to elaborate a little bit on my perspective so that you can take it with you not by way of mitigation or justification, because frankly I'm required by law to do neither, but simply what I hope will be useful explanation. There are sentencing laws, but I still have what's called 'discretion,' which I'm sure you understand."

"I do, Your Honor."

"So, I offer this. I don't think you've hit rock bottom, because I've seen rock bottom. I see it frequently in this courtroom. People who truly have nothing, who've lost it all, what little they had in the first place. And that's not you. I'm talking about folks born into addiction because one or both parents were addicts, who never had a chance to begin with. People without homes or more than the set of clothes they're wearing. People so desperate for the next fix they stole from their parents, their own children. People lucky to be alive. Do you understand?"

"I do."

"And no one in the courtroom. No family. No representation other than what the state appointed. This place empty. You get the idea."

"I do, sir."

"Now because you're who you are, and with the defense teams you've been able to assemble, this court has been quite lenient with you over the years. Not once but three times now you've been put in rehabilitation facilities rather than having to serve time."

"And for that I am grateful, Your Honor."

"It hasn't worked."

"I know that, sir."

"I am therefore sentencing you to a three-year term at the state prison in Corcoran, where you will also undergo mandatory substance abuse treatment."

“Sir, please don’t do this.”

As if in the basest of television procedurals, the judge lowered his gavel with a punctuating smack, after which a murmur rippled through the court. Peter’s counsel, at $800 an hour, rose and faced him.

“Peter,” he said, “we’re going to appeal. That motherfucker let it get personal. Depriving you of your rights. Interrupting you and forcing you to listen to his *interpretation* of what you were saying instead of dignifying you with—”

“Do me a favor, Nathan, and shut the fuck up.”

Behind him Peter saw the studio lawyer rise without a glance, gather her papers, and nod toward her cohort in the row behind. They think I’m finished, he thought. When I come back from all this, and I will, it’ll be with a vengeance the likes of which this cruel world has never seen.

TWO

Eleven-year-old Max Kaiser accompanied his mother one Thursday afternoon to Ken's, the sundries shop near the tennis club to which they belonged in the suburbs of Philadelphia. While she selected her weekly magazines, a riot of primary colors on a Sparta Comics display beckoned.

It was as if he'd been propelled into some other reality, the aesthetics and laws of which transcended his own, and little could have been more propitious. At school not only was he avoided, he was paralyzed from doing anything about it. A mild form of asthma exempted him from sports, so he remained meek of frame while other boys grew the arms, legs, and chests that suggested the men they'd become. Meanwhile, everywhere he looked kids seemed to be developing strategies to succeed. Some were pretty, some were handsome, some good at sports, others at school. Others knew politics and history, gathering around a board game called Diplomacy he endeavored to enter but was ridiculed for not knowing Austria and Hungary had once been a single polity. As these five last-ditch males also constituted the runts of the class, he had no recourse but to consider his situation hopeless. What better refuge, then, than a world in which mutants, outcasts, and the irradiated became those on whom the world depended?

The comic that most intrigued him, the newest issue of which he purchased that day, was *Meteor Team*. It involved a cohort of ne'er-do-wells at a reform school who chanced upon the space rock referenced in the title, transforming each into extreme manifestations of their innermost qualities: the emotionally volatile boy became a raging Adonis; the smart girl could build computers from car parts; the sexually promiscuous lass could control others with protean seductions suited to vulnerabilities peculiar to each target; the shy, but devious, lad could become invisible. The group assembled under the guidance of a wizened, gray-bearded leader named Professor Thaddeus Klein, who not only deduced the source of their newly acquired abilities but had tasted of the meteor himself. Together they endeavored to save an ungrateful world that would have them eradicated as pernicious and deformed. What would be my strength? Max could now wonder, lofting him into fantasies of mental and physical prowess, the cohort of heroic misfits at his grateful side. No longer was he alone.

His mother allowed two purchases per week, usually *Meteor Team* and another Sparta title, along with a twenty cent pack of Fisher sunflower seeds he'd devour in a frenzy while inhabiting the new editions in the front seat of her Renault Le Car on the forty-minute drive to Ardmore where they lived. Since the latest issues accompanied him always to school, other boys, especially those around the Diplomacy game, began to notice. Looking over his shoulder, they'd question him with desperate fascination, his answers evincing an authority that not only astonished but provoked feelings he'd never encountered directed at him: admiration and its more devious extreme, envy.

Soon Max found himself the undisputed leader of a clique for what was developing as his Talmudic knowledge of a seemingly limitless narrative world. For not only did new Sparta issues materialize at Ken's each week, but subgenres, offshoots, entirely new characters, along with outlandish storylines connecting them. Yes, you could live within a single character's or group of characters' successive installments, but to think and speak intelligently, you needed to contextualize within a far greater whole. This effected, on the first night of Hanukkah in the incipient year of his obsession, his parents gifting him the book that would change his life: *The Sparta Comics Character Handbook*.

"This is a thing your mother is tolerating," his father, already on to his third Cutty Sark and soda, responded to the boy's lachrymose glee. "I'd have you reading actual books, which is what I was doing at your age. A life is something you start building early, before you even know you're doing it. And you're not laying a good foundation."

"Isn't that a little harsh, honey?" his mother asked.

"Got it. I'm the bad guy again. Me against you two."

"And have you even looked at this tome?" she asked, hefting its 527 pages. "It's almost all text."

"We'll see if he reads it," he remarked, sipping his drink. Max's mother looked away.

By the age of seventeen, Max still referenced the duct-tape-bound volume along with its yearly addenda, and his comic books numbered just under fifteen hundred. Though he'd always purchased without consideration of future value, he reckoned it had to have reached a multiple of its cost, considering he'd scoured swap meets and brick-and-mortar purveyors to complete collections of his favorite storylines. Once he began working weekends bagging groceries, and then, when old enough, behind the counter of a local record shop, he was acquiring between thirty and forty issues across the Sparta brand a month.

ϟ

He'd also begun to draw, and he astonished his parents by informing them he'd spend the summer before senior year at an arts camp in Maine to which he'd secretly applied. Were he truly to understand this nonpareil of narrative forms, he announced earnestly, he must experience it as a practitioner. Perhaps, he secretly fantasized, it would become his adult pursuit.

At camp, however, he learned quickly that he was not an artist when he beheld the skill, both innate and developed, of the others who'd been accepted. By every metric he didn't measure up: line, shading, proportion, tensility, chiaroscuro, even imagination, which he'd considered his strength. For days he wondered why he'd been admitted, finally mustering the temerity to question the head of the program.

"I was frankly waiting for this," said the plump, shaggy-haired man in his late seventies. "Come."

His name was Clifford Clark, and Max followed him into the common room of an old Colonial that housed not only the faculty but the art books each had brought for perusal and instruction. The man seized a survey of eighteenth-century British art and opened it about a third of the way through to the work of an artist named William Hogarth. He thrust the volume at Max and instructed him to turn the pages and view a succession of images.

"All I'll say is that it's eight paintings, and they go together. Go ahead. Spend all the time you need, and I'm not going to say a thing."

Each work existed within a tight horizontal with a ratio of perhaps 1:1.3, identical in proportion. In the first, titled *The Heir*, a smirking but clearly inculpated young man, his head frothed with curls, was being measured for a suit while two women to his right seemed to look on and quail. Around him, in shadow, other figures toiled variously or observed the fitting with detached interest.

In the second, titled *The Levee*, the same young man stood costumed in a new and expensive ensemble, presumably the one for which his proportions had been measured in the preceding image. An assortment of courtiers now vied for his attention. One played a harpsichord, another held a violin, another presented an enormous goblet, another a fencing sword.

In the third, *The Orgy*, our man reclined drunkenly at a table in a windowless, underground brothel among a half dozen bonneted women in varying states of dishabille. The two nearest were engaged in not only disrobing him but purloining his watch.

In the fourth, *The Arrest*, he traveled in a sedan chair that two officials had halted, it would seem, to detain him for some crime or debt.

The next four paintings depicted the dandy's continuing demise: in one he married a rich older woman, in the next he gambled away her money. He then appeared in prison and finally in what the eighth painting's title announced to be *A Madhouse*.

"Every time I go to London," the teacher informed Max, "I run straight to see these on my first day. They're in Soane's Museum, all eight. They open panels in the wall on the quarter hour and display them in order. And always I'm speechless, because I'm in the presence not only of wonderful paintings but of history, and not only that, a cultural phenomenon. Consider the story being told here. Each frame is packed with information while never announcing the fact. In that first one alone, *The Heir*, what do you see other than the young man being fitted for clothes? Don't look in the center of the work, look around it, especially to the right and above where the light falls away."

The work seemed to contain almost two paintings. On the left, a source of light, no doubt from a window, illuminated what seemed to be a spurned fiancée, pregnant and holding a ring, beside her despondent mother. To the right of them the tailor measured the young roué's upper leg. Yet all around this drama, the scene receded, and not just from an absence of light but of color and contrast as well, nearly all hues succumbing to shades of brown. But within this palette other activities were taking place, perhaps of equal significance should the viewer care to discover them. An official, most probably an accountant, filched a coin from the young man's purse. Behind him a woman on a ladder hung dark cloth for mourning. Another servant cleaned ashes from a fireplace, above which hung a portrait of perhaps a deceased patriarch counting money. In the foreground a hauntingly skeletal cat scrounged in a small chest for food.

Many paintings, of course, told multifaceted stories, but either he'd never been guided to examine one in the way Clifford Clark now urged, or few packed in as much detail as did William Hogarth, an artist of whom he'd never heard. Moreover, seven images followed, each as chockablock with information as the last, seemingly no area within any of the frames squandered in terms of the narrative they collectively told.

"They're like a novel or an opera."

"It's funny you say that," said the teacher. "Stravinsky wrote an opera, with a libretto by no less than W. H. Auden, based on these. Not nearly as good as the paintings, I'm sad to say. In every viewing, I find something new. For instance, you can't see it in this plate in an old art book, but in person it's very clear what the coat of arms is for the family. Right here"—he pointed to a spot above the door in the room in which the heir was measured by the tailor—"three vices clamped shut, and do you know what this says below? It says 'Beware.' Imagine! 'Beware' as the family crest! Or over here in this cupboard." He slid his finger to the upper right. "That's a jack and a spit in there, which is the symbol of hospitality, and it's being locked away. So it's no wonder this boy is going all out with the spending and disrepute." He slapped Max amiably on the back and chuckled heartily. "His father was a miserly tyrant who had no guests over, was completely paranoid, and starved his own cat, the old bastard! But I'll tell you something even better. Hogarth painted these over two years in the 1730s, but more importantly, he also then made engravings of them. You know what engravings are?"

"Um, like prints?"

"Not *like* prints, *precisely* prints. He published them for everyone to see, in other words. On the very day that the Engraving Copyright Act became law in England in 1734! A very big day, because it meant an artist could publish his work widely and profit from it without fear of others aping what he'd done. It also meant more people could own the works. Those comic books you carry around everywhere you go?"

"Yes?"

"Without Hogarth and his pals who helped make that law, you wouldn't have those. So if you haven't figured it out already, with the publishing of these eight paintings and the single story they tell, you have the first comic book. Don't laugh! I'm serious. You ask me why we accepted you? Not every artist is Matisse or Miró or Braque or Picasso. Not every writer is a Hemingway or a Proust. Do I think you'll become one of the greats? Who knows? You might. One can never predict when or how a person will find his or her voice. Do I think it's likely? No. And before you get all despondent, I don't think it's likely any of you will become a great artist. Sometimes I don't even know if there will ever be one again."

"What?"

"There's no room in this world anymore for a Picasso. Painting doesn't hold the cultural importance it once did. Now it's other things."

"Then why are we all here?"

"You're studying art because you want to be famous?"

"No, but I want to feel like it matters."

"Hah. Well, maybe it does, maybe it doesn't. If you're wise, which I hope you are, you're here for the *study* of it as much as the doing of it."

"Don't we learn by doing?"

"Of course. But if you can think and see like a painter or a sculptor or any kind of artist, then we'll have done our job at this silly little camp. Where you look around at the world and organize what you receive in a manner particular to you that you can share. And honestly, Max, it doesn't matter what form it takes: painting, drawing, sure. Or accounting, computing, medicine, insurance, a publisher of comics. When we looked at the drawings you sent in, we saw someone trying to call our attention to aspects of the world that you saw in a way we didn't. Was there a bit of anxiety and wobble in your lines? Sure. Some unnecessary information here and there? Absolutely. An absence of restraint where less would have meant more? Hogarth actually was no genius as a pure painter, but what he did in the larger sense was monumental. When I look at you right now at the ripe old age of seventeen, most of all I see a storyteller, which is why I wanted you to see these. And I wanted you to know that the stuff you're up to with the comics has a relevance that goes way back into some of the most important work in this tradition. These eight paintings, once they were disseminated in print form, were a sensation! And every bit as important, in what went on later in the century and particularly the next, as any work by anyone. Look at painting number seven there. *Prison*. That's a debtors' prison, and after that our rake has only the madhouse as a final stop. There are no more debtors' prisons! Hogarth had something to do with that! If you have your own artist's mind, and you keep trying to refine it, you can have influence inside a life like you can't imagine, no matter what you do, because your brain will work in ways no one else's does."

While it was happening, Max understood he might never have a more important conversation. Not only had what most interested him been valued, even placed in one of art's highest traditions, *he* had been valued.

Rather than fearing or envying the other artists at camp, he set about befriending them. He studied their work, asked them questions as to the whys and hows of it, and even, at the risk of seeming overly solicitous, aggregated fellow enthusiasts to gather nightly in the de facto library to study color plates and discuss varying aesthetic strategies with the teachers. As in middle school, he became a leader, but not just of a marginal cohort of boys hunched over an encyclopedia of superheroes and their villains, but of an entire camp. At the end of the four weeks, though he took no prizes for his work, the faculty bestowed on him the award of First Camper.

"Max Kaiser," Clifford Clark announced, "was our unanimous choice. Never before have we had an artist here more interested in the totality of what we're up to. He not only brought us all together, faculty and students alike, but he reminded us on a daily basis that when artists, each unique in his or her way, share a common goal, we're all better for it. If you can do that in life, Max, you're going to have one hell of an impact."

Back in Ardmore, his mother's summer had been far less salutary. The lights were off when he entered the house, having hoicked his bags the twenty blocks from where the commuter train had deposited him to no parental greeting.

"Mom? Dad?" he asked upon entering.

"In here," she managed from her bed, where he found her alone, a bruise embracing her left eye. "I hope you'll forgive me for not picking you up. I could've worn sunglasses, but that just seemed silly at night."

"Where is he?"

"Moved out. Or thrown out, to be more accurate."

"What happened?"

"He's been carrying on with a woman in Wynnewood."

"What?"

"You're surprised?"

He didn't answer.

"How was your summer? I stopped hearing from you."

"I'm sorry, it—"

"I took it as a good sign. Was it all you wanted it to be?"

"I can't believe you're asking me this when—"

"Just, please."

"It was amazing, Mom."

"I'm so happy for you. But I need to tell you something."

"Okay."

"This happened two nights ago."

"Him hitting you?"

"Other things too. He came home late. I'd known about the affair for a few weeks."

"How did you—"

"Just, please, let me speak. He came home chewing gum, which always made me laugh, especially when he'd been drinking. I confronted him in my usual way, but as he grew more belligerent, the hopelessness of it all just hit me in a way it never had. I'd grown to hate him, really, deeply hate him. And in the morning when he would apologize and cry and beg forgiveness, I realized

I would still hate him. It was like I'd gotten there gradually but suddenly all at once. So I told him I wanted him out. I didn't shout. I was calm about it, and the more he begged and raged, the quieter and more resolved I became. A lot of ugly things were said, mostly by him, including the old stuff about once we had you, there was less room for him, how you and I were against him and that's why he drank, why he saw other women, why his life being a shambles hurt him at his job, why that made him want to drink more, which made him even more vulnerable to cheating, and it was all my fault. I said some things in response that I probably shouldn't have."

"Like what?"

"Like asking what kind of pathetic is it for a man to resent his wife over caring for their child? That this was actually far worse than the philandering because it showed what an inconsequential, small person he was."

"That's when he hit you?"

"In our nice house a man who's a lawyer hit his college-educated wife. But there's more."

"What could possibly be more?"

"I want you to sit down."

He did.

"Max, he burned your comic book collection."

"What?"

"I know. I'm sorry."

"But how could he even—it was—"

"In your room. I know."

"But why would he—?"

"He wanted to hurt me, and probably because of what I said, it was the best way he knew how. I saved what I could."

He ran down the upstairs hall to his bed, where he found remaining from the collection's entirety six single issues in varying states of ruin: an early popular Sparta title called *Major Machina*, a lesser-known one called *Jugular* that featured a clan of vigilante vampires, plus three DC issues and a graphic novel so marred as to be nearly unrecognizable. Except for the *Major Machina*, which remained intact save for a dusting of ash, the issues were now entirely without value. He sat on the floor and bawled.

He'd spent, over the years, just shy of $1,800 amassing the collection. But more than its cost, or the profits lost in its immolation (money that would be paid back, with interest, by his father in the divorce settlement negotiated by his mother's lawyer), it was the seeming destruction by fire of his very future by his own father that so hurt Max Kaiser. With each purchase and its subsequent cataloging, he had envisioned the collection growing: through high school, college, grad school if he chose, through whatever career into which he might matriculate, into marriage and fatherhood. He'd imagined the children, whether male or female, whose interest in them he would seed and nourish, eventually bequeathing to them these physical manifestations of what had given him sole purchase in life when all had seemed hopeless.

He vowed never to speak to his father again, a promise he'd kept through college, his half decade in Los Angeles as a PA on any film that would hire him, and his fifteen years ascending the ranks of Sparta Studios, the company he now, miraculously, ran. *The Sparta Comics Character Handbook* occupied a place of prominence on his office credenza. An eighteenth-century edition of Hogarth's *A Rake's Progress* hung in order on the wall facing his desk.

He had accomplished for audiences worldwide, he often mused, what comics had done for him as a boy, what Clifford Clark exhorted him to pursue as his life's work, what had been adumbrated during those unforgettable weeks at arts camp: he'd organized, from cell after cell to moving image after moving image, a manner of seeing the world that might make sense of the mayhem of contradictions that composed life in a new century. Deride it as simplistic, silly, vacuous, the end of cinema as it had once been known, or any other rhetorical abrasion Max and his behemoth company had suffered, but what had now become known as the Sparta Comic Galaxy, with its dozens of interrelated blockbuster films, constituted a phenomenon in screened entertainment that no one, certainly not Max Kaiser, had ever considered possible.

THREE

Having been left by Margo within the first year of incarceration, Peter met Marci Levy on his third film after lockup—one in fact *about* prison in which he played the head of a drug syndicate running his empire from behind bars.

"Are we getting it right?" she asked after a perfunctory introduction. Petite and tightly built, she carried the authority of one twice her size, as if the set were hers and hers alone, though her presence involved being both representative and factotum of the lead producer.

"That's complicated," he responded.

"Why's that?"

"You could be asking for all sorts of reasons. The script? The extras?"

"Background artists. We no longer call them extras."

"Noted. But is your question aesthetically oriented: costumes, production design, that kind of thing?"

"Start with production design. Does this pass for a prison?"

"Sure, except that it all looks freshly painted. I would distress it more."

"I'll tell Joseph."

"Isn't that the director's job? To talk to the department heads?"

"Not on movies Stan produces. We're very hands-on. Anything else?"

"Wardrobe is good. I had to suggest some things to Jill about the aging on mine, but she listens, and the colors are accurate. They really pop. Prison laundry is a particular thing, and she knew that—actually researched it and is using the obscene ratio of starch to detergent. My biggest note would be that there are about twelve black people."

"We didn't want to seem to be saying that black people are always in prison."

"There are still a lot of them there."

"Yeah, but we didn't want to be one of those movies."

"Meaning what, exactly?"

"That promote the trope of blacks as criminals, especially in a film that deals with drugs."

"Got it."

"Okay, I really shouldn't be speaking to you this way since I'm supposed to be a sycophant like everyone else—who, among other things, are afraid you're going to relapse and completely sink our production—"

"Thanks for sharing that."

"—but could you possibly be more condescending?"

"Yeah, here's the thing. Actually being in prison around lowlifes such as myself, because I was a very fancy lowlife when I was sent away, you tend to dispense with a lot of the pleasantries that used to roll so easily off the tongue. You asked me a very specific question: 'Are we getting it right?'"

"I remember what I asked."

"Seventy-five percent of your extras are white. Plus, what, two Hispanics? This is like no prison I ever saw. Granted, I was only in one. I humbly advocate the converse, which is to say you unmask the inherently racist prison-industrial complex by instead offering a preponderance of brown and black inmates, which is not only powerful but accurate—well, except the prison-industrial complex part, because in my experience, most of the people behind bars, me included, were there because we deserved to be."

"I love that you think we haven't thought about this."

"You think you have, but you haven't. Not in a deep and rigorous way, anyway."

"Fuck you."

"Don't get me wrong. This is the most interesting conversation I've had in a very long time because, I'm not sure why, but I feel completely comfortable saying to you whatever comes into my mind. Also, even though you're utterly wrong on this issue and I'm completely right, you're very smart. Not to mention attractive."

"Wow. First insulting me, and now with the tacky come-on line from the eighties that could have you kicked off this set."

"Were you even born within a decade of the eighties?"

"1988, actually."

"So what was it like being hit on before you were two?"

"What's it like being the most arrogant person I've ever met?"

"I'm just glad to top any list associated with you."

"I'm spoken for."

"Yeah, we're clearly flirting, and I'm pretty certain you're too neurotically moral to do that if you were in a serious relationship. You'd have all sorts of alarms going off telling you what a horrible person you are, and ten minutes ago you'd have fled to the producers' monitor or the DIT tent."

"Trust me, you'd know if I were flirting."

"I also see you around the set. You have the walk of a single person: simultaneously content, because you're comfortable with who you are, and restless, because you know that if you end up in a relationship it'll need to be on your terms, and any guy willing to do that would ultimately bore you, so what sort of relationship would that be? Hence, you're restless."

"Wow."

"Also, I asked Stan."

"You asked my fucking boss. And he told you?"

"If you were interested in a guy, wouldn't you ask if he was seeing anyone?"

"Maybe the guy himself."

"So I'm a chickenshit and I asked Stan."

In a moment uncomfortably reminiscent of the one that led to his imprisonment, an AD approached. "Sorry, Peter, but we need you to get wired."

"Absolutely," he said, before turning back to Marci. "How can I make this easy for both of us? The ADs know where I am at every minute of every day. That's the regime you guys have set up. I'm guessing you have hidden cameras in my trailer. I sure would. If you want to grab coffee at some point off campus, get them to leave me your contact info when this is all done. If not, don't, though I will be utterly destroyed if we can't continue whatever this just was."

She didn't give him so much as a greeting for the rest of the shoot, but on his final day he received a terse card at wrap: "Dear Peter," it said, followed by a (310) number, a comma, and "Marci," the penmanship sharp, absent of curves.

⚡

They met for breakfast near her office on Wilshire in Beverly Hills.

"You think there are too many white people here?"

"I do, actually. Not that you and I are helping the situation."

They spoke until she left for a lunch she wouldn't cancel.

"It's with Stan and the head of the studio."

"About our movie?"

"About *our* movies. We're seeing if we want to keep our overhead deal."

"Stan can't handle Jack on his own?"

"I love Stan and he's been great to me, but we're not even at our car after a meeting and he's forgotten half of what was said. I take notes, which drives everyone crazy. I guarantee you in the meeting today Jack will stop me five times and say, 'Wait, Marci, Jesus, this is a lunch. What did you just write down?'"

"Have they ever tried to steal you from Stan?"

"Please. My second job out here was at Warner on the desk of an executive. A studio is like an eighteenth-century European court. Prerevolution, mind you."

"How?"

"You've got the studio head, who's obviously the king. But divine right of kings so long as the stock price remains high, meaning the movies and the merchandise and the parks make money. The control is absolute, deciding how billions of dollars get spent every year. Underneath him or her you have the heads of each division, so film and TV, merchandising and promotion, theme parks and live events if you're Disney or Universal, and underneath them are the executives. Basically this huge pyramid of striving, with everyone currying favor to advance their own agenda all leading up to that one studio head. Just think about it. The outrageous stakes for all the courtiers. And for every hundred-million-dollar film that gets made a year at a given studio, there are probably forty in some stage of development. Imagine if you had one or two of those as an executive and you're struggling for a green light. The jockeying that goes on. The backstabbing, the pointed gossip, the raiding of each other's talent. Projects with millions against them in development costs just languishing while other shit not nearly as interesting gets made because certain executives know how to flatter the right people and steal talent and play the political game. Or the entire studio's agenda gets sideswiped by the success of some film at another studio. The first Sparta movie was fucking cataclysmic. Suddenly comic book movies were all the rage—still are, obviously—and everything else was sidetracked everywhere. The executive I worked for had gone three years without a film getting shot. Coming into the office just lacerated by it day in and day out. When I got offered a promotion, I said, 'Not on your life.'"

"You and I should work together."

"Is that what this is? A business opportunity?"

"I want to fucking marry you."

"I don't blame you."

"Does that mean it's possible?"

"I'm not really in the market for a recovering addict."

"Oh, but there's so much more to me."

"Sorry, and an ex-con."

"Whom you just paid half a million bucks to be in your film."

"Not me. The studio. Why do you think Stan and I are reconsidering the overhead deal?"

⚡

That Friday he took her to Peppone in Brentwood where they sat for four hours, closing the place down over cappuccinos after dessert and, for her, a grappa.

"You're sure you don't mind?" she'd asked.

"If you wanted to do coke, I'd probably take issue. I never really liked booze. Wasn't my thing."

"What about pot?"

"As a teen like you wouldn't believe. It was my gateway drug, so it worries the fuck out of me. If I ever have children, I'll probably wig out if I catch them with it."

At the valet stand he extended his hand.

"Seriously?" she asked.

"I'm not going to have our first kiss be while we wait for our cars a hundred feet from Sunset."

"Then why don't you come over?"

She owned a two-bedroom on a tiny, manicured plot in West Hollywood. Signed prints by Chagall, Miró, and Clavé adorned the walls of her living room, which she explained away with performed nonchalance as gifts from her father, who was an art dealer. They made out for an hour on her sofa until well past any taste of liquor in her mouth. He didn't dare anything further until finally she rose, removed her shirt, and led him to the bedroom. The sex was deliberate and intense, as if they were performing in a team event. She came in an attenuated gust, shaking on top of him, before collapsing in tears.

"Marci?" he asked.

"I'm terrified," she finally answered.

"Because of my past?"

"Not just that."

"Then what?"

"If you want to know the truth, it's that I'm really into you, and that was amazing, and you're a fucking actor."

"Wow. Being an actor is now worse than having a rap sheet."

He laughed. She did too.

"It kind of is, actually. You're exactly what I don't want, and here we are. How are you feeling?"

"Grateful beyond words."

"This wasn't charity."

The more time he spent with her, the better his life got, as if the trust of such a cohesively decent soul engendered success in anyone closely associated, particularly as pertained to business opportunities. Their movie grossed $30 million its opening weekend on a thousand screens, the preponderance of white bodies among the incarcerated background artists notwithstanding. A month later he was offered a television series, coincidentally the day after he'd proposed to her on a trip to Mendocino. Would he play a smart-mouthed lawyer in a high-stakes litigation firm in Los Angeles who ruffled feathers by taking pro bono cases for the underserved? "No, I like my film career just fine." "Five hundred thousand dollars an episode with a guarantee of twenty-three." "I don't care."

"Television is changing, Peter," Marci insisted.

"This is network television."

"You came up through indies. And then the studio movies you did mostly worked, not just commercially but critically. You add prison into that, as perverse as it is, and you could do an infomercial and people would find it interesting. And do you know what kind of deal this is with them making you sign for only a year? Ride it out and you're set. You have no idea the power of television if it's the right show, the right actor, and the right time."

Two months into his second season Marci quit her job and the two formed Compton/Levy, the production company he'd not only imagined the morning of their first coffee but that now reflected the reality of his professional and artistic life: he was the talent, she ran the business. She also read every script, attended production meetings, consulted on budgets, pored over designs, wardrobe, special effects, and makeup. She helped choose not only directors but department heads. She took a producer credit, no lower than third position, on every film regardless of its provenance. If you hired Peter, you hired Marci, and unlike others in such positions, spouses or otherwise, she earned her status by helping to build her ex-con husband into a global brand.

It therefore surprised neither Peter nor Marci when Max Kaiser called personally to offer him the title role of *Major Machina* in the newest origin story for the Sparta Comic Galaxy. Based on one of the most intriguing of the Sparta serials, it told the story of Paul Kramer, an alcoholic nuclear scientist in the aftermath of the Second World War whose body was rebuilt after a failed suicide attempt that involved driving his car into the wall of a missile installation. Part machine both mentally and physically, his feats of heroism were complicated by a tendency to argue the nuances of any issue, invariably pitting utilitarianism versus individual rights and, being an American, usually coming down on the side of the latter in the struggle against a vaguely, but unmistakably, communist alien menace. This in service of a body that was both lethal and impervious. Given his scientific background, he could also augment his physique with a welter of improvements, much to the dismay of government handlers forever chasing him in an unintended arms race. Paranoid, addicted, fueled by a god complex, he was an id inside of a superego with no ego to mediate. Modern man in the modern world, at least in 1955 when the original comic was written.

But Marci considered Paul Kramer even better suited to her time than the one in which he was conceived. Yes, democracy had withstood its philosophical Cold War antithesis, but who could truly believe in it anymore? The country had now twice elected a reality star whose serial mendacity and pathological narcissism had been baked in from the start, suggesting newly exposed limits to the system's efficacy. The founders hadn't anticipated television, the internet, social media, AI. That Hollywood seemed blind to this, even willfully so, underscored the trenchancy of a character like Major Machina—machine integrated into man—all the more.

On election night in 2016, she and Peter attended a watch party hosted by the actress Claire Fisher and her showrunner husband. The couple had spent for a celebration: Dom Pérignon, balik salmon, easily a half pound of sevruga caviar, then for dinner lamb loin, coq au vin, and a vegan curry, all served on long tables fronted with red, white, and blue bunting. In the great room of a mansion once owned by Stanley Kramer, a twenty-foot screen was lowered, onto which CNN was projected, John King growing decidedly more consternated after each commercial break, as Florida, Wisconsin, and Pennsylvania fell. At 8:30, Marci escaped to a first-floor bathroom and vomited easily $300 of food and libation. In the front hall she couldn't find her shoes.

"These fucking people and their no-shoes policy. Give me a fucking break. Don't have people over! Now I'm searching through this pile like it's the display at Auschwitz."

"I've never seen you this upset," observed Peter.

"And why do you think that is?"

"Either because we elected Trump or because Hillary lost."

"How about the fact that the most qualified person, yes, *person*, ever to run for president was defeated by a man I wouldn't want cleaning my gutters. It's like the country saying we'd prefer a shit stain on the bottom of a shoe than have a woman run the country, so it's basically telling women who are educated and independent and have, God forbid, liberal ideas that are beyond, say, the Twelve Tables or fucking Leviticus that we're always going to be relegated. I mean seriously, the Germans, the British, the Israelis, the South Koreans! The South Koreans have elected a woman!"

It was a perfect truffle of disappointment. While the angriest voters, with their willful ignorance and very real problems, took over, the educated stole ludicrously expensive footwear from one another because a movie star and her producer husband didn't want any scuffs on the terrazzo floors of their Bel Air mansion.

Major Machina wasn't just good as a career apotheosis for Peter, it was right in every other respect. Paul Kramer, with his half-bionic brain and the titanium arms and legs that bested his quadriplegia, saved the world for the good of himself as much as others, a kind of latter-day Meursault in reverse, subconsciously motivated by his emotional afflictions to redeem rather than destroy. What better part could there be for Peter, a man once dubbed the "face of America" who'd then squandered it with addiction, causing so many to question America itself—the same country that had now elected Trump not once but twice? Peter's failings and redemption, like those of all stars, could be seen as universal. Him as a recovering suicidal superhero was perfect: collective unconscious at twenty-four frames per second as we grappled with the existential fragility of being at one another's throats.

"If you actually believe everything you just said to me," Peter responded after he'd read the script and she'd shared her hopes, "I'm going to reconsider this entire arrangement. Because seriously, if you can find all of that nonsense in this, where the villain is an alien called 'Jellyfish,' then I no longer trust what you see in me."

"You're going to deny this is a character you were born to play?"

"I'm going to repeat: villain called 'Jellyfish.'"

"Which you could say about the Penguin, Mole Man, Rorschach. The more outrageous the better. Do you have any idea what Max Kaiser has accomplished? These movies are a mythology the world is growing up on."

"Having me embody any mythology is an awful notion—either for me if my presence is cautionary, because I'm basically saying, 'Don't be me,' or for the culture if I'm saying, 'In spite of it all, be like me.' I do have to admit, though, that the prospect of embodying him is pretty seductive. Physically I'd have to put in some insane time and training."

"You're never going to have titanium arms and legs and synthetic muscles. I think you can give yourself a break. You don't have to drive a car into a missile installation to try and kill yourself either."

"I need to *feel* like I did, *feel* that strong. Why else do a part like this? And his mind is mathematical in ways mine isn't with the ability to augment the design and programming of his mind and body. But still, in so many ways he *is* me. The suicidal ideation, which of course was my demon for the whole first year of being in prison. The paranoia, even though he's smarter than everyone and how that actually feeds his paranoia. The need for control, but the decency beneath the fear that inspires that."

"So you'll do it?"

"It might even be fun."

Marci would be paid $1 million and take the fourth producer card for the film and all sequels, the first going to studio head Max Kaiser and the second and third to individuals of Sparta's choosing. To act in the initial film, Peter would receive $15 million, plus another $5 million to promote. For a sequel, he would be paid $20 million and $7.5 million to promote, for a second sequel, $25 and $10 million. For every $100 million the film made beyond $500 million, Peter would receive a box office bonus of $1 million. Marci and Peter would have approvals over all department heads. The studio would hire them each an assistant (meaning pay the salaries of the assistants they already had). Peter and Marci would fly privately to and from location, with a total of eight trips between them. Each would receive a $12,000-a-week living stipend and exclusive transportation, with approval over drivers, to and from set. Peter would have a triple pop-out trailer for himself, his own hair and makeup trailer, his own trailer gym (as well as a fully outfitted gym at his Atlanta residence), and a trailer for his chef. Marci would also have a single trailer. The studio would arrange for a floor to be laid within this pentagon to create an open-air plaza in which Peter's and Marci's teams could meet, work, and share meals and information.

In return the studio would get Marci's exclusivity as a producer for all of preproduction and principal photography. They would own Peter for all of principal photography plus the month prior. He would provide up to six weeks of free reshoots, a week of free sound looping, mandatory appearances at the film's North American, European, and Asian premieres, and a month of promotion that would include, but not exclusively, travel around the globe where Americans were welcome and safe, all associated junkets and appearances, and his willingness to do interviews on television and for feature stories related to the film—each of these to be vetted by a personal publicist of Peter's choosing to be compensated by the studio.

All this having been memorialized, Peter Compton became Major Machina.

FOUR

The guests in their house on Avenida Ámsterdam in the La Condesa neighborhood of Mexico City always reflected the spirit of Javier Benavidez's parents. They were socialists, both professors at Universidad Nacional Autónoma. Adults would gather at least twice weekly to drink and eat excessively, then harangue one another over art, literature, politics, economic theory, who should rule whom and how, the meaning of truth, happiness, love, and beauty.

His sister, five years older than he, engaged these luminaries as peers, and he wanted nothing more than to be like her. She would produce movies, she told her younger brother, specifically documentaries that could unmask the oppressor class and the devastation it was wreaking on equatorial peoples. By the time Javier was thirteen and she had moved into a dorm a mile from their house at Universidad La Salle, he realized she was as beautiful a soul as he would ever know. She was also the most keenly perceptive, able to unmask artifice no matter the person or circumstance. He was convinced no one would ever know him better.

For his twelfth birthday she bought him a Honeywell Pentax Spotmatic 35mm film camera with a 50mm f/1.8 lens she'd found used at a shop in the Bazar Centilia for 200 pesos. Along with it she gave him six rolls of Tri-X film, then sat him down to explain the basics of photography.

"The film is covered with an emulsion that's sensitive to light. The lens delivers that light onto the film. And you have to think of it that way. Everything is light or level of light or absence of light or reflection of light. No light? No picture. It's the same with your eye. Everything we see is just the play of light off things. Light and shadow. But shadow is absence of light or blocked light. So, it always goes back to light."

"What about color?"

"Light has all colors in it. When we see color it's because a thing we're looking at absorbs every frequency except the color we see, which then gets reflected back at us. But this film I'm giving you is black and white, so you don't have to worry about that yet."

"Okay."

"So the reflection of light off objects and surfaces and shapes comes through the lens, where it's projected onto the emulsion and stored there. We'll call that the recorded image. And the image gets determined by how you manipulate the camera, which means where you point it, where you place yourself, what you focus on, and how you expose the light onto the film. Let's start with focus. You see this ring here?"

"Yes."

"Twisting it changes the spatial relationship between the elements of glass inside the lens. In other words, it moves them closer or farther from one another. Try it."

He put the camera to his left eye and twisted the ring. The kitchen sink and the backsplash behind it blurred.

"Now turn the opposite direction."

They sharpened, then blurred once more. "Okay."

"Now the next thing you concentrate on is the frame. You're looking at the sink, right?"

"Yes."

"And it's in focus."

"Yes."

"So, you move the camera around until it's the version of the sink you want people to see. You can also move closer to it or farther away and from side to side. Anywhere you can be in relation to the sink that feels most interesting to you. It's the object that you want to make the subject of your photograph. Object becomes subject once it's seen or perceived. Just by doing that you turn it into something it wasn't before you encountered it."

He moved around the kitchen, adjusting focus as his relationship to the sink changed.

"By the way, it doesn't need to be from inside the kitchen."

He backed through one of the doorways, allowing the vertical moldings on either side to close into frame. He centered the faucet between them, splitting the image into thirds.

"Right here," he said.

She took the camera and stood where he'd stood, bending her knees to approximate his height.

"Javier, you're a natural. It's confident and formal and beautiful." Still looking into the eyepiece, she fiddled with a dial on top of the camera, then twisted a ring on the lens inside of the one he'd used to focus. He heard clicking as she did so before she handed the camera back to him. "Okay, you're ready to take your first picture. Find the frame again, focus, and shoot. Just press this button."

He did as instructed, feeling the camera spring to life with a tiny jolt and the tightest succession of clicks, like the closing of a minuscule door. It was thrilling.

"Now, come to the table."

She produced paper and pencil from the desk in his mother's study opposite the kitchen and returned to sit beside him. She smelled like honey and earth and the clove cigarettes she smoked outside the high school from which she'd graduate that spring.

"Are you ready? Because here's the most complicated part but also the most exciting." She wrote the numbers 32, 125, 200, and 400 across the top of the sheet ascending numerically left to right. "Every film has what's called an ASA, or speed, and the higher the number, the faster it is, and the faster it is, the less light it needs to register on the emulsion. With black and white there are only these four speeds readily available."

"Okay . . ."

"You're getting nervous, but don't. The more complicated it gets, the simpler it gets."

"How can that be?"

"Because you go back to the first principle I gave you, which is that it's all about the emulsion on the film registering light. Everything goes back to that. Always."

"Okay."

"So, here's the first thing you need to know about these numbers: the lower the number is, the more clear and detailed your image is going to be when it's a printed photograph, and that's because the emulsion on the film, when it reacts to the chemicals that you use to develop it, has finer grains. A picture taken at 125 ASA, a slower film, is going to have more detail than one taken with the 400 ASA film."

"Then why not just always use the lower ASA film?"

"Great question. For starters, remember what I said earlier. The slower the film, the more light you need. So think of slower film as daylight film for now and faster film as evening or nighttime film. Just keep remembering that it's all about light. Everything is light."

"I'm trying."

"Okay. Now watch this." She pressed a button next to the lens, then twisted it from the camera's body before raising it to the light. "Now, look through it." As he did she twisted the same inner ring she'd manipulated before. Again he heard clicking. "What do you see?"

"Something inside the lens is closing up."

"And now?" She twisted the ring the other way. Again clicking. "It opened back up, right?" she asked.

"All the way."

She placed the lens back into its socket and locked it into place with a deft twist. "Now, I want you to put your finger up in front of your face where you can focus on it."

He extended his hand from his eye until the raised digit sharpened into clarity. "Okay," he said.

"So, that's minimum focus for your eye, which means that's as close to something your eye can get and still be in focus. But I want you to tell me if the wall in Mom's study is in focus while your finger is in focus."

As much as he tried, he could not focus on both at the same time. "I can't."

"Okay, I'm going to show you how you can. I want you to squint as much as possible while still being able to see your finger."

"I'm doing it."

"Are both in focus?"

"I guess they are."

"That's what a lens does when it closes up like I showed you. It makes more of what you see in focus. So far so good?"

"I guess."

"All right. Now, believe it or not, I'm about to give you the final piece of all this, and then we can start putting it together. I bet that's a relief."

He gazed into her open face with its sharp dimples in each cheek, the right one slightly higher than the left to match the crookedness of her wry grin.

"Look on the top of the camera." In the center, over the base of the lens, stood a small pyramid housing. To the far right was a lever similar to the one he'd seen her crank to advance the film on her Nikon, and between the two, a small round dial. She pointed to it. "So you see these numbers?" He saw a series atop the dial from 1 to 500. He was clever at math and quickly discerned a pattern that approximated exponential doubling: 1, 2, 4, 8, 15, 30, 60, 125, 250, 500. "Those are shutter speeds. Have you learned fractions yet?"

"Of course."

"So imagine a one and a slash in front of all these numbers, and the fractions are of seconds. What does 30 mean?"

"One-thirtieth of a second?"

"Fuck, *mijo*, you're a little genius."

"Go on."

"So, this is the final piece."

"You keep saying that."

"It really is. Inside the camera is a little curtain on a spring, and based on what number you choose on this little dial, the curtain opens in front of the film to expose the emulsion to light for the time you tell it to, all the way from a whole second to one five-hundredth of a second. And again, it's all about getting enough light onto the film where it can record the image."

"So . . ." He parsed it in his head carefully before speaking. "If I want a lot to be in focus, I have to make the lens squint—"

"Yes, you close it down. It's called the 'aperture.'"

"But that means I have to have the curtain open for longer so enough light can get in to account for the squinting."

"Exactly. And to put it in exact terms, the more open your aperture, the faster your shutter speed can be, and the more closed your aperture, the slower your shutter speed has to be. Now, why do you think you would ever need a fast shutter speed?"

"If you want your picture to look dark?"

She laughed. "Yes, that could be a reason, but you're getting a little advanced now. 'Underexposure,' it's called. But imagine if you were taking a picture of me and I was just sitting here, very still."

"I could use a slow shutter speed. But if you're moving it needs to be fast."

"Exactly, or I'd be blurry. But at, say, two-fiftieth of a second, how do you get enough light onto the film so the emulsion gets the information it needs?"

"By opening the . . ."

"The aperture."

"By opening the aperture really wide, but then less is going to be in focus behind you."

"Can I tell you something?"

"What?"

"You've picked this up faster than anyone I've ever explained it to."

"But how do I know what shutter speed and aperture goes with the film? I mean, how do I get it right?"

"You use a light meter."

"Where do I get one of those?"

She laughed. "I happened to have given you a camera that has one inside it, and it'll help you balance the three factors: film speed, aperture, and shutter speed to get the right exposure for the film you've chosen. With your hands and feet and eyes and that little machine, you've got all you need."

⚡

The Spotmatic accompanied him everywhere—not just to each class at school, including gym, but excursions of any sort. In the lavatory at home he devoted two entire rolls of thirty-six exposures to documenting each object and phenomenon: his sister's toothbrush, the toilet paper, the toilet paper dispenser, the soap, a deceased cockroach, the trash can, his dick while peeing, his feces in the bowl. On walks he learned the neighborhoods of his city: Copilco, Narvarte, Juárez, San Miguel Chapultepec, and his favorite, Zona

Rosa, with its lubricious display at every hour, the whores rarely shy posing in doorways for the plaintive adolescent who fetched up before them, camera in hand.

He also became the de facto house photographer for his parents' soirees, his contact sheets a who's who of artists and thinkers, for, whether denizens of the city itself or simply passing through, the table at Avenida Ámsterdam was a necessary stop. Gabriel García Márquez was a regular, along with the Spanish poet Vicente Aleixandre, the thinker Eduardo Galeano, the journalist Carlos Payán, the artists Rufino Tamayo, Luis Arenal, and countless others. His sister taught him to despise the flash, so he didn't own one, instead pushing the 400 ASA Tri-X to 1600 and bringing candles so close to subjects' faces they feared he'd set fire to their beards. Or he'd focus lamps he'd flag on either side to avoid spill onto the walls, each lighting scheme improvised based on the contours of the particular face. Octavio Paz, whose poem "Piedra de Sol" he'd studied that same year at school, announced upon meeting Javier, by then fifteen, "This is the famous photographer who's going to take my picture for posterity!"

His parents allowed him to curtain a darkroom in the basement where he developed and printed, shimmying exposed rolls onto spools he'd load into a canister, mixing D76 developer from a powder, and printing on a Meopta Opemus enlarger discarded by a neighborhood weekly.

His sister taught him never to crop.

"It's a way of saying, 'You get the image as I composed it when I was standing there in relation to the subject. Honesty. No artifice. The image as I saw it.'"

"Thank you so much, Lucia."

"For what?"

"All of this."

"I need to get my influence in there next to Mom and Dad."

"Dad is brilliant."

"Let's see him go into Zona Rosa or some of the other neighborhoods you do and really suss out what's happening, instead of fondling his cigar and opening another bottle of Rioja with all the trophies at his table. 'You missed Neruda last night!' 'Where were you, *mijita*? Octavio and Marie-José were over! You should have heard her and your mother speaking French!'"

"I love the dinners."

"The way we've been raised is incredible. But we've got to go out and do things with it now. I mean it, Javier. If you waste all your talent and intelligence and fucking decency, I'll come to your door wherever you are and bludgeon you to death with your Pentax."

By the time he'd graduated high school, she was production managing for a national film industry in full flower that turned out not only romances and potboilers for domestic consumption, but had supported the work of Luis Buñuel, for whom she would later produce. In the meantime, their father had died of liver cancer, which won out over the lung cancer also afflicting him.

"I have nothing to complain about," he said the week before his death. "I lived a life beyond what I ever imagined possible. I had a great love that endured for decades, and she gave us four extraordinary children. I don't regret a single drink or cigar because they made it all the more sweet."

His funeral was covered generously in all the dailies. Carlos Payán made sure of it.

Without his father's salary, the family couldn't get by. His parents had spent rather than saved, living well beyond their means to keep the guests coming. Three of his grandparents were still alive, and half his mother's wages went to their upkeep, with Javier and two younger brothers still under her care. Rather than attend college, he therefore went to work, opening his own photography studio from the basement, even though he'd been accepted to art school with a scholarship.

By the age of nineteen he was making twice what his father had as a full professor, photographing weddings, quinceañeras, bar mitzvahs, anniversaries, christenings, centennials. Demand only increased the more jobs he took, Mexico City's wealthy insatiable for his singular acumen in capturing their passages at just the right moment from just the right angle. Within a year he'd taken over the entire basement, as well as his father's former study. He added two Leica Focomat 1C color enlargers to the Omega B600 that had replaced the Meopta for black and whites. The place ran day and night, with four assistants working overlapping shifts.

"So what are you gonna do?" Lucia asked. "Become Mexico City's greatest wedding photographer? Take your four hundred pesos a night from the aristocracy for the rest of your life? That's the monster I created?"

They were sharing one of the last bottles of Priorat from their father's cellar on the back patio, each in their usual seat across from each other at the long table not so much out of habit as in deference to something greater than they, something timeless. Bougainvillea poured purple blooms from the upper balconies, the vines clinging to the home's back wall of mustard stucco. A single light glowed in a third-floor window where their brother Miguel was finishing a paper. Javier thought of the hundreds of portraits he'd shot where he and his sister now sat, wondering if he'd ever publish the book his mother insisted he organize, which would mean permission from each subject or, in the cases of those deceased, their families. Florita, the tabby they fed but did not own, slinked diagonally across the patio, having disposed of half the saucer of milk his mother had left out, as she did nightly, hours before.

"You can go out there and do things with your talent, Javier. Not just in Mexico, but the fucking world. An event photographer? Not even fashion or journalism? Are you kidding me? When you decided not to go to school, I stood up for you, but not so you could do this."

"I made eighty thousand pesos last year, and I'm only twenty."

"Who gives a fuck? The pictures you take are seen by no one but the people who paid you, and even then they just sit on a shelf closed up in an album to be looked at maybe three or four times by the same dozen people before they're thrown away fifty years from now. And the money? You spend it. What next? You're going to marry some bourgeois woman and you two are going to have a house down the street and a little finca in Oaxaca? Raise kids who go to private school, have a fucking maid and two cars?"

"Sounds pretty good to me."

"You do that, you're going to wake up in fifteen years and wonder what you did with the one life you had when you see the people out there your age who are making a difference. You're going to realize you wasted it all."

"What sort of difference does a photographer make?"

"Be a Cartier-Bresson or a Robert Frank or fucking—what's that guy who was at the house two years ago? The Brazilian?"

"Salgado."

"Salgado. That guy. Or be a cinematographer."

"That's a whole world you have to break into. Besides, how'm I going to do that when I've got a business to run?"

"Come to my set tomorrow."

"I have a luncheon I'm shooting."

"What luncheon?"

"A wives of PRI thing. Echeverría is going to be there."

"Okay, now you're just pissing me off."

⚡

The following day he visited her set, having read the script the night before. In it the daughter of a wealthy family fell in love with the driver's son, who hoped to be a great artist. Not only did the girl's parents object, but the boy's parents did as well. The poor marry the poor, the rich the rich. In a rebellious frenzy, the couple eloped to wed secretly at an abbey in the mountains where a Friar Lawrence type acceded to sanctify their vows. Arriving in a rage, the father killed his son for having disrespected him, after which the new bride quickly dispatched herself. In the final shot, the driver (who, for reasons that escaped Javier, had not been arrested, let alone fired) transported his boss to the bank he owned, the two men in stony silence, while the matriarchs stood wailing behind the departing vehicle, the mother of the aspiring artist holding a canvas her son had painted of his fiancée just before their elopement.

"What did you think?" Lucia asked the following morning.

"It's the most ridiculous thing I've ever read. I love it!"

"Wait until you see how it's being shot and acted. You're never going to want to photograph another wedding in your life!"

The entire enterprise astounded him: a roiling hive of complete enthusiasts each sensitive to the interlocking responsibilities of others. Edmond, the director of photography, exercised absolute, but restrained, authority, amiably dispatching those beneath him to set flags, fixtures, and stands inside the restaurant where they would shoot the first clandestine date between the two lovers. What Javier had sought to accomplish in his portraits as a teen, manipulating the equation of exposure, film speed, and aperture to determine what was to be in focus and what blurred to abstraction, applied to the moving image even more, with the added complexity of rendering the apparatus of capturing it all invisible. In his portraits he embraced theatricality, down to having his subjects look straight into the lens. In a movie, one needed to achieve a balance of extremes: what appeared within the frame had to seem both highly subjective and incidental all at once.

"Look at it this way," Edmond explained. "I've just spent forty minutes lighting Amanda's close-up. She has beautiful eyes, which is why the finger light, which I've shaped down to almost a slit, diffused, and then softened around the edges. It accentuates a feature, but then I do all this work to hide the fact there's a light there. Not only the barn doors and the opal and the flags, but the rest of the light on her face with the Fresnels."

"Which you bounced."

"Exactly. Because direct light would be too stark. And I'm going to diffuse the bounce and dim it way down, so the eye light still focuses the frame. You see all that spill on the tables back there?"

"I was wondering about that."

"Usually you'd flag it, but I want some shapes behind her, so instead I'm gonna put up some frames." He paused to shout to his gaffer: "Rodrigo, some scrims." Within a minute grips were setting nets that reduced the background light by two-thirds. "Now look through the lens." Javier did. "I've got a seventy-five on there, which on your still camera is like an eighty-five . . . so it's compressed but not overly so. It gives you intimacy without it starting to look extreme. What we want is something secretive, because they're in the back of the restaurant, trying not to be seen, speaking softly, which you saw in the rehearsal. The seventy-five gives you access, but without the camera being too close, because the audience should feel a bit like they're allowed in, so long as they don't intrude."

In the eyepiece the stand-in, a woman of the same height and stature of the star, sat dutifully still. The bottom of the frame cut across her collarbone, leaving about two inches over her head. It was as if he were beholding a different scene, all the contributing sources of light invisible, the appeal and proportionality of it as natural and coherent as the air: a perfect heightened accident, though every aspect of it manufactured by a lattice of equipment just outside of frame.

As for the actors, Guillermo, a young star whom Javier had seen in at least four films, as well as a telenovela his mother followed, seemed to get along with everyone, while his female costar of the appealing eyes proved the most demanding person on set.

"That's because she's convinced herself she needs to be," explained Lucia. "As smart as she is, she knows that if she weren't beautiful her talent wouldn't mean a thing, which can tend to piss you off. Meanwhile, every day she gets older. It's like having cancer; you'll never escape your own demise. In five years, unless she's extremely fortunate, she'll be nothing, because the next pretty little thing will come along. Meanwhile, Guillermo? His roles only get bigger. All the way until he's sixty, maybe seventy. The movies are everything that happens in real life to the genders, but times ten. Times a hundred. That's why I produce."

The person on whom the actress focused much of her unrest was the on-set photographer.

"This asshole's there snapping away again," she announced between takes. "Can't we play a *pinche* moment?"

"Alejandro," said the AD, "why don't you wait until after, and we'll give you the actors and the set for a few minutes."

"Of course," said the slender man wearing two Nikons. "I'm so sorry, Ms. Vasquez."

"That's what you say every time, but then there you are again, right over his shoulder when we're rolling, and I can't do my fucking work. It's enough I have to worry about the extras bumping into me, and the grips banging stands on my knees, and the script girl telling me, 'No, you raised the fork on this line,' without you snapping away."

"Why didn't Raul say anything?" Javier asked his sister, referring to the film's director.

"He's terrified of Amanda, and she understood that even before we started shooting. She took the movie over in her costume fitting. I watched it happen. Raul, who studied painting when he was your age, sees everything in terms of color. So he and Marta—"

"Who's Marta?"

"The production designer. I introduced her to you this morning."

"It's so many people."

"Raul and Marta and Edmond decided on a palette for the film. Yellows and browns and greens. But most importantly, no reds, so that when the chauffeur kills his son, the blood pops on the screen."

"Wow."

"Cool, right? So the first thing Amanda asks when she goes to her first fitting is 'Why no reds?' She left the fitting without trying on a single dress. Did you see what color dress Amanda was wearing today?"

"Red."

"Fucking scarlet red. Sorry, blood red! But even with someone like Amanda around, making movies is a blast. Now listen, *mijo*, I think Alejandro quit right before lunch."

"What?"

"Do you want the job?"

"I don't know how to take pictures on a movie set."

"It's the easiest thing in the world! You don't have to light! The DP has done it for you! You shoot during the final rehearsal, and if you don't get what you need, you just ask Raul if the actors can play the scene again after the scene's been shot, and you get in there. Just stay out of Amanda's way when the camera is rolling and you'll be fine."

"I have a job. My company."

"We talked about that last night, Javier."

He appeared with the crew at 6:30 a.m. the following morning and furnished stills for the remainder of the shoot. Then for two years, delegating assignments inside his company to assistants eager to oblige, he went from film to film, not only in Mexico City but all over the country. Mostly he worked with Lucia, not because he needed to—it got to the point where every film craved his services—but because it's what the two of them most desired.

In Veracruz, where he was taking stills for a comedy about three couples at a seaside hotel, the director of photography, a septuagenarian named Hector Guriel who had the worst breath Javier had ever encountered (exacerbated by the fact it was alcohol tinged after the midday meal), fell ill. The first AC took over for the afternoon, but haplessly. Not only did he and the gaffer despise each other, but his sense of where to place the camera was counterintuitive to the point of aggression.

Lucia knocked on his door that evening. The director, carrying two thick binders, stood beside her. She presented a bottle of Rioja.

"Do you have three glasses in here, *mijo*?"

"I think so."

"And an opener?"

He produced one, and they moved to his small balcony.

"You're going to take over the camera department," she announced.

"Isn't that up to David?" he asked.

"It's what I want," answered the director with a curt smile as Lucia filled Javier's glass. "Your sister showed me your stills. They look better than my movie."

"They *are* your movie. I shot what you put in front of me."

"So now the only difference will be that your pictures will be moving."

"But you and the DP did all the lighting," responded Javier, suddenly as anxious as he was tantalized.

"Tell me something," the director said, opening the more slender of the two binders to a series of transparent sleeves that revealed eight-by-ten prints Javier had given to his sister the preceding week. He pointed to an image of the film's three couples having dinner by candlelight overlooking the Pacific. "What do you think is wrong with this picture?"

"Maybe I could have been a few paces to my left so that Maria would be less in profile."

"Nonsense. First of all, that's where the camera was, not to mention the focus puller on the other side of it. You were in the best place you could physically be. Forget the framing, which to my mind is pretty much perfect. What else?"

Javier looked to Lucia.

"This is my third film with David, *mijo*. When he wants your opinion, he means it."

"Okay," said Javier, "it's what I always think about our comedies. It's the same with American ones. The shot is overlit. You don't need to see everyone's face all the time. If you look, there are no shadows, even on the parts of the faces turned away from the candles. Where's all the light coming from? It's nighttime. And what's ridiculous is that you could have all the exposure you need in the close-ups, because the candles are all in the middle of the table and the characters are talking to each other."

"You're hired."

He spent a week doing the job to determine if he could actually run a department. Going from self-governance as a still photographer to commanding a team of camera assistants, grips, and electrics, then reporting to a director and the AD, might present untold challenges. He not only met these but relished them. On his first day off he called his team in Mexico City and offered to sell them his entire operation, provided they remove themselves from the family basement within the month.

"You're going to drop all this to be a fucking stills photographer on movies? Are you crazy?" his printer asked.

"Soy el DP ahora, pinche cabron!"

FIVE

Minute by minute and day to day, a director controlled a film in production, and when one pursued bad choices well or good choices poorly, failures tended to abound. But in this case a desultory film, or worse, a laughable one, would be pinned on Peter more than the director or anyone else. Even many of Marci Levy's friends wanted her husband to fail. Why should a movie star essentially born into success with appealing looks and a parent in the business get a second chance, when so many others not similarly advantaged were never afforded a first one? With this in mind, Marci received the news of Max Kaiser's choice for who would direct *Major Machina*.

"First of all, remember we already have Javier Benavidez to shoot, so the movie is going to look fantastic."

"Does this director know that? Javier Benavidez is notoriously temperamental."

"This guy loves Javier. But more importantly, he loves Peter. Secondly, he's been runner-up on three of our films, two of which we should have gone with him."

"Just tell me his name."

"Joel Slavkin."

"Didn't he direct *Incinerator*?"

"That was Joel Rivkin. Joel Slavkin directed *Pleasure Island.*"

"Was that any good?"

"The action sequences were phenomenal. I've spoken with his executive at Sony. Joel is a team player. They loved him."

The trajectory of the director's career did point toward success with Sparta. His movies had become exponentially more commercial, with all impulses to distinguish himself outside the studio system in conspicuous retreat. One could not, in other words, happen upon any of his recent efforts and identify it as "A Joel Slavkin Film." Scenes weren't willfully underlit or photographed from occluded angles. There were no pointlessly interminable shots moving from character to character in and out of rooms and buildings, calling attention to staging and camera work while completely obfuscating the narrative.

He also didn't upstage his stars. When Peter appeared in a film it should be known as "a Peter Compton movie." Sure, *Major Machina* would also be a Sparta title, and toward this she had no objection; let Peter cede a bit of attention to the most powerful cultural engine in the world, but never to a director, unless one of the world's auteurs, of which there were few. As for Javier Benavidez, so long as the man didn't try to take over the film, he'd be an asset, and one she and Peter could control.

For the meeting, rather than choosing a neutral spot, they invited Joel to their home, a dynamic Marci depended on in certain circumstances. In fact, when they'd bought the house, which occupied a hill's summit about a mile and a half north of Sunset in Brentwood, she'd done so with just such interviews in mind. During the first walk-through with the broker, she'd imagined sitting with coffee in the capacious living room facing southwest where light lavished the interior through floor-to-ceiling glass on two sides. To the left over the low, narrow fireplace she'd hang the Diebenkorn, and on the wall adjacent, the Motherwell, so that everywhere a supplicant looked, whether curated by Marci or God, they would encounter beauty. Just beyond the south-facing window, a Saarinen table with six matching swivel chairs would beckon from under the eaves.

"It's so nice out, do you mind if we sit outside?" she fantasized inquiring, which she did after she and Peter exchanged introductions with Joel Slavkin.

"Sure," said the director. "This place is beautiful."

"That's all Marci," Peter offered. "We call it 'the opposite of prison cell.'"

In the warm, dry air, Keith Jarrett's *Book of Ways* playing at just the right volume on the outdoor speakers, they got down to it.

"So Max says you're excited about our little superhero movie," said Marci.

"That's an understatement. I was obsessed with Sparta growing up."

"Which was Indiana, right?" asked Peter.

"Bloomington. There was a comics store near our house. I'd ride my bike there with my allowance and then sit on the curb outside drinking Mountain Dew and reading, I'm not joking, *Major Machina*."

"I was probably stoned on the beach in Malibu," said Peter. "Makes me re-think everything."

"Somehow it all worked out for you."

"Eventually. Thanks to Marci." She chose not to disagree, her eyes on Joel Slavkin's every twitch.

"So," she said, leaning forward in a bikini top covered by a short-sleeved red button-down she'd tied above the waist, "now that we've explored variations on boyhood in America, tell us how you see the movie. Is that a look book?"

The director had been lugging the binder since his arrival, not once relinquishing his grip, even outside, where it remained in his lap.

"My concept," he said, opening it on the unblemished Formica top of lime green, "is one of a time suspended between now and Cold War America. In other words, more the aesthetic of *Major Machina* when it first came out than in the early eighties when I was reading it or of course now. So no cell phones, the cars more nondescript than ultramodern, early computers, yes, but no internet. A time you can't pin down."

"Why no internet, and especially why no cell phones?" Peter asked.

"So that it sets its own terms with the audience for the world we're meaning to create. And there aren't cell phones in the comics."

"But cell phones are part of the other Sparta films, with which, obviously, *Major Machina* needs to fit. The SCG is not one planet, it's a galaxy, if Max Kaiser hasn't reminded you. So how do I then interface with the other characters? What if I work with Meteor Team or become a Disruptor?"

"What does Max think?" Marci asked.

"I didn't specifically say this to him. Or, I mean, I did, but more generally, just in terms of how we wouldn't see cell phones, which is really what I mean, not that they don't exist."

"So if they exist, why wouldn't I use one?"

Their dog, a Bouvier des Flandres, the same breed with which Marci had grown up back east, bounded to the table and arranged himself on his haunches as if he, more than any of the humans, needed to appraise the director's response.

"Sorry. This is Pierre," she said.

"Our fierce hound," added Peter, stroking the panting animal. "So why no cell phone?"

"You're Major Machina. You're wired in without needing an external device."

"So there is an internet. A second ago you said there wasn't."

"There is, just like there are cell phones, we just don't foreground them. That's why it won't be an issue with the other movies. With your cellular abilities—as in cell *phone*, not biological cells—I mean, you have those, but—"

"I get it," said Peter.

"Your cellular abilities are onboard, which basically they were in the original comic. Paul Kramer could radio airplanes, communicate with tanks on the battlefield, read AWACS transmissions when that came around. Why would he need a cell phone?"

"And what about other people?" asked Peter.

"Of course. They have them."

"See, I think he not only has a cell phone, but it's this insane one of his own making. Like with the body the government gave him, he can tinker with it, improve it. It not only communicates with people and accesses data and the web—"

"I've said I don't want to foreground the web either."

"Why do you keep using that word? 'Foreground'?"

"To foreground is to put it front and center."

"Jesus. I know what the word means."

"Look at it this way: you're one of the most compelling actors in the world. The more time Javier and I spend pointing the camera at computer screens and smart devices, the less time we're pointing it at you. The movie's called *Major Machina*. The title is an oxymoron. With the original comic, World War II had just ended, a war fought with machines as much as men. Not trench warfare, but tanks and airplanes, the bomb. A holocaust on a mass scale achieved with crystalized gas that came in canisters from chemical plants. All this in the middle of a century that began with the Industrial Revolution. And in the wake of that, the comic dared to do what the rest of the world refused to: not obsess over the dichotomy between man and machine, not *fear* dehumanization, but *embrace* it by combining the forces into one hero whose very flaws seemed to spring from the friction between opposites. He was named for those opposites: machine fused with man when people were thinking machine *versus* man. But what's even more extraordinary is that in our era the contradiction has become even more relevant, because now we're in a different sort of revolution, this one technological, obviously, where we're actually *manifesting* a version of the print comic, because we're not fighting machines, we're merging with them. What are smartphones, what is the internet, but a kind of man-made extension of our collective brains: all of human information not just accessible in the palm of a hand but more and more attached to us, individuated to us. And so much so that it's affecting our biology, so that brains—less essential for memories of simple stuff like addresses, names of people and things, how to get to places, appointment times—now can focus on other stuff, and so we are literally changing physiologically. And we know this because of brain mapping that shows synaptic activity, blood flow, cell density, you name it. I don't even know my wife's cell number. That just seems crazy to me. And biometrics! Again, think of the early *Major Machina* comics where he's constantly checking his blood levels and oxygen levels and battery power along with his organically alloyed bones and synthetic muscle and tissue. Guess what? We've got actual devices, some of them we wear, others permanently attached for people with congenital issues, that measure heart rate and numbers of steps and blood pressure and glucose levels for readouts at will or that connect right to a person's doctor. And biggest of all, the new frontier: AI. Who the fuck knows if any of our jobs will even exist anymore as creative people?"

"Yeah, I don't buy into that. Actors are unique. What, you're going to AI a guy who went to prison and is now a movie star?" said Peter.

"My point is *Major Machina* was kind of the first smartphone in the imaginations of two genius writers in 1953. Why would Paul Kramer, why would *you*, need to carry what you already are?"

It was clear to Marci that Joel Slavkin was ready to make this film. He evinced just the sort of passion, verve, and intellectual enthusiasm necessary to spend two years conceptualizing, prepping, shooting, editing, and scrutinizing visual effects, sound mixing, color grading and the rest. Day after day of utter tedium, the minority of which would be spent actually on set. He would need to accomplish this with politesse and grace under constant oversight, every decision vetted by corporate ombudsmen wary of any deviation from what they deemed central to their brand.

Directing a Sparta film constituted the perfect converse of authorship: unlimited resources, but the ceding of all meaningful control within a system built to protect itself from the aesthetic caprice of any individual.

But while Joel Slavkin fit with Sparta, his relationship with Peter posed challenges. The guy was perhaps too smart and educated, flashing knowledge and references that would irritate her husband for not knowing them. Marci had learned within months of their courtship that a deep insecurity from never having attended college only intensified as Peter had gained early stardom. While incarcerated, he therefore applied all the time once allocated to procuring drugs, women, and roles to the attainment of knowledge, helping to run the prison library where, under the guidance of a UC Davis professor, he read a broad selection of the Western canon, starting with the Bible (both the Old and New Testaments), then the Greeks, assaying not only Plato, Aristotle, and Thucydides, but Euclid somehow as well, then Augustine, Dante, Locke, Hobbes, Mill, Nietzsche, Marx, and Freud. Along with these he finished every great novel he could, with particular emphasis on the Russians, from *War and Peace* to Gogol, Solzhenitsyn, and all of Dostoyevsky, already a favorite. When the professor, as Peter's sentence neared completion, insisted he fashion a course load ex post facto representing all the material he'd assimilated to form the basis for a degree, Peter surprised him with a furious dismissal.

"Not a chance."

"Seriously? What's the downside?"

"You don't know Hollywood. I'll get, 'Wow, that's amazing,' all while they're secretly looking down on it. The thing I hated most about my job before I got locked up was the condescension, even while I understood the scripts better than anyone I ever met as an actor. Usually understood them better than the directors and producers too, where I was teaching them about the historical context or the central conflict because I'd actually done the research. No, *I'm* my degree, and without the meaningless piece of paper."

"You know what, Joel," Peter said, to Marci's astonishment, "you're making a lot of sense. But to be clear, when I said I wanted Paul Kramer to carry a phone, it was as Paul Kramer, because of course the guy lives two lives, and one of them is incognito. The phone is a prop, part of his human costume. That way no one says, 'Why doesn't Paul Kramer have a phone?' But a prop he uses, because people need to get ahold of him, even though he *is* a phone, but also much more. Ultimately he wants to belong."

"Okay, Peter. Now that's brilliant. This is the reason you're the guy to play this role. You get the dichotomy. Paul Kramer loves that he's Major Machina, but he's also burdened by it. He's human and wants the stuff humans want: love, simplicity, a nine-to-five job, stability, a family. But none of that is possible because he's too tormented. So what does he do? He saves the fucking planet. I don't want to piss you off with what I'm about to say—"

"You won't."

"But your life, the things you've been through . . . Your addiction and imprisonment were just as public as your stardom. Not to mention the disparity between how a star is treated and how a convict is. It's like two lives in the same person. And just to put your mind at ease, look at this." He opened his binder to a page toward the middle, revealing an image of Peter as Paul Kramer in his Major Machina incarnation, with an insert detail of Major Machina's eye making a phone call on a keypad internal to his augmented brain. "Here he is dialing a number, which, by the way, I've spent hours with this disciple of Ray Kurzweil who thinks this is where we're headed."

"Singularity? Yeah, just like all the hand-wringing over AI, I think that's a load of shit. The central claim, which is immortality? I mean, for one thing, machines break down, and for another, humans are motivated more by the desire to reproduce, which is its own kind of immortality, than to live forever. Every piece of literature, every conceptualization of not dying, is characterized not by happiness but by misery. Dorian Gray, Rip Van Winkle. Freud was right: what we really want to do is fuck and die."

"Can we put that in the script?" Joel asked. "That was brilliant."

"Put it anywhere you want. You're the director."

Marci could only sit back in wonder. The movie had suddenly become quite assuredly real. Joel Slavkin had flexed when challenged and could even depart with not one but two victories: the first, having secured the job; the second, having prevailed in an argument with Peter. He has no idea the ugliness with which that little win will resurface, she thought. But leave that for another day.

SIX

“I’M BEING ENTRUSTED to direct what could be a billion-dollar franchise,” Joel Slavkin said to Annie the night he was officially offered *Major Machina*. Their three kids had been put to bed upstairs, the eighteen-month-old in his crib in the nanny’s room, the four- and six-year-old daughters in their adjoining billets across the hall.

“It’s the highest you can go,” she confirmed, sipping from a petite stem of 1995 vintage port his manager had sent over that afternoon. He’d looked it up on numerous websites, and the $125 price point felt well short of appropriate for the $200,000 she would earn from the booking. She’d better amp up the holiday gift this year, he thought when pulling the cork.

“Just remember, now you have Peter Compton to deal with.”

“He doesn’t scare me.”

“Not to mention his wife. Don’t forget, she’s represented at my firm.”

“They loved me.”

“They love everybody, until they don’t. That guy needs to be worshipped. Constantly. Don’t forget that.”

“Jesus, Annie, I’ve been dreaming about this moment since I was sixteen years old in Bloomington. I mean, fucking Bloomington, and now this.”

“I love you, honey.”

“Why did you say it that way?”

“I want you to be happy. I want you to succeed.”

“Isn’t that what this is?” he asked.

She sipped her port.

⁂

They'd met when he had just finished mixing his first film. It was the week after Thanksgiving, and they found themselves standing together at the Avalon Hotel bar on Olympic. He'd arrived with his producer to celebrate, and unsurprisingly found himself abandoned when his companion ran into an old girlfriend carrying a vial of hash and a pinch hitter.

"I'm Joel," he offered, when his future wife and a friend turned to face him. Each wore a simple dress, one red, one black. Both drank white wine. The woman in red held hers expertly by its base.

"I'm Annie," she said, switching the drink to her left hand with a dexterity that struck him as strangely sensual. "And this is Arlene."

"What do you guys do?"

"We're in law school. UCLA. You?"

"I'm a writer-director."

"Anything we've seen?" asked Annie.

"I just finished my first feature. Hopefully someone will buy it. We're going to Sundance. I found out last week. Competition."

"Congratulations," said Annie. "What's your film about?"

"It's a sort of supernatural thriller."

"And you said you wrote it?"

"With a writing partner, but from my idea."

"But you directed it." Suddenly he felt as though he were on a witness stand.

"Exactly."

"What's the plot?"

"You sure you want to—?"

"I asked, didn't I?"

"Okay, so it takes place in Indiana, where I'm from. There are these crop circles that everyone thinks are being done by local kids as a prank, which is accurate, because my friends and I actually made a short when we were in middle school where we used lawnmowers and made giant circles in a field near my house to make it look like an alien landing, and people started freaking out on airplanes flying over. It made the papers and everything."

"So, this was based on you and your friends?"

"Kind of. In this movie, though, the kids turn out to be actual aliens, which you only realize in the second act, and by the end they've taken over the town. It's sort of a metaphor for our paranoia about people who are different from us."

"Sundance is a big deal."

Ever so subtly, without the woman in black seeming to mind, Annie moved closer to him, turning what had been a triangle into more of a shallow curve. She had straight blond hair, full lips painted red to match her dress but slightly outdo it, and an angular face that became less so when she smiled. Her brown eyes turned slightly up at the edges and focused noticeably while listening. In two-inch heels she reached exactly his height, meaning a difference of no more than an inch were he to step from his Blundstones and she from her pumps. Both women were lean and familiar to the sun, probably runners. Perhaps he'd even passed them when driving through Westwood in the Fiat 500 he'd bought used upon moving to Los Angeles two years prior.

"Did you make the film in Indiana?" asked the woman in black.

"This past summer, actually. It was insane being back home, but what I always dreamed of. I'd had the idea for this movie in my head for, like, ten years."

"I thought you said you wrote it with a partner," Annie pointed out.

"Wow, you really listen."

"Of course I do."

"But yeah, a screenwriter friend of mine from AFI."

"Is he here too?"

Does she need corroboration? Joel wondered. Yet her fierce need to square the facts charmed him.

"No, the fucker. He's off directing his own film now. In Malaysia. He hated standing around with someone else making all the decisions when that's what he wanted to be doing. He won't even be at Sundance."

"So this is a big moment for you."

"I mean, I could stand here and be all aw-shucks, but when we were making the film, all I could think about was premiering in Park City."

"I'm gonna go get more wine," offered the woman in black. "You guys want a refill?"

"I'm good," said Peter, checking his Dos Equis to confirm that half remained.

"No more for me," Annie assured her. Perhaps further inquest required sobriety.

"I love how you hold your glass," he said.

"It's so my hand doesn't warm the wine. A thing my mom taught me."

"Classy mom."

"That's true."

"Is she a lawyer?"

"A painter."

"And your dad?"

"Silicon Valley. A CFO."

"And what year are you at UCLA?"

"Third. Almost done."

"Are you going to stay in LA?"

"I've already got a job lined up. The firm where I interned last summer."

"So you'll be an entertainment lawyer?"

"Why else be in LA? I'm certainly not going to be a divorce lawyer."

"I guess there are a lot of those out here too."

"I want to be in the business. I grew up addicted to movies."

"You didn't want to be an actress?"

"Vulnerability to the decisions of others isn't for me."

"Are you single?"

"You should know I fit all the clichés of my future profession."

"How's that?"

"I like to argue, I have fancy tastes, and I hate losing."

"I definitely have no issues with the first and last of those. Not sure about the middle one in my present reality."

"You did get a film into Sundance."

They dated for two years before he proposed, though they both knew where it was headed within six months. He loved most of all her dogged stability, accomplished through a rigidly structured life that contained habits and needs neurotically catered to that he did nothing but admire, even when they inconvenienced him. Indeed a runner, whether they slept at his apartment or hers, no matter the hour of their having retired the night before, she was up at 6:30 for her four miles, the times of which she recorded dutifully in a notebook now kept in their kitchen drawer. She drank wine nightly, but never more than two glasses, and a two-shot macchiato each morning. Otherwise she ingested no substance that might alter her mind. She avoided refined sugar militantly, ate very little bread, and no red meat. Life to her was about winning arguments and advantaging deals for her clients. Anything that impeded this was to be shunned.

Ten years in, they had three kids. She made partner just before their third anniversary and now represented many of the top producers, directors, and writers in Los Angeles. She took to motherhood as she had the law, with a focused zeal that bordered on maniacal. They still had sex, but only on Sunday mornings instead of her run, as allocating those thirty minutes imposed least impactfully on her time. What he missed by way of caprice and warmth she made up for with undeviating fealty to all she held dear, which blessedly included him. Yes, at times he felt like a client, but with Annie there was no better relationship to have.

Major Machina would be his seventh feature, and he'd have just shy of $160 million to make it. Twenty of that would go to the lead actor (including $5 million for publicity), another seven to remaining talent, and five more to producing fees, but he'd come a long way from having $70,000 for his fourteen shooting days in Indiana a dozen years prior.

Why then, a month into soft prep for a $160 million Sparta movie, was he as unhappy professionally as he'd ever been?

"Why do you think?" asked his therapist.

"I keep thinking about Jordan."

"Go on."

"When we were at AFI, he was begging to partner with me. I was the guy. People were comparing me to Spielberg, Paul Thomas Anderson, the Coens. He skips Sundance, goes off to Malaysia to make his first feature, and that was it. Now he's got this reputation as an auteur."

"Your movies do very well."

"I haven't written my own material since my first film, and Jordan has an Oscar. He's been nominated for Best Picture twice, Best Screenplay three times. When we run into each other he just oozes condescension."

"Is this about you or him?"

"You think it's about me?"

"That's the part of it that concerns me. I don't treat Jordan Levinson."

"I mean, just that alone. I only need to say his first name and you knew who he was."

"We talk about him every week."

"Have you seen his movies?"

"Why is that important?"

"Answer the question."

"I saw *Dark Passage*."

"Which, by the way, was an idea we developed together in school, so again. And if you don't believe me, he called to make sure it was all right that he went with it. In movie textbooks a hundred years from now I won't even be in the index. Jordan will have his own chapter."

"How would you have your life be right now if you could?"

"Making my own films instead of other people's."

"*Major Machina* isn't at some level your movie?"

"Do you know why it came to me?"

"Why?"

"Because Max Kaiser and the studio, and especially Peter Compton and his wife, want a person with few of his own ideas who will let himself get pushed around."

"If I were to ask Peter Compton or his wife why you were hired, do you think they'd confirm that assessment?"

"Absolutely they would. And I even kind of won an argument with the guy in the interview—which, right there, the actor had to approve me. Little did I know how that one moment would come back to haunt me. I haven't prevailed in a dispute since, almost as if he despises me for having been right about something. You're making a face."

"At the risk of crossing a line, I sit with a lot of people in here, most of them connected to your industry, and 'director who doesn't have his own ideas' seems like an oxymoron."

"Then I'd say a) you're meeting with some very high-end directors, or other people who look at directors the way directors want to be looked at but aren't, b) the directors you're treating make films outside the studio system, probably self-financed, or c) you're mostly treating actors who think the person giving them orders must be the most powerful person on the project. I never thought I'd make more money than my lawyer wife. We used to joke about me being a kept man. Now I actually do. But those big paychecks come with an inverse quotient in terms of actual control. I make a huge amount of money to do a job no one wants."

"Again, this just doesn't jibe with reality as I understand it. Your job is what almost everyone covets."

"Then everyone is a fucking moron."

"Do you have a dog?"

"No, why?"

"I think, given the stress you're under and the hours your wife keeps, it might be a good idea."

"I'll be keeping worse hours than her once *Major Machina* really starts. Especially during prep. Then I'm going to be in Atlanta. This is a year and a half of my life, minimum."

"This dog would be with you much of the time."

"Like a therapy dog?"

"A therapy dog is a trained animal. This would simply be a dog."

"But really, a therapy dog?"

"You might need to get it licensed so it can go with you certain places."

"How is that not a therapy dog?"

"The idea is a being outside of yourself that you care for and who reciprocates in a way that reassures, brings comfort. It lives with you, you take it to the office, to the set. It'll help with the anxiety."

"This isn't anxiety. I'm unhappy. Unfulfilled. Living a life I don't want to be living."

"Whatever you want to call it, Joel, it'll help. Get the dog."

SEVEN

As the plane arced toward Hartsfield-Jackson, the flight attendant appeared.

"Anything I can get you, Mr. Compton?"

"I could use a coffee, thanks, Cheryl."

Across the aisle his assistant texted on a phone in her left hand while swiping at an iPad with her right.

"Hey, Jay, what do I have this afternoon?"

"Just the walk-through of the house."

"How long should that take?"

"I can do it if you want."

"Where is it again? Marci showed me pictures, but—"

"Edgewood. You're close to everything, but it's not in the middle of it all. And I checked out the neighbors. You'll be left alone. Not like Toronto."

"Did Marci decide when she's coming?"

"Monday."

"Make sure she gets this same crew."

"Already done."

They touched down on a far runway, taxiing alongside a Boeing 777 emblazoned with the Delta logo. He stared up at the bloated machine, thinking he could mark his entire career through the variety of air travel alone. Early on flying coach in complete anonymity, trudging past boldfaced names in first class willing himself not to stare. Then the inaugural dispensation of frontmost seats when he was flown from New York on a test deal for a network show he didn't get. Back to coach for several years. Discovering for the first time he could do blow in the bathroom at the back of the plane. Getting blown under his blanket by a single mom on the red-eye east while her four-year-old daughter slept next to them. Back in first class as he started to book films. Doing blow in the front bathroom a wall away from the cockpit. Fucking his first wife in that same bathroom. Flying coach with that wife to the premiere because the studio wouldn't pay for a plus-one, his part one scene too small. Flying coach moving back to LA when she insisted they not squander cash. More film roles, so riding regularly in first to Vancouver, Toronto, Winnipeg, and especially New Orleans—in a single year three films in the Crescent City. Suddenly realizing the searching eyes of actors were finding him on their way to the back. For four years always up front, more than occasionally recognized but afforded privacy. Lots of blow in the front bathroom, once with a flight attendant he screwed so hard from behind he thought it might be mistaken for turbulence.

His third relapse and arrest. The years in prison, neither first class nor coach. Out of prison, divorced, and no out-of-state work while he endured parole and started dating Marci. Plenty of cars: first driving on his own to see his PO, go to meetings, get tested, visit his agent, meet directors, most of whom he failed to persuade he wouldn't relapse. Two believed him, and their movies were good, both locally shot. Suddenly once more in demand. Back-to-back films outside of California as soon as he could leave the state, and again flying first class, but now sober.

Then the television show and a level of fame he'd never imagined possible. Even with an escort he couldn't walk ten feet in an airport without being hassled. "I'm your biggest fan." "My mom is your biggest fan." "My sister won't believe I met you." "I'm a lawyer too." "My sister's a lawyer." "My dad's a lawyer." "I'm married to a lawyer." "Will you sign this for my daughter?" "Will you sign this for my dad?" "My brother-in-law?" "My son?" "My granddad?" "Make it out to Ellen." "To Jill." "To Joe." "To Wilbur." "To my cat." "To my goldfish" (yes, that had happened). "Sign my shirt." "My hat." "My pants." "My tits."

And the pictures. It began within seconds of exiting his car on the departure side and didn't abate until curbside at arrival, the final anodyne smile while standing outside the SUV just before he closed its door. What, he perpetually wondered, could be the value of pixelated evidence someone had met him for long enough to extract a smartphone from a purse or pocket and stand idiotically with him to snap a selfie? The interactions rarely varied: a quick acknowledgment of who he was via some perfunctory assurance of veneration or vacuous affinity followed by "Can I get a picture?" at which point he stopped while they fumbled with the device to put it in reverse mode, and then the two of them would stand staring at their image while the assailant jammed his or her thumb at the icon of a button. To decline provoked not only bafflement but frequently rage, especially when fathers or husbands were involved. "Are you serious, dude? All she wants is a picture. To me you shit and piss just like the rest of us. But she fuckin' loves you, and you just ruined that by being a selfish asshole." On it would go until he was out of earshot—that is, if he weren't followed. Thrice airport security had become involved, albeit in two of those cases his own belligerence catalyzed aggression.

On planes he was trapped. "Are you and Jane going to have an affair?" "Are you and Li going to get together?" "What's it like being the sexiest man in America?" "How do you learn all those lines?" "Were you ever a lawyer in real life?" "How do I get into acting?" "How do I get into television?" "What's your favorite part of a woman's body?" "What's your favorite part of a man's body?" And his favorite, asked by a gentleman of seventy with a honeyed twang: "What's it like to be loved by every soul you meet?" No more sex in bathrooms aloft, as he was now constantly watched. A curtain drawn to separate the seats from the galley might have helped, especially if the dalliance were to involve a flight attendant, but the pursuit had lost luster. Airplane lavatories provided little room and reverse-aphrodisiac odors. He took to declining all offers, despite the erstwhile frisson of sex at 350 miles per hour thirty thousand feet above the planet. His predilection for excess notwithstanding, Marci had become too important. Their marriage needed to last. Not once had he betrayed her.

He now flew only privately, even when travel didn't involve work. No ticket counter, no lines at security and the gate, not even the inconvenience of a crowded first-class lounge. On the plane a flight attendant for you and you only, beverages and food stocked to your specifications, cars that drove you to and from the plane with you never having to touch a piece of luggage. And above all, not encountering a single person you didn't know who wasn't there entirely for your needs.

⚡

George, the Atlanta Teamster hired at his request, met them planeside in an electric Porsche Cayenne. The vehicle represented acquiescence to Marci, who had converted their entire fleet to EVs in 2019. As for brand and color, he loathed the ostentation of oversized American SUVs, electric or not, and always required silver on location for increased anonymity.

"Those two bags should go in the back seat," he heard Jay Lynne instruct the copilot as Peter shook his driver's hand.

"Hey, George," he said. "You see that Falcons game?"

"What kind of question is that? Penix was twenty-three for thirty-seven. Two forty-nine and two TDs. And against the Ravens defense."

"Last I heard, Lewis and Suggs retired."

"Penix is the most underrated quarterback in the league." George had been a linebacker in the NFL for eight years, mostly with the Chargers, but also the Eagles under Buddy Ryan.

"Let me ask you something," Peter said as he settled in the back seat and the car began to move. "In a cover two defense, if you're the Mike linebacker, are you essentially a spy with a dual-threat quarterback?"

"Back in the eighties and nineties, no. The Mike would be big and strong, but slow. They were run stoppers. That's where the Tampa Two came from where you could roll the safety up and put another tackler in the box against a Michael Vick or a Randall Cunningham, those types of guys."

"Who would be the spy then?"

"That's either that safety you bring up or another linebacker in a three-four. And he becomes a hybrid. Every team calls it something different. Back then it was the 'rover' or the 'dog.' Now the 'cheetah.' And he shifts all over the place. That's that guy, Venables, I think, came up with 'cheetah' when he was the coordinator at Clemson. But yeah, at Auburn, where I played, it was just the 'Mike,' and you were pretty much it between the line and the secondary on a run play whether it was the quarterback or not. If they came through the A gap or the B gap, that was on you at the second level."

"Unless it was a blitz."

"That's right."

I can talk to anyone about anything, thought Peter.

"How's Marci?" asked the driver as he plotted their route on his touchscreen. "I hear she's headed down in a few days. She staying for the shoot?"

"What do you mean? She's one of the producers."

"Of course she is."

"And don't tell her you hear she's staying awhile like she's just here to visit. I won't hear the end of it."

When they pulled up to the house, he couldn't resist a headshaking grin. One couldn't glimpse a single brick or window from the street, from which a long, winding driveway pierced a thick stand of eucalyptus trees. He would also be ten minutes from his favorite Italian restaurant in the city. The home itself, a modern two-story with immense panes of glass looking onto a lawn befitting a country club, had a pool and two outbuildings beautifully proportioned to the main structure. To enter the front door, one traversed a succession of cut marble squares lifting from a koi pond scattered with lily pads.

"How the fuck does Marci find these places?" he asked Jay Lynne.

"Trust me, I put about twenty options in front of her before this one."

He pointed to the two extant buildings. "Have you chosen your bungalow?"

"Based on the photographs, I think the one farthest from the pool. It had the better kitchen. Ace will go in the other one," she said, referring to Peter's chef, "since he'll get the kitchen in the main house."

"Have at it."

"Let's get you unpacked first."

The master suite took up the entire second floor, with windows on three sides looking out across Freedom Park toward the Carter Library and Museum. He chose the smaller of two capacious walk-in closets outfitted with dozens of wooden hangers and three banks of drawers with slender nickel handles running parallel to the carpeted floor.

"I think this closet might even be bigger than mine at home."

"That's because it's empty. When I put your clothes up you'll see it's a little over half the size."

"Now you're just embarrassing me. Which bag did you pack my gym clothes in? I'm gonna work out."

"The smallest of the three. And the shoes are in the compartment along the bottom."

He dragged the soft trunk into the closet and closed its two doors. After choosing a T-shirt and shorts, he stripped naked. All I'd have to do is open one of those doors for a gag, and she could sue us for all we have. He shook the thought and regarded himself in the mirror. At fifty-one he looked better than ever. His obliques stretched in defined ridges across his stomach with Cartesian symmetry, and above them his pectorals pulled his skin into broad plates. His penis, which had been described by a plurality of partners, including his wife, as one of the larger and more well shaped they'd encountered, drooped poetically beneath a tuft of trimmed hair crowned by the triangle of his inguinal ligaments. I'm like the fucking *David*, he mused, turning to inspect his pert ass. He slipped the trunks over his dick, manipulating it with his left hand to hang comfortably inside the mesh of the running shorts. Exiting the closet, he found Jay Lynne perched on the bed scrolling through emails.

"Joel Slavkin wants to have dinner tonight. What should I say?"

"I guess I should."

"Arrabbiata?"

"Might as well dive right in."

"I'll call Giovanni. They're saying eight thirty. He has a tech scout."

"Eight thirty is not happening if he wants me in shape to play this part. Make it for seven and act like you never read eight thirty. If he pushes back we tell him it doesn't work. How's that for a shot across his bow?"

"You're the boss."

In the kitchen he opened the Sub-Zero refrigerator for the bottled rainwater he knew would be there, then made his way with a jaunt in his step to the basement that a week before had been converted to a complete gym per Jay Lynne's precise instructions as to layout and brand. He was officially on the ground. Production could now truly begin.

MAJOR MACHINA

EIGHT

Peter Compton's refusal to accommodate his tech scout could only be construed as a claim to status Joel needed to rebuke. Ten minutes' tardiness, along with an underwhelming apology referencing directorial responsibilities, would suffice. Let the star sit alone while diners gawked.

He eased the Cadillac XT4 rented by production into a parking space across the street, his dog not with him, as he'd had his assistant deliver her to the pet-friendly apartment he was renting in midtown. His therapist had been right. The animal gave him comfort.

He scanned the eatery, known as the top Italian restaurant in Atlanta, but couldn't locate Peter in the grid of tables crowded with happily, voluble diners.

"Are you Mr. Compton's guest?" the bearded host queried.

"Yes."

"We have you at the chef's table."

He was led through a crowded bar where a superfluity of women, their backs mostly exposed in an array of cocktail wear, chatted with beefy men in blue and white oxford shirts, their pressed blazers draped on arms or the backs of high chairs. Most of the men, some black, some white, drank beer or bourbon or both, the women martinis, sidecars, white wine, Manhattans.

"Right through here, sir," said the host.

He heard Peter before he saw him, laughing performatively at a table for six lodged in a nook jutting into the back wall of the kitchen and surrounded on three sides by casement windows. A triumvirate of slim candles stood in silver holders spread evenly lengthwise down the center of five boards milled at least a century ago, no doubt for a farmhouse in the area. Peter sat in the booth farthest. A man who was clearly the chef stood over him with the glistening carcass of one of the strangest sea creatures Joel had ever beheld.

"You're just in time," Peter announced. "This is my director," he then said to the chef with something of an edge. "He's late because he's busy getting the production ready for yours truly, and far be it for me to interfere with that."

"Pleasure to meet you. I'm Giovanni," said the man in an accent unmistakably Southern.

"This is his place," said Peter.

"It's gorgeous," Joel admitted. "What a kitchen."

"Yeah, that's one of the requirements I had when I opened. Space, and worker friendly. I learned that when I was studying in Italy and then especially in New York, where the kitchens were cramped like you wouldn't believe. And I wanted a chef's table."

"I thought you put this in for me," said Peter, perhaps half meaning it.

"Had I known you at the time, I probably would have."

"What's a chef's table?" asked Joel.

"Just what it sounds like. A spot in the kitchen either for us after hours or my personal guests. When he's in town I take to calling it Peter's table. He can have it whenever he wants. Here. Check this out." He reached to a ledge along the grid of windows behind Peter and produced a copy of *Gourmet* magazine, on the cover of which appeared Giovanni in the booth where Peter now sat, with Peter and Marci opposite, the table resplendent with pastas, meats, and a charcuterie board. The headline read: "Giovanni Pierson Brings Southern Italy Back Home: At the Chef's Table with the Comptons."

"That was last year," announced Peter. "They flew me and Marci down for the shoot on the Condé Nast jet. For one night. It was fucking ridiculous. So over-the-top."

"And we haven't had an empty table since," said Giovanni. "Have a seat!" He gestured to where another setting faced Peter with utensils for at least four courses. "I was just showing Peter what you guys have in store. Off the menu. Just for you. It was line caught this morning in Florida, and my guy sent it up with the day's red snapper."

"What is it?" queried Joel, already nauseated by the sycophancy. His strategy for marooning his star had failed utterly. In fact, appearing late with Peter in the throes of attention from the owner-chef had situated the director for denigration, not the other way around. It was as if the actor had been ten steps ahead of him.

"This is a hog snapper," said Giovanni of the fish that glistened as if just removed from the sea. Its mouth extended like a pig's snout, and above its eyes rose a cockscomb of yellow spines descending toward its dorsal. It looked to be just under two feet long from nose to tail but was tall in the middle with stripes of burgundy-tinted brown from just over the mouth down the pink body. Accents of yellow played along the tail and pectoral fins.

"If you ever see this on a menu," Giovanni commanded with a gravity bordering on ridiculous, "order it, because outside of Florida, no one ever has them."

"How are you gonna prepare it?" Peter asked.

"Simple, simple, simple. Salt, pepper, and garlic, pan-fried in grapeseed oil. Onions cooked in the pan just after, olive oil drizzled on the top with a touch of local lemon, and right to the table. This is one where you don't get in the way. Save all the stiff-pinkie shit for the rest of the meal. Trust me, you guys are gonna leave happy."

"This is why I did two hours on the circuit today," offered Peter. "Otherwise my director here is gonna have a coronary."

"Don't worry about me," said Joel, lifting his hands defensively.

"Both of you, please! Peter's assistant sent me a list from the nutritionist weeks ago. I'm hip to the rules. That's why the fish. I'm gonna take care of you guys."

"I never doubted it," said Joel.

"All right, back to it. See you both in a bit. Nice meeting you—what was it, Joe?"

"Joel."

"Joel!"

"So," Peter said when Giovanni had left, "you get it all sorted out today? Everything good?"

"I wouldn't say it's all sorted out, but thankfully we have a week and a half. The locations are fantastic."

"I've been seeing the pictures. I have some questions about the bank exterior."

"Agreed. We'll shoot that in New York. A lot of the establishing shots up there, in fact. Two days with a drone and you won't know the difference."

"Yeah, I hate drone shots."

Here we go, thought Joel.

"Every time you see one in a film now, it's its own thing. 'Okay, here comes the drone shot,' I always hear myself say. Like the helicopter shot used to be: 'Oh, wow, they were able to get a helicopter.' I love in *The Shining* where Kubrick, who was obsessed with every little detail, actually left a helicopter shot in the beginning of his movie even though—"

"There was the shadow."

"Stanley Kubrick! Of course, now they've erased it digitally. Anyway, do your drone shots. Go crazy."

"Thanks," Joel said, immediately regretting the implication the actor had approval over such decisions. "Plus, Peter, you'll be back in California by then. We're shooting all that after we wrap down here."

"Why not just get a second unit to go up to New York while we're shooting? Then you can edit it all in with your exteriors here and make sure they work."

"Yeah, we're considering that," said Joel.

"Gets you home sooner, and we don't have to spend on hotel and per diem. I'm sure there are outfits up there that specialize in second unit. And they've got the rebate. I'll get Marci to talk to the studio. You shouldn't have to go up there. We put some guys in front of you, you make your pick, and boom."

Joel's anger began to well. Not only the tone, oozing with sugary largesse, but the fact that Declan Morris, the line producer, had voiced the same sentiments four hours earlier. None of them had the generosity to infer that Joel intended New York to be a reward. They were scheduled to wrap in Atlanta on a Wednesday, giving him a day to pack, after which he'd fly to meet Annie on Friday and they'd have a weekend at the Lowell, her favorite hotel in Manhattan. They'd eat at Fleming that night. Saturday they'd wander galleries in Chelsea, perhaps buy a painting on impulse, maybe purchase her some jewelry at Ted Muehling, eat at Fleming or Gabriel's, see a play. Monday morning she'd fly out early after a 5:00 a.m. run, and he'd be ready for two days of shooting, with a couple of nights on his own to meet friends. And all of it, save for the play and the art, charged to the studio. Somehow Peter Compton knew this and wanted it taken from him. Only certain people should sit at the chef's table. I have to change the subject, Joel thought, or I'm going to reach over and stab him in the face with my butter knife.

"So, how's your place here?" Joel asked.

"We've got to have everyone over once Marci's here. The owner is some billionaire lawyer. Made his dough against the tobacco companies and now lives half the year in Argentina breeding Paso Fino horses. Great kitchen. Great gym. Has everything I need. I love shooting in Atlanta. People ask if we support the boycott, but fuck that. If you want to have influence, stay engaged. Come down here and make a pro-choice movie using Georgia tax dollars. That's how you stick it to them."

"What's the studio's position?"

"Are you kidding me? Max Kaiser would shoot in North Korea or fucking Xinjiang if you gave him a rebate."

"Xinjiang?"

"The Uighurs? Repressed Muslim group in China. Keep up with me here, Joel."

"Oh, right." Now I want to murder him. Does the guy ever stop flashing his intelligence? It was in every article: "Peter Compton Read More in Prison Than You Will in a Lifetime" announced one subheading he'd encountered, too repulsed to assay the two-thousand-word profile.

"I mean, seriously," continued the actor, "thirty cents on the dollar? For a nine-figure Sparta movie? We come in here, and we just rape this state. All you hear in LA is how we should help the needy. Meanwhile, if you add it up, Georgia is kicking in about fifty grand alone to help put me up in this lawyer's spread for four months. Imagine where else that money could go."

"Well, I guess the idea is—"

"You don't have to explain it to me, Joel. The Keynesian multiplier. For every buck spent, you get a buck fifty back. But does that fifty grand on a fancy house for a movie star really give seventy-five grand back to the community? The owner is spending the money in Patagonia, not here. Who else? The yard-man? He's gonna keep up the grounds anyway. The housekeeper? Sure, but the studio's paying her minimum wage, and she's probably an illegal anyway—at least until Trump finds her—because they pay through the broker and not her directly, so that money goes back to Central America untaxed. Ace, the chef I brought from LA? He doesn't come with the house or even the city, and he buys his ingredients at Whole Foods, which, last I heard, is not a Georgia company, so sure, they spend here to build the store, plus they buy and hire local, so fine, I'll give you the groceries, but are they specific to that fancy a residence? I think not. Giovanni?" He gestured to the chef at the Garland twelve-burner twenty feet away. "And his staff? I'd be eating here if I were staying in a hotel. So you tell me."

"I guess you have a point."

"But fuck that." He changed his tone. "I saw the schedule on the plane."

"Okay."

"You really want to start on the stage?"

"We'll be ready. Besides, that's always—"

"I'm sure we'll be ready. I mean, obviously. You've had what? Four months?"

"More like five. But I also like to ease the crew in. Get the kinks out with an easy couple of weeks before the hard stuff, especially on a tentpole movie like this."

"Yeah, I know the philosophy."

"You don't agree with it?"

"It's not that I don't agree, it's just a missed opportunity."

"How's that?"

"To see what everyone's made of."

"This is going to be a tough shoot regardless, Peter. Tons of night exteriors on big, dressed locations with a lot of background. Plus water elements. We'll know what everyone's made of by the end of it."

"When it's too late, in other words. It's better to get a sense up front, so we figure out where the studio needs to give us more support. Besides, you're thinking in terms of crew. Some of those scenes you have in that first week are pretty dialogue heavy."

"Don't you want those out of the way?"

"Let's start on the lake."

"We go there the fourth week."

"Why not flip them?"

"That would be a terrible idea." He regretted the adjective the moment it left his mouth.

The actor wobbled his head as if to dislodge the offending modifier. "Give me a second." More cranial shaking. "Nope, you're going to have to help here by explaining what you just said, otherwise I'm gonna need medical attention."

"I shouldn't have said 'terrible idea.'"

"But you did."

"First of all, it's September in Georgia."

"Yeah?"

"It's still going to be extremely hot and very buggy, especially in the late afternoon when we'll be murdered by mosquitoes."

"So, you're going to make a scheduling decision for a hundred-and-sixty-million-dollar movie based not on your actors and what's best for the film, but on a preponderance of insects that can be eradicated by bug repellent, and how the temperature might be uncomfortable for the crew?"

"Plus, you haven't been to that location, Peter."

"I've seen pictures."

"It's a production nightmare. Base camp is over five miles from set, and then there's a drop-off with the crew vans about a hundred yards from the shoreline, so cast and equipment on Gators back and forth. Pre-rigging alone will take two days."

"Grip and electric will thank you. Instead of stretching the department thin while we're working some other location, or worse, killing their weekend, they get it all done during prep."

"Peter, with all due respect, that's just not how it works. We've been building on the stages already for weeks. There's been no work done at the lake at all."

"There's no build at the lake."

"We have the water tower, plus moving condors in, and all the rigging. Platforms out into the water for the crane, plus grading the shoreline, putting two roads in to get people and equipment in and out."

"All of which can be done in a week. I mean, seriously, you just listed moving in condors. Since when is that considered a build?"

He found himself uncertain how to proceed, the notion of reorienting the schedule in such a wholly unproductive manner simply too ludicrous to consider. He might as well be trying to describe an elephant to a seahorse. He decided to pivot. "Plus, we won't have Ron."

"Fuck Ron. He's got to be down here for the scene at the missile installation, which is when?"

"The beginning of the third week."

"When's he scheduled to get here?"

"I'd have to ask the ADs. Four or five days before. He hasn't been fit yet."

"He'll be happy to come in early. I'm sure he's staying at the Four Seasons. Didn't he just get divorced?"

"I think so."

"And if he can't, we replace him. It's a great role. I can think of ten guys who'd be amazing. Maybe even better. The last thing we need to do is make decisions based on Ron Huston's schedule. He's lucky to have the part."

"He's been nominated for an Oscar."

"So he's told me. And all of my friends, enemies, acquaintances, and fellow humans. And I mean, seriously, for what?"

"Have you seen footage of Hemingway? And didn't he gain forty pounds?"

"Okay, now you're starting to piss me off."

"Not my intention."

"Eat a bunch of bread and pasta, get a good makeup and hair team, sit in front of the camera saying amazing lines written by a great screenwriter—who actually *deserved* the Oscar he got for that movie—under the eye of an auteur director and his first-rate DP and editor, and you're suddenly a great actor. I'll have to remember that."

"I believed him."

"The suicide? He spends the whole movie in and out of bars, going to bullfights, bragging his ass off, happy as can be, which yeah, you can say overcompensating, putting on a face or whatever, but not what I saw in the acting. And the writing standing up everyone went on about? That's what Hemingway fucking did! That's the actor?! And, buddy, I'm a fucking addict. I didn't buy the alcoholism for a second. I don't even know what that was. The minute we got to Key West it was like a parody. You don't have the DTs when you're drinking, you have them when you're *not* drinking. And slurring the words? Please. I'll tell you what Ron was great in, though, was *The Poplar Tree*."

"Jordan is a friend of mine." Anything to change the subject.

"You're friends with Jordan Levinson?"

"We were at AFI together. He cowrote my first film with me."

"Great filmmaker. I mean, seriously great. And I don't say that lightly."

"You should work with him."

"Tell him to offer me a part. Seriously. I'd work with him for scale. Marci and I would produce him."

"I will, but he has his own roster he likes. He loves Ron Huston."

"And that's what I'm saying. That's when Ron has been his best. It's stylized. I don't buy him when the character has to be real. And I love Ron. He and I did a film together about five years before I was locked up. A piece-of-shit thriller for Screen Gems that paid him half a million dollars. This was before his nomination. I was so baked at the premiere I don't even remember it. Woke up at Shutters alone in a suite naked with a condom still on my dick. I shit you not."

"Wow."

"Very different times. For me and everyone. And any recovering addict who says he or she doesn't miss certain aspects of the days using is a fucking liar. And don't worry, I like life more now. That doesn't mean I don't have a hankering now and again." He paused, then said with a mercurial smile, "I'll call Ron and tell him we need him here early. In fact, I can't wait."

"Please, Peter. Javier and I, not to mention the AD, want it the way we have it."

"I'll talk to Javier."

"You know Javier?"

"I can't call our DP?"

"You can, but—"

"Do you know how many films I've done?"

"I respect your level of experience, Peter, but you've got to respect mine."

"Not when you want to wimp out and start on the stage. Let's push the envelope with this thing, go hard into the paint."

Thankfully Giovanni approached with two thick porcelain spoons atop petite matching saucers. Once "wimp" had been uttered—a word describing what Joel most feared about himself—he wanted to forget the butter knife and simply break Peter's perfect, formerly coke-snorting nose.

"Sorry to interrupt you guys, but I've got the amuse-bouche."

"Is this the quail egg?" asked Peter.

"You know it, dude." The chef turned to Joel. "I made this for him the last time he was in Atlanta. A poached quail egg atop our house cured bacon on a nest of polenta and chive." He set a utensil and saucer before each of them.

What a despicable species we are, thought Joel. People starving in this city, and I'm about to eat a poached quail egg on bacon in a "nest" of buttery corn. The single bite was so exhilarating he resented his conscience for inhibiting complete enjoyment.

"Are we pleased?" asked Giovanni, underscoring the unconscionable remove with the first-person plural.

"Amazing," Joel responded.

"If you like that, you're gonna love what we have in store. Any food allergies?"

"Uhm, no," Joel answered.

"You're looking at me like I'm out of my mind."

"Well . . . I mean, so no menu?"

"Oh, absolutely. Peter said just whatever I wanted to make you guys within the rules of his diet for the film."

"Trust me, you don't want to order from the menu," interjected the actor. "What, you're gonna eat what the dopes out in the main room are served?" He grinned wryly. "Totally up to you. Just don't think I'm sharing any of my hog snapper."

For three months I'm going to be dealing with this, thought Joel. I can't even eat the food I want.

"And give him a glass of wine."

"Oh no, Peter. I'm good," said Joel.

"You don't drink? Of course you do. I saw you at Max Kaiser's house. Look, when I used to get high, I didn't wait to make sure what others in the room were doing, so I made a deal with myself when I got clean: I was never going to inhibit the behavior of people around me."

"We've got an insane Chassagne-Montrachet. I just bought a case for our reserve list," said Giovanni. "It'll go great with the snapper."

"The guy's a bona fide genius," said Peter when Giovanni had departed. "And did you see how crowded it is out there? What he does is so smart. Italian food, obviously, and he lived and studied over there for nearly a decade, but then he came back and applied it to the best of what's here. You're getting the freshest ingredients from Georgia and Florida and South Carolina. Italy's are better, mind you, but the point is all locally sourced. Nothing canned or frozen, and the pasta's all handmade. This is the real deal. Trust me, I've been in the best restaurants over there."

"I'm sure you have."

"I had dinner with Berlusconi."

"Amazing."

"Two years after prison, almost to the day. I'm at the Hotel de Russie in this insane suite—doing a junket there for the film Marci and I met on—and the publicist gets this engraved card inviting me to the Quirinal Palace that night for a state dinner with Angela Merkel. And they fucking put me at their table—hers and Berlusconi's. I mean, of course they did, right? They weren't going to have to talk about the debt crisis with me sitting there, although if they had I would have chimed in for Italy as a fellow black sheep. The guy was already a fossil at this point. But the formality. The waiters in these red greatcoats and tails with matching vests and white ties and white gloves. Everything on bone china. Crystal glasses. In America the old shit—and I'd probably been to the White House maybe three times at this point—but in America the old shit is nothing compared to Europe. Popes lived at that palace. Napoléon was there. And man, did I want some champagne when they made the toast, whatever, to the lasting friendship of the two countries, and I'm right there at the main table, Angela Merkel telling me what a fan she is."

"Unbelievable."

"But if I'd taken a sip of the bubbly, three hours later I'd have been down in the EUR scoring coke, and you and I wouldn't be sitting here. At a certain point I had to understand that. Not wanting to be back in prison also helped. Speaking of which . . ."

Giovanni approached with two crystal stems and a greenish slope-shouldered bottle beaded with perspiration. Suddenly Joel felt relieved Peter had insisted he imbibe. Otherwise how would he endure the next hour and a half of bullying interspersed with tales meant to inspire envy and awe?

"So," announced the chef, "we have the 2010 Les Chaumées. Straight from the Côte-d'Or on the northern hillside above Chassagne."

Joel examined a label of a yellowed cream with black letters boasting *Premier Cru* above *CHASSAGNE-MONTRACHET* before it was swept back by the chef, who cut the foil with a small, curved blade hinged from the top of his waiter's pull. He extracted the cork, then held it to his nose before handing it over. Joel took it between thumb and forefinger, inanely aping Giovanni to give it a smell.

"Seems great, I guess," he said.

The chef poured an eighth of an inch into his own glass, then twisted the stem until the scant portion had coated its inside. He added an inch more and brought the goblet's outer circumference to his nose. "Melon and pear. A bit of honeysuckle." He pooled a sip behind his lower incisors and inhaled rapidly to inspire a loud sputtering. After a theatrical swish, he swallowed. "Yup. Gargantuan fucking wine." He poured an eighth of an inch for Joel, then, just as he'd done with his own, turned the stem horizontally and rotated. "We prime the glass, so you get maximum nose." He poured another three inches. "Taste."

Joel did. The taste was faintly sweet but sharp. He sensed the apples the chef had promised, but little else.

"So?" asked Giovanni.

"Yeah."

"'Yeah' is right. The winemaker is Philippe Colin. He and his brother have adjoining parcels but very different philosophies. Philippe lets the soil do the work. 2010 was a motherfucker. Bad winter and a very wet June, but good heat in September, especially in Chassagne. What I love is the minerality." He took another quick sip. "I get oyster shells."

"Hey! Guys!" announced Peter. "I'm over here. The guy who can't drink!"

"Oh my God," proclaimed Giovanni, "I'm such an asshole. Sorry. I've been waiting for a case of this for about a year now."

"It's all right, knock yourself out, but me and Joel have some items to go over, so pour yourself and your waitress a glass of that, leave Joel the bottle, and we'll see you when you bring over your next insane concoction."

"You got it, though Jane will have to wait for what Joel doesn't finish," said the chef, refilling his stem up to just below its maximum circumference. "See you guys in a bit."

"Sorry about that," said Peter when Giovanni had left. "Can you really taste oyster shells?"

"Sure."

"Bullshit. But the thing is, he can."

"I bet that's true."

"Which is my point. He can figure out that taking a quail egg from a farm thirty miles from here and poaching it perfectly down to the second and combining it with polenta, chives, bacon, and a little salt probably harvested and dried from the surf by monks somewhere in the Mediterranean in a perfectly proportioned bite is gonna make your taste buds tell your neural receptors to go insane. And then to pair it with a wine that evokes apples and the shells of mollusks."

"I know where you're headed, Peter."

"I've been doing this a long time, and like he knows how to make food, I know how to schedule a movie."

"So do I."

"Okay. We both know what's best for the crew. You think I don't, but I do, because I want this film to succeed just as much as you do. Just as much as Max Kaiser and Sparta do. Probably more, because I've been down, way down at the bottom, meaning I appreciate the top in ways you guys can't imagine and hopefully will never have to. I don't want to start on the stage. As I've said, you lose the opportunity to test production, but also to test yourself."

"Peter—"

"No, just listen. You also need to think of your actors. Yes, the crew is important. But people don't go to see films because of the fucking gaffer or the dolly grip or the poor idiot who has to drive the Gator from the van drop-off two hundred yards or whatever it was you said to the set. Jesus, that you even mentioned that. Those people work their asses off, but they're interchangeable. I'm not. Jennifer is not. Ron is not. Who's making the most of anyone on this film and also gets participation in box office gross—not the net, mind you, but the gross? Me. And that's not because I'm everybody's best pal. I know the studio is terrified of me, and you're sitting there wondering why I of all people got to meet Angela Merkel and sleep in the White House, and I don't fucking blame you."

"Peter—"

"But whether you like it or not, they love me out there." He gestured to his left, where, behind the wall, the restaurant teemed with "dopes" ordering from menus, nearly every single one of whom knew the actor's name. "And when people go to see this movie on opening weekend, it's going to be because of Sparta, yes, but also for what I can do when a camera is pointed at me. I'm a brand, and I protect that brand. Before you came on board I worked on the script to make it what it is. Anything that's funny, I came up with. Eighty percent of the science? Me. The entire B-story for Ron's character? Mine and Marci's. But most importantly, Joel, you are here because of me. They came to us with you. I watched most of your films, including the first one about the crop circles—brilliant script, by the way, so it's no surprise Jordan Levinson wrote it—"

"Cowrote it. From my story."

"Apologies. But I watched your movies, called around, and you were at our place a week later with your look book speechifying about cell phones."

"I'll change the schedule, Peter. It's not that big a deal."

"Thank you. And can I tell you something?"

"Sure."

"This is going to be a fantastic experience."

Joel reached for his empty stem, not realizing he'd been sipping steadily since Giovanni had left. The star watched as he seized the bottle from the ice bucket and poured. *He can't be as indifferent toward my drinking in front of him as he advertises, but I need this. I'm going to need it every night.* He sipped in silence. Since he'd eaten only the quail egg, polenta, bacon, and chive, the alcohol soothed his vanquished being all the more. *I amount to absolutely nothing,* he thought with a masking smile, as a tear leaked from his eye.

"Jesus, Joel," said Peter. "It's just a fucking schedule change."

"I know," said the director. "I just feel so lucky to be making this film, and with all your support."

"Of course, man," said Peter, clearly not believing a word of what the director had just said.

NINE

What had happened to Joel Slavkin? Peter wondered as he returned to his makeup trailer from the morning's blocking rehearsal. Including the ten-minute ride from the pond on the Gator to the road where George waited to drive him to base camp, the trip had taken a good twenty-five minutes. Why had the director chosen such a difficult location? Why had Declan Morris allowed it? The setting was stunning, with its unblemished ring of oaks, willows, and maples surrounding a fittingly bucolic pond, but couldn't much of that have been accomplished digitally?

He'd had such confidence in the man after their first meeting. Yes, there'd been the dispute over smartphones, but at least that demonstrated a degree of mental agility and politesse. While this had persisted in the weeks following, there had been hints of instability. Foremost was the therapy dog that suddenly accompanied the director everywhere. Wisely he had not brought the creature to Brentwood, or Marci would have shown him the door before the bottom of the hour, given her obsession with canines and what they indicated about their male owners. In this case it was a bichon frise no more than a foot and a half in length and eight inches tall with trimmed white hair stained brown below the eyes from a persisting ocular drool. Of late a skin condition spreading along its underside inspired the wearing of an oversized horn to prevent it from licking the afflicted areas.

"That is seriously your dog?" Peter asked the first time he saw it.

"Yeah. She's hypoallergenic, which is better for Annie, plus she doesn't shed, and it's a really friendly breed."

"So she's a therapy dog?"

"What? No."

"But you bring her everywhere."

"Yeah, well, she doesn't like being at home alone."

"Your wife can't take her to work?"

"They don't like dogs running around her firm."

"Will you bring her to Atlanta?"

"I plan to."

"In the cabin or below?"

"In the cabin, I guess."

"So, she's a therapy dog. As in licensed."

"Well, if you want to be technical, yes, so she doesn't have to be in with the luggage. I mean, you have a dog."

"We do."

"And do you have her travel with the luggage?"

"Kind of a different situation with us."

"Because you travel private."

"Because we travel private."

Whenever Joel was seated, the animal occupied his lap, a perch it demanded with a series of piercing yips and leaps, as if in danger of being swept up by a raptor should she spend a moment on the ground.

"Can the dog not be in the middle of our blocking rehearsal?" Peter had asked an hour before. The snake wrangler had just removed four copperheads from the woods, and Peter wanted to toss the animal into the bag that held them, even hold it himself to experience its struggle against the ravages of a dozen venomous reptiles.

⚡

"How did we not realize this guy was such a fucking weirdo?" Peter demanded of Marci.

"He's a smart weirdo."

Why was she always pointing out the man's intelligence? "I'm less and less convinced. Besides, you have him wrapped around your finger. He can't even look up when you're in the room. What is that?"

"I am what I am. Are we done here? Because this location is a nightmare. Everyone told you, including Joel, that we should have started on the stage."

"He said he could handle it. We're going to learn a lot today."

"I've got Javier telling me we'll be lucky to get a shot off before ten thirty, which already puts us an hour and a half behind. Jeremy and Charisse are in their tent sharpening their knives."

"Was Declan with them?"

"He'd been summoned."

Jeremy and Charisse made up the producing duo on the ground for Sparta. Both were terrified of Peter. With Marci they maintained a healthy cordiality. Charisse, who was black and just four years younger than Marci, had even initiated weekly lunches in LA during which the two women shared tales of coming up in the system before Me Too and BLM. But both Marci and Peter understood that regardless of such overtures, her loyalty lay with the company that gave her her credit. Her name appeared ahead of Marci's on the call sheet, just as it would on screen. It had been the last point in Marci's deal.

"You're not going to win this one, ever," Peter advised. "She's been with the project since the idea stage. Plus, imagine operating inside this system as her."

"Welcome to my life. You don't think everyone on set looks at me, including those two, and says I'm only here because of you? You think anyone bothers to look on my IMDb and see how many films I produced before Compton/Levy?"

"So, you should be a little more sympathetic. Besides, ultimately you'll have more say."

"You're dreaming on that last one."

"I'm the star, baby."

"*A* star. In a whole galaxy."

"No stars, no galaxy."

"I wouldn't say that around Jeremy."

"Jeremy needs to know it. On the phone with Max Kaiser every half hour cutting us off at the knees or asking Javier about his lenses like he knows what a Panavision C Series even is."

"Maybe he does."

"I thought Javier was going to belt him. I mean, what is Javier Benavidez even doing here? Does he have any idea what he's gotten himself into? He and I are going to have to protect not only each other but the integrity of this film."

"What does that mean?"

"Here's the thing, Marci. If you look around on this film at the leadership positions, you're going to see few people with our in-battle experience on a project of this size, and I'm beginning to fear that Joel Slavkin isn't one of them. It's me and Javier. We need to be there for him, or you and I are going to be sinking into a morass. It's our film."

"I think Max Kaiser would dispute your characterization."

"Who insisted we start out here instead of on the stage?"

"You, obviously."

"I needed to learn if the Joel who sat on our patio in Brentwood was the real Joel."

"He seemed pretty real to me."

"You should have been there this morning when Jennifer didn't want to have her back to the water."

"What was the issue?"

"Jellyfish."

"The character, I hope."

"Her objection was that she knows he can come from the water, so she would never have her back to it. She was right. And Joel says, 'Well, it's a freshwater culvert, you don't assume that.' But the point is that Jellyfish—the character, not the Cnidaria—"

"The what?"

"Cnidaria, the phylum of jellyfish."

"Jesus, Peter, you're such an asshole."

"Because I do my research?"

"Go on."

"The character of Jellyfish can thrive in water regardless of the sodium content or lack thereof, even though salt water is the natural habitat of his nom de guerre."

"So, what happened?"

"Joel got anxious, picked up his animal and started fondling it, kept trying to convince Jennifer because he'd of course already storyboarded the scene, and now he'd have to find a different background or switch the axis or move video village and the base for the crane, which of course is what we ended up agreeing to do, and that's why we're now an hour and a half behind. And can you imagine what happens tomorrow when we're shooting in the water. Lucky for Ron it's about ninety degrees. Kind of disgusting, actually."

"I'm aware. I was on with Ron's manager for an hour yesterday wanting to know if we'd tested it."

"Tested the water?"

"Yes."

"Have we?"

"Every week since Joel chose the location. And we've paid two farmers to water their cattle elsewhere. Ten thousand bucks."

"What's the issue with cows drinking out of the pond?"

"When they piss and shit in it? You are aware that a huge amount you have no knowledge of goes into every decision we make. There's this whole legion of enablers so you guys can do your thing. Are you going to be all right? I'm going to set."

"Check in on Javier. He's worried he's going to take the blame with Jeremy and Charisse for having to move the crane."

"Javier is insufferable. They should never give out Oscars."

Once Jennifer had confided in her indulgently receptive makeup artist, anxiety regarding her character's status in the scene as written and staged took complete hold. When the cast returned to a set and crew eager for the first shot at 9:45, she was in a state of turmoil.

"I'm sorry, Joel. It's just . . . I mean, Peter may be fine with it, because he's of course Major Machina and can, whatever, deal, and maybe he's a step ahead, but my character just isn't. She's supposed to be this marine biologist teaching at Stanford, and she's standing there by the water when this creature could materialize at any time? It makes no sense."

"But she's *facing* the water now, and like you just said, she's with Paul Kramer."

"So what? She's with a man—who at this point she doesn't even know is Major Machina—so that makes it all right?"

"Paul Kramer, yes."

"It just makes her seem like a ditz, and that's not what I signed up for. Why are women always not smart, victims, or both? I have to call bullshit when I see it. Actors have to be able to do that without feeling like they're being difficult."

"No one said you're being difficult."

"I see how everyone is looking at me."

"That's in your imagination."

"So now I'm the crazy, paranoid actress too?"

"No one said that either."

"How about we add a line?" asked Peter.

"Such as?" said Joel.

"More lines for you?"

"Actually for you, Jennifer. Of the proleptic variety."

"What does that mean?"

"Taking an argument away from the audience. We make your character cognizant of the danger. Something like, 'Paul, I'm not comfortable here by the water.' That's when you move to where you can see the water, and maybe I stand closer to where you were going to stand, thereby protecting you."

"That makes her weak."

"Then I don't protect you. The important thing is you'll get a line suggesting your character knows she's in danger."

"Maybe I can say, 'I know we're by the water, but I don't care. This is too important.'"

Jeremy appeared, Charisse beside him. The pair complemented each other exquisitely: he, tall, white, bespectacled, and handsome with thinning hair; she, short and equally comely with a thick mane of dreads.

"What's this about line changes?"

"Jennifer was just concerned—"

"We heard," answered Jeremy, pointing to the cans hanging around his neck. Even after three decades wearing body mics, Peter still forgot that every word an actor said was available to others, especially directors and producers hungry to learn what performers really thought about the project and, more important, them. "Nobody's changing any lines until they're approved."

"It's six forty-five in LA," said Peter. "Who's going to approve a change right now?"

"We can shoot it both ways," Joel submitted.

"What, then you just do a take with the line to shut me up and the original version is what ends up in the film?" asked Jennifer.

"Jeremy," said Joel, "is it really going to make a difference if she shows a little strength here? Strength and smarts? What do you think, Charisse?"

"Any dialogue changes have to be approved in LA."

What no one was asking, of course, was why Jennifer had waited until the threshold of shooting to protect the strength and dignity of her character. It seemed to happen on every film: actors withholding script issues until there were hundreds of crew members and millions of dollars of equipment arrayed and primed. Only at a thousand dollars a minute did a thespian's analytical faculties reach peak acuity.

"Jeremy," Peter offered judiciously, "you guys are here as Sparta. I mean, who in LA other than Max is going to weigh in with more authority than you two? Seriously, isn't that the point of having you here instead of people more junior? You're the fucking A team. Can't you just approve the change?"

"He's got a point," said Charisse.

"So, what's the line being proposed?" Jeremy asked.

"That I say, 'I know we're by the water, but I don't care. This is too important.' It tells the audience my character knows there's a danger that Jellyfish will materialize. Otherwise, I'm a marine biologist from Stanford standing like a moron where he could just appear and pull me under. Of course this still doesn't address my issues with why are we by water in the first place."

"Because a disturbance has been located here," said Joel.

"And besides, if you say that," said Charisse, "then it's not a surprise for the audience when he does appear."

"Exactly what I was thinking," offered Jeremy.

"But really?" said Peter. "At this point, whenever characters are standing by water, the audience is basically just waiting for Jellyfish. Three scenes ago he took down six Apache helicopters over the Skagerrak."

"Have we figured out where we're filming that?" asked Charisse.

"Halifax," said Joel. "It couldn't look more Scandinavian. The location scout sent pictures yesterday."

"We're shooting it on the stage," interrupted Declan Morris, who'd been lingering behind Joel without anyone realizing it. "I've already arranged for the plates. And with a team in Denmark, not Canada, so you're welcome. I spoke with Javier."

"You spoke with Javier and not me?" asked Joel, tightening the grip on his dog.

"It was the weekend."

"But I don't understand. How do we even—"

"We shoot the helicopters in San Diego at the naval base, the actors on the stage here with some e-fans, and composite them with the plates from Denmark."

"Javier agreed to that?"

"I cleared it with Anton and Nazak. It's nothing for those guys."

"How was this decision made without me?"

"By me being a line producer and saving, minimum, half a million dollars not having to get us to Nova Scotia and put us up for a week and organize a fleet of Apache helicopters to fly over the water of a Canadian fishing village in the middle of winter."

"I told everyone I didn't want to do it digitally," said Joel. "Once again you went behind my back."

Honestly, thought Peter, if people knew such conversations took place, they wouldn't see movies. They'd boycott us all. There'd be a sterilization program.

"Declan," said Peter, "can we just stay with the subject at hand?"

"I didn't bring up the Skagerrak. Joel did."

"I did, actually," volunteered Charisse.

"Let's discuss it at lunch," said Peter.

"Joel and Jeremy and I will discuss it at lunch. You don't need to worry about it," said Declan pointedly.

"I'll choose what I worry about, not you," Peter retorted, regretting his sudden aggression. He reached into his pocket for his cell and texted Marci: "YOU NEED TO GET TO SET NOW PLS."

"I don't see adding the line," said Jeremy.

"And I don't see acting the scene without it," responded Jennifer. "Again, this is not the part I signed on to play."

"I respect that, Jennifer," said the producer, "though I would point out that this scene has always been set here." He read from his sides: "'EXT. ESCARPMENT OVER SWIMMING QUARRY—DAY,' with the lines as scripted."

"Exactly," she responded. "'ESCARPMENT OVER,' which implies distance, height. I wasn't thinking I'd be, like, two feet from the surface. I mean, look at this. And it's a large pond, not a quarry. I was picturing huge granite cliffs. Mountains even."

"In rural Georgia?" asked Peter.

"You know what, Peter? Enough with the condescension. I don't like throwing this around, but I'm in Mensa."

He kicked at the dirt. To his left Jeremy inhaled audibly, as if internalizing Jennifer's membership in the world's sanctioned society of geniuses demanded extra oxygen for his own sub-Mensa brain. Behind him Charisse stared at the actress slack-jawed, probably half in astonishment and half doubting the announcement's veracity. To her left stood Declan, his face a mask of disdain for everyone present. And finally, there was Joel, by now practically strangling his bichon frise.

Marci appeared. "Hello, everyone. Sorry I'm late to the discussion. What's going on?"

"Well, first of all," offered Peter, "were you aware Jennifer is a member of Mensa?"

"I wasn't," said Marci. "That's fantastic. Did you just find out? Is that why everyone's gathered?"

"It came up tangentially," said Peter. "We're caucusing because Jennifer has observed—rightfully, I think—that her character wouldn't stand this close to the water."

"I thought we'd solved that."

"Jennifer would like a line exhibiting her concern. Our colleagues at Sparta are reluctant to allow it without papal dispensation."

"You know what?" said Jennifer. "I'll be in my trailer, because now that everyone is here, this has become very public, and I feel exposed. James!" she shouted, summoning the assistant director, who at six-four and black stood a good ten inches taller than the diminutive and resolutely Caucasian Joel. "Could you please make sure there's a van?" She marched toward video village, beyond which waited several all-terrain buggies to ferry cast to the road a quarter of a mile through the trees.

"Joel," said Peter, "now is when you follow her and keep her from a twenty-five-minute ride back to base camp at this ridiculous location, so that we can actually get a shot off before lunch."

"I'm not sure what to say. Her points are valid, just poorly timed."

"You apologize that it got public, tell her you understand where she's coming from, and promise you'll fix it. Meanwhile, we're going to figure this out."

"This is why I wanted to start on the stage, by the way."

"Yeah," answered Peter, "and this is why I wanted to start out here."

"So you could break the crew?" asked Declan.

"Did you really just say that to me? With an ironic tone?"

"Any irony was unintended. I meant what I said."

"The crew has done great. And they look pretty relaxed to me." Around them an array of electricians, grips, PAs, and makeup, hair, and wardrobe assistants stood or sat sipping coffee and sodas, some swiping at flies, others their smartphones.

"I think I have a pretty good sense of what's going on now," said Marci. "What's the line she wants to say?"

"I typed it into my phone," said Charisse, handing it over.

Marci looked. "I don't get the issue. Stick it in the scene, and if it doesn't get approved, you cut it in the edit."

"Jennifer's Mensa brain alerted her to that specific vulnerability, which for obvious reasons did not appeal to her," explained Peter.

"But that's true about any line. Scenes can be reshot, removed; lines that were never said can be inserted off-camera. I mean, seriously. Let me go speak with her."

"Nothing would make us happier," said Peter.

They finished the scene before lunch, Jennifer's new line rewritten thrice by the time they shot her close-up. By then the latest two of the script's eight screenwriters had been awakened and briefed in Los Angeles. With their input, Paul Kramer now joined the marine biologist in voicing wariness near water given the liquefaction tendencies of his nemesis. Max Kaiser commented in a brief FaceTime at 7:45 Pacific time that the scene had actually been improved, vindicating the impulses of the exacting female star.

As he walked with his plate of halibut marinated in ginger and low-sodium soy sauce to meet with Marci, Joel, and Declan regarding the helicopter set piece in the seas north of Denmark, Peter felt relief. He and Marci, not Jeremy and Charisse, had demonstrated leadership and finesse. It was arranged that Joel would henceforth arrive to set half an hour early to consult with Peter regarding each day's work. Sooner than he'd imagined, the film's nucleus had gravitated toward the plaza between his four trailers, away from the lunch tent frequented by the producers and the gnashing hoi poloi.

TEN

The more Javier experienced the American studio system, itself a microcosm for the very worst of the country itself, the more he wondered why he'd ever aspired to live and work there. Why hadn't he gone to Argentina? Spain? Colombia? In fact, as much as he'd grown to abominate the political and social venality that embodied life in his native country, not to mention the assassinations, kidnappings, and collateral murders, he often fantasized driving down to the border at San Diego and shouting, "Turn around, you idiots! Go back to your impoverished and endangered lives and count yourselves lucky!"

He'd never intended to leave Mexico, but it had become essential. Once his sister had secured him his first DP job, he had not once wanted for work, to the extent that for three years he always had his next film lined up before he'd completed a current project. The surfeit of offers brought choices, allowing him to graduate from thinly disguised telenovelas and insipid comedies to films with far bigger ambitions.

His eleventh film was his riskiest, an overtly political work produced by his sister about homelessness in Mexico City told through the eyes of a young boy being raised by his *indígena* mother in Ciudad Neza. Shot on 16mm using mostly short ends his sister scrounged from any production she could beseech, the movie never reached much of an audience, though it did screen at a number of international festivals, including Rotterdam, where Javier won a prize for cinematography, a plaudit that surprised him because he'd mostly lit the film with practical sources and bounce, and had had to push two stops for most night interiors since the director wanted a wider depth of field to make the film more environmental. He hadn't gone to the festival, but a week after learning of his award, he received a phone call from someone who had.

"That film is one of the best motherfucking things I've ever seen, dude," said a voice that couldn't have been much older than his. "Not just the lighting, which was like Rembrandt or fucking Caravaggio, but your framing. I kept looking for mistakes. And I know it was sixteen, but you *went* with the grain."

"I didn't have a choice."

"I want you to shoot my next feature."

"You haven't even told me who you are."

"Alfredo Huron, and you and I are going to be partners for life."

Javier had never met anyone like him. To begin with, he was physically enormous: easily 275 pounds at perhaps five feet six inches, with a thick goatee and a pair of round Trotskyite frames perched on a wide, misshapen nose. He was both hideous and rivetingly attractive, to the extent he couldn't walk the street or enter a room without provoking stares. Unlike Javier, who'd grown up among academics but attended public school, Alfredo's father was one of the largest wool manufacturers in Mexico and had sent Alfredo to Sierra Loma, the most expensive international school in Mexico City. Groomed for college in the United States, he astounded his parents by opting to remain in Central America for film school at the same institution Javier had shunned. There he'd fallen in with two other young filmmakers who were the talk of the city's arts community for their thesis collaboration, a modern-day adaptation of Lorca's *Blood Wedding* set in Oaxaca that Alfredo had directed. It took the top prize at Rotterdam, which is how Alfredo had seen Javier's work.

The young director, Javier soon learned, was obsessed with monsters.

"From when I was eight and already weighed a hundred and ten pounds, I didn't need mirrors because the whole world was telling me how to see myself, and it wasn't pretty. You can't believe how lonely I was or the kind of bullying I got. And private school kids are the meanest, because they have the biggest need to steal and repress so they can have even more."

"Even more what?" asked Javier.

"More everything!" Alfredo responded with infectious delight. "You have to understand, it's not the indigent and the fucking poor who are the most aggressive about possessions, it's the ones with the most. And when you're a cruel little boy, the easiest thing to steal from another boy is his dignity. I loved creatures because I could empathize with them. I'd sit at home weekends and draw comics or make figures out of clay. Then when I was fourteen I saw *Allegro non troppo*. In every one of those creatures on the march I saw all of us, and suddenly anything was possible. I started shooting stop-motion animation, first with drawings, then with clay. It was like I could go more into myself but get outside of myself at the same time. And it was a way to say fuck you to the bullies, because I could create shit that not only amazed them and freaked them out, but one day they'd have to pay to see, and then maybe think twice about the way they treated me and people like me who were suddenly explaining the fucking world to them."

His new script, set in an unnamed fascist dictatorship, told of a young girl with a curious soul whose body is taken over by a woodland troll eager to destroy her family and the town in which it resides for having displaced him from his ancestral lands. The allegorical twist lay in its ultimate sympathy with the troll. In the end, the town is destroyed, the fascistic land-grabbing humans are in retreat, and the creature sunders from the girl to make her his bride.

"You go from Lorca to this?" Javier asked when they met for lunch in La Condesa.

"What could make more sense?"

"And this is a fantasy movie. I've never shot anything close to that. You could get anyone. An American maybe. Someone from Europe even."

"When I could have you? A *pinche* Mexican?!"

❧

As he was completing photography on the film, only the fourth he'd done that his sister didn't also produce, she took on a project that would alter both their lives. Made by a preternaturally brash thirty-year-old writer-director, it chronicled the misdeeds of a small-town mayor who treats his backwater fiefdom as his personal bank account, siphoning funds not only from the town coffers but local businesses as well, all while wearing a PRI pin. In the end, having murdered the local sanitation head for insufficient obeisance, he commandeered a garbage truck down the main street of the town waving the party's flag.

"Clearly the film hits a nerve," she said brashly to the group from IMCINE who visited the set demanding production be shut down. When she didn't relent and submitted the finished film to Cannes, the government wouldn't allow the print to be shipped, causing the director to go to the press. *La Prensa* wouldn't publish, but *La Jornada*, a daily recently founded by the same man who'd written her father's defining obituary, did. She also managed to have it screened for the selection committee at Toronto, smuggling a print overland, where it was accepted to premiere at the 1988 festival.

In the meantime, she was blackballed, informed she would no longer be hired in Mexico. She began receiving threats at home, at her office, and on her car, the windshield of which was smashed. When none of this inspired compliance (the director by this time had fled to Bolivia), the authorities turned on Javier. For the first time in his life, while he was color timing Alfredo's film, he didn't know what his next job would be. One night, after a late session at the lab, he was beaten at gunpoint and instructed that should his sister not respect party wishes, he'd be wise to find another line of work.

"Go to America," Lucia insisted.

"And leave you to face this alone?"

"I did this, not you, *mijo*."

"You wouldn't leave me in this kind of mess."

"I wouldn't have let you get into it in the first place."

"That makes no sense."

"We're different people. I'm a fighter."

"What am I?"

"An artist. If I could do what you do I'd trade places in a second. When you were twelve years old I saw it. Why do you think I gave you that camera you were using better than me a week after you got it? Your talent is too big for this country."

In the winter of 1990 he moved to Los Angeles.

Everyone who saw his reel insisted it was as strong as any they'd viewed, especially given the scant resources with which he'd created the images. Nevertheless, he found himself stuck. All sets were unionized, and he had no way to break in other than as an apprentice, an entry point that didn't interest him.

Finally, an American production designer his sister knew agreed to introduce Javier to his agent. "I've seen your stuff, and it's good," the man said matter-of-factly on the phone. "A little extreme, but good. Let's meet."

He bought a suit at Ross Dress for Less for seventy-nine dollars that his wife then tailored. He wore it with loafers, an off-white button-down, and no tie. An assistant ushered him into a small second-floor office from a nondescript lobby in a low-slung, cheaply constructed building on Wilshire seven blocks east of La Cienega.

"Sorry about the mess in here," said the trim, balding man in his forties, "but it's been an insane week. It's crazy what the video market has done for our industry, which is both good and bad, of course, because, yes, more films and, with cable, more TV, but for you guys—DPs, production designers, costume designers, makeup artists—less of it is ultimately seen in theaters, so your work isn't appreciated the way it used to be, meaning on the big screen and here in this country. I guess you'd all take the paying jobs, though, right?"

"At this point."

"I like your reel. The last couple of clips from . . . I forget the movie—with the little girl and the monster. And the stick insect with the wings."

"It's called *The Dwelling*. A director named Alfredo Huron. He's fantastic."

"Seems that way. What's happening with it?"

"He takes his time, and there were a lot of issues with sound and effects, plus getting the music right. We're waiting to hear from festivals."

"So how can I be of help?"

"Well, Clarke said . . . I mean, the thought was that . . ."

"That I would bring you on?"

"You said just now that you like my reel."

"I do, but Jesus, what do you think this is?"

"I don't understand."

"I have a few Brits and some French clients, even a German guy, but I get them on shows because there are certain directors who want that sensibility, especially if they're working in Europe with European crews, or they're snobs and we seem to have a thing about Europe here. But I start pushing a Mexican to do anything but the gardening, producers are going to look at me like I've lost my damn mind. No offense."

"None taken." In truth he wanted to rip out the man's larynx.

"It's not me, you understand, it's just . . . I've got twelve DPs on my list, and I'm not adding another unless I know I can help him, not to mention make some money for all the time it would take, which in your case would be a lot. Have you thought about teaching? Maybe there's a community college in the area that caters to Spanish speakers. And again, this isn't about your talent."

He didn't shoot a frame for five months other than stills of his children while his wife worked nights for a cleaning service in East LA that did janitorial services downtown. While she slept most of the day, he took care of their two sons, neither of whom was old enough to attend school.

When Alfredo called to inform him *The Dwelling* would show in competition at Cannes, he didn't think much of it other than a tinge of resentment that the producers refused to fly him while supplying airfare for three of the actors and the film's editor.

"Seriously?" he asked Alfredo. "I mean, the actors I at least get. But Alfonso?"

"He sits in a room all day with a Steenbeck and a Moviola hanging strips on the fourth perf then goes home to his wife and kids and minds his own business. You've got a rabble-rousing sister and producers completely beholden to their buddies in PRI."

"I can't get away from these motherfuckers. And then in America I can't get work because I'm Mexican. How do I win?"

He could only laugh when he answered his phone on a Sunday morning the third week in May, his wife asleep in their bedroom after scrubbing latrines all night at a bank building on Fourth Street. It was Alfredo informing him from Cannes that he'd won for best cinematography.

"It's the only award the film took, motherfucker!" the director shouted with a gusty laugh. "Not director or screenplay, but cinematography! It serves those assholes at PRI right! You're going to be in all the papers in Mexico, and they can't do a thing about it! And guess what else? Sony Pictures Classics bought it for America, and they're going to go for Best Foreign Film, dude. You're going to be up for a fucking Oscar!"

"There's a best foreign cinematography award?"

"No, Javier. They're going for Best Cinematography period! In the whole fucking world!"

On certain sets, and *Major Machina* was certainly one of these, Javier actually cursed his sister's stubborn decency. Had he not left Mexico, he might perhaps still have been considered an Oscar candidate for *The Dwelling*, but given the amount of in-person pandering he'd done to get nominated, let alone win, he certainly couldn't imagine owning the statue. As it stood, he didn't even consider *The Dwelling* his best work at that time, just the most striking, and of course it was associated with the only of his early films ever to show outside of Central and South America.

After winning, he had his pick of not only agencies (he opted not to sign with the one who'd have had him trimming hedges) but projects as well, including commercials at $5,000 a day when he wasn't shooting a film or television pilot. He and his wife moved to a three-thousand-square-foot Spanish Mission home in Santa Monica on the corner of Twenty-Fourth and Georgina where they enjoyed a year and a half more of marriage until she tired of his being perpetually on location and began sleeping with a neighbor, an out-of-work screenwriter she met walking their dog one morning while Javier was in Prague.

Now married to Alma, an Argentinean painter who enjoyed the solitude of a husband periodically away, his life was more or less in order. Both his sons had graduated college, and one now worked with him as co-owner of an equipment house in Van Nuys.

Why then did he continue to do jobs he knew from the outset he would loathe? Why did he find himself in Atlanta, the city that, because of the state's tax break, now doubled for everywhere from Saigon to Khartoum, alone nightly in his Cabbagetown loft surrounded by artwork he despised and living underneath a drummer who thrashed on his kit at all hours? He should have shunned Sparta from the start, but Joel Slavkin struck him as sufficiently clever to navigate the challenges of working with such a leviathan. Difficulties began ten days before photography when the increasingly feckless director informed him that instead of starting on the stage for a week of mostly three- and fourhander scenes, they would begin at the most difficult location of their shoot, a stagnant culvert hundreds of yards into snake-infested woods.

"I hate the idea," Javier told Peter Compton in an unexpected phone call from the star meant to enlist the DP's support. "I don't think Joel likes it either."

"I don't care what Joel likes."

"Isn't he the director?"

"This is a Sparta movie. Max Kaiser is the director."

"Max Kaiser is not my director."

"Javier, you and I both know that no one, including me, is on this film without Max's approval. At least tell me you're not going to stand in my way on this, that if we switch to starting at the quarry—"

"It's not a quarry. More like a snake sanctuary leading to a morass of cow shit."

"I saw pictures. It looks great."

"You can't smell pictures, or see not one but two venomous snakes sunning themselves like models in Saint-Tropez on the walk out."

"Come on, Javier, back me on this. I'll owe you."

"Owe me what?"

"Supporting you when you need it, which trust me will be worth your while."

"This is starting to feel like I'm dealing with a cartel."

"Are you really going to cause a problem on this?"

"Fine. If Joel agrees we can start at the bovine sewer."

"What is it with your vocabulary? You speak English better than most native speakers."

"Imagine me without the Mexican accent."

"The accent makes it more impressive, actually."

"Mexicans aren't supposed to be intelligent?"

"Are you kidding me? I've read Márquez."

"Gabito was Colombian."

Javier's gaffer and key grip now wanted to slaughter the DP. In the former schedule the shit swamp was a month in, meaning a separate crew budgeted to do all the pre-rigging while the first team was occupied with main unit. Now, instead of prepping the stage in relative comfort, they'd spent a week in the woods.

"Do you have any idea what you're doing to my people?" Javier asked the line producer Declan Morris, who had pitched up at the production office in a silver Audi R8 he'd purchased over the weekend. "And what's with the new car?"

"I waited to buy it here instead of in LA with the markup and the California sales tax."

"You're not mentioning the deal Sparta has with Audi."

"Our deal is with Cadillac."

Javier could sense a swell of defensive anger, so he pivoted to the more pressing subject. "You're fucking my crew."

"You signed off on the quarry."

"If you people keep calling it a quarry, I'm going to bring a gun to set."

"Don't make jokes like that."

"When I agreed to the scheduling change we still had a pre-rigging crew."

"And why would I double up like that now when all your guys would just be sitting around. This saved us forty thousand dollars."

"You were budgeted for the forty thousand."

"Don't say shit to me like that when all you see is the camera budget. I look at where I'm over in every department, including, by the way, yours, with the hot and cold running Steadicam and C-camera crew who are going to do nothing but loiter at the craft service table eating pistachios day in and day out."

"The Steadicam doesn't cost you anything unless it comes off the truck."

"Yeah, and because it's following us, Joel's going to be requesting it for every scene. You forget that you have to deal with me, but I have to deal with the studio, and on every single item. It's like Chinese water torture with you people. Janine with her two extra seamstresses, Kate with her construction budget going up fifteen percent each week, and hair and makeup every time Charisse gives a note about Jellyfish's head extension. Or if Joel adds a dozen extras suddenly, they need just as many day players to handle hair, plus an extra trailer. I have to think of every dollar."

"Is that why you're buying sports cars?"

"Again about the car. What are you getting at?"

"It was a joke."

"Yeah, but tell me what the fuck you're getting at?"

"Jesus, Declan, *calma te*. Can we please—?"

"No, Javier, I said no."

⚡

By the time they'd prepped the manure pond anticipating nights with easily five miles of cable, six condors, eight 18K HMIs, ten 6K PAR HMIs, twenty-five LED panels, ten Maxi Brutes, four twenty-foot frames and their lifts, seventy-five C-stands, and the flags and screens to go with them, it was as if they'd been shooting for a month for all the enervation and rage, not to mention the half dozen snakebit grips and the two others downed with dysentery. Setting the crane had been the worst of it, requiring a platform to handle and level track in five feet of water, meaning the hiring of a local construction crew to drive piles into the silt. And all of this accomplished with a crew that would then shoot for seventy-plus days, half of them exteriors in the summer heat. The entire process brought to mind some sort of ancient great works project—the Almuñécar Aqueduct, Chichén Itzá, the Colossus of Rhodes—for all the drama and casualties. The structure had toppled twice, nearly drowning one of the contract workers and breaking the leg of another. Yet it had been completed, replete with dolly track laid out and leveled in the early-morning hours (thanks to a two-hour pre-call), the Zebra head assembled and ready to be attached to the end of the Supertechno30+.

"So, Javier," Joel had said at 7:30 a.m. "There's a problem with the crane."

"Something I don't know about? We can be up within thirty minutes whenever you decide to do the establishing shot, which based on what we agreed shouldn't be before eleven a.m. because of the shadows."

"Yeah . . ."

"What's the issue then?"

"Well, Jennifer, and I believe she's right by the way, doesn't think she'd be so close to the water."

"Is this a joke?"

"And like I said, I think she has a point, because if Jellyfish—"

"Please stop."

"I don't like your tone."

"My tone?"

"We're on the same side here."

"There are no sides. We're making a movie."

"I'm aware of that."

"You think I can just move that platform to wherever you and your actress want it?"

"I didn't say the platform, I said the crane. This is just for the close-ups and now the tighter master."

"Does Declan know about this? And Jeremy and Charisse and Marci?"

"At this stage I'm just telling you."

"So, just to be clear, to pull out the crane and stage it—where am I supposed to stage it?"

"I was going to leave that up to you."

"In the fucking woods with the snakes? In the sewage?"

"The snakes have been cleared."

"Do you know how many? Just this morning?"

"I was dealing with the actors."

"More than half a dozen. And that's just thirty feet on either side of the path. The fucking wrangler has a bag full of them. And don't tell me the swamp has been cleaned, because it stinks."

"I'm told those are methane deposits from under the silt."

"It's cow shit."

"The water was treated, and there haven't been cows near here for a month. We're not putting an actor in water that isn't safe."

"Meanwhile I've got two grips who can't eat a cracker without pissing out of their asses three minutes later from building the *pinche* platform that's now useless."

"A director should be able to restage a scene. And, Jesus, I'm asking you to move the fucking crane, not the platform. Why do I have to keep telling you that?"

"So I move the crane to where it can't be seen, a few of my guys get bit by copperheads, but it's okay, we've got that fat medic over there who, when I asked her for aspirin earlier, it took her half an hour to bring it to me. And when she finally waddled over, she apologized, saying her bunions were killing her. Her fucking bunions. But at least we have her, and I saw on the call sheet there's a hospital that's only thirty-eight miles away. Thirty-eight miles! I worked in Malaysia in a mangrove swamp and the hospital was closer. So we move the crane off, which means disassembling it because there's no room for it in one piece in the woods, and that takes forty-five minutes. So, to be clear, to then reassemble it and level the track is an hour and a half. Tell me how you're going to get all your coverage and still have us ready by eleven thirty? Because lunch is at noon, and we're not shooting from the crane after one. I'll start seeing my shadow."

"We'll get your shot off before lunch."

"You won't. I saw Jennifer at the camera test. She's a monster, and I get it, but with you catering to her every whim this is going to be a disaster beyond words."

"Where did you learn your English?"

"What?"

"Never mind. It's just you speak—"

"Everyone with this. Mexicans can learn other languages! It's truly amazing!"

"I didn't mean—"

"Reorient the coverage so you're not shooting down the shoreline."

"The crane shot wouldn't cross the axis."

"Isn't that a good thing?"

"I want the disorienting gesture."

"It's a huge establishing shot! No one will even notice your *pinche* gesture!"

ϟ

By the time the grips had disassembled and moved the jib, and the actors had had their second private blocking rehearsal with yet more bickering and line changes, it was 10:30. Pushing the establishing shot until after lunch had now become certain. He'd be ordered to shoot since any shadows could be removed digitally. This would be the right call (other than Joel telling the actress she needed to stand by the water and deal with the obstacle, which would actually make her performance, and therefore the film, more interesting), but it rankled Javier no end. He wished digital photography and digital effects had never been developed. A room shot digitally made one wonder who'd just departed it, while one shot on film provoked anticipation as to who might enter.

"That's nonsense," said one director with whom he'd shared this theory. "The emulsion of film, which has an absence of information that's native to it, keeps us off-balance. The image is incomplete and that's ultimately what we want. Less information subjectively delivered. Art is not reproduction. It's an object or story revealed in essences. Why do you think we still love black-and-white photographs and black-and-white films to the extent we do? So much so that you can take most color pictures and make them black and white and they become better images? Or you can take a black-and-white photograph and deepen the blacks and increase the highlights and it's more interesting? Or time a color photo and make it look like three-strip with higher contrast and more saturation and it's better? Our brains don't want all the fucking details. We want the artist embracing constraint. I'm not a fucking primitive, but there's an aesthetic event horizon between reproduction and abstraction where making great images lives, and digital photography pulls us away from that to a thing that's no longer art. It's more like a combination of video and, with all the digital effects added on, cartoons."

With Sparta one had no choice. The entire storytelling apparatus, from the requirement of IMAX to the preponderance of effects shots, was geared toward digital capture. The genre required it to the extent that every setup was duplicated with a plate shot, absent of any actors, for the purpose of digital augmentation. Additionally, each performer was required to be scanned digitally. This involved standing in a half-sized trailer outfitted with more than two hundred digital cameras on floor-to-ceiling hexagonal grids that fired in a strobe of flashes timed to the shuttering. The resulting images were then fed into a computer and filed for digital compositors, an army of whom, spread across the globe from Romania to Malaysia, would then produce effects without further need of the performer. There's going to be a time, Javier predicted, when they don't need any of us.

⸙

Eleven thirty came and went, and they owed not one but two close-ups, meaning the crane shot would now occur at 3:30 or later, when the shadows would be so long he couldn't adjust frame to minimize their intrusion.

"It's a shot we could have gotten with a drone anyway," announced Declan.

"We're not using a *pinche* drone."

That's when Peter found him.

"You see that?"

"What?" Javier responded.

The actor pointed to where the director sat texting in his tent, the dog with the horn on its head at his feet. Javier couldn't decide whether the animal's presence indicated confidence—like wearing an outlandish article of clothing or a preponderance of body art—or utter emasculation.

"I did a movie with Herzog once," said Peter.

"I assume you mean Werner."

"In Louisiana for the tax credit. He told the crew, 'I don't want to see any phones on my set unrelated to the work. If you're caught texting or scrolling videos or arranging dinner, you'll be sent down the Mississippi on a raft.'"

"That's probably good advice."

"I knew this would be a test, and Mr. Therapy Dog has failed it. We're not going to make our day; you're taking the brunt of it because Max is going to see the dailies with crane shadows that embarrass you; Jennifer doesn't trust him and, frankly, neither do I. Not to mention the fact that the crew despises him for starting us out here."

"We're here because of you."

"He could have told me to fuck off, that we were starting on the stage. He didn't. Fine. I prevailed because I think easing a crew in is always a mistake and there were some scenes on the stage I wasn't ready to shoot. But I'm just an actor. He didn't have the backbone to put me in my place."

"So he's texting at the monitor and the day has been a disaster. What can I do about it?"

After wrap he was summoned to one of Peter's four trailers, which he reached, after admission by security, by walking a parquet plaza resplendent with standing lamps, café tables, and chairs, where a half dozen subalterns of Compton/Levy toiled on laptops, sucking from smoothies prepared by Peter's chef.

"The first thing we want you to know," Marci began once Javier had taken a seat on the sectional sofa, "is that with Peter and me it's about having each other's backs."

"Okay . . ."

"You're nervous," said Peter. "Don't be. Are you familiar with Occam's razor?"

"Always do what's simplest?"

"Well, that's the, forgive me, common misinterpretation. Really it's meant to apply to different hypotheses that reach the same conclusion. It says that the simpler route to a thesis should be preferred because fewer steps in a proof make it less vulnerable to fallacies."

"What does this have to do with being a DP on a Sparta movie?"

"The three of us in this room represent the simplest way to make this film happen the way it should."

"Are you firing Joel and taking over as director? Is Marci?"

"Of course not."

"Then it seems to me you're making things more complicated, which is the opposite of your parable. Joel is the director."

"What I'm envisioning is that you and Joel and I become one by being a team of three—plus Marci, of course—where you and I guide him."

"Then why isn't Joel here?"

"He's meeting with Declan about tomorrow's work."

"If we're all now one, why aren't we with them?"

"Because Marci and I wanted to talk to you and make sure you're on board."

"I'm not participating in a coup."

"We don't see this movie succeeding unless there's strength and confidence and, frankly, competency at the top," said Marci.

"Tell me what that looks like to you," Javier requested.

"Power loves a vacuum," answered Peter. "Mark my words, within days you're going to be hearing from Jeremy and Charisse how to light Jennifer's close-ups. But not if we're standing side by side. This may be a Sparta movie, but I'm the face of the franchise. Instead of abandoning Joel, you and I hold him close and protect him."

"You mean control him."

"Better us than Sparta. Or imagine if Sparta gets rid of him and puts some stooge in who's even worse. And you want to know something? I like Joel. He's just in over his head. Shame on us. He impressed us when we met with him."

"And, by the way," added Marci, "my husband's not going to say this, but there are worse fates than having Peter as an ally. He's going to be meeting with Joel every morning now. Give it a few days. You'll see."

ELEVEN

"Any calls?" Joel had taken to asking his local assistant between setups. She'd just graduated from the Savannah College of Art and Design after growing up in Augusta, where her father was on the board of the country club. An aspiring screenwriter, she'd also dabbled in acting. She was also striking: blond and easily four inches taller than he. Why had every aspect of his life come to feel compensatory?

"Jordan Levinson called again. He said it won't take long, just the next time you're on a break. I can't believe you know him."

"I do."

"He's why I want to be a screenwriter."

"He'll be flattered."

"Joel! How's the land of Sparta?" his erstwhile collaborator asked after the first ring and without saying hello. "I'm so envious."

"No, you're not."

"More people will watch your movie than anything I've ever made."

"I'm not sure if that's true or, if it is, how that's a good thing on any level."

"It's good for you."

"I'm on set with a very unhappy DP and a lead actor I want to strangle, so it's not a great time to expose to you why the only emotion you should have for me is pity."

"What are you, about two months in?"

"Something like that." Had he been speaking with anyone other than Jordan, he might have described the inexorable diminution week by week of what little power he ever had. One day had blended into the next, every scene a struggle to negotiate not only the picayune quibbles of his two lead actors but what seemed to be the coopting by Peter Compton and his wife of every relationship he had with department heads. He'd expected this from Sparta; it's why his therapist had insisted on the dog. But being relegated down another couple of echelons had never been contemplated.

"You've called twice this morning, Jordan. What's up?"

"I'm firing my lawyer."

My God, thought Joel, is he really going to encroach on the only refuge I have left, my marriage? Will he now be in my home, where I'll have to listen to deals being negotiated for the life that could have been mine? Why, other than out of pure malice, conscious or not, would he be asking what he's clearly about to ask?

"It's in the middle of a contract, which is why the bit of urgency. But I got to thinking, Who is the best attorney around? And of course it's my old pal Joel Slavkin's amazingly brilliant wife. But I don't want to call her if you're not comfortable with it."

"Why wouldn't I be comfortable?"

"You know how people are. She's your wife, maybe you'd feel like it was some sort of line that shouldn't be crossed . . ."

It was as if he were imploring Joel to admit, "You know what? I *am* kind of uncomfortable with it. There are thousands of entertainment lawyers in LA, many of them extraordinary, and I really wouldn't be good with Annie representing you."

"Jordan," he instead heard himself say, "nothing would make me happier than for her to work with you. Two of the most extraordinary people I know in league with each other? I just want to be around for the results."

"Are you sure about this?" she asked on the phone that night.

"We're a partnership. What's best for you is what's best for me."

"What makes you feel like representing Jordan is what's best for me?"

"My own feelings about the guy aside, he's one of the most respected directors of our time. Your reputation is incredible, but the more of these guys you have, the more of them you'll get. Plus, he's doing TV now as a producer.

He's also . . . what did I hear? Selling his own espresso and vodka? You'd be representing not just him but an entire brand."

"Why does it sound like you're using this to beat yourself up?"

"Beat myself up for what?"

"I'm not taking him on."

"Now you absolutely are."

"It's my choice, Joel."

"And I'm telling you that if you don't I'm going to feel even smaller than I already do."

She arrived on the last flight from Los Angeles that Friday. Both avoided the topic until Sunday morning, when he woke to an empty bed (on their one day for sex) and found her in the kitchen at her laptop.

"Give me half an hour with this contract."

"Jordan's?"

"Joel . . ."

"Just tell me."

"Have you heard of something called attorney-client privilege?"

"I don't care."

"A few years ago he optioned a book that Paramount has decided to make."

"Which is?"

"*Light in August.*"

"A book he hadn't read until AFI, when he asked me what piece of literature I would most want to make into a movie, and I said *Light in August*. Un-fucking-believable. For all his reputation as the great 'auteur,' that guy has never had an original idea in his life. How much is Paramount giving him to make it?"

"I'm going into the other room, and this conversation is over."

"I want to know."

"The more you talk right now, the more unappealing it is."

She finished her redline while he walked the dog twice around the block, avoiding the eyes of pedestrians as they beheld the plastic horn. He now wished he could euthanize the creature, which had grown so attached to him he had to carry or hold her perpetually or she'd bark relentlessly. He'd nearly been evicted because of it.

"I'm sorry," he told his wife upon his return. "Obviously my frustrations are not about Jordan."

⚡

"How are you going to make this a better experience?" she asked that night over dinner at the Optimist.

"Our marriage?"

"Let me put it another way. What are you going to do to stop being a pussy on this film?"

"It's hopeless, Annie."

"What's making it so difficult?"

"Oh, let's see. I told you about the daily meetings."

"With Peter in the morning."

"What about the fact that those happen in his own area of base camp, garrisoned by security guards who, to this day, look at my ID, then announce me over the radio on Peter's own dedicated channel. His assistant alerts Peter, who then approves my admittance. I walk across the square they've laid out, past the chef's trailer where a local barista Marci hired is setting up, and into his makeup trailer, where I sit beside him while his face is tended to, and don't get me started on that process, which is—why it takes not two but three dedicated artists just to get Peter Compton to look like Peter Compton, you'll have to explain to me. There's no prosthetic work, no wig, no facial hair, no aging up or down, so why three people? I'll tell you. One to handle hot towels and the moisturizer, another for makeup and concealer, the third for hair. Or why did we have to shut down for the entire morning last week while a dermatologist was called in to look at a fucking blackhead? His diagnosis? It's a blackhead! The treatment? Something called a fizz mask that had us down for another forty-five minutes when they could have covered the fucking thing with base. 'No, that would clog the pore further!' I was told by the stooge in charge of the hot towels. It was like conferring with Anthony Fauci at the onset of COVID. I honestly thought Peter was going to be rushed to the CDC by ambulance and escort."

"Go on."

"So while he's being tended to, I present the day's schedule, shot by shot, defending my choices while his makeup artists, the assistant, and the hair lady listen. Am I sure I don't want to flip the shooting order and do what's slated for the afternoon in the morning? What's the coverage for this scene going to be? What's the master shot I have in mind? How am I going to get the performance out of Ron in this pivotal moment? How do I intend to stage it? What lenses am I going to use? Will it be Steadicam or dolly? Did I clear that with Javier, which, I don't quite know what the arrangement is, but he and Javier have some kind of cabal going that they claim is for my benefit."

"Cabal, Joel?"

"Basically the way it works is that if one or the two of them disagree with how I want to cover or stage a scene, they overrule me, as if directing the film weren't my job but all of ours, and decisions, at least the most impactful ones, are decided by majority vote. And since Javier and Peter will always agree with each other, I'm always outvoted. So I sit there in the makeup trailer—and half the time he has his eyes closed, by the way, because they're steaming his skin and applying all sorts of toners and creams—"

"Do they shave him?"

"He shaves himself, if you can believe it, though the makeup artist in charge of concealer and the rest dons magnifying glasses just for the task of finding individual whiskers he might have missed. These are razed with a state-of-the-art micro electric German contraption I was informed was purchased for twelve hundred dollars on the Touch of Modern website. Not by Peter, of course, but the film, but he'll then keep it because once he used it no one else can. So after thirty minutes of merciless inquest, complete with jokes, mostly at my expense that his little audience of minions laughs at dutifully, I'm dismissed, after which, as instructed, I meet with my AD, who jots down what I've written, and we begin our day. And that's just how it starts. The remainder, minute by minute, hour by hour, is a succession of humiliations large and small, almost all of them delivered publicly on set, that abate not at wrap, not even when I get in my car, but when I silence my phone for the six blessed hours of sleep I get so that I have any prayer of surviving another day without them calling for the paddy wagon."

"Jesus, Joel."

"And did I tell you that he—Peter, I mean—brings crystals and sage to set?"

"You didn't."

"The crystals he places around the perimeter as a purifying shroud. The sage he burns like he's some kind of shaman. It's, minimum, a ten-minute process, which sounds like nothing but is significantly expensive with this sort of crew because it adds up over the day, especially when I'm constantly racing the clock. But everyone treats it like they're lucky to be in the presence of such a spiritual being. Or the guy who follows him around with a suitcase—I'm not kidding you, a suitcase—full of vitamins and proteins, plus these innumerable contraptions to measure every aspect of his health, from his pulse down to the millisecond to his glucose to his lungs, his breath. It's fucking crazy. But of course it's not, because what it does is further assert his centrality, and that's what Peter Compton requires. Everyone needs to know that the set is his and he's the most valuable asset on it. When Alice called me last weekend for help with her *Of Mice and Men* paper, you were worried I didn't have the headspace. I actually felt some relief, because finally I was in a position of authority. This movie is a bloodbath."

"What can I do?"

"You came and visited."

"I could have been nicer."

"Taking Jordan on was my fault. I could have told you no."

"The fact is, Joel, not even Jordan has the control you think he has or that you fantasize for yourself."

"That's just not true."

"He's got budgets that limit him, he needs stars for his films like anyone else. I'm speaking out of school, but there are mutual approvals on his department heads when he does a studio film."

"But when Jordan goes onto a set it's his show. It's gotten to the point where I'll choose a lens, I'm not joking, and we'll set up the shot where Javier and I agree, and Peter will look at the monitor with the stand-in—this guy Cody who's a complete pain in the ass, don't get me started about him—and Peter will say, 'Shouldn't we push in a bit and maybe boom up?'"

"And what do you say?"

"'This matches Ron's close-up,' or whoever's, to which Peter will answer, 'Yeah, but the movie isn't called *Jellyfish*,' or name the scene partner. One day I got so exasperated I said, 'You know, Peter, there are some actors who don't even want to know where the camera is, much less the lens size and distance from the floor. They just want to play the scene.'"

"Jesus, Joel."

"To which he responded, 'Oh yeah? Well, there are some directors where I don't worry about it, and you're not one of them. Now go text behind the monitor so Javier and I can fix your mistakes and let you take credit for our work.'"

"He said that?"

"He did, sweetheart. The shaman actor with the crystals and sage who is, of course, a drug addict and an ex-con the world now worships. So please don't tell me I'm just like Jordan or Jordan is just like me, because it's fucking bullshit."

"I'm not the enemy here."

"I'm sorry. And if I hear 'The movie is called *Major Machina*, not *fill in the blank*' from him again, I'm going to throw myself from a bridge over I-85 into oncoming traffic. I contemplate it every day at wrap. I can show you the exact one. I'm terrified of when we go into full nights. There'd be a certain poetry to offing myself at dawn."

"Don't speak like that."

"You think I'm joking."

"Then what are you doing this for, Joel?"

"I'm supposed to quit? Plus, I look at the dailies and they're good. Peter, for all his prancing and bullying, crystals and sage, is still an amazing actor. And he's incredibly smart—a fact he'll be the first one to remind you of—and hard-working. The guy's running himself ragged. I keep telling myself that maybe it's like how women describe childbirth—incredibly painful, but then you'll forget just how extreme, so you'll do it again."

"Please don't ever compare making a movie or anything to having a child. I honestly hate that rhetorical epidemic."

"Noted."

"Can you speak with Marci?"

"And say what?"

"'Tell your husband to give me some space.'"

"You think she'd be receptive?"

"Marci is shrewd. She's also the world's foremost expert on Peter Compton. She has to be. Without her he'd not only not be where he is, playing this part and on the verge of becoming one of the top five movie stars in the world, but he probably would have relapsed."

"You think?"

"Do you have any idea the pull of that disease? You're a fantastic director, Joel. The only difference between you and Jordan is the path you chose to take. You went the studio route, and between you and me, Jordan would never have succeeded in that world the way you have. And by the way, Jordan has never been paid what you have."

"Even if you combine the writing and directing?"

"Never. And part of the reason is because you can deal with people like Peter in a way that Jordan never could. It's part of the deal. Listen to me. Peter and Marci need you to be your strongest and best version of yourself, because guess what? Jeremy and Charisse are on yor ass now—I mean, I'm assuming they are, and the only reason you're not mentioning them is because Peter is so much worse—"

"Correct."

"Well, it's nothing compared to what's coming once you're done in Atlanta."

"Sweetheart, I've directed studio movies before."

"Not for Sparta. Remember, I represent James Finn and went through the entire *Python* debacle. These people are terrified of actors, and they don't know equipment or how to choose a location, let alone stage a scene on it. It's kind of hilarious, actually. But what they do understand is post. When Max Kaiser and his people take control with their test screenings, which, by the way, are all in-house because they're terrified of spoilers, Peter and Marci are going to need you. It becomes like an echo chamber, and you guys will have no real empirical support to back up your ideas. If that means getting Peter to back off and give you space to operate, you have to do what it takes to get that for yourself."

"And if she tells me to go fuck myself?"

"Marci's too smart. Trust me, she won't."

That week production moved to the stage. He could at least look forward to several weeks of driving onto a lot, parking next to his trailer, and strolling onto a set unexposed to the challenges of weather, snakes, insects, and paparazzi.

Annie had left Monday and it was now Wednesday. He'd awakened at 4:45 a.m. to give himself plenty of time to feed the dog, review the day's scenes, peruse his notes and shot list, and stop off at his favorite bakery for an almond croissant and macchiato. This would afford fifteen minutes in his trailer before the compulsory meeting with Peter at 7:00, after which he'd have a good half hour to speak with Marci before the 8:00 a.m. rehearsal.

The dog, however, saw the morning differently, refusing to eat her breakfast even after two slices of bacon he'd taken time to fry and chop had been added to the four-dollar can of organic food specially designed for the animal's worsening skin condition. Instead she shat easily a half quart of diarrhea on the bathroom rug. Once he'd rinsed it and chucked it into the washing machine, then had gathered the animal and his belongings, he was easily twenty minutes behind schedule. By special arrangement, the local bakery allowed him to purchase his goods early before it opened at 6:30, but the croissants still weren't ready at 6:15, adding yet another five minutes to his tardiness.

"You're late, Joel," murmured the actor from underneath his towel.

"Sorry, Peter."

"I watched the dailies last night. What are you going to do about Ron?"

"There's a performance in there."

"We'll only be certain when we're cutting." More and more frequently the actor anticipated the edit with the first-person plural, foreshadowing weeks locked in a room struggling for control of a process the studio would render unbearable all on its own.

"I think we'll be fine. I've always got you and Jennifer to cut to, not to mention the various guards. And when he doesn't go up on his lines he's pretty good. Did you want to go over the day?"

"What's the plot of this movie, Joel?"

"Uhm . . ."

"Twenty-five words or less, give or take."

"Faced with world domination by an alien being who will poison the lakes, rivers, and seas unless mankind achieves universal peace, Major Machina, with the aid of a brilliant marine biologist with whom he has fallen in love, must save a flawed world."

"More than twenty-five, but still pretty good. When I least expect it, you impress the hell out of me." He turned to his assistant and the two makeup artists. "Wasn't that kind of amazing? Seriously, Joel, if you brought that kind of clarity to set, we'd be making *Citizen Kane*."

"I'm trying, Peter."

"I know you are. Why do you think I asked for the plot, simply told?"

"I'm really not sure."

"When I was in prison I studied with a professor named Reuben Shapiro. You've never heard of him, but he's one of the most incredible people I've ever met. We read Aristotle together. Every story needs to be seen in terms of its narrative trajectory, which Aristotle insisted be described in terms of a single protagonist whose story has a beginning, middle, and end, with a moment of what he called *peripeteia* that reverses the hero's story and leads to a tragic denouement."

"But this isn't a tragedy. You don't exactly end up poking your own eyes out because you realize you've killed your father and slept with your mother."

"How about our Joel, ladies? Pulling out the Sophocles reference."

"Amazing."

"Let's not give him too much credit. Probably the most famous tragedy ever written, and the basis for one of Freud's seminal doctrines." He again addressed Joel. "Obviously it's not a tragedy. But the rules of the narrative arc are the same. Today we're filming a scene in which Dr. Stanton, played by the hypersensitive Jennifer Taylor, and Paul Kramer, played by yours truly, realize their affection for each other is more than platonic."

"You kiss."

"We do. And it changes everything for Paul. Suddenly he realizes that what Jellyfish doesn't understand about humanity is that, yes, we're flawed, but sometimes beautifully; even the superheroes among us are susceptible to unexpected passions that have nothing to do with some collective utilitarian reality. You know what 'utilitarian' means?"

"I think so."

"Greatest good for the greatest number. Jay Lynne, order a copy of *On Liberty* by John Stuart Mill for Peter. Have it sent to the production office."

"Done," said the young assistant.

"I really—"

"You'll read it after we've locked picture."

Were I to tell people this happened they wouldn't believe me, thought Joel. That this clown got to stuff his brain in prison with pretentious allusions he only half understands is enough to make me want to murder his sentencing judge.

"What I'm getting at," he continued, "is that this scene should be intense. Don't worry about Max Kaiser or what Jeremy and Charisse say. Fuckin' let Jennifer and me go at it. I've already talked to her and she's game."

"There's an intimacy coordinator."

"Yeah, I know, but fuck that."

"It's required by Sparta. Also the union. She's been hired."

"If that woman says a word to me, I'm going to bolt my trailer door until she's on a plane back to LA. Intimacy coordinator. I mean, can you believe someone is actually paid to do this? That people call it a profession? That our industry buys into this manufactured need? Look, women have had it terrible—though, let's be honest, that didn't stop Marci. She did fine. But actresses, sure. It's awful how so few of them get meaningful work past their twenties, and during their twenties it's all about fuckability. If I had a daughter who wanted to be an actress, I'd lock her in a room and feed her under the door. But does this mean that the women whose parents failed them and who've chosen this profession need some closet sex fiend on set asking them if they're okay every three minutes and getting between them and their scene partner right when shit's meant to get interesting? On the last film I did, and I am not making this up, this woman would not stop whispering in our ears. Finally I said, 'You know, the way you're purring at us, you're actually more like a fluffer.' And the woman reported me! The intimacy coordinator, not my scene partner, went to the producer! And she walked away with ten fucking grand in a settlement because I'd apparently harassed her."

"As I said, Sparta requires it."

"Just keep her away from me. Better yet, I'll have Marci handle it. I don't want you getting sideways with anyone. You're going to have Jennifer to deal with today, and we don't want *her* lodging a complaint; you'll get served by Mensa. Speaking of Marci, don't you have a meeting with her?"

"I do."

"What's that about? Me?"

"Why would I have a meeting about you?"

"Oh please, Joel. I've been your worst nightmare. Annie was here this weekend, wasn't she? My guess is you were complaining to her, and she told you to talk to Marci about getting me to back off. It's fine. It's smart. Annie is smart. I wish she were my lawyer. You married the right woman."

How can so many despicable qualities aggregate within one functioning being? Joel wondered as he carried his dog across the parquet. There's that saying between smitten lovers that the depth of their affection proves the existence of God. Peter Compton does the opposite: his presence, when juxtaposed with the suffering he causes, proves there is no God.

TWELVE

Marci could think of at least three men on her freshman hall whom Joel Slavkin brought to mind. What did each share? She was the precise woman they fantasized meeting when setting off for Penn. One of them she dated, a boy from St. Louis she met moving in. Already on campus for varsity soccer, he appeared shirtless from showering, his broad chest and loose hips moving in leonine rhythm as he centered himself at her door in only a towel.

"You need help?"

"Shouldn't you get dressed?"

"I could do that," he answered with a wide smile revealing teeth straightened by an orthodontist who'd no doubt belonged to his temple. "But I've gotten really fast at that, so I'll be back soon."

She had thought of men as dogs—not in the debased sense as marauders in a pack, but more as pets—for some time, really since reaching puberty, when she began to test her power to seduce and control. It happened first with her father's friends, whom she'd watch will themselves not to stare when visiting, especially in the Hamptons around the pool or before dinner when drinks were served. Her lips, eyes, and breasts seemed of particular fascination, but they also spoke often of her hair, which she kept long and came clearly from her Sephardic maternal side, with thick curls that splayed out in a feral diaspora of dark brown.

"How's school?" they would ask, more interested in the sound of her words, the way her lips formed them, how her body moved when she gesticulated, than the utterances themselves, a thesis she tested by willfully making no sense when she spoke and watching them nod encouragingly as if her incoherence conveyed truths they'd been desperate to learn.

"Are you thinking about college yet?" they'd wonder prematurely in her ninth grade year, when her breasts had grown to three-quarters of their present size.

"I'd like to stay on the East Coast," she'd respond. "Or maybe Stanford, Pomona."

She could practically feel them tumesce as they reconsidered their entire journeys. Why had they married the women they'd married? Why had they settled for the Wall Street life? Why weren't they young again? Why couldn't they begin anew and wed a girl like the one in front of them who wouldn't mutcher and complain, demand they have lunch once a week? Why couldn't they have lost their virginity to Marci? Or better, why couldn't she lose her virginity to them with all their knowledge and experience instead of to some high school *schlep* who'd fumble with her bra, not know where and how to touch her, would ejaculate the moment it all began?

They would follow her, desperate for any scrap of attention, or simply stare unwaveringly as she moved through a room. A few were mastiffs or Dobermans, fierce and loud, overimpressed with themselves. Others more like sheep dogs or Saint Bernards, cumbersome and gentle. Some were small and angry about that, compensatory with their aggression like Jack Russells. But to a man they'd heel to her attention, panting at her feet for whatever she'd choose to provide by way of conversation or simple proximity. Two had overstepped and tried to kiss her, each during the summer after eleventh grade. She'd rebuked the advances and told no one, though both had engineered retreats with their wives to Manhattan the following morning before breakfast.

The soccer player from St. Louis was more the retriever type, loyal, generous, kind, just smart enough not to bore her, eager to fetch prizes—snacks late at night, the odd necklace or bracelet—and put them solicitously at her feet. The sex was the best she'd ever had, if only because she'd not encountered such an athlete from among the boys at Collegiate and Browning and Dalton she'd dated on and off in the city, but also because of his obsession with pleasing her, to the extent she'd need to discourage overstimulation. As for what she did for him, she'd never been lavished with such vocal display. Neighbors on their hall nicknamed him "the Hyena." What appellation she'd earned, she could only guess.

They dated for four months, but nine weeks in she caught him looking at her over dinner at a Chinese restaurant off campus and realized that, for all his confidence and swagger, she had all the power. And why? Because though she'd fuck him like a maniac, though she'd sucked him off until he'd screamed at four in the morning on the quad, though they did for each other whatever each wanted, it was clear that what he saw in her, for all its perversity, was an intensely fuckable version of the woman who bore him.

She shared this epiphany with her roommate and another girl she'd befriended on the hall, and of course with friends from back home, along with the conviction the relationship needed to end.

"Are you out of your mind?" her older sister shouted over the phone. "That's the sweet spot, Marci. You'll never do better. He's attracted to you, which, of course, why wouldn't he be? You're a little Semitic goddess. But he looks at you and has a conscience! Jewish boys fucking adore their mothers, but they're also terrified of them. It's a whole thing. I mean, have you seen Jacob around Mom?" she asked, referring to the brother between them in age.

"I don't want to be some boy's mother. In one week he went from Labrador to spaniel."

"You and your ridiculous dog thing."

"Says the woman who married an Airedale."

"A Jewish Airedale who's obsessed with me! Which, trust me, is insane with how good-looking my husband is and that he's loyal the way he is."

She broke up with her Lab turned spaniel and moved on to two German shepherds in succession, then a poodle, then the MBA candidate (a rottweiler) who cheated on her. And it was always the same until Peter: she was a sex mom. There was no other way of putting it, and it repulsed her.

And yet the concept, so long as it remained only that, had its advantages, and with men like Joel Slavkin she was always reminded of this. In short, though the director had married a fiercely attractive blond lawyer, he lusted in ways beyond his control for Marci. At a certain level it was only human. Should he have chosen a Marci, he would have been distracted by an Annie: cold, withholding, as rigorously perfect as an equation. But with Marci's assent for the fifteen minutes it would take to bed him, the man would throw it all over: his wife, their children, directing the movie for Sparta, directing any movie at all. And why?

To this cockapoo forever risking glances from behind his tortoiseshell glasses with his fine high cheekbones, thinning hair, and hawklike nose, Marci was the most lethally dangerous being imaginable. He could disagree with her, not trust her, learn to despise her, but she would always ultimately control him with her beguiling combination of Semitically sexual maternal power.

She'd been predicting Joel's request to meet for weeks. Her husband had become too openly restrictive, at times even abusive, lately critiquing blocking and staging in front of other actors and the crew, in addition to the persisting questions regarding angles and lens choices.

"I'm honestly starting to wonder why I'm here," Javier had remarked to her and Jeremy and Charisse at least half a dozen times. "Because if it's just to carry out his orders and get between him and the dog owner, you can do a lot better. Hire a psychologist who's good with animals."

Peter was becoming unmanageable, perhaps even vulnerable to old impulses. They had under three weeks left to shoot, but these were important weeks, with the big UN scene yet to be filmed, one that involved Paul Kramer's Saint Crispin's Day exhortation to the planet that they come together in solidarity to quell the alien menace. Effecting behavioral change through Joel offered the most propitious alternative since it would also embolden the director for postproduction, when Sparta would pose challenges that would make those associated with Peter seem nugatory.

The question upon waking had been what to wear. She needed the director to have his wits about him, but also be enough on his heels to carry out her solution without argument. The result was a pair of tight denim capris that clung halfway down the leg and ended to reveal most of her shins and calves. On top, a loose-fitting long-sleeved black V-neck she'd bought at Fred Segal just before setting out for Atlanta. He would have little temptation to gawk, but enough of her would show to keep his imagination firing. My problem, she thought as she shaped her eyebrows, is that while I love men, understanding them has become too easy, and the more I know, the more sympathetic I become, which of course makes me all the more appealing. What other women find off-putting, I find poignant, even at times endearing. Should I not pity Joel Slavkin for having to encounter daily, on a set where he's being persistently humiliated, this seemingly better version of what his life might have been? Of course, I'll get mine in fifteen years when much of this evanescent allure has waned.

⚡

Samantha, her assistant of four years, allowed Joel and his bichon frise into the trailer just after seven thirty.

"Peter! May Sam get you anything before she leaves? You want breakfast?"

"I ordered something from catering."

"Oh my God, why did you do that? Let Ace make you something."

"Yeah, but my breakfast tacos, which I actually love, will go to waste. Plus I had an almond croissant about an hour ago."

"Seriously? What? You're worried about your weight? You're at least five pounds skinnier than when we started."

"Ten, actually."

"Someone will eat your tacos. You've got to let us get you something. Ace isn't working with the same budget as those guys. His eggs alone. It's crazy. He found this farmer who feeds his free-range chickens marigolds. You've never seen yolks like this. And the taste. Like the hens laid them in Eden. He also found a baker in Buckhead who makes a seven-grain bread that Peter and I love. I get two poached eggs on toast with sliced avocado and fresh ground pepper. Why don't we have Sam order the same for you?"

"Sure."

"And some fresh-squeezed juice. What do you like? He can do grapefruit, orange, blueberry, raspberry, blackberry, pineapple, strawberry, and I think acai. You name it. Or a combination."

"Whatever you like."

"I have apple, grapefruit, lemon, and blackberry with a shot of ginger. Same as in LA every day. It's tart, but I haven't gotten sick in five years."

"Sure."

"And you have your coffee."

"Yes."

"Okay, Sam, put it in motion. Joel and I are gonna get to it." After Samantha had left, Marci said, "She's amazing. We negotiated an associate producer credit for her on this, but in ten years she'll be hiring and firing us all. Movies are one of the last industries in America with an actual apprentice system—well, except for actors. Actors can crash the party. Look at my husband, although you can argue he served his apprenticeship at the feet of his father on all those sets. But that girl is brilliant. One thing I love is ambition. One thing I hate is stupidly impatient ambition. She gets it. Not once have I ever sensed resentment, no matter the task. She's getting our breakfast right now. That's what she's doing, and with a smile on her face."

"She should join us."

"No, Peter, I want this to be just you and me. What's on your mind?"

"Well . . . honestly, Marci . . ."

"Honesty is what I want."

The dog barked and he raised it to his lap. With its cone, the animal looked like a bullhorn attached to a body and four legs.

"I don't want to be directing this film anymore."

"Okay . . ."

"Your husband has defeated me."

"Peter has tremendous respect for you."

"That's just not true. I know you're mostly in the producers' tent—and thank you for that—protecting the quality of the film from the Sparta folks."

"They're harmless. And actually both of them are very smart. He'd never admit it, but Peter listens to them. Especially Charisse. I shouldn't tell you this, but they're talking with Max about your jumping on to the *Hawk* franchise."

"That can't be true."

"I wouldn't lie to you."

"I know you wouldn't, Marci. You've been amazing."

"Look. No one ever said it was going to be easy directing for the SCG. If it were, you wouldn't be paid what you're getting paid to be taking it from all sides while still putting everything of yourself into it you can. I watch you every day. I see what's up."

"I just can't believe they would want me back."

"It's the results that count, and who can argue with those?"

"Nobody ever says dailies are bad."

"I've seen directors and DPs and actors fired over dailies."

"But they have to be pretty terrible."

"Yours are excellent. I just want to be clear here. You say you don't want to be directing the movie. Does that mean you're quitting?"

"Honestly, if I could I would."

"Okay. Whew. I'm gonna take that as a no. The first thing you need to know is that, whether it seems so or not, Peter is capable of hearing criticism. You may not believe me, but the guy is truly decent, and he has a conscience. I wouldn't be with him if I didn't believe that."

"Of course not."

"You can't be afraid to let him know how you feel and how his crowding of you is getting in the way of your doing your job. If you let him know how his behavior is making you feel, he's going to hear you. Remember this about most actors: they can't stand not being liked. Jesus, their whole being craves adulation, or they'd be doing something else. That goes for the smart ones and the dumb ones, the mean ones and the nice ones—well, maybe not all the mean ones—but it certainly goes for Peter. Everyone gives me credit for his sobriety. It's partly me, but more than that it's his success and the fact that he's loved out there and doesn't want that to stop. What I worry most about with Peter is what happens when he's no longer one of the most famous people on the planet. Or if he still is but for not good reasons. You've got to stand up to him."

"May I ask what that sounds like?"

"'Hey, Peter, your intrusiveness leaves me no room. It also humiliates me, which makes it less likely I'll risk exposing my ideas for fear of having to endure your shooting them down in a way that's public and ugly. I'll also go so far as to say that when you do that, it makes you look bad.' You add that last part, and trust me, he'll listen."

"Can you really imagine me saying any of that to your husband? Let's be honest. From the moment we disagreed about whether Major Machina should have a phone, he's done everything he can to try and undercut me, from making fun of my dog every chance he gets to forcing me to change the schedule, which everyone knows was a disaster. I mean, should I have just caved when we first met and Paul Kramer carries a phone? Maybe. Perhaps I should have known your husband doesn't like to be challenged, especially in front of his wife."

"Wow."

"Sorry, maybe that was too—"

"If you can be this frank with me, why can't you do it with Peter?"

"Forgive me, but Peter can make my job difficult in ways you can't. I mean, I guess you can maybe fire me, but at this point, like I said, I'd welcome that."

"Only Max Kaiser can fire you, and both Peter and I would fight him like hell on that. Not only would I never do that, I'd hire you again."

"Now you're just saying what you think I want to hear."

"I don't ever do that, Joel. Honestly, what can Peter do that has you so afraid?"

"He can show up two hours late. Refuse to say his lines. Sit in his trailer and not come out. Stop taking my direction. Turn the cast and crew against me. Turn Sparta against me. Actors have a tremendous amount of power in production. I don't have to explain this to you."

"He's done none of that yet, and we're well over halfway done. My husband is difficult, but one thing he also is, at least since he became clean, is professional."

After a brisk two knocks, Samantha entered carrying a thin bamboo tray with two identical breakfasts on ceramic plates with stainless steel flatware. Between the plates stood two slender glasses filled to nine-tenths with pinkish juices that foamed at the top.

"Wow," Peter remarked, rising to help the assistant, who was clearly practiced with such a precarious load.

"We figure, why eat off cardboard?" said Marci. "Plus, so much plastic ends up in the oceans. It's sort of a cause of ours."

"Anything else, you guys?"

"No, Sam, this is all great."

"I'll just be out in the square then," she said. "I've got about seventy emails to answer before we go over to set."

"Knock yourself out. You've had breakfast, right?"

"Before you got here."

She exited, closing the door. Marci watched Peter taste his drink through its paper straw.

"My God," he said.

"Now try the eggs."

He did. "Jesus. I've had fresh eggs before, back in Indiana, but nothing like these."

"And what about the color?"

"The yolk really is like marigolds," he said, seemingly close to tears. It wasn't just this simple apogee of culinary aesthetics, but life in her proximity.

"Here's the thing, Joel. Peter and I aren't selfish with what we have. All this"—she gestured, rolling up her sleeves to expose her forearms—"the trailer, what Sam just called our square, the food, yeah, it goes on Peter's perq line and the studio groans about it, but it's not just for us. Had I known you were eating from catering every morning I'd have fixed that in a second and Ace would have been cooking your meals, because you're on our team. The same goes with your leadership of this project. Sure, Peter needs to feel like he's calling a lot of the shots on set, but he also knows that you need to be able to do your job. Let yourself be known. And I'll tell you what else, I'll be there to back you when you do it."

"You'd do that against your own husband?" It had the slightest hint of suggesting she escape her current life to begin one with him.

"If I suddenly earned the reputation of putting Peter over our projects, no one would bring me on as a producer. I'd maybe get the title, but I sure as shit wouldn't be sitting in the tent next to Jeremy and Charisse, and I wouldn't have my direct line to Max Kaiser. When it comes to production, I've got to be my own girl. Take a bite of your eggs."

"Oh my God . . ."

"Take another. It's what I call the two-bite theory. The first surprises you, the second you can really appreciate." He would disrobe on the spot if she instructed him to and without a moment's cunctation. "So what are you going to do, Joel?"

"I'm going to tell Peter how I feel. I'm going to push back."

"And I'm going to be there to support you."

When Peter asked about their meeting, she responded vaguely, revealing only that the director sought a less humiliating relationship with his star.

"Did he say anything about Javier?"

"Just you, Peter."

"Is something wrong? Are you worried about the make-out scene with Jennifer?"

"Peter, please. Knock yourself out." For her strategy to work she needed, without explicitly saying so, for him to understand that if Joel spoke up, Peter wouldn't necessarily have her as an ally.

In the first hour and a half all went smoothly. She watched the camera rehearsal from the producers' monitor and even listened in her Comtek as Joel directed the scene without Peter questioning his guidance. He didn't even object to the presence of the director's dog.

This changed once the scene crossed into intimacy, though the contretemps began not with Peter but with his female costar.

"This is not going how it was written on the page," she announced. "In the script, I make the first move, and it feels like that's suddenly not the case. He keeps beating me to the kiss."

"Yeah, that's on me," said Peter. "I just thought it was a bit disempowering in a weird way for you to initiate. Joel and I discussed this yesterday morning."

"Where was I?"

"I'm guessing you were getting into makeup."

"And how is it disempowering for my character not to start things?"

"Well, because—"

"No, I want to hear from Joel, not you. Joel is my director, with all due respect."

"By all means," Peter responded.

When Marci joined them alongside the intimacy coordinator, Joel was holding the dog. He glanced at Marci, then turned back to Jennifer and Peter.

"What Peter and I discussed is that if you break traditional norms it sort of suggests that Paul Kramer is irresistible."

"Traditional norms?"

"That the guy initiates."

"What is this, a Production Code film?"

"That's funny," said Peter.

"Maybe I'm just not getting it here."

“For you to kiss him first,” said Joel, “suggests he has some sort of magnetic power, or to speak to the converse, it suggests you’re powerless.”

“He’s a good-looking guy—oh, hi, Marci, this is kind of weird.”

“Would you rather I step away?”

“No, it’s fine with me if it’s fine with you. I mean, not when we actually do the scene—”

“Of course not.”

“I mean, just because—”

“I get it,” said Marci.

“If you look at the rewrites that came in this morning—” Joel continued.

“There were more rewrites?”

“They were in your sides. Did she get sides?” he asked James, who stood behind him.

“I did,” she said, “but I didn’t look at them. I got the double goldenrod revisions last week and those are in my script, which has all my notes. With revisions coming in every day I can’t transfer everything. I get in this place while I’m shooting where there has to be a cutoff, otherwise, I’m just not here. My brain just can’t turn shit off. It’s just the kind of thinker I am.”

Please, Peter, don’t make a joke about Mensa, Marci said to herself as she watched him consider doing so then repress the impulse.

“The idea was,” he instead said, “that I make the first move, and you remark on it in a way that gives you the upper hand, sort of turning the scene on its head and surprising us by putting Paul Kramer off-balance. It’s actually really cool.”

“So I have new lines, and this is the first I’m hearing of it?”

“There were sides—” said Joel.

“I don’t want to hear again about the sides.”

“And the double buff revisions—”

“Fucking emailed to me yesterday! I mean, seriously. Based on a conversation involving a scene I’m in with Peter but in which I wasn’t included. I’ve been treated better as a guest star on network television.”

“Jennifer,” said Joel, “you absolutely have a point, and I want to take full responsibility. You were treated disrespectfully here, and I’m sorry for that. For me to say it won’t happen again—”

"Would be utterly meaningless since I have two shooting days left. This movie has been one humiliation after another. I get it. He's number one on the call sheet. But every day I come in, and you guys are on this whole 'bro' kick, jerking each other off, which, like, Jeremy and Charisse tolerate because they've got to protect the brand, which is bionic Peter Compton—and seriously, since the implication in this PG-13 movie is that we fuck, how does that even work? He's Major Machina, but he's got the actual goods, or was his dick reconstructed?"

"Again, actually quite funny, Jennifer," said Peter.

"A second ago I was 'funny,' now I'm 'actually funny'? As if it's a surprise that anyone but you is capable of a witticism?"

"It was more addressed to the point that you haven't been much of a jokester on this."

"Yeah. What a laugh riot it's been every day having you mop the floor with me."

"For my part, I want to say that I wasn't aware of any rewrite either." It was a voice Marci didn't recognize but, with a glance, learned to be that of the intimacy coordinator, a slender woman in black tights and high-tops with a dark hoodie worn unzipped as if she were warming up for a floor routine. "I got the script I was given a week ago, and that's it. No rewrites. Jennifer's trust has been violated here."

"Oh God," said Peter. "She didn't check her email or look at her sides. That's on her, not us. Sure, Joel and I had a meeting yesterday, which we do every morning, and lines were changed, but so what? And it's not like she didn't have the chance to object. She's doing it right now."

"More than lines, actually. The entire scene."

"No, Jennifer, not the entire scene. And if someone would just get you the sides, you'll probably like the scene more now. I keep saying. And it's not from me or Joel, it's from the writers in LA and approved by Max Kaiser, along with of course Jeremy and Charisse."

"But not me!"

"It wasn't intentional!"

"What she's saying is that it doesn't matter if it wasn't intentional," said the intimacy coordinator. "She doesn't feel heard or respected, and if she's not respected, if she's cut out of the process, how can she trust anyone, especially today? Trust is essential to the physical experience, whether real or played for the camera. You guys have broken that trust and it clearly needs to be repaired, if that's even possible. You have an actress who feels unsafe."

"Okay, look—what's your name again?"

"It's Aviva. That's the third time I've told you."

"Sorry, Aviva. You'll forgive me. I'm playing a title character in a franchise movie here."

"Respectfully, that doesn't mean you disregard the needs and feelings of your female costar when it comes to a scene in which, perhaps more than any other, you need to have consideration and empathy."

"I wasn't—okay . . . I wasn't talking about that. I was explaining why I didn't remember your name."

"Maybe that's part of the problem."

"Excuse me?"

"You're allowing your importance to this project, which no one disputes, and the demands that come along with it to inhibit your ability to consider others."

Marci remained silent, too interested in how Peter would respond to try to de-escalate the dispute.

"Is somebody going to remove this woman from the set now?" he asked loudly. "Or am I done? Because if I have to hear another word, I'm going to behave in a way that'll have me back in prison, which I really don't want. I mean, honestly"—he turned again to Aviva—"do you actually hear yourself when you say such insipid nonsense?"

"Mr. Compton, you can insult me personally as much as you want, though all you do with such attacks is show how frightened you are. Fortunately being your therapist is not my job."

"You're right about that."

"There does remain the problem of this scene. Before moving forward we need to clear the set of everyone but you and Jennifer and me and go over it together, which is what I was trying to do this morning when you had me banished from the stage."

"No, banished would mean you were there in the first place. I had you refused entry altogether. We weren't rehearsing the so-called intimacy part of the scene yet, and since your entire job is one big racket, I didn't see any reason for you to be anywhere near where actual work was being done."

"All right, enough," said Joel, perhaps the sole observer insufficiently curious to allow the feud to go further. "Aviva is actually right, Peter. We need to clear the set of everyone but the four of us."

"Meaning, just so I get this right, completely ignoring what it costs per minute when everything's added in—"

"That doesn't stop you from blessing the set."

"Excuse me, Joel?"

"I'm just saying sometimes we pause. This is going to be one of those times."

"Wow. Okay, you went there. Interesting. So we'll all huddle on the couch here for more idiocy from this completely useless person who, if she hadn't opened her mouth when I was in the process of apologizing to Jennifer—who, let's be frank, should apologize to the production for not reading the changes last night or looking at her sides this morning—but if she hadn't opened her psychobabbling mouth we'd be doing a camera rehearsal right now, but instead we're gonna stop everything and unload our feelings. Don't you see how this works? There's an issue that doesn't need this woman, but she picks and pokes at it and irritates it further so that she can then assert her value. In other words, she creates the problem she then claims only she can solve."

"I'm sorry, Peter, but I don't find your characterization to be accurate. We fucked up. We made changes to the scene—sure it was rewritten in LA and signed off on by Max—but we didn't consult Jennifer, which was pretty stupid of us given the current climate."

"Could somebody, anybody, please explain to me exactly what happened in this industry? In this country?" asked Peter. "I spent three years in lockup and came out to pure fucking insanity, leading, I'm gonna go ahead and say, to the second election of Trump as a clearly self-destructive effort to put a stop to it. Why is this individual—excuse me, *Aviva*—even here? Sure, we fucked up. Jennifer, I'm sorry. I thought it was weird, especially given the fact that you're twelve years younger than I am, that you were throwing yourself at me in this scene, so I said to Joel that I didn't fucking buy it, that it was the same old shit, *seeming* to give the woman power while in actuality just reinforcing the appeal of the man. If you read the sides, you'll see that I make an advance on you, Jennifer, and you push me off as being presumptuous. Yes, we end up making out—which is *all* we do in this PG-13 movie—but it's on your terms, not mine. And Paul Kramer, Major Machina, the superhero, gets pretty humiliated in the process."

"Maybe I should read the pages," Jennifer said.

"Would that be all right with Aviva?" asked Peter.

"Yes," responded the intimacy coordinator.

"And what about you, Joel? Are we good with her actually reading the sides, or would this be yet further evidence of our misogyny?"

"Enough, Peter," said Joel.

"No, really. Because after all, a printer ejaculates ink onto the page, which might be seen as a phallic gesture."

"She should read the scene."

James offered a set from inside his GoldFold, and while Joel, Peter, and the crew waited, the actress read.

"I do still have some issues," she finally announced.

"We'd love to hear them," said Joel.

"She says, 'You think just because I invited you up here it means you can kiss me? That somehow I'm interested in you?'"

"Not a great line. Agreed. But you don't buy it?" asked Peter.

"She's not stupid. Of course she invited him up because something might happen. My sense in moments like this, not that I'm some kind of expert, is: my apartment, my terms. You don't ask for a drink, you wait until one is offered."

"So, you're saying you like how it was with her starting it?" asked Joel.

"No. I just don't think there needs to be all this discussion between them. It's just like at the water. You guys think you're putting forth some version of what a strong woman is, but here you just make her seem naive and prudish. She wants to fuck the guy, but she wants to control how it happens. That's it. Why not just cut all this dialogue. Have him try to kiss her, have her deflect it, push him off or whatever, and then she initiates it once he feels repudiated?"

"Initiates it how?" asked Peter.

"Physically. She kisses him."

"Is that okay with you, Peter?" asked Aviva.

"Oh my God. How about this: if it isn't okay, I'll say so, and I'll tell Jennifer or Joel. You don't exist."

To Marci's surprise, Joel spoke before she could. "Peter, Aviva is a part of this crew. Whether you like it or not, she's going to be here. I want her here, the producers want her here, and I'm guessing Jennifer wants her here."

"Wait," Peter responded, "because I keep trying to square this. You've chosen right now, today, finally, to assert yourself. And in defense of this person?"

"You can't say to a crew member she's not welcome on set."

"I fucking say it all the time, Joel. I say it to the B-roll team when they're in my eyeline, or to Javier's guys when they're tweaking lights or putting sandbags on C-stands during a rehearsal, or to Elise when she comes up with the script while I'm trying to concentrate and wants to correct a line or is bugging me about continuity. You kick everyone off set when we rehearse a scene before showing it to the crew. So why can't I tell the woman who inhibits all sexual spark—everything the scene should actually be about—that I don't want her in my fucking ear?"

"Because one," said Joel, continuing to radiate his sudden authority, "you're speaking to her in a manner that's disrespectful and personal, and two, yes, you're free to express a preference that direction come from me, or that Jennifer express directly to you what issues you might be having, but you cannot—I will not allow it, in fact—say who is and who is not allowed to be here. Only I can do that."

"Who the fuck *are* you? I mean, seriously. Where did the sudden assumption of authority come from? Your conversation with Marci?"

"I think we should let the crew grab coffee," asserted James. "This is feeling like—"

"Feeling like what?" asked Peter. "A real conversation?"

"James is right," said Marci. "It's a discussion that should happen between the people actually having it, without an audience, without anyone, including you, saying things publicly you'll later regret."

"There's nothing I've said or will say that I'm going to regret, of that you can be assured."

"You're making us all uncomfortable, honey. No one wants to hear this." She glanced at the gawking crew to discover the opposite to be true.

"You think I don't want them to hear?" he said, turning to face them. "You want to know something, everybody? Just in case it hadn't crossed your mind? The person who has the most at stake on this movie, the person who will actually take the biggest hit if it fails, is me. Not Jennifer. Not Joel. Not my wife or any of the producers. Not any of you, but me."

"Peter, please . . ." said Marci.

"No, seriously." He raised his voice to dispel any ambiguity as to whom he wished to address. "Go out there and look at my base camp, which I know everyone makes fun of, and ask yourself why. Why all the trailers? Why the common area we've set up so all of our people can meet and share ideas and info. First of all, make no mistake. I pay for all that, not the studio. Yes, they handle the invoices, but trust me when I say it's baked into the cost of having me around, meaning if I forwent all of it or most of it, I'd get an even bigger salary than I already do, so I effectively lose money by having it. It's skin off my hide. But why then *do* I have all of it? And given how seemingly great I have it, why would I get a bit cross with a woman coming onto this set and disrespecting me and my process? Actors are the only workers on a movie who when they're working, everyone stops and watches them. Imagine that when you're setting a flag or laying dolly track or changing the battery on a radio mic. That everyone stops to watch you. But it doesn't stop there, because then some guy comes up and tells you, in front of everyone, 'No, do it again, but not like you just did, that sucked. Do it this way.' And so you do, then he says, again with everyone listening, 'No, more like this.' And there are people whispering in his ear with still other suggestions, and meanwhile everyone else is *thinking* suggestions and judging you and wondering not just why you ever became a star but why you got the part, thinking deep down at some level that they could do it better. And don't claim otherwise, because I know. But not only on set are you being scrutinized and corrected. You're being filmed every take, and everyone will watch that too, because there are dailies, even the takes you fuck up. *Especially* the ones you fuck up, because they'll even make blooper reels. But that's acting. What I signed up for. Fair enough. But now multiply it times a hundred. As Major Machina in the film of the same title, I'm supposed to be a certain weight, my skin is supposed to be clear, my hair perfect, and I'm meant to be here every day with my lines learned and my character filled out and be relaxed and in command.

Because if I don't and I fail, this big engine won't keep running with people buying tickets to see me so that you all can get hired to do your well-paying jobs. You think I'm exaggerating? You think, Who gives a fuck about Peter Compton? This is a Sparta movie! Guess what? At the end of the day it really ain't. Trust me when I say Max Kaiser would not green-light a nine-figure movie—no studio will—without a star. And so the star becomes this kind of avatar for all their hundred-million-dollar excesses. Am I replaceable? Sure, but honestly, not beyond a person or two. You could have one of a handful of so-called bankable names play Paul Kramer, but right now, guess what? I'm the guy, and guess what happens if I fail? Sparta? They'll go on to make other films in their so-called galaxy while I'm implicitly trashed for not having had the goods. Moral of that story? I'm fucked, because just as America and the world love their stars, they also love to see that tracer of light burning in the atmosphere. And I know, because I was once that tracer and somehow came back from it. Yeah, I'm up here at the top, but believe me, I'm standing on the head of a pin. The point is, you want me comfortable and you want me happy. So, when I say I don't want some charlatan snowflake airhead woman whispering moronic shit in my ear or in anyone else's ear on this set, I think I have every fucking right, because in the end, I am this movie, not her, not Joel, not even Sparta, and with all due respect, not any of you. I'm the guy who has it all on the line."

Marci had waited for the slightest caesura in which to impede this tirade, but there simply was none. Moreover, having experienced more than a few such caffeinated outbursts from her husband, she knew not to come near the invective spray. As for what he had said, it wasn't just the unhinged nature of it or the self-aggrandizing tone, but the sloppiness of the argument that astonished her. For starters, underpinning all of it was the implication that Peter had somehow been forced into the position of movie star, as if, like a kind of Jesus thrust into it by dint of immaculate birth, he had to take responsibility for the sins of an entire industry.

The justification for his (and her) village of trailers had been especially unnerving. He would have an argument if the rest of his life didn't cohere with how he expected to be treated when acting. As yet without children (they intended them soon, with Marci approaching forty), they lived in a seven-thousand-square-foot house on a four-acre lot in perhaps the city's most exclusive enclave. Peter had two full-time assistants, one exclusively for his schedule and another to eradicate all other inconveniences. He flew only private, having become a savant at laying off such liabilities on studios or businesses by conjuring obligations wherever he wished to travel. "Find me a club or store that's opening," he would demand of his manager, "so I can get a plane to New York next week," and there they'd be, Peter drinking seltzer with cranberry and lime at 1:00 a.m. in a VIP booth, his picture in the *Post* the following day, the jet provided.

For just the two of them, they employed three housekeepers so that not a waking hour didn't occur without help. From the spartan life of prison, he'd gone to not having laundered a garment, changed a light bulb, cut a blade of glass, washed a dish, or even answered a door in at least six years. He had his own gym in their "basement," though what usually connoted a cement floor, cinder block walls, and a preponderance of vermin was, in their home, more like a private athletic club, with floor-to-ceiling windows overlooking $20 million homes. It contained the best equipment available, including two Technogym treadmills, an Aviron rower, a Peloton bicycle, a heavy bag, a speed bag, and a sparring ring. Two trainers alternated days Monday to Saturday, with boxing Tuesdays and Thursdays, and weights and cardio for the intervening sessions. They employed two chefs for the Brentwood house and Malibu, where the housekeepers also traveled, depending on where the couple chose to sleep.

Other than in the gym, the extent of manual exertion in which Peter involved himself was occasionally to drive his own vehicle, but this an inconvenience endured only in Los Angeles with his 1961 Austin-Healey or on vacation in Europe, where the assistant would arrange a sufficiently agile vintage roadster. To pay for staff, groceries, and cleaning products, as well as the upkeep on two homes, without raiding their now considerable savings, Marci had calculated they needed to generate $4 million per year in income. Lately this had been easy, though the number did startle her.

Peter was also not accurate in predicting the demise of his career should *Major Machina* fail, if only because the film *could not* fail. The entire enterprise of the Sparta Comic Galaxy was designed to support each of its planets for sustainable life, simply because one had to visit all to breathe on each. There was too much narrative information spread among the storylines for it to be any other way, just as in the original print comics. Regardless of its quality, much of the negative cost of *Major Machina* would be recovered within five years of its release worldwide. This was true even though Sparta films were no longer grossing what they once had—proof in itself that underwhelming results would never be ascribed solely to Peter.

Worst of all, however, was the implicit denigration of the crew and what each of its members did. "Unlike me, you're all replaceable," he had stated unambiguously. "I have everything to lose; none of you does. I deserve all my blandishments and pay; you deserve the absence of the former and your meager apportionment of the latter."

A silence ensued of the sort she'd experienced too often on movie sets when a person of status chose to inveigh publicly regarding a perceived misstep or slight.

Finally Joel spoke. "Okay, everyone, we've heard Peter out. It's not my job to say whether I agree with what he said or not, though I will offer that I don't like raised voices on my set, no matter whose voice that is. But we all heard you, Peter, and I think everyone recognizes that being a star comes with its challenges and responsibilities. But so does being a gaffer, a wardrobe assistant, a set decorator, a dolly grip, a PA, a director, a producer, a DP. What's most important is that we accept that each of us has a common aim here, which is to make a wonderful film. We know that's what you want, Peter. But you need to know that's what we want too. No one is against you."

"I'm not saying anyone is against me, Joel. I just don't want this woman directing the scene. I want you directing it."

"And that's what I'm going to do, so let's get on with it. James, clear the set so we can go over these new lines, figure out which of them is going to be cut, per Jennifer's notes, which I think have merit, and inform LA. Let's then make sure both she and Peter are comfortable, with Aviva's participation, and then we can rehearse and shoot. Could somebody please take my dog?" It was the first time Marci had seen him pass the animal to another, in this case a PA who gathered it, along with its cranial horn, to depart with the rest of the crew.

As Marci joined the exodus, Joel spoke once more. "If it's all right with the actors, I think the producers should stay, just in terms of whatever writing changes are to be presented. And that includes Marci."

Within ninety minutes, half of which involved cutting lines and rehearsing and the other half lighting, they'd begun to shoot. What suggestions Aviva had were told to Marci and Joel, who then spoke to the actors.

At lunch Aviva quit.

"Not only have I never been so disrespected, I don't think I've ever experienced someone so completely unaware of the impact he has on others."

"On behalf of the production, please accept my apology," Marci responded.

"I'll be fine, trust me. When HR gets through hearing from me, I'll be more than fine. But for you and Charisse to stand there and let that happen to another woman was outrageous."

"Don't go there. If you were a white male in your position, Peter would have treated you just the same. My husband is an equal opportunity offender."

"I think you're fooling yourself."

Am I? wondered Marci when the woman had driven her black Chevy Volt off the lot. I love Peter. I remain *in* love with Peter, but were his issues with the intimacy coordinator—a position that even as a woman Marci found maddening, given how the endless discussions inspired by the position consumed production time—evidence of some deep atavism in the man with whom she was spending her life? The being whose fame benefited her so profoundly? And what did that suggest about her own perhaps outmoded predilections? Was she herself somehow obsolete, a subscriber to a worldview becoming steadily less helpful, even corrosive to progress?

But then again, what of Joel taking control of the set? Had she not urged the assertiveness he'd so uncharacteristically summoned? In that light, even while questioning herself for a diminishingly relevant worldview, she'd rarely felt as powerful. Solely because of the forty-five minutes she'd spent in her trailer with this heretofore diffident man, he had handed off his emasculating animal and steered a course from her husband's tantrum, glancing repeatedly her way as he did so.

No, Marci was the opposite of inhibitive to progress. At least as far as this movie was concerned, she'd proven herself essential to it.

THIRTEEN

Declan Morris had hoped since high school, when he'd seen Terrence Malick's *Days of Heaven* at the Paris Cinema in Boston, to be a writer-director, but his father refused to bankroll an undergraduate film degree at NYU.

"I'll be damned if I'm going to pay nine grand a year for you to watch movies."

"Film is what interests me."

"Films make money, don't they? I mean, that's the aim?"

"An aim. Yes, they do."

"Then study economics so you can understand how and why."

Out of spite he instead chose comp lit, which seemed to hold even less vocational promise, even while satisfying his father's preference for text over image. Upon graduation he followed a girlfriend to Los Angeles, where she'd been accepted at UCLA for postgraduate work in English. Having grown up in the Valley, it had been a dream of hers to live, as she put it, "where the area code begins with a three or four, not an eight."

When they broke up two months into her first semester, he moved in with a high school friend who was also trying to make it in film. Now I'll be able to write a script, he told himself. But every day a blank screen waited for slug lines, scene descriptions, and dialogue. After three weeks, needing money, and lonely beyond words, he was hired as an assistant property master on a nonunion comedy paying its crew a hundred dollars a day and on which his roommate was the location manager. The job was simple enough, though it had the very opposite of appeal given that he was only ever recognized for incompetence, usually when a prop wasn't delivered to an actor before or after a take, or when it was set improperly before action was called.

"I said put it with the knife's handle facing out, not in!"

"Sorry. I didn't understand that's what you meant."

"How else could I have put it other than 'place it with the handle out'? It's not that fucking complicated."

He resisted the impulse to suggest that he and the actor, who was nineteen and the film's lead, discuss Laclos and the cultural forces that influenced one of the last epistolary novelists.

He did, however, enjoy preproduction when he and his boss shopped for props throughout Los Angeles, drinking beer and smoking pot throughout the day, and snorting coke when it became available, the latter of which delighted him most because under its influence he could imagine the life he still most desired, that of an auteur. Plots for movies would spread out before him with irresistible simplicity, and in describing them to others similarly impaired, he could see himself, completed script in hand, having his pick of agencies, followed by bidding wars for his singular vision.

But the drug was expensive, and since it was required for such inspiration, he needed more of it, and for that he had to work, meaning long hours suffering the abuse of performers and having only weekends to write. Fridays were usually either splits or full nights, so he didn't wake on Saturdays until after one, often with a hangover from revelry to celebrate the completed week. By the time he got to his computer, it was after three, and he'd need to finish by six to go out. Saturday nights were usually a blowout, meaning sleeping until one on Sundays, waking hungover, often with a woman in his bed or in some woman's bed. He'd then do his laundry, watch football, and turn in early for his five a.m. wake-up on Monday. Thus, what writing he did accomplish during the three-hour Saturday window never seemed to inspire with the same verve as at its idea stage. Also, by developing these plots aloud with a drug-fueled cohort, he denuded them of their power. On the page they felt flaccid, derivative, uninspired.

As a crew member he was never late and more diligent than most. He was also good at his job, so the work kept coming and in whatever capacity he chose. Tired of props, he managed locations for three films in a row. He then switched back to the art department, where he set decorated. He worked as a second AD running base camp on a couple of horror films, then was asked to AD a comedy by that movie's same producer. Suddenly he was one of the most sought-after nonunion ADs in Los Angeles. One producer hired him for three films in a row, then took him to lunch after the last of these wrapped.

"Declan," he asked, "how long have you been at this?"

"At what?"

"Movies."

"I guess seven years. Maybe eight." He hadn't written a page for the last three. At a certain point the humiliation had become too painful. He'd also proposed to an actress he'd met on one of the horror films, though at the time he was having his doubts.

"What's the issue?" the producer asked.

"Mainly her career obsession. I mean, I know it's tough being an actress, but this is beyond anything I ever imagined a human being doing in pursuit of a single goal. It's not just the four hours at the gym every day, and the combing of *Variety* and *The Hollywood Reporter* and the sending out her résumé—"

"She lost her agent?"

"She says he doesn't work hard enough."

"Go on."

"But it's the constant talk about her career, about this person and that person, and who is doing what, and why wasn't she seen for this part when so-and-so was. Then there's the acting class three times a week with this guy who's more like a guru than an instructor. I met him at an art opening. As in his own. He paints too, and he coerces his students into buying his work. He doesn't even really teach acting. He's more like a career adviser. He'll tell students they have to book jobs or he's booting them from the class. Meanwhile she's shelling out thousands of dollars so she can be berated for not having gotten work that week."

"Declan, what are you doing?"

"What's that supposed to mean?"

"First of all, don't marry this woman."

"I love her."

"You don't love her."

"That's a little presumptuous."

"Look, I'm not sure why Courtney and you have ended up together. Maybe you've got a huge dick. She's gorgeous and you're handsome, but not at her level. It's not going to last, and you know it. She'll eat you alive on her way up, and if she doesn't succeed she'll blame you for it. You lose either way. That kind of person, and notice I don't say woman, but that kind of person will betray anyone and anything to get what they want. A guy like you, you need someone who's stable and reliable and decent. A female version of you. Which leads me to my second point. What do you really want to do out here?"

"Work in movies, obviously."

"In what capacity?"

"You really want to know?"

"I'm asking."

"I want to write and direct."

"Do you have a script I can read?"

"I'm working on one."

"What about an old one? One you've finished."

"Nothing I'd want to show you."

"Why not?"

"The one I'm working on right now is at another level."

"Are you really working on a script right now?"

"No."

"Have you ever finished a script?"

"I just told you. Of course."

"Then why not show me?"

He stared at his plate, too embarrassed by the dissembling and its increasingly humiliating consequences to answer. Why can't it be a minute ago, he asked himself, and I can just say I want to be an AD, get into the union, and spend my career scheduling, approving call sheets, running sets?

"Let me make this easy for you," the producer continued. "Being a writer-director seems like it's the holy grail. Maybe it is, but I doubt it. Most of the guys I've seen do it once, maybe twice, they end up directing for hire, usually in television, and they're miserable. But sure, you're gonna say you watch Steven Soderbergh and that feels like the most amazing life imaginable. How old are you?"

"Thirty-one."

"Be honest. Have you ever finished a script?"

"No."

"I'm going to be very hard on you right now."

"Go ahead."

"Being a writer-director is never going to happen for you."

"You're right." He'd never truly admitted this, even to himself, and it felt suddenly as though the most important part of him had died. Either that or he had finally just become an adult. Perhaps both.

"And thank God," the producer, whose name was Stuart Goldman, continued, "because the last thing you want is to end up a bitter failure."

"I'm really curious what you're going to say next."

"There's a wonderful place for you in movies, a place that can put you in the proximity of some extraordinary people doing interesting work. But more importantly, you can know, even when others don't, that without you those movies never would have been made."

"What is it exactly you have in mind that justifies your having stripped from me any dream of becoming an auteur."

"Please don't use that word."

"'Auteur'?"

"The French came up with it to dismiss what they saw as the industrialization of an art form by the studio system, even though those studios funded the very creation of the medium. Single authorship in movies is a myth, which is another reason why you're better off not being a writer-director, so you're not drowning in unearned adulation. Most directors are dicks. Spoiled beyond words and stinking with self-importance. Honestly, what do they do?"

"Are you really asking me that?"

"Okay, fine, it's a huge job in terms of casting and helping determine what the movie will be. But who *makes* everything happen? It's not the director. A movie really concretely happens because of a particular breed that's becoming more and more rare."

"Producers?"

Stuart contorted his face in disdain. "When you say it that way, it sickens me. So many people appropriate that title without deserving it. A real producer should be able to budget, schedule, and hire crew, not just choose material and get a writer and director on board then call it a day. That's producing? Fuck off. Trust me when I say the nuts-and-bolts stuff is what really makes a film. To put it in context, for *Teeth*," he said, referring to the horror film they'd just shot in Oxnard, "who do you think found the DP, the costume designer, the script supervisor, the production designer, and you, the AD? Which, trust me, is just the start of it."

"You."

"I also signed off on all the locations and came up with the entire production plan."

Declan now wished he'd truly perceived the bitterness in Stuart's voice. Had he allowed the depth of sentiment to register, he might have pursued his professional life differently, for he now understood that what inspired Stuart's frustration was utterly true: to be a line producer meant to be involved in every aspect of a production but get credit for very little of it.

"Just what is it you're suggesting?" he instead asked, missing the opportunity to recommend that Stuart see a therapist rather than promote his thankless career to others.

"I want you to work with me as my UPM on the film I'm about to do. It's an indie with very little money, and I need someone I can trust."

"I can't manage a production."

"You'll be great at it. You've worked in how many departments now? Locations, art, assistant directing. I mean, it's everything but dolly grip."

"I've actually done that too."

"Jesus."

"And transpo."

"How far did you go in math?"

"Calculus in college."

"Any accounting?"

"That I stayed away from."

"You pay your own bills, or do you have a business manager?"

"A business manager? I'm barely in my thirties."

"You're gonna do this. And while the director and so-called creative producer are prancing around at the premiere basking in all the glory, you'll sit quietly a few rows back and know hands-on how every single physical decision made and every dollar spent came together to cause each moment to happen on that screen. You'll know every crew member. You paid them and fed them, put them up in hotels you chose. You *made* the film in the truest sense, and knowing that is a feeling like none other."

He broke up with his fiancée, about whom Stuart had been right (at present she'd done little acting professionally, had two ex-husbands she blamed for this, and a new career as a dental hygienist), and he went to work for Stuart Goldman. Together they made easily two dozen films, and his phone contained the cell numbers of the top craftspeople the world over. He shot in Australia, New Zealand, South Africa, Jordan, Spain, France, Hungary, and eight of the fifty states.

Stuart long retired, *Major Machina* marked Declan's fifth consecutive film for Sparta. In addition to enjoying the largesse and éclat of cinema's most successful brand, he'd done just as his mentor had advised in his personal life, marrying the most stable woman he could find, a psychologist from San Diego he met through friends. Her name was Ellen, and together they had two sons and a daughter. Though it seemed clear they'd never divorce, mostly he experienced his family more on FaceTime than in person. At times he felt as though he barely knew his wife, and his kids looked measurably different each time they appeared on-screen, if they chose to do so at all.

And for what? Everyone, it seemed, was his enemy. While between jobs, Max Kaiser lauded him no end; during production, the calls were anything but friendly. The studio head's Dobermans berated Declan for overruns no matter how small, for cost report discrepancies, for location and equipment issues, and, of course, for scheduling shifts that seemed to metastasize daily. As the studio's on-location enforcer, he was in turn despised by the other producers and department heads, who saw him as punishingly bottom-line-oriented and therefore an enemy to quality, as if staying on budget meant anything other than having enough money in ensuing weeks to ensure consistent results through the film's completion.

Most directors would hardly speak to him, so intense were their paranoia and disrespect. As for crew, they approached him solely to complain: their overtime wasn't right, the AD was calling "grace" too frequently, craft services was inadequately healthy, craft services was too stridently healthy, catering didn't offer enough vegan choices, catering didn't have enough meat, the food was too sugary, too salty, and why were there no fresh juices? Why no espresso? Who chose this location? Who chose that hotel? And then the actors and their agents: all day with the questions about accommodations, schedule, flights; complaints about makeup, hair, wardrobe, their trailer, their driver.

But about one aspect Stuart Goldman had been right: when considering the actual nuts and bolts of making films, there was no position more exciting than his, if only because there was no delusion involved.

Writers? While he'd once hoped to generate scripts, they rarely came to set for disinterest in their input that often bordered on aggressive. As for directors, the other occupation that had appealed, they interacted sporadically with producers, whom they largely tried to avoid for fear someone else might have an idea worth considering, and they rarely addressed crew other than by way of vapid exhortation. Instead they spoke almost exclusively with actors, the AD, the DP, and other department heads, and occasionally the script supervisor when confused due to their own incompetence. Otherwise, they sat behind their exclusive monitor or marched self-importantly around in a pale charade of leadership. The most challenging part of being a director was becoming one. Once that had been achieved, it was all delegation. Actors acted, a costume designer put clothes on them, makeup and hair made them look right, a DP photographed them, a mixer recorded their dialogue on locations designed and dressed by an art department, and an editor cut it all together. In postproduction VFX artists and compositors conjured further astonishments while a composer wrote music. Foley artists and sound supervisors enriched the track for a final mix to play in 5.1 surround sound joined to an image digitally graded by a colorist. What did a director do other than respond yes or no and occasionally adjudicate disputes?

To Stuart Goldman's credit, Declan wanted no other job than the one he held. Why then did he wake each morning in a state of dread at having to be in the presence of Joel Slavkin, Peter Compton, his flirtatious vixen of a wife Marci Levy, Charisse, Jeremy, the loathsome Javier Benavidez, and the rest of the perpetually restive *Major Machina* crew?

For starters it had to do with what he now abetted. At sixty years old, he'd poured more than half his life into what for him, at least in terms of the films he worked on now as a full-time employee of Sparta, was the most cynical of businesses masquerading as an art form. After all, what ultimately was a superhero movie other than a series of set pieces stitched together with horrific dialogue explaining their terms? One needed to know why this character could fly, why this one could liquefy, this one control another's thoughts, this one create force fields, and on and on into the furthest reaches of the ludicrous before all the mayhem involving such peculiar abilities resulted in the titillating wreckage of city blocks.

It had for years struck him that the true demise of his country, perhaps the beginnings of its bariatric death throes as a polar force, coincided with the ascendency of the superhero movie. The genre seemed both symptom and accelerant of cultural stupidity. With the comic serials that were their antecedents it was fine; at least the consumer brought certain acuities to the exercise, such as being able to read, analyze images, fill in lacunae between cells. A Sparta movie eliminated all of this with overlit scenes suffused with capricious violence and performances devoid of all subtlety. An audience member simply received: all work done for it in a stultifying tide of idiocy.

Not by coincidence, most nationally defining phenomena seemed to mirror this. Our leaders, elected or otherwise, became more stupid and venal, our sensitivities dulled to the extent that nuance seemed to have fled all discourse. We saw one another in starker terms in every arena from the social to the cultural, whether around race, religion, gender, party affiliation, educational and economic class, or geographical region, and we did so with destruction the natural recourse rather than civil debate and comity.

No, one couldn't blame superhero movies. To do so would be silly, but one could put them in the vicinity, and as more than manifestation. Said another way, for Sparta films to have been grossing $200 million on their opening weekends, often ending their American theatrical runs easily doubling that number, meant at the very least fifteen million tickets purchased, which didn't even include the number who'd then view the films on other platforms after their theatrical runs. This suggested that, based on the population of the United States numbering three hundred million, easily 10 percent saw Sparta films. Even accounting for the fact that many of these viewers were not yet of voting age, one still couldn't help but ascribe some sort of confluence—going both ways—between the state of the culture and the success of the movies, a symbiosis of retardation undeniable. Sparta films, now in their fifth "echelon" of narrative coalescence in which Major Machina would be introduced as the eventual leader of a new team of Disruptors, had plateaued and were even, by some estimations, on a glide path back toward Earth, with American grosses now rarely exceeding $300 million. But ultimately did this matter? The damage had been done; the SCG, as both cause and result, was a microcosm of America, and in no way was this good.

To make matters worse, Declan recognized the brilliance of casting Peter Compton as Paul Kramer from the outset. Max Kaiser had clearly understood what the brand needed: a piece of titular casting that felt dangerous and chic. What better choice than an ex-con? But at the same time, did Declan—who had once hoped to create in the genetic line of Hitchcock, Scorsese, Altman, and Malick, filmmakers who effected true aesthetic advancement in the form—want to be participating in the resurgence of Sparta?

⚡

He passed the Audi dealership on I-285 as he drove back from a location scout in Sandy Springs during preproduction, having left Joel Slavkin, his dog, and the despicably arrogant Javier Benavidez to make it back to the production office in Javier's rental. His time with the director and DP had not been pleasant. The two men were wired and voluble in the way creative people can afford to be when the cost of things is of concern only to others. It was just past 2:30 p.m., and he'd decided to spend the remaining hours of the day working from the apartment he'd rented in midtown. Who would know that the boss had stopped off to peruse automobiles?

At least a dozen cars occupied the glossy white floor lit with LED panels set to a crisp, cool kelvin to balance the afternoon sun blazing in from windows that faced the highway. A salesman named Barry "Buzz" Bremer with a wide, flat face and the bearing of one who'd spent time in the military approached with easy strides. Declan stood over the automobile that most interested him, a low two-door race car in a grayish teal.

"You walked right to it," the salesman said in a gruff drawl. "The R8. There's not a better ride on the floor. I like to say the only reason you don't buy it is if you need more seats, because in terms of performance you're just not gonna do better. And not just in this showroom but anywhere, unless you want to spend three times as much, and even then I'd buy this vehicle. It's all there on the sheet: 562 horsepower at 8,000 rpm, twin turbo, 3.1 seconds to sixty, V-10, dual-clutch transmission, all the bells and whistles, and if you want to push her hard in the aftermarket, there's an outfit in Dallas can get you to sixty in 1.3 without touching the engine. I've got the article from *Road & Track* if you want to give her a gander."

"I'm good. Just looking."

"No laws against that. You from the area?"

"Los Angeles."

"A lot cheaper buying a car here, that I can tell you. Taxes too. Then you drive her back, save on the airfare, what I always say."

"You sell to a lot of out-of-staters?"

"Sell to whoever."

"I think my wife would have something to say about my showing up with this in the driveway."

"You ever owned a sports car?"

"Right after college. I had a Fiat Spider I bought used when I moved out to LA. Spent half its time in the shop."

"Fix It Again, Tony."

"Exactly. But I loved driving it."

"This car here is a whole other level. What they call a supercar, but one us normal folks can own. Buy her right off the floor. Feed her the premium stuff, keep her tuned up once a year, you'll have no troubles. Ever. You can't beat German engineering. Even still. Americans, Italians, Japanese, the Brits, the Swedes, the Koreans . . . they'll always be spreadin' it on a burger."

"How's that?"

"Playing catch-up."

"Got it. But yeah . . ."

"What?"

"The German thing's a whole other issue with my wife."

"She Jewish?"

"Exactly."

"Long time ago."

"She won't even travel there."

"Copy that. Of course, I'm all about engagement."

"Uh-huh."

"I'm kind of a history buff. Military history, so you'll forgive me. You go back, what set the Germans off was blame after World War I that wasn't entirely justified—don't get me wrong, they started the war in certain respects, but interlocking alliances were just as responsible, otherwise a world war doesn't happen just because some idiot kills a prince in Sarajevo. Hitler came to power on a platform of restoring pride in Germany. No Treaty of Versailles, and Hitler doesn't arm the Ruhr or invade the Sudetenland."

"Wow. You really know this stuff."

"Like I said, bit of a buff."

"Did you serve?"

"A dozen years. Parwan Province. Bagram. Before that Fallujah. And still do. National Guard. And look here, not to brag, but I'm good at whatever I take on, which includes cars, and I'm a patriot, so a part of me'd rather be selling Yukons or Navigators. But I want to push the best, so here I am. And as for the German thing, I'm not saying your wife's wrong, but we get a lot further with forgiveness. The way I see it anyway, but hey, that's just me."

"So, what's the story with test-driving one of these?"

With Buzz in the passenger seat, he turned left from the parking lot and within minutes was on the access road to 285 curving south and west. The car drove tight and low, but what he most appreciated was its cohesion. The power engulfed him, as if he were welded into the alloy. He could feel the asphalt in his hands as he moved through five of the seven gears in the dual-clutch gearbox.

"Take this exit up here," said Buzz as they approached Doraville.

He released his foot from the accelerator and downshifted with a suddenness that whipped the vertebra from his craniocervical junction down to his coccyx.

"Yeah," said Buzz with a chuckle, "like I said, different kind of machine. You'll learn about that. You gotta ease off it slow. You're on a racehorse now. That's why they call them supercars."

Declan paddled through the gears onto I-23 toward Norcross.

"Now you can really open her up."

Within seconds they hit ninety miles an hour. It in fact frightened him how the car seemed so effortlessly to accelerate, as if the entire machine had been shaped from a single frame with no need for rivet or screw.

"You ain't gonna hurt her. Let her rip. We've got a good relationship with the police from here to Duluth, so don't worry about that, long as you keep her under a hundred, but trust me, there's a lot more this engine has to offer. If you want to do the asking, somewhere around Flagstaff between here and LA, you can be up at one-seventy without seeming like you're stressing her at all. Rear-wheel drive, of course. Engine's right behind you, in case you didn't notice."

"It's like a racecar."

"'Like'? It is," Buzz assured him somberly in a manner that suggested an intimacy only possible between two men on a Georgia highway in a high-performance automobile. "5.2 liter, 8,700 rpm. Fixed damper suspension for long trips. Just watch the abrupt changes in speed, which, like I said, you'll get used to. And guess what? After this year it's over. Gonna stop makin' these for gas only, meaning if you take good care of her, she only goes up in value, so you're talkin' about an investment too. Tell that to the wife."

"You mean they're going electric?"

"Electric, hybrid. Either way there's gonna be a battery involved."

"What do you drive?"

"Funny you should ask. A Ram 1500 TRX, which I mainly purchased because I've got a boat I haul around, and then what I'd call a lesser Audi—an A3 40 sedan I get through work—that my wife uses. When I say lesser it's a great car, but not like this."

"Gotcha."

"How do you feel in that seat?"

It was as if he were reclining in an Eames lounger at ninety miles an hour sitting comfortably still. The leather was black with red stitching that sat up from the flat matte patterning. The belts were of a thick crimson herringbone that harnessed him fast to the seat. The rest of the interior was black and chrome with dials and high-resolution digital gauges easy to the touch. The existence of such an automobile seemed almost unfair. What saved him, of course, was the cost. At $171,000, he needn't worry, other than to feel a tinge of guilt at having wasted a salesman's time.

"May I ask what you do?" queried Buzz.

"Movies."

"Figured as much, given you're from Los Angeles. You're an actor?"

"Oh God, no."

"Writer? Director? I don't know much about the field."

"A producer."

"Now that's interesting. I've always wondered: Just what does a producer do? You're basically the boss?"

"That sort of depends on the project and how it's set up. In my case, I hire everyone and manage the budget, the scheduling, all the locations, all the equipment, all the invoices. Everything goes through me."

"So you are the boss."

"The studio's the boss, but on the ground, exactly, I am. But don't tell the other producers or the director that, because then they'd have to face their self-deception." As he said it Declan despised himself. My God, he thought, has my frustration reached the point where I'm exposing it to a car dealer?

"I'm gonna say something right now, and I hope you won't take it the wrong way."

"What's that?"

"You deserve this vehicle."

"Buzz, you don't know how much I agree, but I can't afford it."

"You'd be surprised by the financing plans we've got."

"I've never believed in the logic of that. Sure, you stretch out the payments, but there's a reason you guys like when we finance. In the end it puts you ahead, or you wouldn't do it."

"We do it because it gets folks to buy the car."

"Yeah, well, if I could beat the spread on the interest, sure, but I can't, so I lose in the end."

"I could introduce you to a good stockbroker."

"I've got one."

"Look, Declan, it's none of my business, but how old are you?"

"You're right, it's none of your business."

"My apologies. I overstepped. I'm gonna tell you I'm forty-nine. That's right. About to turn fifty. When I purchased my truck earlier this year, I asked myself, when I was about to settle for a standard, no bells and whistles F-150, I said, Buzz, if you could have any truck out there, what would it be? And there was no doubt: it was the Ram TRX with the Hellcat."

"The Hellcat?"

"Under the hood. You're talking about the most durable, dependable truck on the planet with as powerful an engine—the one Chevy's got in the new Challengers, the Dodge Chargers: 700 horsepower turbocharged Hemi V-8, 6.4 liter—and does not break down. Excuse me, but a fuckin' monster. Not getting into the details, but yes, it was more expensive. Strike that. Stretched me to the limit. As for my wife, well, let's say there was a raised eyebrow or two, but now she can't get enough of stepping up into that cab. So ask me if I regret it."

"I don't need to, Buzz. And you're a great salesman, but that's not the point. It's actually truly about what I can afford. It would be more than a stretch. Really."

"You're gonna tell me that you're down here working for a studio—which studio, by the way?"

"Sparta."

"The comic book movies?"

"Yes."

"Oh man. Which one? It's not *Viper*, is it?"

"No."

"*Retribution Force*?"

"A new one."

"Are you allowed to say?"

"*Major Machina*."

"Knew it. I read about that."

"You did?"

"Peter Compton, the guy with the drug problems. Or former drug problems."

"That's right."

"Well, in terms of you, a man knows what a man knows, especially as it pertains to his own finances, and I'm the first to admit, this is an expensive car. It's just, you carry yourself like a fellow could afford it. Not a bad thing."

They drove back in silence. When the car had been handed over to the garage for cleaning before being restored to its place of prominence, a softening light came through the showroom windows where traffic had stalled to a standstill on 285.

"Well, Declan, it sure was a pleasure."

"I'll never forget being behind the wheel of that car."

"That, I can tell you, is true." Buzz paused, then stepped forward conspiratorially. "Look, if there's any way I could get my two boys onto your set . . ."

"I'm afraid it's not allowed."

"I imagine it's like Fort Knox over there."

"Something like that."

"They sent a blast out to reservists about working security."

"Doesn't surprise me."

"My sons were begging me."

"You should have."

"Like I said, happy right here. Don't want to strap one on to protect a bunch of actors anyway."

"It's more about protecting any images from the set from leaking out."

"I can't tell you how many Halloween costumes my wife's got in boxes down in our basement from those characters. I guess they make money every which way."

"That they do."

"A little more of that came your way, you'd be driving that R8 off the lot."

A hundred and seventy-one thousand dollars, Declan thought as he sat in the black Cadillac CT6 production was renting for him thanks to Sparta's promotional deal. In addition to the discount for Cadillacs appearing in the film, thirty cents of every dollar would come back from the state, meaning the actual cost to Sparta was forty dollars a day. Too bad we don't have a deal with Audi, he thought. But what then? The Germans would give me a discount? Peter

Compton, maybe, if he agreed to drive it around LA. What about Buzz if I snuck his sons onto set? Would he knock off $5,000? With the thin margins of car sales, that would probably erase much of the dealership's profit. Would the filial glee be worth it to the man? Call it $166,000. Still way beyond Declan's range. After taxes it would erase well more than half his salary for the year, and with his wife limiting her patients of late, they needed his earnings.

There *was* the rebate. He laughed out loud at the ridiculousness of it. Suddenly the car would cost $115,000. And if it were true what Buzz said about the model being discontinued, he could always sell it in Los Angeles for near its cost, perhaps even a profit. The same would be true if his wife became enraged imagining the descendants of Nazis manning the robots at the factory in Neckarsulm (for some reason Buzz had referenced the place of manufacture repeatedly).

⚡

Never having started the Cadillac, he reentered the showroom, where he found Buzz supervising a young mechanic as he nosed the supercar back under its devoted LED panel.

"Come back for a last beholding?"

"Let's speak in your office."

The deal Declan proposed was simple, and as with certain rare and uncannily propitious offerings, it would benefit everyone. Declan would arrange not only for the young spawn of Buzz Bremer to visit set, but the boys would be extras. Moreover, he would guarantee their appearance in frame with Peter Compton.

"How do I know they won't be edited out?" asked the dealer with a sudden and somewhat off-putting comprehension of postproduction perils.

"I'll pick a scene the movie can't do without. You leave that to me."

For such consideration, Buzz would knock not $5,000 but $7,000 from the sticker price of the R8. The two would then draw up an invoice for $164,000, not to Declan personally but to Atlanta Jelly LLC, the shell company for *Major Machina* set up by Sparta for public and liability remove, $100,000 of which Declan would pay the following day by personal bank wire, and the rest in installments at 3 percent amortized interest, to end within twelve months.

"It's billed to the film, but you'll pay?" asked Buzz.

"That's the idea."

"And who signs for the loan?"

"I do."

"So I check your credit for the financing."

"That's correct."

"But on paper it's the movie buying it. I'm beginning to understand."

"We don't have to discuss that."

"I'm just trying to figure out all the ways this is gonna come back and bite me in the ass."

"It isn't. The dealership gets the money, you get the commission, your boys get to be in a movie and be the envy of all their friends. You move this car off the lot, and you're father of the year. The rebate is my problem."

"And when the State of Georgia comes around asking questions?"

"What did you know?"

"The checks aren't coming from where the bills are!"

"They will."

"You just said you were responsible for the first installment and the loan."

"The checks will still come from the movie."

"And just how are you gonna fix that?"

"Let that be my problem."

"You sure you want to do this, my friend?"

"Buzz, I need to do it."

The following day he called his broker and liquidated $80,000 of stock. His wife looked regularly at their bank statements but left the equities portfolio to him, which is what would allow the transaction to escape near-term discovery.

"Are you sure you want to liquidate nearly half the position? I mean, Jesus, you could give me a little warning. Some of this is gonna be a fire sale and the rest not exactly tax advantageous. It's been a bad week."

"It's not close to half. Find some companies that are overvalued, or do what it is you guys do and take a tax loss."

At noon that Sunday he drove the car off the lot, the vehicle charged to the movie, but not so his overseers in Los Angeles would ever know. Declan had already been hired to stay on through postproduction, so when it came time for the rebate, he'd long have isolated the liability as a blip and could capture the funds before they were perceived, funneling them off to himself and erasing all evidence of their having existed. His assistant wouldn't even know. As for the line item, he'd sneak it in at the right time during production. The liability would disappear within hours. As further padding, he would also pay himself the rental fee that would have gone to the Cadillac. At $399 a week, he'd be knocking further thousands off the bill, not to mention what he'd pocket for the first-class airfare back to Los Angeles he wouldn't spend. By the time he wrapped, the negative cost might dip below $100,000. Moreover, what a figure he'd cut arriving on set each day in such a ride.

As for the chicanery, what the studio itself did was far worse, bilking the State of Georgia for tens of millions it could easily have afforded to pay, only to fatten profits of billions per year. Moreover, Declan worked harder than anyone he knew, devoting himself to how such larcenous budgets were spent, setting up shell companies within shell companies to move spending into the state in whatever mendacious ways possible. Why not get some of his own compensation by doing the same with a car purchase?

His impulsiveness did, however, inspire pause. It was as if owning the vehicle were some sort of metaphor for a transition in his life far more significant. What that was he couldn't fathom. Once you have the car, he kept saying to himself, all will become clear.

FOURTEEN

From his first hour on the film his sister produced that started his career, Javier had observed how the lead actor could set a tone. Peter Compton, with his insistence on private blocking rehearsals for every scene, his constant berating of his stand-in (admittedly one of the most cloyingly deluded people Javier had ever encountered), his need to view every take of every setup, his compulsory meetings with the director each morning, his ever more picayune and acerbic critiques of Javier's frames even while "purifying" each set with crystals and incense—all of it announced it was his set, with production there to serve him. Any sense that he and Javier would conjoin with Joel Slavkin to support the director's authority had long since dissipated.

Why did Ron Huston not bother to learn his lines? Because Peter carried his sides during rehearsals, then constantly shouted "Line!" at the script supervisor, whom he'd turned into his personal serf: "Where was my hand when I said this?" "When did I pick up the glass?" "When did I put it down?" "Did I start walking on my left foot or my right?" And should the poor woman not have an answer, the public flogging was instant.

"You have one responsibility, which is continuity!"

"Actually, Peter, that's not true," she replied. "I take notes for the director and editor. I'm responsible for lettering and numbering the takes, recording lens sizes, making sure we don't cross the line and that each scene is adequately covered."

"*And* you're supposed to tell the actors when they did what so that the editor and director, who according to you now couldn't survive without all you have to offer, can actually put the film together."

It took one day for Jennifer Taylor to experience this before she too needed a peek at every take, before she too no longer found it necessary to know the text, before she too began questioning Joel Slavkin's every decision, before she wondered aloud at the monitor why she was in silhouette in the master while Peter enjoyed an abundance of fill.

The set had become like a middle school recess with a half-blind octogenarian substitute French teacher proctoring. Javier had no one to whom he could complain. The two producers from Sparta had little interest and responded only by lavishing him with meaningless praise. Marci Levi was married to the cause of all duress. And most important, Declan Morris, with his ridiculous car, loathed Javier, and Javier, him.

"That this is a Sparta movie doesn't mean you just order up every toy you want and Max Kaiser pays for it," he had announced in one argument. "None of you ever thinks how your decisions ramify."

"Were you ever in a camera department?"

"Yes, I was."

"Well, a little knowledge is a dangerous thing."

"What did you just say?"

"It's Alexander Pope."

"Who?"

"The eighteenth-century British poet. Quoting Confucius who said, 'Real knowledge is to know the extent of one's ignorance.'"

"Cut your budget ten percent and get the fuck out of my office."

They now communicated solely through his key grip, first AC, or gaffer, depending on the specific concern.

Regarding set dysfunction, he could call the studio, but his relationship with them had soured after an exterior shot outside the High Museum one afternoon as an amber sun slanted through the trees surrounding the Woodruff Arts Center. The response was ecstatic. The following morning, however, they'd filmed at the same location under thick cover in a cold gloom. He thought nothing of it until two days later, when Declan approached with feigned concern.

"Los Angeles is furious."

"Why? The homeless crisis?"

"Your dailies. The ones from the museum exterior."

"They loved those. I can show you the email."

"Not the ones from the next morning. They wanted to know why, when they told you how great the other ones were at the same location, you then went in the complete opposite direction."

"And how would I do that when it was the next day when the light, from the sun and clouds, which I can't control, was completely different?"

"I wouldn't know. Remember, 'a little knowledge is a dangerous thing.' I'm just a budget guy. Anyway, they want you to get with a colorist and make it work."

"Anything I would do right now with some random idiot is going to be ridiculous."

"They're not asking."

"How would they have responded if you'd called them that day and said, 'Sorry, Benavidez doesn't want to shoot because the light doesn't match'?"

Two hours later Charisse and Jeremy beckoned him between setups.

"We heard you refuse to color the scene."

"Because the studio has no sense of how exteriors work, and I'm frankly insulted that they send the *cabron* with the race car with their demands, which if you haven't looked into how he could afford it, then you're not real producers."

"Look," said Charisse, "you know and we know that there are a lot of executives back in LA who, when they look at the dailies, feel like they need to say something to feel useful. What I've learned is that it's best to placate them or it only gets worse."

"What I've learned is that when you give in you just reinforce their outsized view of themselves."

"Then what is your suggestion?"

"What I'm doing. To fucking refuse. If they don't like it, they're free to get another DP."

It was the first time he'd ever threatened to leave a production, and it felt liberating. Why had he never considered it before? He could simply walk away. What really would be the consequences? For every job he took, he turned down at least five. As for having quit a Sparta movie, with many it would be an act worthy of respect. Did Sparta films even matter anymore? Everyone kept claiming this one would, and never count out Max Kaiser, but was it really true?

"Javier, no one wants that," said Jeremy, with his preternatural calm. "We'll take care of it."

With under a month left, he still didn't know how he could muster the patience to endure. To exacerbate this, his knees seemed perpetually on the verge of giving out, as if all the cartilage had somehow drained to his toes. I could quit over that alone, he began telling himself. No one would have to learn it was because Joel Slavkin wouldn't take charge and direct, that Peter Compton had occupied that vacuum with his self-serving pseudo-intelligence (embodying the converse of the Confucian notion that true intelligence was an awareness of what one didn't know), or that the studio continued to hector him in a genre that was quintessentially disposable.

Peter Compton's outburst finally decided it. At a cost of approximately $60,000 an hour of production time, meaning $1,000 a minute, the actor had denigrated the crew while simultaneously humiliating the film's intimacy coordinator. Javier had waited years for the reckoning that was Me Too, especially given the depredations suffered professionally by his sister, who had been raped twelve years prior while shooting in Brazil in the Amazonian port city of Belém. The consequences? Not only the local authorities but the Mexican production company blamed her for walking near the Ver-o-Peso Market stalls at night. Javier was convinced men needed to shut up and allow women not only the opportunities they deserved in a chauvinist industry, but the protection required when asked to engage in even the most chaste physical encounters on set.

He approached Charisse at lunch and asked that he meet with her and Jeremy in their trailer. He did not invite Marci.

"I'm sorry, but I'm finished."

"All right, Javier. Let's just talk this through," answered Jeremy. "It's been a rough morning for all of us, and I'm sure especially you, given all the pressures you've been under."

"This isn't about the pressures. I don't want to be around that motherfucker anymore or the movie he's directing."

"Joel?"

"Joel I gave up on when he agreed to start out at the sewage pond because Peter took him to a nice dinner. It's Peter. And his enabling wife, who stood there just now while a crew member was humiliated. I'm sick of Joel's dog getting in the way when we're trying to move the camera, I'm sick of Ron Huston and his yelling at my gaffer because he talks on his walkie during a camera rehearsal, and most of all I'm sick of putting up with all of it for a movie I would never go see. This business this morning was the final straw. I'll give you the rest of the week to bring someone in and get them up to speed, but at Friday wrap, I'm done. And I know you think, 'He's threatening to quit again, it will be over in an hour,' but this time I mean it."

"Javier, you can't do this to us," said Charisse.

"Forgive me when I ask, but do what? Anyone could be shooting this movie at this point."

"You've brought a look no one else could. And Peter loves you."

"He would love anyone photographing him twenty-four times a second."

"And Marci loves you. Just yesterday she—"

"Yesterday she what? Told her husband to go and kill Duncan?"

"Who's Duncan?"

⚡

At wrap Marci found Javier by the monitor speaking with the script supervisor.

"I know Peter told you we buzzed him on take three," he was saying, "but otherwise it was the best one, so you should definitely label it as a print so Joel has it."

"Javier, Peter and I would love to take you to dinner tonight."

"I'm sorry, Marci, but it's been a long day. All I want is to get to my apartment, order takeout, and watch La Liga. Let's meet in LA when all this is over."

"Please. Notwithstanding your comparing me to Lady Macbeth, it can't end like this. You're one of the greatest artists with whom either of us has ever worked. And I mean ever. That you want to leave is nothing short of devastating. Whether you stay or not, the film's entire look will be because of you. At least let us say thanks here and now."

What intrigued Javier most about Marci was her mind. She was a manipulator to be sure, but an instinctive rather than a calculating one, which made her not only more dangerous but blameless as well. Everything about her was fair and decent, yet she would always end up ahead, no matter the cost to others. To top it off, even in this moment, he couldn't help but like her.

"We'll send a driver. Your agent told us you like Spanish reds."

"When did you speak with him?"

"This afternoon."

"I guess that's why I have six messages."

"He was, to say the least, surprised."

⚡

"When Sparta calls to meet, you say yes," that same agent had shouted on the phone from his office on Civic Center Drive when the request for an interview came in. His name was Mark Diamond, a no-nonsense blue-collar soul with a law degree who stood at an even six feet under a carapace of dark hair. "And when you get the offer, you push for as much money as you can get. And guess what? They've budgeted for that. You also check as a diversity hire. Or half of one anyway. Brown is not black, but you've got the stupid accent and you never shut up about being Mexican."

"At least seventy percent of Sparta films are CGI. Why do they even need me?"

"Max Kaiser wants to open up the trades and see that once again Sparta landed an Oscar winner. He wants not only the look you'll bring to the film—"

"Please stop calling it a film."

"Max is a genius. The Cecil B. DeMille of our time."

"It's a movie about a guy defending the world against what sounds like the most ridiculous villain ever put to paper."

"That didn't hurt the comic."

"In the 1950s."

"He's called Jellyfish, but that's just a form he takes. He's got a pretty interesting philosophy involving a form of scientism."

"What is scientism?"

"The idea is that we will always argue over right and wrong when there is no moral truth because anything can be argued. As in it's all just words. We have laws against murder, but the state justifies killing when it calls it 'execution,' would be an example. Scientism removes ambiguity so everything is calculable. What's right is what can be proven—proven to be true, proven to benefit, proven to solve hunger, alleviate pain, save the planet, you name it."

"When your country goes the way of all other empires, people like you will be example number one. The best and the brightest went into entertainment and finance—two pursuits that advance absolutely nothing but themselves."

"America is not an empire."

"You're fooling yourself."

"And secondly, we're not in decline."

"The Roman Empire lasted five centuries. America's peak was 1989."

"And what about the fact that you are also participating in this unproductive and self-serving enterprise called entertainment, our greatest export?"

"I come to the empire as an *other*. I'm accelerating its demise by participating."

⚡

He entered an empty establishment save for a tall hostess in a cocktail dress, spaghetti straps on slender shoulders grazed by a bob of sandy hair. Three waiters stood smiling behind her near a vacated bar. Peter and Marci occupied a table along the wall to the back near a bank of windows facing a patio, also bereft of diners.

"I guess this place isn't very popular," Javier said, sitting down.

"More like too popular," said Peter. "I usually sit at the chef's table, but Senator Warnock and his wife are back there, and for obvious reasons we couldn't get Giovanni to dislodge them."

"Giovanni?"

"The owner."

"What does that have to do with the fact there's nobody here?"

"We wanted privacy," said Marci. "It's tough when there are people around."

Jesus, Javier realized, they bought the place out.

"This way we can speak freely," said Marci. "Too many times we've been out, and an hour later everything Peter or I said was on the internet. Or the time we were eating at a steak house in Mississippi, and as we were leaving people were taking Peter's dessert plate, his knife and fork, his napkin and his placemat."

"Marci and I have a lot to say to you, which starts with my apologizing for today. I don't know what happened. I just snapped. What I did was tactless, injurious, and irresponsible, not to mention disrespectful to the contributions of others, especially you."

"Okay," said Javier, uninterested in proffering a word that would allay any guilt the actor might be feeling.

"But first things first," said Peter, beckoning a waiter. "Could you have Jack bring over that bottle of wine we brought?" He addressed Javier once more. "My driver went all over Atlanta looking for this. Finally found it in Buckhead."

A tallish, dark-haired gentleman in a seersucker suit, who Javier determined must be the sommelier, arrived with a high-shouldered bottle the label of which the cinematographer recognized, though he'd only ever drank it once, seven years prior at the San Sebastián International Film Festival when invited with Alfredo Huron to dine with the president of the Provincial Council of Gipuzkoa.

"The Dominio de Pingus 2011," the man announced in a languid drawl. Javier remembered googling the 1999 vintage upon returning home from the festival and blanching at the price point of $1,800. Given the increasing renown of the estate and the banner year of 2011, he couldn't imagine this bottle having cost less than four figures retail.

"I don't know anything about wine," Peter announced, clocking Javier's response. "Wasn't really my thing, but we heard about your tastes."

"We wanted to impress you," added Marci.

"I appreciate it, but I'm happy to go without," answered Javier, conscious of Joel Slavkin's report of the meal, no doubt at this same restaurant, where Peter had plied him with white Burgundy to effect the schedule change that to Javier's mind had set the entire production on its unmanageable course.

"Come on, if we're really going to be saying goodbye to you, let's at least do it in style. Whatever you and Marci don't polish off, I'm sure Giovanni will enjoy, though if I have to hear him describe the taste or go into the history of the vineyard I might flee. Right, Jack?"

"I'll plead the Fifth, particularly since I make my living doing that," answered the sommelier as he carved away the top of the bottle's foil.

He looks like an ice cream salesman, thought Javier. How can I take a word this man says seriously?

As if on cue, the sommelier raised the cork to his nose, then primed the glass in front of him with a Lilliputian portion he used to coat the goblet's interior. "We prime our glasses here so the olfactory—"

"I'm aware of the technique," said Javier. It was an act he had first experienced at a restaurant in New York that he found the apogee of pretension. He loved wine, and his father had taught him his old-world tastes. But bottles opened for dinners at Avenida Ámsterdam were never discussed, and his father disdained the ritual of tasting himself before pouring for others. He might as well have been offering water or tea.

"Mr. Compton, you brought the wine, so perhaps you'd like to speak on its behalf."

"All Marci and I did was tell my driver to find the best bottle of Spanish red in Atlanta, so you go ahead."

"Tell us everything," said Marci, "and ignore what my husband said about Giovanni."

"Very well. In the early nineties a Danish winemaker named Peter Sisseck goes to the Ribera del Duero and selects for his new experiment the Hacienda Monasterio in the La Horra area," the ice cream salesman began, almost as if the speech were an obligation, so prevalent was the lassitude. "Plants old vines, spends a few years cutting them back for a more concentrated yield. Tempranillo, of course. Wholly biodynamic. No fertilizer, no pesticides. All wooden barriques. Calls it 'Pingus,' which was his nickname growing up. He brings his '95 vintage to the '96 *en primeur* tastings in Bordeaux, where *the* Mr. Robert Parker gives it a hundred and slaps it on the back cover of *Wine Advocate*, and suddenly the secret's out. I assume you'll be doing the tasting?" he asked Javier.

"Marci and I both."

"You'll get all the hallmarks of a Ribera tempranillo," the sommelier continued as he poured. "Nice concentration of fruit, but almost chewable tannins and terroir. Deeper and richer than to the north in Rioja, but a Pingus drinks like no other wine in the region for delicacy while somehow maintaining real power. Violet and spice, but the smoky peat the region's known for."

"Well, how is it?" Peter asked after Javier took his first taste.

"It's amazing," he answered. In spite of his almost aggressively indifferent delivery, the sommelier had described the wine accurately.

"What is it about wine?" Peter asked.

"What do you mean?"

"Especially in Hollywood. The obsession is ridiculous. And if you're at someone's house, forget it, with the cellar and the opening the bottles, and again, because it's usually the men, the dick measuring over what's being served and what this guy has had and that guy has had and where. I mean, seriously, we're just a bunch of assholes making movies."

"Well, I will leave you to it," said the sommelier.

"Take a taste before you go," said Marci.

"Yes. Please," said Javier.

"I'd appreciate that." He took a glass from a nearby table and poured himself a demure inch and a half, giving it a quick smell. "Yes, indeed. I thank you." He stepped away without tasting, clearly having noted Peter's twice expressed disdain for garrulous oenophiles.

And that's just it, thought Javier. He completely humiliated this poor guy and didn't even pause to realize it.

"I will say this," Peter offered. "Hearing all the discussion does make me regret not having partaken while I could, if only to understand what the hell people are going on about."

A waitress stepped to the table. She was young and perkily energetic.

"How are you tonight?" asked Peter. "It's Jane, isn't it?"

"That's right," she responded with a smile before turning to the rest of the table, her red ponytail shifting like the hand of a metronome. "So, I know Giovanni has Peter's dietary preferences, and yours as well, Marci. Sir, is there anything you'd like to tell me in terms of food allergies or what you'd like to avoid? If not, Giovanni is going to prepare a meal suited to what I understand to be a pretty extraordinary bottle of wine you guys have toted in."

"No allergies or restrictions on my part," said Javier. "Whatever the chef thinks is right."

"Great. Giovanni will be out in a bit to say hello. In the meantime, anything I can get you, Peter?"

"I wouldn't mind an Athletic."

"I'll be right back with that."

Javier took another sip of his wine and thought immediately of how he and his sister worked through the bottles of Crianza, Priorat, and Reserva his father left behind in the year after his death. He then remembered, as he often did of late, the faucet he photographed with the first roll of film she gave him. He wished he'd said to Peter moments before that wine is the drink of memory, that more than any other sensation, the taste of a good Spanish red connected him to all he once imagined he could be.

Jane returned with Peter's nonalcoholic beer and poured it into a tall pilsner glass.

"Amazing," the actor said regarding nothing in particular as he raised the libation and the three of them clinked. "To a gorgeously photographed film."

"Yes," said Marci.

"I appreciate it" was all Javier could muster.

"Javier," said Marci, "we don't want you to leave."

"That's an understatement," said Peter. "There's no movie if you leave."

"I can't imagine how that can be true," he answered. "The two of you are this movie. You've systematically made that happen, probably since the day Peter was offered the part. I'm sorry to put it that way, but for better or worse it's a fact."

"We're all working for Sparta, Javier," answered Marci. "I think that had a lot to do with Peter's outburst today. The fact is, if we could control the film the way you think we do, or better still, if the one who *should* be controlling it were, which is Joel, then we'd be a lot happier. The reason we're the way we are is because we care."

"I partially believe that."

"You should completely believe it."

"When I walk on a set," said Peter, "and I feel like the wrong decisions are being made, or worse, no decisions, I can't do nothing. Did I fuck up today? Yes. My apology to the crew later was sincere."

Javier had experienced many such clothes-rending atonements in the wake of actor outbursts, but Peter Compton's on that day, which occurred after lunch, had to have been one of the most manifestly insincere he'd ever witnessed. Though it had begun and ended with heartfelt contrition, the content between sagged with self-justification that only confirmed the delusions of its speaker: that the crew needed to understand what pressures Peter was under; that he felt watched, judged; that having been in prison rendered him socially inept at times and subject to outbursts; that none of it was personal; that no one could understand what it was like to be him. He wept in conclusion, which of course provoked scattered applause, but what meaning did tears have when spilled from the eyes of an actor?

"You have to understand, Javier," said Peter, taking a sip of his denuded IPA. "I've had many ups and downs. But I have never, and I mean *never*, had what happened today happen. This film . . . I don't know what it is . . . it's just different. Yes, it's been tough with Joel like he is, but I'm not against him. I'm certainly not against you. I'm not even against that moron Declan Morris, strangler of all creativity."

The server reappeared with three small plates carrying proportionally sized forks and what appeared to be cubes of charred beef on wilted beds of dark green.

"For your amuse-bouche, Giovanni has prepared seared and lightly smoked Wagyu filet on sautéed local spinach topped with Le Marche truffle oil."

"Why would you want to leave this film, Javier?" asked Marci when the waitress had left.

He shimmied the utensil beneath the spinach and took the portion in the one bite for which it was intended. The chef certainly knew how to combine tastes, though the server had failed to mention the flakes of fleur de sel that bridged the sear and smoke of the perfectly tender meat. After taking a sip, he studied his wine, twisting the stem to perceive the retreat from darkest red to translucence where the liquid pooled in his half-canted glass.

"We're sitting here in this restaurant," he began, "and by the way, that little bite was amazing, as I'm sure will be the rest of the meal. And that you would do all this"—he gestured to the empty room—"just so we could have privacy, it's not obviously what I'm used to."

"We want you to feel appreciated, which obviously you don't."

"Whether I'm appreciated is not what's important, Marci." He took another sip, then put down his glass. "Peter talked today about the pressures facing him when he walks on a set. He did that in both speeches."

"I did," said Peter.

"You have to understand that others of us are under pressure too."

"We absolutely do, Javier," said Marci.

"I'm not talking about the studio or what the film is going to look like or getting my next job, though of course all of that is at play. I'm talking more about from myself. Peter, you've lived an up-and-down life, but so have I. Getting run out of my country, existing hand to mouth in LA, losing a wife to this business because I was always away. And through it all I've always asked myself, Is it worth it? Or lately, because I'm becoming older, Has it been worth it? My father used to think, when he was at a party in Mexico City: Would I rather be at home reading? And if the answer was that he'd prefer to be in his study with a book, he would leave, with or without my mother. When I shot my first movie with Alfredo and then later when it started to seem like I would actually win the Oscar, all I dreamed about was to be able to shoot movies where I had all the tools I would need to create extraordinary images. I would do this in big vistas and close-ups with the luxury of waiting until the sun was perfect and I had the ability to move the camera wherever and however I wanted. This is what I've devoted my life to from when I took my first photograph with a Pentax SLR. And it's mostly been better to stay at the party than to go home to read. I don't know exactly when it happened, but things have changed, and the prospect of being in my living room with my wife and a glass of wine, though certainly not as good as this one, and my Galeano or Cortázar has suddenly become more enticing. This movie has been a kind of watershed for me."

A largish man wearing a pale apron over a black T-shirt, blue jeans, and red high-tops approached the table. "Peter Compton and his amazing wife. Once again, you've emptied the place!"

"Trust me, at considerable cost."

"Giovanni, this is Javier Benavidez, our DP," said Marci.

"Pleasure to meet you, Javier. And sorry not to have been out yet."

"We know. You've got the senator," said Peter.

"Who is dying to meet you, by the way."

"Send him out."

"I was hoping you'd come back. Not this second. They have a ways to go. I need him to feel like this was the night of his life. The Restaurant Association is hounding me to get in his ear about some legislation. Six months from now when I'm sitting in his office in Washington, he'll remember meeting you more than anything he puts in his mouth."

"Fine. But we're in the middle of something here, so in a bit," Peter said to the chef, visibly annoyed at having to yield status to a US senator by being the one to visit the other's table.

"I can take a hint. And thanks. I'll owe you one." He gathered their three plates. "I'll be back with your fish course in a few."

"Javier, tell us why you're unhappy," said Marci when they were once again alone.

"Do you realize, Peter, that you give me notes on an almost hourly basis?"

"I talk to you as a collaborator."

"You didn't conceive the shooting strategy or the look, coordinate a color palette, spend months looking at references. You didn't choose the department heads—"

"We did have a hand in those, actually. Marci especially."

"Joel and I had been conferring for months," Javier continued. "Before shooting I actually liked the guy, even when he showed up with the dog."

"I want to kill that animal," said Marci.

"But Joel's dog, you and your notes and your outbursts, none of this would matter. I don't even know what it is to be a cinematographer anymore. You either shoot these huge movies with all this interference and insanity, but that's the only way your work ever gets seen on the big screen, or you shoot smaller films where there's less at stake so you're left alone, but those films are only ever seen on home screens that haven't been calibrated properly, so your image looks like video half the time and all the work you did is irrelevant. It isn't film anymore in a theater either, of course, it's digital, but at least there's projection from the back of a darkened room. Some incredible images are being made by some amazing DPs now. But what's the point of all that if the only way I can work with the full potential of what movies were meant to be is to participate in an iteration that gets more and more corrupted and cynical by the year, and is more prone to interference by people at cross-purposes with what real artists want to do?"

"Wow," said Marci. "That was a lot."

"So, to what's important!" announced Giovanni, the chef's timing in his own restaurant so maladroit Javier suspected it might be a special acuity. He carried two plates, and Jane followed with another. "We have here some line-caught Georgia coast pompano pan seared in garlic, grapeseed oil, sea salt, and lime, then drizzled with olive oil from the dear old island of Ischia. For the garnish, chive, rocket, and nasturtium, all local, in that same olive oil and a Modena balsamic. And for a pairing, Jack has opened a bottle of 2011 Puligny Montrachet—same year as your Pingus."

The sommelier appeared with a slope-shouldered bottle and two stems.

I was right. They're going to try and get me drunk, Javier thought.

"I'm fine with just the red," he said.

"Not at Peter's table. This is on the house. I'm not going to leave you without the option to have that fish with this wine."

Skipping the glass priming, the sommelier poured a full portion for Marci, then did the same for Javier.

"I appreciate it," said Javier.

"Now, back to the galley. You guys enjoy."

Javier prepared a bite, the slightly blackened skin breaking at the touch of his fish knife. Were it not for his dinner companions and the pretension roaring from the histrionically folksy chef, it might have been one of the better meals he'd had in years.

"You want to know something?" asked Peter.

"Sure," said Javier.

"I'm completely with you about the changes in what we do, especially in terms of how movies are consumed. This is going to sound horrible, but before we put in our screening room—"

"Oh God, Peter," said Marci. "Don't be that guy."

"I know. I'm sorry. Yes, we have a screening room. Seats sixteen, so not huge. But before then Marci and I only saw the movies that were important to us in theaters. And with our system it's still not the same, because we're in the room alone or with a few friends instead of strangers, and there's also no substitute for the sound you get in a great theater. My ideal? Mann's Chinese."

"TCL," said Marci.

"What?"

"It's called the TCL Chinese. Not Mann's anymore."

"What the fuck is TCL?"

"It stands for 'The Creative Life,'" said Marci. "A Chinese company."

"The Chinese own Mann's Chinese now?"

"*Some* Chinese. I don't think it's the CCP."

"Wow. Okay, fine. So the TCL Chinese, and I'd fill every seat for the collective experience. It goes back to the ancients. I don't give a fuck what the movie is, it's better as catharsis. Or Artaud. Theater is plague."

"Get on with it, Peter."

"Marci and I started our company because we want to do real films. Would I trade five Sparta films and, whatever, a hundred million dollars for being in *Apocalypse Now* and working for scale? In a second. But when I went to prison and was scared out of my mind for what was going to happen to me—everything from being molested to fucking killed—you know what saved me?"

"That they knew you from movies."

"Exactly. But it wasn't the art films—the ones that were important to me. It was the studio stuff and television. Like that scene in *Sullivan's Travels*, when the director wants to make his socially conscious films, so he goes on the road incognito and learns that what the people really want is just to be entertained because it's their only escape from how shitty their lives are. 'You were in *Scorcher*!' they would say, or 'Man, we've got the motherfucker who did *Cobra Mission* on our block!' or, the one that really sold it, 'Nobody who played Slade Butcher is gonna get a hand laid on him unless it's to bless him.' The most ridiculous character name I ever had in what until then I considered one of my worst films, a pure money grab. And sure, I was glad it looked like I could survive—which, believe me, after the first few weeks that shit wore off quick and things weren't so easy—but the real lesson I learned is that when I did those movies because of the paychecks in support of a lifestyle that centered entirely on drugs and pleasure, but at the same time was looking down on the people who made and saw them, I was being an asshole. They were part of these people's lives, and who was I to judge them for that? And who was I to judge the movies themselves for actually serving a purpose, especially for a bunch of criminals who'd been stripped of everything else?"

"I'll go a step further," said Marci. "Your sister is a producer. You told me that early on, right?"

"An amazing one."

"Mine is a pediatric surgeon. My brother is an M&A lawyer, but he teaches at Lehman College gratis as an adjunct and runs a Big Brother program in Harlem. Both my siblings live in the city within a mile of my parents. Peter will tell you that as he and I have become more successful, a part of me has felt increasingly more unsettled, especially when those most important to me, my family, seem to like the movies we do less and less. I actually hate when they come to LA now because the judgment is frankly unbearable. Enough to change it? Absolutely not, because mostly I've grown to love my life. Screened entertainment is the most powerful narrative technology man has ever created. The only other phenomenon that comes close was the printing press, and by the way, people inveighed against the results of that as well, claiming anything other than the Bible would corrupt readers. So you can go on with your Savonarola routine, but I'm not with you."

"That frankly offends me."

"Forgive me, Javier, but what's the difference?" she asked.

"Savonarola was fighting the Renaissance. I don't think that's what's going on here with Sparta films."

"He's got you there," said Peter, laughing.

"And I'm not asking that we make bonfires of the films I find objectionable. I just don't want to work on them."

"But what did you think this was going to be?"

"I grew up in a family where to be a creative person on a large scale was considered a kind of priesthood. I don't want to tell you who was around our dinner table in Mexico City. And I think about that and that I'm putting up with all this humiliation to work for a conglomerate owned by another conglomerate making movies that barely entertain with you guys bossing me around all day and Peter yelling at the crew, and it starts to make me ill. It's a fucking no-win situation."

He could sense her welling anger and was oddly grateful. He needed to be challenged for the unrelenting judgment to which he'd been subjecting himself over the past month. A dressing down from Marci, whom he considered smarter than her very clever husband, was perhaps just what he required.

"All right, I've honestly heard enough," she began. "First of all, these movies don't 'barely' entertain. If they did, the two so-called conglomerates you mention—because I don't know how Sparta is a conglomerate other than that Max Kaiser makes features and TV, but whatever—anyway, if these movies are so deficient, how do they make so much money for the businesses that make them? Are you going to say because the unprecedented audience for these films is stupid? I really hope not, because then you're just like every other hypocritical person in Hollywood—and trust me, I used to be one of them—who claims to be socially conscious but secretly despises the people they're purporting to want to help. Sparta films entertain on a scale that is almost unprecedented as a brand, except for perhaps Disney, another 'evil' conglomerate. Well, guess what, bub? I grew up on Disney films. I fucking *loved* Cinderella, and I was a lit major in the Ivy League who marched for choice and did sit-ins on campus for women's rights, and I've never voted for a Republican in my life. But did I like having clear moralities in narratives crafted for little girls to grow up with? You bet your ass. And did I, in college, suddenly realize that Cinderella's reward is to get to marry a handsome prince and how fucked up that was? Or that her nemeses were a stepmother and stepsisters, pitting women against women? Of course. But I wouldn't trade the tears I cried as an eight-year-old identifying with the little girl who's treated poorly by everyone except the Fairy Godmother and gets to win in the end because she's, above all, a decent person. That story made me better. I watched it easily two dozen times. The movie we're making—I'm sorry, I'm going to say it—is not stupid, it's smart. *Major Machina*'s hero was based on an alcoholic nuclear physicist whose addiction prevented him from participating fully in the incredible atrocity of the nuclear bomb who then killed himself, he was so disheartened and confused by what his work helped accomplish. That's the source material. Is it updated for our movie in a sometimes hackneyed way? Stripped of some of what made it originally compelling? Sure. Is the villain a sea creature? Yeah, though I'd argue that's going to provide some pretty insane imagery if you'd get over yourself. The point is, Javier, when I'm up at night doubting myself and my choices, I'm ultimately reminded that regardless of all the flak that thinking people like us put in the air for ourselves, I'm getting to influence what hundreds of millions of people will see. And not only will they experience what we create, they'll talk about it, argue about it, because we're going to make sure it's as goddamned compelling as we can."

"They should be arguing and thinking about other things."

"Who are you to determine what people should and shouldn't do? And what other things, Javier? Honestly. Let's be real. World hunger? Homelessness? Joyce? Who the fuck was it Peter said a second ago? Artaud? Neruda, who next thing I know you're going to tell me was at your dinner table back in Mexico?"

"Twice, actually."

"Okay, that's just ridiculous. But, and I'm not ashamed to point out what's true: we're talking about a world that elected Trump twice, Boris Johnson, Berlusconi."

"Whom I met, by the way," interjected Peter.

"Exactly. The world elected those people," said Javier, sublimely uninterested in a sidebar concerning the star's encounter with Italy's most repugnant politician since Mussolini.

"And we either accept that fact," retorted Marci, "and engage with it, or just consider ourselves superior and serve up coastal agitprop, which trust me, no one wants to see, not even you and me. And stop shitting on this movie, because we stand behind it. My husband brought himself back from the brink."

"I'm aware."

"He's playing a guy fighting not just bad guys and his own government, but his own awful demons. I get to be at the monitor seeing this incredibly talented man find all of that within himself, refracted through the modernization of a comic that every outcast boy in America was reading sixty years ago, and filmed by you in a way that, even though you now report to us that you hate your job, is fucking brilliant. Your use of shadow to show his inner conflict? You think we don't see that? Talk about it at night when we get home? Tens of millions of people will see the ambiguity and conflict you're painting on my husband's face for the character he's working his ass off to bring to life. And if you don't see that as a good thing—that well into your life you're doing something that impactful—I don't know what to tell you, because in lesser hands, which is to say pretty much any other DP on the planet, all those people wouldn't get the nuance and the vulnerability and the humanity and all the things you're trying to bring out. Why am I so worked up? Because if you quit, we lose all that and so does our audience."

She's Svengali and Mesmer and Jeanne d'Arc all in one, Javier thought.

"Welcome to my wife," Peter said somewhat fecklessly, though with unmistakable charm.

"My husband screwed up today. He knows that. This has been a tough shoot for you even before then, and you've explained why. We hear you. Please stay on, with Peter no longer murmuring in your ear."

"No more of that," the actor assured them both.

"And with Joel back in charge, which, trust me, I'm working on. I'll also speak to the studio about their notes. You get back to the streamlined basics, and I promise you this will end up something you'll be proud to be associated with. And by the way, art films and commercial films? To my mind movies are best when there's no wall between those two, and people like you and Peter can make something of this scale also be thoughtful and artistic and intimate. You do that, then this film, which is a celebration of individualism, selflessness, and redemption, is going to be the furthest thing from how you've been construing it."

"What am I supposed to say to all of that?" he asked.

"That you've heard her," said Peter. "That you've heard my apology. That you're willing to take us at our word. That you're going to stick around and help us finish this thing."

FIFTEEN

Over the several months following its purchase, rather than alleviate his unhappiness, the car coaxed a deepening emptiness within Declan Morris that comments from others only exacerbated.

"Is that your Audi outside?" Joel asked. "Javier told me it was, but I didn't believe him."

"Why didn't you believe him?"

"It's gorgeous. Insane, really. I just didn't think you were the type."

"What do you mean? What type?"

"I don't know, to drive a car like that. I wouldn't even know what to do with it. Did you have it shipped out? Javier didn't say. It looks new."

"I bought it here," he offered without thinking. Why hadn't he simply lied? Plenty of producers had their cars trucked to location.

"You went to a dealership in Atlanta? Jesus. Were you planning to, or was it an impulse?"

"A little of both. I mean, I've always loved sports cars. Do you want to go for a ride in it?"

"I mean, sure."

He drove them five miles down the Buford Highway to a working lunch over barbecue, where the director exhibited nothing but further befuddlement.

"Seriously, if I showed up with that car, Annie would call the couples therapist."

"But why?"

"It's, like, the whole middle-aged guy with the sports car thing. If you don't mind my asking, how much was it?"

"I'd rather not say."

"Did you talk them down at least?"

"It helped that they're discontinuing the model. The guy was really trying to move it."

"Too bad you can't rebate it. Then you'd really have gotten a steal!"

"Jesus," Declan answered almost too quickly. "Can you imagine the state auditor when a six-figure sports car came across his desk? He'd fucking choke on his latte."

"So it was six figures even with the discount?"

"Oh God, no," he lied. "I was just saying if you bought, like, a Maserati or something, I mean really went for it, because if you were going to do it, why not really do it?"

He decided not only never to offer anyone else a ride in it but to curtail discussion altogether. Yet given what it was, could he even accomplish that?

Jeremy, something of a buff, was especially querulous.

"You bought an R8? That's a crazy fucking roadster. I drove one at the dealership in Pasadena. It's not a bad price point for the amount of car, especially when you compare it with the 911 Turbo Cabriolet, but you're paying another eighty grand minimum for the Porsche. Careful where you park it. If you're in midtown, leave it at the Four Seasons. They love supercars out front. Definitely don't leave it on the street anywhere, though, unless you're in Buckhead, but even there. You'll get keyed for sure. You're gonna let me drive it before we wrap, right?"

"Of course."

With Javier, the less he and Declan got along, the more curious the Mexican became.

"I just think it's a little strange that the guy who's giving me shit about man days and pre-rigging, nickel-and-diming me on every little ask, can afford the most expensive car of anyone on the movie."

"What does one thing have to do with the other?"

"You don't apply the same stringency to your own expenditures."

Nothing irritated Declan more than Javier's vocabulary for its message of intellectual superiority.

"Javier, what the fuck are you talking about? One is my money, the other is Sparta's. Go buy whatever the fuck kind of car you want. Eat at Bacchanalia every night for all I care, so long as it's your money."

"So that car is all you? Your money as a producer?"

"What the hell are you even getting at?"

"Don't forget, I'm from Mexico. We wrote the book on this kind of thing."

"I still don't—"

"You didn't use your position somehow to get a deal? Otherwise, why now? And why here? Why put that kind of money into a vehicle you're going to have to beat the shit out of driving all the way back to LA or that you'll have to pay to have shipped? Either you had some dealer by the balls here—you saw him buttfucking his cow—or it's a quid pro quo."

What recourse did he have now but to minimize their interactions and, whenever possible, accede to the DP's overages without argument?

Peter Compton, however, introduced a level of inquest that exceeded all others. The car became his obsession.

"Just tell me again," began one conversation in the snack area of the production office four days before principal photography. "You're coming home from a location scout and you just pop into the Audi dealership?"

"We've been over this, Peter. Yes. That's what I did. Why is it such a big deal?"

"I'm just interested anthropologically."

"That a man decides to look at cars, sees one he likes, it'll make him happy, he can afford it, so he goes ahead and buys it?"

Crew members began to linger, pretending to graze the crudités and granola bars, clearly drawn by Peter's inquisitional tone.

"This is not just any car, Declan. And you of all people. Our line producer. It's all Javier talks about."

"It's starting to seem like it's all anyone talks about. You are aware we're trying to make a movie here."

"Good one. And yes. Which is kind of my concern. The optics of it. Here we are, a hundred-and-sixty-million-dollar film being subsidized by the State of Georgia. And lo and behold, the producer of the film taxpayers are pitching in a cool forty million dollars or so to get it here—and not just the producer, but the one signing the checks—is driving around in a hundred-and-seventy-five-thousand-dollar supercar."

"Trust me, I didn't pay a hundred and seventy-five thousand dollars."

"Tell me about that."

"That's just not what the car cost."

"I looked it up. You got some kind of deal?"

"I bargained them down like anyone, but one-seventy-five wasn't even the sticker price."

"Let's be generous and call it one-seventy then."

"I'm not going to get into what I paid for it, but it wasn't near one-seventy-five."

"And leaving aside your average denizen of the Peach State, what do you reckon the gaffer thinks? Some of the grips? The boom operator? The assistant costume girl, when we're calling grace every day, and doing walking lunches on ten and a half hours you're always asking the shop steward to stretch so you don't have to pay meal penalties? You think it's a good look?"

"Really, Peter? You're gonna go there? Because let's talk about your five trailers over there, or the house we're renting for you at fifty k a month, or your two assistants and your chef and your doctor on call with his suitcase full of vitamins following you wherever you go."

"I'm the artist. You're management. And what I have I fucking share. Check the bucket on Five-Dollar Fridays where I Venmo a thousand bucks every time. Or the espresso truck I ordered last week, the pizza I had delivered the week before. And all of it out of my paycheck, not Sparta's, so don't come back at me with the lobster you're gonna have them make at catering when we're halfway through. Or Sushi Friday or whatever. You go ask the crew what they think of me, and I don't think you'll get an unkind word. Then have someone ask them what they think of you. As for where I live here, sure it's expensive, but try and be me for a second where you can't go anywhere without being hassled and see if you wouldn't want the compound you have to live in to be as nice as possible since you basically can't ever leave it except to come to work."

"I don't begrudge you anything, Peter, just don't begrudge me."

"Yeah . . . I'm sorry . . . it's just . . ."

"What?"

"Why'd you buy it here?"

"Why is everyone so interested in that? It was cheaper."

"Come on. A sticker price is a sticker price. There has to be a reason, and please don't say it was on impulse, because not even I would lay down that kind of scratch on an impulse buy."

"Maybe that's the difference between you and me."

"Hah! You're telling an addict about impulse control? I don't think so, especially when, if you analogize it, I'm figuring, no offense here, that you spending a buck seventy on a car would be like me spending ten million."

"Fuck you, Peter."

"I've hit a nerve, haven't I? Something's rotten in the state of Declan."

Not a day went by without some version of the same conversation with the star. He's a bully, a congenital predator, Declan finally determined. If it's not Joel Slavkin or Jennifer or Javier, it's me, and for whatever reason, more and more I seem to be the easiest to separate from the herd.

It culminated a week before they were to shoot Paul Kramer's scene with the Stanford marine biologist in which the actor would make out all afternoon with an actress a dozen years his junior. Declan had begun to fantasize about her, an obsession he was able to bring to fruition at will thanks to the Cialis he was taking to quell his sleep-interrupting urge to urinate the bottles of Chardonnay he was polishing off nightly. Jennifer, he often averred to himself, is the one exception: her, I would give a ride in the car. If I park near her trailer, perhaps she'll inquire.

"What's it like driving it?" she might ask.

"Do you like antiquing?" In a Google deep dive, he'd learned she collected vintage dessert spoons.

"Wow, Declan, I do, actually!"

"How about this? We can hit this insane flea market this weekend in Decatur and go in my car."

To his astonishment, she approached him behind the monitor before he could even execute his plan.

"Declan, is that your car? I think it's an Audi, parked in base camp?"

"It is indeed." The blood rushed to his face.

"Wow."

"I know, right?"

"It must have been expensive."

"Actually, I got a pretty good deal, and also, it's about to be discontinued."

"I sure hope so."

"Why's that?"

"What's the gas mileage?"

It was fourteen miles per gallon in the city, a statistic he had no interest in sharing. "I really don't know."

"Is there a reason you didn't buy electric?"

"I'm actually quite climate conscious," he said, incredulous that the conversation had so suddenly turned from flirtatious to inculpatory.

"Oh yeah, and how's that?"

"Well, since you ask, my wife and I are installing solar panels on our home. And she drives an electric car."

"But you bought a gas guzzler?"

"You know, the Chinese and the Indians, not to mention poor forest management resulting in wildfires, have more than negated any of our new electric and renewable standards."

"Where'd you pick up those statistics? Fox News?" Actually he had, but statistics were statistics.

"May I ask you something?" he asked. "How did you even know anything about my car? It's nowhere near your trailer or the makeup trailer."

"Peter pointed it out to me. He said you paid over two hundred thousand dollars for it."

"Well, he's wrong about that."

"Where it's really exorbitant is in the price to future generations."

A grinning Peter joined them. "What are you guys talking about?"

"What is it about my car, Peter? And how can I get you to stop hassling me about it?"

"Jennifer is very concerned about the environment. And this is not a frivolous person we're talking about. She's in Mensa."

"Please just answer my question."

"Unfortunately, Declan, I got a bad vibe off you from the moment we met. You're one of these guys who hates creative people. I get it. You work your ass off. More hours than me in production. More hours than Javier. More hours than pretty much everyone but Joel. But who'll ever know that? It's sort of like fishing. The line producer drives the boat miles out to sea, he prepares all the baits, sets the outriggers, looks for birds and seaweed and driftwood so he can find the big game, does all that work for the jackass that chartered the boat. But when the two-hundred-pound sailfish is caught, who gets his picture taken? The fat slob who sat in the chair getting catered to. And if that fat slob sets the world record, will credit go to the boat captain, without whom the fish never would have been found and even hauled in because the captain set the drag on the reel too, and reversed the boat when the so-called fisherman was running out of line? No. It'll go to the fat slob. But here's the thing. The fishing boat captain has to want to be a fishing boat captain. He needs to love the sport for the sake of the sport and be fine with never being recognized. No one made him put up his shingle. He chose that life, and since he did, it's up to him how he feels about it. You don't want to watch me get credit for catching the fish on the set you did all the work to help make possible—although let's be clear, you didn't pay for it, and you didn't write the script or make a single overarching creative decision—that's your problem. But don't resent me because I'm the face of it and not you."

"I don't resent you, Peter. I barely even think about you."

"I catch your glances. I see how you look at Ron and all the other actors. To you we're a bunch of entitled divas who do less work than anyone. Never mind that acting is work. In fact, I work my ass off at it. But your love of all this, the making of movies, has to be bigger than your resentment, and with you it's just not. When you bought the Audi I knew it. The two-hundred-thousand-dollar car—"

"It wasn't even near that, and you keep—"

"Fine, the—what was it you said a few weeks ago?—hundred-and-fifty-thousand-dollar car—"

"A lot less than that, actually."

"For that car to have cost a penny less than a hundred and fifty thousand dollars means you somehow used production. And please, I don't want to know, because I'd have to report you or be an accessory, and I don't want to go back to jail. But ultimately it's the car itself. If it were an MG or an Austin-Healy or a Morgan or an old Mustang, it would suggest a true love of cars, like a true love of film production. But it's a fucking fresh-off-the-line supercar. The only thing worse would have been a McLaren. Now, if you'll excuse me, I've got to get back to set to make sure Joel and his dog have a plan for the next scene."

Such a deft analysis from the self-absorbed star consumed him in a storm of self-recrimination and fear. Should the actor alert Marci Levy or Sparta to his suspicions, Declan would soon be answering some profoundly inconvenient questions. Why had he been so stupid? He, who had built a career on unwaveringly stolid sensibilities, had walked into a car dealership off the highway ringing Atlanta and, without so much as a contravening thought, engendered a lethally risky scheme to purchase a vehicle he now understood to be utterly ridiculous.

He stopped calling his wife, texting to explain that it had nothing to do with her or the children, that he loved her as he loved no one else, but that he simply couldn't speak. Should his strategy for purchasing the car be exposed, he determined he would have no choice but to end his life, so extreme would be the humiliation, destroying not only his career but any dignity he possessed. His wife considered him the most honorably reliable person she'd ever met. Yes, she derided his outlook as "constipated," his need for structure and control "beyond anal," and his sense of humor "marginal at best," but she adored his decency, his reliability, his unwavering ethics. Their three children, while they probably secretly relished those times when he was away for the corresponding laxity in discipline and parental expectation, perceived him as a paragon of dependability.

His daughter had once informed him, "Dad, you've made it nearly impossible for me ever to find somebody. No guy will ever measure up to you." Now what would she say?

⚡

The night before Peter Compton's outburst he slept fitfully, knocking back his usual bottle of Chardonnay, plus an extra glass for good measure. This had him pissing every other hour in a foggy delirium until finally, at 2:30 a.m., he took an Ativan and half an Ambien. He woke to the alarm four hours later and headed to set. In spite of the requirement of an intimacy coordinator, the scene would involve no disrobing, no simulation of sex or even foreplay other than passionate kissing should the actors drive it that way. He stepped inside the UPM trailer to go over cost reports, sign a few checks, and look at the schedule.

His assistant, a lost twenty-something who was the son of a friend, brought him his second macchiato from craft services as he stepped onto the parking lot to walk to set. He passed his car without looking at it.

Upon opening the interior stage door he heard the raised voice of the intimacy coordinator. She seemed to be arguing with Peter or perhaps Jennifer, Declan couldn't tell.

As he approached from behind the dense ring of crew, James, the black AD who stood at six-four with not a hair on his head and presented as perhaps the most sane and measured individual on set, was urging that everyone take a break. Declan was about to step forward in support of this when Peter Compton raised his voice insisting he be heard, and not just by those nearest, but by the entire crew.

Acting more on instinct than in service of some cynical gambit, Declan, observed by no one, not even those now beside him, who were too rapt by what seemed to be an impending meltdown by the film's star, edged behind a forest of C-stands, lifted his iPhone, punched its video lens setting to x3, and began to shoot. Yes, at any moment a crew person, or, far worse, Marci or Jeremy or Charisse or a member of the security team, might perceive his raised device, but somehow he knew none would. Star meltdowns were simply too captivating. It wasn't so much the content of what the actor was saying but the stridency of his delusion that epitomized to Declan the monumentally overblown, misguided, and self-important enterprise of making movies. He simply had to document it.

Let Peter Compton accuse me all he likes. Let him deride me, accurately or not, for who and what I am. Let him ridicule me for the car I'll sell when I get to LA without my wife even knowing I bought it. With a few taps on this phone I could destroy him and this entire project. No, not Sparta—though that would be a service for which not only film history but the trajectory of our culture would thank me—but the brand that is Peter Compton and the screen iteration that is *Major Machina*, most definitely.

And I just might.

I just might.

SIXTEEN

Max Kaiser had been up since 2:30 a.m. when the phone awakened him. On the first ring he knew it concerned *Major Machina* with its unrelenting drip of problems: scheduling changes, cost overruns, friction between director and star, a restive DP. Yet the dailies were extraordinary. If we can just hold on for the final month of production, he kept saying to himself, we're going to have a movie that might restore Sparta to where it had been in echelon three, when the superheroes came together in a triptych of films that had broken nearly every box office record worldwide.

"Sorry to wake you," Marci Levy said from Atlanta, where it was 5:30 a.m.

"Is this going to be a long conversation?"

"Definitely not short."

"Let me go into my office," he said, rising quietly so as not to disturb his wife.

"You can take it in here," she said.

"It sounds like I might need to pace."

He had met Melanie his junior year at Oberlin when they were both twenty and caught each other's eye across a Harkness table discussing Gogol. Their first date involved walking from her dorm room in South a quarter mile to the Feve in a blizzard so fierce it took them twenty minutes to navigate the conservatory buildings and parking lot. A dual-degree candidate in viola and art history, she'd grown up in Marin County, where her father had retired from a career in finance to build furniture and her mother taught high school music. She was wholesomely un-Jewish, fair skinned and freckled with sandy-blond hair, and a disposition that had no forced diaspora in its ancestry. From that first date, where they discussed everything from his father's alcoholism (why to this day he'd never taken even a sip, including during the toasts at his own wedding) to her love of Aaron Copland and John Singer Sargent. Though the opposite of the malcontent rebel he imagined dating, particularly at Oberlin, he was utterly smitten. They'd rarely spent a night apart since.

He put Marci on hold and walked past the bedroom doors of their daughters to his office overlooking the ocean. They lived on a promontory in the Palisades in a house inspired by a section from *The Fountainhead*, one of Melanie's favorite novels. In the scene Howard Rourk asserts his prowess with a hastily drawn structure extending vertically from a cliff. Once they'd bought the land, she'd made every potential architect read the passage and propose an iteration. The winner had been a woman completely unfamiliar with Ayn Rand who urged a post-and-beam solution cantilevered to extend the cliff not only upward but outward, with alloyed buttressing painted the color of the rocks to make the entire home, even with its preponderance of glass, seem like an extension of the geology itself. He stood holding his office handset at its southwesternmost point as if on the prow of a ship.

"Okay, Marci, I'm ready."

"Can you go to your computer?"

"Give me a sec." He strolled thirty feet from the window, where he'd hoped to follow the lights of a tanker approaching the horizon. He sat. "I'm there."

"Type in my husband's name."

"Oh shit."

Before him appeared an entire page of links with the words "Tirade," "Temper Tantrum," "Meltdown," "Screaming Fit," and the like, along with stills of the actor gesticulating in front of the *Major Machina* crew. The vertical aspect ratio assured the existence of an iPhone video.

"You need to watch it," she said.

He did.

"Marci, I'm going to ask you something, and please understand that to lie will only hurt us both."

"You want to know if he's using again."

"That's correct."

"I can tell you categorically that he's not."

"Then what could possibly have provoked this? I mean, Jesus. This is a guy who purifies every set with incense and crystals."

"It was a combination of things. First of all, Peter can be volatile. It's residual from prison. But it was the intimacy coordinator."

"That you're going to have to explain."

"He was away for a few years. Sometimes it shows in very ugly ways."

"Hasn't he been out for over a decade?"

"Sure."

"When did this go up?"

"About four hours ago."

"And when did the tirade happen? Why wasn't I told about it?"

"Yesterday morning. It was a long day."

"So there's been this much spread in that short a time. And in the middle of the night?"

"People are going nuts."

"How's Peter?"

"He doesn't know yet."

"How can that be possible?"

"He's asleep. Him I can deal with. At least I think I can, so long as I can convince him not to do a deep dive into all the horrible things people are saying. What he endured during the trial was pretty ugly, although this time I haven't found anyone defending him. It's more Sparta I'm worried about, and I wanted to give you guys the chance to get out ahead of it."

"Who the fuck shot it? And why would they share it?"

"Really, Max? This is the world we live in."

"But if they were caught they'd be fired."

"You can't blame the idiot who pressed record. You have to blame Peter, me, Charisse, Jeremy, all of us, for letting him go on like he did and not shutting it down."

"Why didn't you?"

"What can I say? My husband is compelling to watch. We were, as they say, caught up in the moment. Shame on us."

"No offense, Marci, but why do actors do this to themselves?"

"That I can't answer. But here's what you have to understand about my husband, and maybe it's true about all addicts. I've come to look at his disease as finding all sorts of ways to express itself. Just as an example, do you know how much coffee he drinks during the day? It's staggering. I talk with him about it, and he says, of course, 'I'm still me at some level. Would you rather I be hitting a pipe?' He also needs to be the center of attention. Always. And when he feels himself losing that status, with all the turmoil going on inside his demented and brilliant mind, wired on caffeine, he snaps. That's what you're seeing on that tape, not that he didn't have legitimate reasons in the moment to be frustrated. But he fucked up, and he hurt the project and he hurt himself. It was monumentally childish and stupid. This is what he's capable of."

"And what do you do when it happens?"

"I love him and forgive him and help him repair this."

"What does that look like?"

"Well, first of all, you should know that he did apologize to the crew later in the day."

"Okay."

"But in terms of the video, I've already written a statement for him when he gets up. Essentially it exposes how awful he feels for the outburst, that of course he respects what intimacy coordinators do and what the crew does, that he was completely in the wrong."

"I didn't even know we had intimacy coordinators anymore."

"What, they were there to mollify women until George Floyd was killed and then we moved on to that? Of course we still have intimacy coordinators, Max."

"Will he put it out?"

"He will."

"And then what?"

"I've done a deep dive, and in every instance where outbursts on set go viral, there are two factors that can make them short-lived. One is if the work is great. As you know, we have extraordinary footage. Not just with Peter, but with all the actors, the sets, Javier's photography, Joel's staging. You guys putting out a thirty-second teaser would be incredibly useful."

"Of what?"

"I don't know, Max. Get with your marketing guys. Obviously it'll have to involve Peter, but he's doing great work."

"No one disputes that."

"All I'm suggesting is to cut something together. A snippet with him and Jennifer, obviously. Him and Ron. Him in his lab. Not now, but a month from now after this hopefully levels off a bit, so it seems like you were always going to do it. And not a scene with dialogue or too many static close-ups, or there'll be memes where they take part of the tirade and stick it in his mouth."

"What else?"

"Well, this is trickier, but remember a few years ago when Chris Rabe flipped out on the DP?"

"Chris was in the right, Marci. The guy let him crawl through a heating duct with vermin droppings in it."

"Exactly." In the film, shot in Bulgaria, the volatile British star had played an American spy working undercover with Armenian arms dealers. Among other infractions against the environmentally conscious thesp was the Romanian DP insisting they burn tires within the chimney stacks of the factory in which much of the film was shot. Not only had the actor tired of breathing in burned polymers, but he couldn't imagine anything salutary for the planet in their release. When the DP announced to him as he choked on mice droppings that they needed to remove an ND filter and shoot again, the resulting philippic was recorded by a crew member.

"You couldn't tell McFadden?!" he screamed, referring to the director by his last name. "You couldn't say the exposure wasn't good as soon as I got into the fucking duct!? And now you're laughing? It's fucking funny to you? Eating rat shit?" He then uttered the sentence that gave the screed its oft-quoted crescendo: "McFadden, either this tire-incinerating Ceausescu motherfucker goes, or I do!"

"Once it got out that Chris had a legitimate beef," Marci continued, "people were more forgiving, especially on the environmental stuff. Stan and I had an overhead deal with the studio at the time. Trust me, getting that information out was a coordinated effort."

"You're saying we manufacture some excuse for Peter? What? Was Javier driving a car that runs on coal? I wasn't aware Peter was environmentally conscious."

"We are, actually. And not 'manufacture,' *find*. We make it so that enough people take Peter's side in the outburst that there's a countervailing narrative, instead of this one-sided deluge we're seeing right now."

"What do you have in mind?"

"Give me a few hours."

⚡

When Max began as an intern in 2002, Sparta Comics was emerging from bankruptcy. It had been acquired by a toy manufacturer named Boaz Gutterman, an ex-member of the Israeli Special Forces who it was rumored participated in the assassination of the Palestinian leader Abu Jihad in Tunis in 1988. The Israeli was to be admired for having understood the value of the imprint's IP and how it had yet to be exploited in the new century. But, strangely, filmed iterations didn't interest him beyond licensing titles to studios for Saturday morning cartoons and the occasional feature. He hoped to concentrate on publishing, trading cards, and, of course, toys, the business that associated him with Sparta in the first place as a fabricator of action figures.

As a boss he was unstable, tyrannical, unflinchingly chauvinist, and miserly, known to fish paper clips angrily from trash cans in the New York office for reuse. Nor would he allow bottled water, snacks, or a coffee machine. He bivouacked his staff not in Manhattan but across the river in Long Island City, where the rent was half the price, in a cheaply constructed high-rise in which at least one window imploded each year during hurricane season. Employees groused about furniture purchased from a nearby building in receivership, and Max heard tell of used desks arriving with half-devoured sandwiches rotting in drawers and, in one case, a bottle of urine.

In spite of his indifference to film, Boaz did need some among his ranks to handle incoming licensing queries, and it was in this department Max caught the owner's attention, quickly moving him to Los Angeles, where the young enthusiast soon advocated they no longer license comics to studios. With his *Sparta Comics Character Handbook* to prove it, he convinced Boaz that when it came to films, Sparta needed to control its own IP with a coherent library of movies all its own. Thus was the Sparta Comic Galaxy born, with a thirty-one-year-old Max Kaiser in charge.

"It won't be rosy," his former partner Boaz Gutterman warned him thirteen years and twenty films later, when Grand Studios offered to purchase Sparta's film division, along with screen rights for all Sparta titles, for just over $4 billion, or $32 a share, with a stock swap to boot. "Though for me it's going to be pretty nice." Not only would Boaz cash out, but all remaining assets (the comic books, trading cards, logo, and print licensing) would be assured persisting value thanks to the free advertising of Sparta films.

"Why not for me?" asked Max.

"You're the one in charge of the movies, aren't you? Running a studio inside of a studio? It'll be like captaining a single-engine motorboat in the pool of a luxury liner in a hurricane."

He had experienced examples of what Boaz had predicted for him, but few like this. It was space Sparta had never occupied: public turmoil. Max despised discord of any sort, having learned (also from Boaz) that solidarity and a softly applied autocracy made for the most propitious results. For his entire leadership tenure he had exercised such power successfully, keeping conflicts and disruptions within the "Sparta camp," as he called it, with overt reference to the winning side of the Peloponnesian Wars that gave the imprint its name.

Even the divide between Boaz and him that had led to Boaz's expulsion had been kept mostly within. It began in the year leading up to the Grand Studios purchase and involved expansion into a new manner of superhero content, specifically films that would feature women heroes in title roles.

"Look," the Israeli said to Max when the former intern suggested a film based on *Meteor Girl*, the early '70s offshoot comic from *Meteor Team*, "I love women. I thank God for women. But the box office does not love women as lead characters."

"Women headline movies all the time."

"With action movies, not as much. It's not believable."

"I don't even know how to process this. Especially from you, who served in the Israeli army that makes female service compulsory. You come from one of the most gender progressive societies on the planet."

"I served with women, but there were limits. When it came to the fighting up close, we didn't have them going up against men, and thank God, for all sorts of reasons."

"But *Meteor Girl* was—actually, still is—a successful comic. She kicks ass and readers love it."

"Readers. Exactly. Take a look at the drawings. She's better than a Playboy bunny. That body isn't even real. I wish it were. It's no wonder it sells so well when ninety percent of our clientele is young boys, or men who are still young boys."

"So, they'll go see a *Meteor Girl* movie. And so will a lot of young girls. And women."

The resulting film outpaced all but three Sparta titles for profits, given its low budget relative to the bloated extravaganzas associated with the studio's male stars.

That same week, Grand Studios made its overture toward a purchase of Sparta. It had flown in Boaz on the private jet for a lunch at Langer's Deli on Alvarado and Seventh near MacArthur Park.

"We could have met at your office," he told Bruce Simkin, the studio head. "Or on video conference. Why all the ceremony?"

"You call this ceremony?" answered the dapper man opposite Max and Boaz in the button tufted vinyl booth. "Person-to-person interaction is how we do business at Grand, and always have since Joe Langley back in the twenties. Besides, with the numbers our lawyers are discussing, I didn't think the remove of video was appropriate."

"You talk about Joe Langley," said Boaz. "What do you think he'd say about a Jew running his company?"

"I'd like to think he'd have liked me and that some of his better principles still exist."

"Like anti-Semitism?"

"He wasn't an anti-Semite."

"He tried to hire Leni Riefenstahl and had his head frozen like a steak."

"He met with Leni Riefenstahl but never hired her, and he's buried, with his head, in Glendale, though I'm not sure manner of burial has anything to do with not liking Jews."

"So what qualities?"

"We're still a family-oriented brand. The Grand logo means something in a way that no other studio can boast. We also think there's an overlap between your approach and ours, which is why it makes sense for us to bring you under our umbrella."

"All I have to do is look at our profits," said Boaz, "to see how it makes sense for you. I'm not sure what's so great for Sparta."

"Well, first there's the purchase price, which will be significant for you, Boaz, for taking a company out of bankruptcy and accomplishing, along with Max here—"

"My wunderkind."

"Your wunderkind. Accomplishing with your wunderkind what you have. But you'll also retain control over it because we'd want the two of you to continue running it."

"Running Sparta?"

"Well, let me be clear. Definitely the larger company, which will remain yours. We're only interested in the film studio, which, yes, we'd also like Max and you to continue to run, but in this case more efficiently. There'd be redundancies between your studio and ours we could eliminate."

"Suddenly you're firing my workforce?"

"Is that a bad thing? Reduced personnel means more money for us to invest in supporting more Sparta films, which, by the way, with our presence in television means more platforms for even more content."

"More, more, more."

"I would have thought you'd admire what he had to say about streamlining costs," Max remarked after the meeting. "Hasn't that been a mantra of yours?"

"About saving. For him it's about making. People attack Jews for being money obsessed. It's not because of greed but fear. Fear that when we suddenly need it we won't have it. And this goes to exactly why what we have that Grand wants is so valuable."

"You're making no sense."

"The thing about Americans, and maybe why I love it here, but it also makes you heartless at times, is that you're not weighed down by tragedy. Vietnam aside, which was fought halfway around the world and mostly by poor people who couldn't get out of it, you have no real losses in your history. No Holocaust, no bombed cities, no attacks across the border, no real national pain."

"Slavery."

"This you did to yourselves. Not the blacks, obviously. But it doesn't make you think, and I'm speaking as part of your broader identity, mind you, that at any moment everything you have could be taken from you, that devastation is a mistake away either because you trust others or someone wants what you have or hates you and wants every single one of your kind dead. And again, please don't say 9/11. Horrible, but one day of terror from very far away. Now I'm not saying what I describe makes for the best mindset in the world either, or the best people, but most humans outside of America wake up every day, and inside, their DNA thinks to themselves that at a moment's notice everything could vanish, vaporized, both big and small. Here, so long as you have a little gelt, it's just not the case. This was especially true after the Second World War, when the comics this studio wants to pay us billions for were written. In no country but America could such nonsense have been created. Nonsense I love, mind you, but nonsense all the same, because countries and people that have suffered real tragedy can't see the world in terms of good and evil, superheroes and villains."

"I'd think it would be the opposite."

"Wrong. The people of Europe saw evil happen all around them in the presence of others they trusted and even thought were good but were co-opted by other forces that are so deeply and malignantly human we can't even understand them. They learned that evil was their neighbor who they never considered evil. And that neighbor's neighbor. And what happened in Eastern Europe after the war, with every citizen every other citizen's enemy, don't even get me started on that."

"I've never heard you speak this way."

"The reason these comics exploded, and the movies even more, is because the rest of the world wants to have the absurd privilege of seeing things the way Americans do, even though it's utterly simplistic and naive and perhaps even dangerous philosophically. But it's what everyone wants. And the best thing about America, the absolute best, is that all of this optimism here and this American exceptionalism, as they like to call it, which I believe in, by the way, is coming mostly from immigrants. Creators and thinkers from elsewhere, or their parents from elsewhere who have just enough tragedy in them to make things interesting, so you have heroes like Thaddeus Klein who are alcoholics, or Paul Kramer in *Major Machina*, alcoholic and suicidal, driving himself into a wall to try and kill himself. Or the vampires in *Jugular*, or Hephaestus who's hideous and angry. But make no mistake, it's all in service of a worldview we might wish were true but has very little to do with what our species is really about. It's all the dream of us or the nightmare of us in certain instances, but never really us."

"But, Boaz, Americans aren't the only people who make comics and movies. Maybe the big superhero movies, but that's because we have the resources to support them."

"Financiers cross borders. Look at me. There's no market for superhero movies in any language but English. And a superhero almost always has to be American, because only an American would be believable in a genre that is so specifically American. Comics were born here, after all. And so, by the way, were movies."

"What are we doing about Grand?"

"We do the deal. A bargain for them, too good for us."

"You obviously don't like Bruce Simkin."

"I don't like the way he thinks. When everything gets down to shareholders and P&Ls, the product gets safe, homogenized, bland, because the only thing worse than not making enough money is losing money. Or—and this you have to worry about more than anything, I suspect—he doesn't know when to stop the exploitation of a product. There's such a thing as overexposure of a thing. Trust me, we're not just going to be making movies for this guy. It's going to be television with a lot more hours to fill. If we don't watch out, there's going to be more of our content than the world out there has the patience for."

"What about you?"

"I'm the one who's expendable."

Boaz had been right about every aspect of the deal, from its price point, a relative discount for Grand and a boon for Sparta, to its exploitation of Sparta IP across all media. The result of this overextension was that at the moment of Peter Compton's meltdown, the movies were now worse, the storylines overextended, and the common aesthetic lacking not only the coherence but the standards of narrative quality it once had.

Most tragic, however, was how Boaz's prediction of his own departure had been realized, as well as Max's agency in it.

It had occurred to Max at the time of *Meteor Girl* that a heroine would constitute but the start of Sparta's foray into more diverse casting; that just as the writers of comics in the sixties and seventies had introduced not only women but people of color, Sparta Studios would now do so. Specifically he imagined a film iteration of the all-black comic *Dark Lion*, introduced by Sparta in 1973. He would wait two to three years after *Meteor Girl* to push resources toward production.

This changed, however, when, on his way home from work in the summer of 2017, he was driving south on the 405 toward the Sunset exit when he heard a report on NPR about a black teen shot in the back three times by a policeman in Topeka of all places, the very epitome of Middle America memorialized in *The Wizard of Oz*. The boy, an honor student with a track scholarship to the University of Kansas, somehow matched the description of a man three times his age who'd just robbed a convenience store at gunpoint.

Locked in traffic north of the Getty Museum, he listened to the teen's mother wail. It didn't even sound human, so atavistic was the maternal despair. A succession of such incidents, like school shootings years before, had proliferated of late, with blacks profiled by officers and the resulting altercations too often ending with the person under suspicion perishing then and there, or in one case in the back of a police van careening through the streets of Baltimore. Yes, he understood the predicament of policemen, many of them people of color themselves, making quick decisions in peril, but when bullets entered from behind, or when chokeholds lasted through the act of subduing a suspect into something lethal, it was difficult not to infer more sinister forces at work.

He decided he'd move *Dark Lion* ahead of all other Sparta titles, including a Hephaestus origin story and the third installment in the highly profitable *Jugular* franchise. Though myriad micro-decisions in every film, including wardrobe choices, line changes, design elements, music cues, and the like, had been impacted by cultural trends, this would mark the first time an event or movement nudged Max off his broader plan for how the Sparta Comic Galaxy would be revealed. It constituted its own kind of risk, but one he needed to take. Moreover, he sensed the possibility for tremendous reward, financially and otherwise.

He arranged a meeting with Boaz at their usual spot in Long Island City, though Max insisted he cater the lunch, venturing to Liebman's Deli in the Bronx where his grandfather had once taken him as a boy. There he bought four beef franks from the current owner himself, Yuval Dekel, formerly the drummer for the thrash metal band Irate, which Max had seen in 1996 with friends in the East Village, even chipping a tooth (long since repaired) in the mosh pit.

"Yeah, it's great to see you up here," the unlikely restaurateur said enthusiastically, handing over the takeaway bag, the entire exchange provoking in Max a sense of wonder at the peregrinations of adulthood. This man he'd last seen shirtless, sweaty, and feral, thrashing on his kit at the Pyramid Club, was now bald as a stone and gray-bearded, presiding over pickles and brisket, while he, Max, ran a film studio. The deli owner seemed even more content than he, and certainly less anxious on this particular day given the challenge Max understood to be ahead of him.

"It's a superb hot dog," Boaz reported after a bite slathered in mustard. "But I'm not sure worth heading all the way to the Bronx. Did you take a cab?"

"I had the car stop on the way from the airport."

"So what's this big news you have for me that you hitched a ride on the Grand jet?" asked Boaz, looking out on Manhattan from their shared bench.

"You already know. Jeremy told you."

"By the way, who is this Jeremy?"

"One of the smartest producers who's ever worked for me. I'd trust him with any project."

"Our audience doesn't want to see a bunch of *schwarzers* in a superhero movie."

"Please don't use that word."

"It means 'black people.'"

"It's derogatory."

"We're still not making *Dark Lion*."

"It's time, Boaz."

"You didn't shoot this black kid in the back. You didn't ever own slaves, nor did your family, who came over from Europe forty years after the slaves were freed."

"Twenty-five."

"So twenty-five. You won't even let me use the word I now won't use, you're so good."

"The movie will make money."

"Maybe in certain cities in certain regions of the United States, but these are the most expensive places to advertise, and you won't make back what you spend. No one in Europe or South America or Asia wants to see this."

"The biggest movie star in the world is black."

"He's half black and very handsome. Like Obama, who thank God is no longer president."

"Both are considered black. And any movie star is handsome."

"You want to right all these wrongs, volunteer at an after-school program, give the tens of millions you make away to every black family you see, but not at the expense of what we've built."

"Go back and look at the history of Sparta. They were always right in step with the cultural changes going on in the country, not behind them. These movies are America, as you've said yourself. You're being conservative, and that's rarely a good thing when it comes to art."

"The primary concern of our pictures, far more than the comic books, is to make enormous, unheard-of amounts of money. When a director comes in to interview and says he wants to make some big statement, that's when you and I have the biggest arguments. I cannot support this."

It was the lowest he'd ever felt running Sparta, because at a certain level he knew Boaz to be right. After all, why had Grand paid $4 billion to add the studio to its empire? It was business, and any conceit that claimed otherwise was self-deceiving. He also had to accept that in spite of Boaz's warnings, not once had he considered whether the Grand purchase and all consequent efficiencies would make the films better.

The following day he took the Grand jet back to Los Angeles, during which he prepared a white paper for Bruce Simkin outlining why Sparta needed to make *Dark Lion*: not only for moral reasons, but profit potential as well. Just as the blaxploitation films excoriated by Junius Griffin (who had coined the portmanteau) had crossed over to a white audience, Max was certain a black superhero film could do no less than transform what the genre of superhero movie, as created by Sparta, meant. The culture was frankly begging for it.

"Are you going to bring Boaz around?"

"Bruce, I want to do this whether I drag him along kicking and screaming or not."

"I'm not sure I understand."

"It's so important to me, and so important to Sparta and frankly the country in my opinion, that if we don't I can't see myself continuing at the company."

"You're asking me to choose between you and Boaz."

"That's up to him." Though he knew Boaz to be stubborn, he couldn't imagine him leaving the film division on such terms. But that's exactly what the old man did.

"The fact that Bruce took your side against me I can deal with. I even expected such a moment. But you spent a mere two hours with me making your case, with your fancy hot dogs from the Bronx, which weren't even as good as Gray's Papaya, by the way, for all you probably paid for them, and then went straight to that gonif in a Valentino suit without the courtesy of my even being in the room. It's all yours now, the most valuable part of the company I saved. May no one ever do to you what you've done to me."

He hadn't heard from Boaz since, not even when *Dark Lion* became the third-highest-grossing Sparta title in its thirteen years and certainly its most successful under Grand ownership. A sequel would follow *Major Machina* within the year, so long as Max could steer the company away from its present and very public difficulties.

⚡

"I'm going to need Cynthia and her team in the office at six a.m.," he informed his assistant an hour and a half before the designated time. "Tell them it's not optional. This is an in-person situation if there ever was one. I need all of them in the same room on the Zoom."

"Do you think they know what happened?"

"More people will have watched this footage online by noon LA time than voted in the last election."

"I hope that's not true."

"It's a lot closer than you think."

SEVENTEEN

Peter loathed waking to find Marci not beside him. She'd been rising early to get her own time in the gym since he refused to wear headphones while blasting Nirvana. What better music for playing a suicidal character with a God complex?

He reached for his phone to discover it missing from his nightstand. Instead was a note written all in caps: "IN THE KITCHEN. BEFORE WORKOUT." He stepped into his gym shorts and donned a black cotton T-shirt to be soaked with sweat an hour hence. Whatever Marci needed to discuss would require quick dispatch, as he hoped to arrive at the makeup trailer early for his daily meeting with Joel. Though he respected the director's sudden display of authority, he couldn't help but perceive it to have been partly responsible for his outburst. Had the man remained his feckless self, Peter could easily have doused all interference from the consultant. So many such hires, from fight coordinators to dialect coaches, from intimacy coordinators to crane operators, strolled onto stages and blundered ahead without getting a read as to who was in control.

Ultimately he didn't regret a word he'd said. He even suspected the film would be better off for his outburst. It would certainly focus the work. The standing ovation he received for his impassioned apology following lunch had probably brought him closer to the crew than he'd been before the day began. Should he have suppressed his concern for the movie? Should he not have exposed such devotion publicly? Yes, Javier had almost quit, but the Mexican was just as temperamental as Peter in his way, which perhaps accounted for the universal adulation inspired by the dailies. It was more important that a film turn out well than that everyone get along.

In his apology he'd insisted that he more than anyone needed to be better. "You all look to me to lead," he'd announced, "so when I don't display good behavior, no one does. Why should anyone have to? But what I need to say is that for all my importance as the face of what we're up to, with my picture on billboards and the month I'll spend on talk shows and traveling the world shilling for all this—and trust me, it's not as fun as it might look—I am not this movie so much as *we* are this movie, and that applies to all of you. When I act out, it makes it like it's all of us acting out. I make not only myself look bad but all of us, because we are one. I want to be clear: I couldn't do what I do without every one of you. And when I seem to forget that and separate myself, it hurts each person watching me right now. The fact is"—and here he broke down—"I love each and every one of you, and I always will, the evidence of it in every word and gesture of mine captured by these cameras. The film is the result of all our work. I could not be more proud than to be a part of that, and that I seemed earlier not to pay this set the respect and decorum it demands is something I'll regret for the rest of my life."

"What did you think of what I said?" he asked Marci afterward.

"What's important is what the crew thought."

"They certainly applauded."

"That they did."

"Why am I sensing a tone?"

"Look, Peter, what do you want me to say? You apologized, and publicly, something not easy for anyone. Let's leave it at that."

"But what?"

"Did you have to talk so much about yourself again? And did you have to cry?"

"Did it at all strike you that I and my behavior were the topic of the hour? I mean, tell me how under these circumstances I was supposed to not speak about myself, which, by the way, was entirely self-critical if you were at all listening. And the tears were sincere."

"Forget I said anything."

She left the set early to roll calls at the production office, including one with the accountant about a $100,000 line item that had appeared and then disappeared in the latest cost report like a blip on a radar.

"Will I see you at home?" he asked as she made her way to the stage door.

"That is where I'll be sleeping," she'd answered flatly.

I'll sort this out later, he thought. But she didn't pick up when he checked in during the afternoon, finally texting him just after five to report she was still dealing with LA.

"Anything I can help with?" he wrote back.

"No. Eat without me. I'm ordering takeout here."

"How did it all go?" he asked when she finally called.

"Declan says he's taking care of it, that it was his mistake and he'll fix it, and why is LA so concerned anyway?"

"Is he right?"

"No. It's a hundred thousand dollars, first of all, an even sum that showed up and was gone within hours. How does that happen? And secondly, we need to know what for."

"If it disappeared, what's the difference?"

"Think about it."

"Thirty grand on the tax credit."

"Do we claim it? Do we not claim it? But there's a bigger problem." She then instructed that instead of her eating at the office they'd be meeting Javier at Arrabbiata. "I just spoke to him at the monitor."

"You're here?"

"I came back to deal with this."

"Did you get the chef's table?"

"Not available."

"Marci, I really don't want to be out in the room. Let me call Giovanni." For $15,000, he'd bought out the restaurant. This would include their three meals, and he could bring his own wine.

"Can we talk about today?" he asked before the cinematographer arrived.

"If you weren't my husband and just the star of this film, I would have said, 'What a fucking asshole,' during the first speech. I also would say, 'Yeah, but there's no one else on the planet who could crush this role the way you're crushing it.'"

"You really think I'm crushing it?"

"I just want you to stop hanging yourself. You're one of the biggest stars in the world. It was like using a cannon to shoot a fly."

"What else was I supposed to do? I mean, if I'm a cannon and not a fly-swatter, how do I kill the fucking fly?"

"You find someone who can be a flyswatter."

"Who?"

"Me. Or better, Joel. You say quietly and off to the side, 'Hey, this lady is destroying our work, let's you and Jennifer and me figure this out.'"

"You're always right."

"Here's Javier."

Buying out the restaurant, half of which would be charged to the film as part of their entertainment budget, had proven worth it, though it meant for a late night, meaning he'd only slept six hours. One challenge after another, he thought as he entered the kitchen to find Marci at her computer, her iPad on its stand beside it, texting on her phone.

"Jesus. Six thirty a.m. and already at it on three devices," he said.

"Sit down, Peter," she answered, not looking up.

"Did Javier change his mind?"

"Just give me a second, please."

Her phone rang just as she finished her text.

"Hey," she said into it. "No, all of them. This is war room shit." She paused briefly. "He just woke up. Yeah. Give me half an hour." She punched off and pointed to the chair opposite her at the vast dining table that dominated the Atlanta kitchen.

"What's going on? I've got to get downstairs."

"You're not working out today."

"Why so curt?"

She turned her laptop to face him, having googled his name and only his name filtered by "news." Every link seemed to promote either reportage or video of his outburst, a few others of the apology that followed.

"Does Sparta know?"

"They do."

"Am I fired?"

"No, Peter, you're not fired. Even Sparta isn't going to piss away the ninety million dollars they've already spent."

He scrolled through a few of the posts, catching words and sentences. "Jesus. People hate me."

"I wouldn't call it hate."

"'Peter Compton shows why actors are the most hideous human beings alive.' How about this? 'If you didn't already hate Peter Compton, just watch thirty seconds of his whining, self-aggrandizing, clueless speech where he humiliates a female crew member today on the set of *Major Machina*.'"

"Please stop."

"Oh, this one looks good. It's long, so please don't interrupt."

"Peter."

"'Let's just be honest. Peter Compton should still be in prison getting buttraped'—spelled as one word, which I don't think is correct, but I'll continue. 'Most Americans, on three strikes laws alone, would have spent at least ten years in lockup, but he was out in less than three because he's rich and famous. Here in this video,' and the word 'video' is blue for a link, 'he proves himself to be like all addicts: hideously self-absorbed and uninterested in anyone's needs or feelings but his own. He's everything that's wrong about this country. We spend hundreds of millions of dollars making idiotic action movies, paying narcissists like him tens of millions so we can distract ourselves from climate change, homelessness, hunger, income disparity, racism, and the rest while he complains about his five trailers and personal chef and having to keep fit and that, oh my God, people are watching him and filming him! Poor Peter! Take him and his carbon footprint and burn him alive in the sewage pit that is Sparta. At least he has exposed Hollywood for what it really is. The guy should honestly just die or better yet kill himself and the world would be a better place.'"

"Are we done here?"

"Trust me, we're just getting started. Oh! This one is about my apology speech. The one you said was too much about me. And it's a news item, so perhaps it'll be a little less of an attack." Once again he read: "'On the heels of the leaking of actor Peter Compton's outburst on the set of the Sparta Studios film *Major Machina*, a video of his apology to the crew has now surfaced, perhaps, if it were even possible, making matters worse for the megastar who revived his career to even greater heights following his stint in prison for drug possession in the 2000s. In what was meant to be contrition, most have observed that he merely repeats what he'd said during the offending outburst, referring to himself as the film's raison d'être—'" Peter stopped reading. "Did I do that? Did I say 'raison d'être'?"

"Not that I recall," said Marci flatly.

"I didn't think so." He continued: "'Unfortunately for Mr. Compton, though some of the words do make clear his regret, his tone in the video has struck most as insincere in spite of what have been called "fake" tears toward the end. Said one industry insider, "You sort of feel like the whole thing is a performance by a guy who just doesn't get it. Yes, he says he's sorry, but it's still laced with self-pity, like someone who just broke your nose talking about how hard it is to have a temper and that his hand really hurts." Reached at her home in Atlanta, where she has reportedly retained counsel, Aviva Wilson, the intimacy coordinator whose contributions for how a love scene between Mr. Compton and the actress Jennifer Taylor was to be played set off the volatile star, stated, "I had hoped that Me Too had stopped the abuse of women on set. Not only did Peter disrespect his female costar, he sought to humiliate a woman doing her job in front of an entire crew. I stand for all women in this industry and in all work environments when I say enough is enough."' Okay, I'm done with this article, because now I'm just getting angry all over again. How about this one?"

"No, we're finished." She took the computer from him.

"You've got that right."

"We're now about damage control."

"I'm over, Marci. I'm done." He rose, sensing the urge to vomit.

"You're not done, Peter."

He detoured to the sink when the bathroom proved too distant and let go. She watched in silence.

"You okay?" she finally asked.

"I can't go to work today."

"You have to, Peter."

"How do I face the crew? My fellow actors? Fucking Joel, who now has this over me. And Declan, who's just going to gloat behind the monitor. I mean, seriously. Oh my God. Everyone's eyes on me." He threw up again, this time in three spasms, seemingly the entire meal from Arrabbiata into the stainless steel basin. She rose to stand beside him, detaching the sprayer from its holster to corral the malodorous ejecta down the disposal.

"Here. Have a glass of water."

"What I want is a fucking drink. More than a fucking drink."

"Well, that's obviously not happening. Come and sit."

"I don't think you understand."

"You in particular have come back from a lot worse."

"I have to watch the videos."

"No, you don't."

"I need to see what it is I'm dealing with, what people are seeing, so that I can truly gauge this."

"Fine, but you have to calm down first."

"Don't fucking tell me what I have to do!"

"I'm on your side."

"I can see it on your face! You're thinking I had it coming, that it proves everything you said yesterday!"

"What you see on my face is someone who has been up almost the entire night and who has a very long day ahead of her trying to fix this."

"Fix what *I* did!"

"That's not what I said, but if you want to put it that way, sure, fix what you did. But that does not mean I'm against you or feel vindicated or anything like that. I want to solve the problem, and the sooner we can put our energies into that the better."

"Then let me watch the fucking videos!"

In footage of his sentencing hearing he at least recognized himself. He even admired his own pluck in importuning a man who had so much power over him. With films in which he appeared he would watch himself twice, first in a private screening (before picture was locked if possible for any editing notes) and then at the premiere, should he have liked the performance. He never viewed the talk shows he did. The entire enterprise embarrassed him with its dissembling format suggesting an unrehearsed, freewheeling conversation that instead indulged topics chosen beforehand by a producer who then prompted the host.

His speech to the crew constituted a nadir. Even his voice embarrassed him, a good octave higher than he wished, as if the sonorous gravity normally present in his characters were some sort of mask to conceal the weak hysteric he truly was. He beheld a person unhinged, bereft of any connection to the reality of his listeners. Moreover, the arguments he made lacked rhetorical savvy, especially his ham-handedly proleptic attempt to explain away aspects of himself others might find objectionable, the most glaring example being the good five minutes justifying his on-set accommodations. Far from denuding any attack against him, he seemed to be exploiting the topic to boast of his importance and power. And wasn't the mark of real status an easy restraint from its actual deployment, and likewise a hesitancy in ever mentioning its existence for the absence of any need to? And yet here he was, gesticulating like a histrionic, punishing an audience of crew members that could only be described as puzzled and, in some cases, quietly amused. He even felt something akin to pity for the intimacy coordinator, whose name he'd once again forgotten in spite of just having read it.

The apology was even worse, his register now elevated to the point of simpering. In atoning for his earlier self-importance, he appeared now only to amplify it. While confessing the abuse of power as the film's lead actor, he brandished it more blatantly. Even his tears, which to him had seemed the speech's apogee for inspiring such a prolonged ovation, now appeared cynical, manipulative, insincere. Likewise, the applause was actually tepid and short-lived. They had stood? They were already standing! Marci had been right; the second speech only reminded his audience what a narcissist he was.

"Why didn't you stop me?" he asked her.

"Tell me how I was supposed to do that?"

"By coming over to me and pulling me away. By actually trying to make eye contact and giving me a look to say, 'Stop,' or 'Tone it down,' instead of just staring at the fucking ground. If I can't count on you for that, what's the point?"

"Peter, you really don't want to go down this road."

"Because I'm right?"

"Because nothing I could have said or done would have made a difference. You want to blame me for your behavior, go ahead, but both of us know that's completely unfair."

"Do we?"

"Do you have any idea what it's like to be married to you as your producing partner slash enabler slash handler slash the woman on your arm who makes it all possible but whom nobody wants to speak to? Who gets cropped out of pictures and moved down the line on the movies she produced and made happen because you happen to be next on the carpet?"

"Wait, so that's what this is about?"

"Don't you dare say that. You screwed up yesterday, very badly, and I've been up trying to deal with it while I let you sleep. And you ask me, essentially, 'what's the point'—your words—of my existence if I couldn't get you to stop making a complete ass of yourself in public, the implication being that's all I'm here for, to protect you from you, when I do all the shit work and run all the interference so that you can be Peter Compton? I knew what I signed up for. But don't you dare denigrate what I do by implying my main purpose is to manage your infantile behavior."

"I'm sorry."

"Look, Peter, whoever put this out wants to destroy you and destroy the film. Don't let them. If you and I fight each other, you lose by far the most important resource you have. Strike that. The only resource that's yours and yours alone. Now you've got to let me take the lead. You have to trust me, and you have to do exactly what I say."

"Which is?"

"I've written a statement from you that Sparta and your publicist will put out in two hours when it's six a.m. in LA."

"May I read it?"

"Of course you can read it." She punched it up on her screen.

"This is a PDF," he said.

"I put a Word document in front of you, we'll be wrestling over the keyboard for hours. You want edits, which you honestly shouldn't, then you tell them to me and I decide whether we make them."

He began, wincing already at the first sentence.

> Yesterday, on the set of the Sparta Studios film MAJOR MACHINA being shot in Atlanta, I behaved in a manner

> that embarrasses me profoundly. I did a disservice not only to the movie and its crew, but to my fans and to myself. While there were extenuating circumstances, I choose not to reference these because they are irrelevant. What *is* relevant is my behavior, which reflects neither who I am nor who I wish to be. I must therefore take full responsibility for all that I said and apologize without any excuses. What has become clear to me is that I've lost sight of who I am and want to be, which is, put simply, an actor devoted to finding the humanity in each role I play. I do this for the making of films that engage and/or entertain. Those are the basics. I need to get back to them. The stories we tell must always be bigger than the people who tell them, and that includes me. My actions yesterday negated that sentiment in a way that's now poignantly clear to me. As a show of my remorse, I hereby pledge $1 million of my salary on MAJOR MACHINA to the Abused Women's Shelter of East Los Angeles. While I understand this does not make up for what I did in response to an intimacy coordinator simply doing her job (and I apologize specifically to her as well), I hope it demonstrates my commitment to becoming more the man and artist I hope to be. Above all, what I did should be seen as no reflection on MAJOR MACHINA or the extraordinary crew and consultants toiling daily to make it the worthy addition to the Sparta Comics Galaxy I know it's going to be.

"Okay, for starters, a million dollars? You realize that after taxes and commissions that's ten percent of my salary?"

"Peter, we're not going to argue this."

"I hate myself right now, but half of what I said about that ridiculous meddling woman was true. And they were just words."

"You're gonna pay it. More specifically, *we're* going to pay it. Five hundred thousand dollars of it is mine."

"The rest of the statement is enough. Let me restate, more than enough."

"Without the pound of flesh, it's just words. We're paying it."

"All right. Let's just table that for a moment. You've really got me prostrating myself here."

"Um . . . yeah . . . I do."

"Please don't with the arch tone. It's going to really piss me off."

"What, are you going to stand here in the kitchen and give another speech? You *need* to prostrate yourself. That's the way these things work. You have to leave your critics no room to find more fault. They feed off your resistance. You don't offer any, they starve for fuel and move on to the next victim. The more you fight, the longer this goes on."

"But honestly, Marci, having watched the video—no, the videos, because the apology is just as lame as the fucking tirade—what's the point? This is worse than the drug conviction, because at least then people could identify at some level, either as addicts themselves or people related to one or friends with one. What's to empathize with here? I come off like a monster. And Jesus, maybe that's who I am, and no wonder I hit the stuff, otherwise I'd have to face it."

"That's not who you are, Peter."

"Then how did those words come out of my mouth?"

"You were under duress."

"I'm not giving away a million dollars, especially when we're really going to need it."

"With what we're making on this film, that you're going to have to explain."

"Who's going to hire me again?"

"People will forget. The movie will come out, it's going to be huge, you'll do sequels, you'll have more opportunities than you've ever had."

"Marci, do you understand the internet? Those videos are out there now. Forever. Our children, if we ever even have children, will see them. Did you read those posts? And they're just the beginning. It's fucking viral. Who is ever going to take me seriously now in any role? Oh my God . . ."

Incredulous there could be more of last night's meal, he returned to the sink. She joined him with the sprayer, as if swift removal might hasten his recovery. The inanity of the gesture infuriated him.

"Just fucking leave it!"

"You might want to smell your own barf, but I don't."

"Then go into another room."

"We have to solve this, Peter. And we have to do it soon, or the outcome you're fearing becomes more likely."

"At this point, fuck all those people. You think crucifying myself makes it all go away? Like spraying my vomit down the sink? Well, you're wrong. All it does is add my voice to the condemnation, which, by the way, since you clearly agree with them, it doesn't surprise me you'd take the position of having me basically confirm what's being written."

"You just said yourself that you come off horribly in the videos. This is a way of making that less the case. Plus, it's only part of it. You're going to have our publicity team and Sparta's publicity team devoted completely to putting out other information that changes people's perspective. This statement prepares people for that. You notice this sentence here? 'While there were extenuating circumstances, I choose not to reference these'? Well, just because you choose not to doesn't mean others can't."

"And just what were those circumstances?"

"We've got a Zoom in two hours and we're going to figure it out, but any number."

"One example, Marci. Just one."

"Okay, that you've been getting up every morning at five a.m. so you can work out and then meet with the director before work, and over the past two months of doing this, you've had an average of four and a half hours of sleep a night and it caught up with you."

"But that wouldn't be true, would it?"

"It's true enough. You've been waking up every morning at five thirty. Often earlier."

"But I've also gotten my turnaround most days, and when I haven't I've been given forced calls at a thousand bucks a pop. Let that get out. That I'm flipped a grand every time I don't get twelve hours off in addition to my twenty-million-dollar salary, of which you now want me to forfeit two million when taxes and commissions are figured in."

"Let's get that straight, Peter, the million dollars won't come from this job. We'll liquidate stock."

"Excellent. Let that get out too."

"You've worked your ass off in this part. What are we arguing about here?"

"It's an exercise in futility. I've basically committed hara-kiri in public, and you want me to publish a statement as if I'm still alive and then give away money on top of it."

"Here's what this looks like, and I want you really to listen to me. If you do nothing, you really are ruined, because you're right about one thing: this is very public and it's very big. It not only involves a huge crew on a huge movie, and all the idiots watching online, it involves hundreds of millions of dollars, and not one but two major corporations when you count Grand."

"Grand?"

"Peter! You are on video excoriating a female crew member as the star of *Major Machina*, which means you're tarnishing Sparta and therefore Grand, as image-obsessed a company as there is. If you don't make a meaningful effort to make this right and you let this get out of control even more than it already has, then you are exposed to a world of pain that makes what you're feeling right now seem like a pinprick."

"You're saying they'll sue me?"

"If you've behaved in a way that impacts their bottom line and they can claw back your salary or some of their losses for breach and signal to the world they're on the right side of condemning gender-based abuse, of course they will. Sue you, blackball you, both. You don't show serious remorse, you'll truly be done."

He'd never felt so trapped. Worse than prison. What could he do? Either nothing, come what may, finally speared below the ribs on the cross to which he'd nailed himself, the last of life drained from him in a trickle of his own toxicity, or expose himself with further contrition that, Marci's optimism notwithstanding, would result in yet more derision, not to mention the smug satisfaction of those already relishing his demise. And the million dollars to an abused women's shelter? How to interpret that other than that he considered himself such a perpetrator? A rapist, a batterer, an assailant. The idea that publicly deriding a person being paid $200 an hour to do nothing but interfere with the good and honest labor of others was akin to physical abuse nauseated him beyond description.

"Marci, it's Thursday. Call Declan. Tell them to spend the next two days doing inserts and second unit. I'll take today and tomorrow and the weekend off, and we'll work through this, I promise. We'll find another way, and in the meantime, just like you said, people move on to the next thing."

"You're going to put out this statement today, let me take the next steps, and you're going to man up and go to work."

He lowered himself to the floor and curled into himself. Tears began to pour as he rocked back and forth. "I can't, Marci. I can't. Please don't make me. Please. Please."

"You have to make it right. You'll do that, and we'll get through this."

"Don't you have any feelings?"

"I can give in to your hysteria, and by doing that confirm your panic, which would be completely unhelpful, or I can make this better."

He despised her certainty in the assumption of complete power. Since the moment they'd first spoken long ago she acted as his equal, though every circumstance of their reality as a couple asserted his value and importance over hers. How had he allowed this? "Please!"

"Sit up."

He did.

"Listen to me. One thing you were right about yesterday is that this movie can't go on without you. You're the one person on that set about whom that can be said. I could quit tomorrow, Joel could, Ron or Jennifer could, Javier—you name the individual, and the film could and would go on. Without you, it doesn't. So, what does that mean? It means that everyone, no matter their disposition toward you and what you did yesterday, needs for you to recover. Remember something, Peter. We're in a shitty business if you just look at it simply as a business, and that's especially true for the workers. Most actors don't make a living. Most writers and directors barely do, given where they live, which is New York or LA. As for the designers and technicians and everyone on the crew, they go from job to job eking it out for what amounts to a lower-middle-class life at best that has them on the road most of the year in shitty hotels working twelve-hour days when it's all going right or working as locals barely getting by. And to do what everyone does—from a grip to the lowliest PA who hopes to be an AD or a producer or a director one day—takes ability and smarts and grit that if applied to any other profession they'd make more by multiples, and life would be far easier and more convenient. But it's seductive and glamorous to say when a movie comes out, 'I was a part of that. I was there when it was happening.' Yes, there are exceptions, and we're two of them. But for the most part, instead of money it's another kind of remuneration—psychic, social status—call it what you want to call it, but that's the reward. And, of course, they're more fulfilled being a part of telling stories than sitting behind a desk. But guess what? Without the movies and the TV shows actually getting completed and seen, it doesn't happen, and without you, this particular movie doesn't get done, and they don't get that essential part of their payment. You really want to make this right, get back to work and give that to them without another word. And finally I'll say this. Watching your meltdown yesterday will be the most significant moment in many of their lives. They'll tell the story a thousand times, dine out on it for decades. But guess what? You'll be the subject of that story, and even in that scenario, I'd rather be you than them."

"I'll send it," he said. "I'll send what you wrote or write without changing a word."

EIGHTEEN

When the video of Peter's second speech appeared online, few could have been more surprised than Declan Morris. It was just before three a.m., one hour after he'd leaked the first clip, and the internet was so fecund with responses he couldn't keep up. Within an hour there were seven hundred listings and thousands of comments, and those were just the ones in English. He'd long since ordered in pizza and, forgoing the chardonnay, was well into his second six-pack of St. Pauli Girl.

Who filmed the apology? he wondered. Considering the angle, he couldn't determine, since it was from the direction of the craft service table, meaning it could have been anyone unsated from the lunch of tri tip, grilled salmon, and a forlorn vegetarian lasagna. In fact, Declan himself had just made an excursion to the truck for an espresso and his daily ration of freshly baked cookies. This suggested the culprit to have been near him when raising his or her phone. But who other than Declan despised Peter Compton to the extent they'd risk so much by recording the actor's apology in the presence of a security apparatus that rivaled the Stasi?

What Declan also couldn't square were the responses to the actor's contrition. Honestly, I almost feel sorry for him, he thought as he scrolled through the succession of ungenerous comments. This could finish the guy. The question is, do I want that? How will it reflect on me that on a film I line produced, crew members (one of them me) disseminated an actor meltdown that ended a career and perhaps sank a franchise before its first installment was even completed? Just as with the car, have I impulsively abetted my own demise?

But I'm getting ahead of myself. Sparta will do all in its unprecedented power to protect its investment, and therefore Peter Compton, which isn't even to mention the resources Grand will commit. The fact is, Peter will come out of this fine, perhaps even better for it, if his post-incarceration life provides any sort of template. His wife, along with Max Kaiser and the rest, will plot a deft strategy, beginning with the actor making a statement and then soon someone publishing heretofore unknown circumstances that somehow exculpate the star. His dog had died that morning. He'd just been told his brother has cancer. Or something related to the set: The intimacy coordinator had actually started the conflict by making an unrequited pass at him. The DP had been on his nerves all week and he'd had enough. He had food poisoning from catering and just wasn't himself. They'll use bots and perhaps AI. Declan had seen it over and over. Short of sexual assault or racial offenses, and these only lately, movie stars were impervious to lasting damage.

A boon to Declan, however, came in how Peter's public excoriation might distract from the $100,000 aberration in the cost report. While he'd expected questions, he'd also counted on forbearance given his impeccable relationship with the head of production in LA. In fact, he would have described it as downright chummy, praise having overwhelmed every phone call and Zoom. "Honestly, Declan, if we could have you on every film we would!" he'd been told that very week. "Your work is clean and comprehensive, everything costs what you say it will, and when it doesn't, the cause or culprit is identified. You manage to keep department budgets in line even with all these overruns, which with some of the folks you've got on this one is downright miraculous. Javier Benavidez alone. That egomaniac never met a piece of equipment he didn't need."

But the $30,000 that might be recovered from the unaccounted-for outlay seemed to focus the accountants in a way Declan hadn't anticipated. He deflected initial inquiries casually in an email, even blaming himself. "Sorry about that one," he'd written. "It was a placeholder before I checked with Casey," the accountant in Atlanta. "You probably remember that from the old days when we'd tread water while the numbers balanced, always knowing they would! It's why I miss you!"

But the Sparta ombudsman required provenance immediately. His name was Arthur Lofton, and Declan had actually given him his first job in the industry on a movie in Santa Fe a dozen years prior. "Look," he'd instructed the twenty-nine-year-old who'd just left a job at Arthur Andersen, "I know you're going to tell me accounting is accounting, but not this accounting. Here we have a different boss each time out depending on the film and the studio, and each one has unique requirements in terms of the numbers and how they're presented. It can get very tricky."

"Numbers are numbers."

"Not in movies, because a lot of money is made and lost based on how costs are allocated."

"Overhead? That sort of thing?"

"Sure, but every deal has its fine print, every studio its way of financing, every state certain negative costs they will and won't rebate. Now let me be clear before you run back to your accounting firm. I'm as honest a line producer as you'll ever meet, but in a business that's all about telling stories, we don't shy away from the notion that a budget is also a story. A deceptively forensic story."

"Like a crime scene?" the young accountant asked with only half a laugh. "And how can something be 'deceptively forensic'?"

"Once it's there for the auditing, and you have to assume that every budget will be audited by a multitude of parties, you're providing the history of how your movie was put together. But like with history, it's written by historians, meaning it's always subjective."

"Give me an example."

"On this movie, what for one person might be a job in Los Angeles, for another is a job in New Mexico. Both can be true, but the choice is huge. Suppose you're the studio accountant, not the location accountant. You make eight grand a week for the year. In New Mexico that could be rebated for the shoot, preproduction, and wrap-out, but we'd have to fly you out and put you up and pay per diem. Costly, yes, but all of it rebatable and far less than twenty-five percent of your eight grand weekly salary. Is there a way to have it both ways? Maybe. After all, you do need to confer with your location counterpart, look over the books in person, see the physical evidence of how money's being spent. Wouldn't it be best to put you on the New Mexico payroll and let the good people of New Mexico pay a quarter of your salary? The eight thousand dollars a week are a fact; where you put them is another matter altogether, so fly the accountant out for a few visits and call him a local."

"I see."

"And to a certain extent New Mexico wants you to do that, because the more money they can say was spent in the state, the more robust their program looks, meaning more films come, and more evidence for the legislature when the rebate bill comes up. But rebates are just one example. In some cases the more expensive you make the movie once it's been budgeted, the better you're doing your job, because studios also have investors, and I'm not talking about stock positions but actual financiers who come in with film funds on specific big-budget movies. And the higher the negative cost, the later the net profits get realized, meaning the more money goes to the studio. Sometimes your job is to go over budget even while you're actually under budget. You'll get calls you can't believe berating you for your discipline when costs can be billed to others and paid to the main entity. Your task on each film is to do the accounting *for that picture*. You suss out how the prevailing entity defines and promotes its terms, and you account accordingly."

Sparta loved its Georgia rebate, even more so since the Grand purchase that had their accountants answering to the larger studio. Accordingly, the $100,000 had become a cause.

"What I'm not understanding," Arthur informed Declan, "is what the number was a placeholder *for*. I know you. It was there for some reason. It can't have just appeared."

"Obviously, but you've been in production. I'm getting it from all sides down here. It might have been something in the art department—a stage rental before we moved to the bank location. It could have been the condors for the week of nights."

"Again, a hundred thousand dollars? And, Jesus, how can you not know?"

"Why are you breaking my balls over this? The numbers all work."

"The numbers don't work. We were a hundred thousand dollars off, which has an electronic trail, and then we weren't. It's like an alien sighting."

Even Marci Levy involved herself, as if she understood movie budgeting, let alone how to read a cost report. The entire situation infuriated him. For a mere forty-five minutes the overage had represented a transportation line item that

Declan printed for Buzz Bremer at the dealership. He presented this alongside the Movie Magic budget page called up on the dealer's office computer. This so that Buzz could furnish a signed invoice that Declan sold to an in-state broker who'd then bundle it with the many other rebates he'd redeem. Declan had his car, his check, and the liability was gone, none the wiser. It should have been so simple.

He woke at 6:30, sleep-deprived but not feeling it. After an hour in traffic he arrived at the stages strangely eager. It would be a fascinating day.

Base camp was quiet, and so far as he could tell from a glance beyond the security detail at its entrance, Peter Compton's town square was empty, though the actor's driver waited along the western edge in his silver electric Porsche Cayenne. Marci's Cadillac Lyriq was parked behind it, along with the vehicles of Peter's makeup team, his and Marci's assistants, their chef, and Peter's trainer. He strolled to the Sparta pop-out to check in with Charisse and Jeremy. They need me now, he thought. Who else can hold this production together?

"Jesus, Declan, thank God," Charisse confirmed when he entered. "You got my text?"

"Of course. Quite a night. Did they find out who did it?"

"Security is on it. They will. The set photographer handed over all his images, and they're making a map of where everyone was standing right before Peter freaked out. That'll at least narrow it down to a dozen or so possibilities we think, just because of the angle of the video."

"That's brilliant." While he might have worried, given how this could place him in the vicinity of where the clip was shot, he'd been in such a thicket of crew members he doubted its number could be winnowed to fewer than two dozen, no matter how zealous the investigation.

"Anything I can do to help?" he offered.

"We appreciate that," said Jeremy, "but obviously no one is more incentivized to figure this out than Steven and his guys. This thing is the worst breach of security in Sparta history."

"Whoever did it must really hate Peter," said Declan.

"What's important," responded Jeremy, "is that we press forward today with the work. It's not our job to handle the fallout. We've got under three weeks left, and like it or not, the most difficult locations and scenes are behind us. Can you imagine if we were working on the original schedule? Maybe Peter was right pushing so much stage work to the end."

"I'm not sure about that," said Declan. "Just speaking as the guy who had to handle the budget ramifications and the fiasco that was the culvert. And we do still have the UN with huge page count and tons of background."

"Fair enough," said Jeremy.

"But Peter meant well," Declan quickly added. "I've certainly never met an actor who concerns himself more with production. The guy is everywhere at once."

"That's certainly true," said Charisse.

A silence ensued as each ruminated on the peculiarities of Peter Compton.

"So," said Declan, "what else?"

"Jeremy is going to speak to everyone at call this morning."

"No big admonitions," Jeremy assured him, "just a quick reminder that cameras are forbidden on set and how leaks hurt us all. But mostly it's going to be about the incredible work everyone has done, including Peter, and how the best revenge against the forces who'd like to see us fail is to deliver a film worthy of Sparta and all it stands for."

"Have you guys seen Peter this morning?"

"I have, and I've spoken to Marci. They're putting on a good face, but it's pretty tense over at Camp Compton. Peter was all smiles during his morning meeting with Joel, but it was about the most painful smile I've ever seen."

⚡

Just after 8:00 a.m., a call went out on the walkies for everyone to gather on the stage, where Jeremy soon stood before them.

"So, we've had a breach," he began, "and I'm sure many of you have been on the internet and seen the results. Charisse and I had a choice: to address it with you all or ignore it, and after speaking with Joel and Marci and Peter, we decided it best to speak of it head-on." After a cursory but vehement warning about cameras on set, along with assurances of anonymity should anyone come forward with information regarding the dissemination of the video, he continued. "I've always hated when folks compare what we do to the military in terms of making a film as going into battle and what have you. The fact is, unless there are stunts or vehicles or armaments involved, lives aren't at stake. That said, in many respects we can learn from the military in terms of loyalty and cohesion. And I can tell you this: there's no one I'd rather have directing this film than Joel Slavkin, no one I'd rather have shooting it than Javier Benavidez, no one I'd rather have designing it than Kate Johannsen, no one I'd rather have managing our budget than Declan Morris, no crew I'd rather have than each of you, no producers I'd rather work with than Charisse and Marci, and no one I'd rather have leading this cast than Peter Compton. We're a unit, and we need to be there for each other. So let's get back to it and finish production on this movie."

Just as the applause crescendoed, Peter stepped forward, causing it to abate. "Jeremy, may I say something please?"

The producer hesitated, glancing at a somewhat nonplussed Marci Levy, who looked at Peter, clearly eager to discourage her husband from uttering a sound. On this day he would play the costumed iteration of his character, which entailed a smart period suit with geometrically shaped patches of green where digital effects artists would paint in the mechanical augmentations normally concealed by his civilian clothing. He had the sartorial bearing of one visiting his tailor at an intermediate moment in the design stage, wherein certain measurements needed to be taken and decisions made before the outfit could be completed.

"So, Jeremy is right," he announced. "We're not saving lives here. We're making a movie. I've got to say, however, that in the last twelve hours it has felt like my life was just about over. But I showed up at work today, and here you all were, ready to keep going. Having watched the videos that were posted, I wasn't expecting anyone to be here given the performance I put on yesterday. Performances! They were, to put a word to it, grotesque. As I wrote in the statement that's going to be released in an hour or so, that's not who I am. But at the same time, I said what I said, and so I have to own up to the fact that I was the one saying what I said and not anyone else. I assure you, though, it's not who I'll be moving forward. That you all had the faith in this project today to come to set just gives me such hope and fills me with such . . . such . . . I don't know . . . such . . ."

Spasms of emotion began to shake him to the point he could no longer continue. The guy could sure cry, thought Declan.

"Such . . . such . . ."

Marci spoke. "Peter, I think they understand."

"Marci, I love you, but would you please . . . ? I just want to . . ." he managed to half exclaim. But again he was unable to finish, so consumed was he by his gratitude for the crew having shown up. What else would they have done?

"Peter, I think—" Marci endeavored again to say.

What happened next occurred in a haphazard manner that under any other circumstance might have seemed comical. As she stepped forward, the actor gesticulated, merely to assure her, his right hand instead striking her squarely in the jaw. Though lean and strong, she was petite, weighing perhaps 120 at five foot six. Peter, who worked out daily in a circuit that included a rower, a pull-up bar, a Peloton, and extensive weights, all of which Declan had rented and paid to have installed in the actor's compound, had the physique of a cornerback, taut with a body fat index that couldn't be above 5 percent given his strict diet and the fact he didn't drink. She received the blow with an audible pop and simply dropped. Declan wondered whether the actor had broken her neck, given the fact she'd been moving toward him when struck, amplifying the blow's power.

Shrieks erupted as those nearby rushed to her inert body.

"It was an accident! It was an accident!" the actor kept screaming, mostly ignored as the medic was summoned. Marci never lost consciousness and, far from having her neck broken, was more stunned than lastingly hurt. Within a few minutes she stood groggily, her husband embracing her, smothering her with regret.

"I'm sorry, honey. I am so sorry. I get everything wrong. I'm such a fuck-up. I don't deserve you. It was an accident. I worship you. I'd be nothing without you. Please forgive me." It went on and on, taking the form of fervent prayer, as if Marci were the actor's sole and exacting deity and this his day of repentance.

"It's okay, Peter. It's okay. Shhh. It's okay. I know you didn't mean to," she said finally, "just please, give me some space." She turned then to those closed in on her. "Everyone, just give me some space."

She tested her jaw as tears made their way down her cheeks toward the pull of the earth now firm beneath her feet.

"Everyone, I'm okay," she then proclaimed slowly to the crew. "I'm okay . . . we're all okay. It's time to stop talking, to stop apologizing, to stop thinking about what's done. We've got so little left to shoot, and then we'll all go back to our lives and on to the next thing. Let's make the most of these remaining days, because, believe it or not, we're going to miss this insanity. I'm going to go and regroup. What my husband did was an accident. I know it, and all of you know it. I don't want anyone to follow me."

"The medic is following you," Declan announced.

"Sure. Sally, but no one else. Remember what Jeremy said, and let's all get back to it!" She even managed what could be construed as a smile.

With that she moved to her husband and whispered in his ear. He registered it with some astonishment and nodded. Then she kissed him full on the lips in front of everyone before walking toward the stage door, the medic huffing behind with her kit.

NINETEEN

ONCE IN HER TRAILER, already having had her eyes examined with a penlight that temporarily blinded her, the nurse now taking her pulse, Marci had time to consider certain truths. The first was that she still loved her husband—perhaps, as utterly bewildering as it was, as much as she ever had. But how could this be? Yes, he had struck her without meaning to, but should that even make a difference given the fact he had done so in the act of resisting her impulse to help him? Or worse, trying to silence her? No, it shouldn't. She'd been dropped by a flick of his hand, a careless or, more to the point, oblivious gesture, compelled by behavior of hers that had clearly annoyed him. He was culpable.

I also loathe him, she suddenly thought. And I pity him for his stubborn, selfish fragility and the extremes between which he so regularly vacillates: crying one moment, rejoicing the next, wrathful, then just as suddenly contrite to the point of preverbal. A man who was incarcerated, utterly forgotten while the world spun on, then hopped back aboard to become one of its biggest stars. Able to marry me at a time when I was interested in absolutely no one. Perhaps we haven't had children because he is effectively my child and I understand this physically at some level, the way female gymnasts often can't conceive for what the sport demands of their bodies. That's what I am. An emotional support gymnast. His lover and his mother—exactly what I've sought my whole life to resist.

Yet even still I feel the need to help him. None of it makes any sense, especially since I wake up every morning feeling good about myself and the choices I've made. I love being a woman, even while the fact I've yet to have children feels irrelevant to who and what I presently am. I have the perfect balance of both nurturer and commander. Not only did I instill in Peter the hope and confidence actually to show up on set today, but I'm the reason he's the lead in this film to begin with. This is the sort of complete person I want to be, and it's frankly inseparable from my gender, because no man I know—and especially not my husband—would be able to impact a production in such a thorough and multifaceted way.

Her assistant knocked—she could tell by the careful firmness of it—sharp enough to be heard, but not the door-rattling carelessness of the base camp ADs.

"Come in!"

Samantha's head appeared in the cracked door.

"Are they at it?"

"Yes, but your husband keeps wanting to come see how you are."

"Please make sure he doesn't until Javier has the set for lighting after the master and all of Peter's coverage. Tell him I'm fine and that I love him and to remember what I said before I left the stage. And by the way, if you want a definition of men, it's that when a woman gets hurt because of them they still manage to make it all about them and their needs."

"Noted." The door closed.

"Ain't that the truth," said the medic. "My ex-husband is the same way. He got us in an accident six years ago and I broke my collarbone, and I swear, from my own hospital bed I was making sure he had food in the fridge and someone to feed the kids and take them to school. Meanwhile he was screwing the neighbor from three houses down. In our own bed."

"I'm glad you're not still married to him."

"That don't mean he still don't act the victim. Somehow I was the bad guy for not being able to get over it. One of my kids won't even speak to me. And she's the daughter, if you can believe that one."

"That's heartbreaking."

"She'll come back to me once she's got children of her own."

"I'm sure she will."

Her jaw felt as though it were no longer attached to her maxilla. It was five minutes before nine, when she needed to be on the Zoom with Sparta publicity in Los Angeles. She trusted no one to look after her and Peter's interests more than herself, and she was shrewd enough to understand that at this moment those needs aligned almost entirely with Sparta's (not necessarily Grand's, but that was a separate issue). Whether Sparta could be made to understand this would become clear soon enough. "So, Sally, not to be rude, because as usual you've been amazing, but I've got a Zoom."

"Wait, are you joking me right now?"

"I'm not."

"Honey, you just got clocked. Honestly, I should be taking you to the hospital for X-rays. I know it wasn't intentional, but your husband is a very strong man."

"I assure you I'm okay, and if my jaw were broken, you and I both know that I'd be in more pain than either of us could imagine. Nor would I be able to speak. You've also checked my pupils and asked me all the questions in the concussion protocol."

"But still, it's my job to treat anyone who's hurt on this film."

"Not only have you performed it beautifully, you've done so with thoroughness and grace, and I'm going to make sure you work on every Sparta project here for which you're available, and at your full rate. You'll swing from one to another like Tarzan. No, Jane."

"I'm not just saying this, but you are one of the most amazing people I've ever met."

"Thank you, Sally. It's nice to hear that right now."

"I'll leave you to your Zoom."

⚡

"Okay," Marci said aloud. She checked the Apple watch that had two years prior replaced the Rolex Oyster Peter had given her for their fifth anniversary because the analogue piece didn't text, count steps, and double as a phone. She moved to the door and opened it to find Samantha waiting at the table nearest.

"You have two minutes to get me a fresh latte and be here for the Zoom."

"Already done," responded the assistant, raising a second beverage that sat before her on a round table with a faux nacreous top of the sort encountered at outdoor cafés throughout Europe. Samantha had scoured Atlanta for them at Marci's specific direction.

A dozen faces appeared on the screen, five of them in a single conference room in Los Angeles at Sparta, along with Max Kaiser, who sat behind his desk in the c-suite two floors above. That it was 6:00 a.m. there underscored the seriousness with which the company was taking the challenges that lay ahead. Also present were two publicists from Grand (in their homes), along with three who worked with Marci and Peter. Other than Max Kaiser and Brad Klein, one of Peter's flacks, all attendees were female and mostly in their late twenties and early thirties. Two notable exceptions were a sixty-seven-year-old Sparta lawyer named Sherry Klotzman and Peter's lead publicist, a freckled woman in her late fifties with a riot of graying hair so thick it brought garden shears to mind. Her name was Marnie Applebaum, and she'd founded and still owned a company called Anonymous PR, long considered the industry's best.

"I've read the statement Marci wrote, and it's excellent," Marnie began. "Has everyone else looked at it?"

"We have," said Cynthia Ackerman, Marnie's counterpart at Sparta, also in her fifties. "And jumping right in, I guess we have some issues with it."

"Which are?" asked Marnie.

"We're concerned with what it says about, or, to put it another way, doesn't say about, Sparta."

"Is it your contention Sparta is somehow implicated in what Peter did?"

"If you read some of the posts, it certainly is. Plus it was our set."

"I'd say most of the posts are personal attacks on Peter. He's the issue, not Sparta."

"Most but not all. You're obviously reading it from your client's point of view, and I have to read it from Sparta's."

"What is it you want, Cynthia?"

"Just a sentence in there about the integrity of Sparta and how his words were no reflection on the company, which if worded right could actually further advance what you guys are already trying to do."

"Don't you think it would be overkill?" asked Marci, mindful of concealing her rising anger. "I mean, we've already got in there 'I did a disservice to the movie and its crew.'"

"That doesn't name Sparta."

"Is this why there's a Sparta lawyer on the phone?" asked Marci.

"We felt it important that Sherry weigh in on any statement put out at this point."

"The point being that if my husband separates his behavior from Sparta publicly, then Sparta is less exposed?"

"It has been Sparta policy since I came here five years ago that when statements go out associated with any controversy or misstep that they be vetted by legal," insisted the lawyer with the lassitude of a rote response. "There's no special consideration here."

Marci despised all attorneys other than her own. "That's obviously bullshit," she said. "I know there's already threat of a suit from the intimacy coordinator. Peter's not exposing himself more than he already is."

"This isn't about that, Marci," said Cynthia. "It's more about the statement not just being about Peter but exonerating Sparta as well. Separating his behavior, if you will. Again, the perception could be that this was our set, Peter our employee."

"Then Sparta can make a statement."

"We are. But do you really want it diverging?"

"That sounds like a threat."

"You're the one who brought up separate statements, not us. Our interests are aligned here."

"I agree, but it doesn't sound like you really see it that way."

"We'd rather our statement be in concert with Peter's. In fact, I can read to you what we've got, but it's predicated on the addition we'd like added to Peter's statement."

"Read it," said Marnie.

"Jane, do you have it?"

"I do," said Cory, one of the women in her late twenties. "It's very short."

"Go ahead," said Marci.

"'Sparta regrets yesterday's outburst on the set of *Major Machina*. While we stand behind our star Peter Compton in his personal apology to the film's cast and crew, his words and much of his behavior in the incident run counter to the beliefs of our company. Sparta remains devoted to gender equity in every aspect of what it does, from its products to its work environment.'"

"We have no problem with that," said Marnie. "In fact, we appreciate your support of Peter."

"We're still going to need the additional mention of Sparta from him," said Cynthia.

"I'm sorry, my husband is just not going to crucify himself even more than he's already intending just so Sherry here can tell Max Sparta is impervious to a lawsuit, which at this point none of us is anyway."

"That's exactly right," said Sherry. "None of us ever is, otherwise I'd be out of a job."

"How about in the section from Peter's statement you quoted we just add 'and to Sparta Studios' after 'disservice to the movie and its crew'?" said Marnie.

"Sherry?" asked Cynthia, dispelling any ambiguity as to why Sparta needed the additional language.

"That works."

"Fine by you, Marci?" asked Marnie.

"Sure," said Marci, writing in the chat to Marnie, "These people are hyenas."

"Agreed," came Marnie's response, followed by: "But smart to agree."

"Okay," said Marci. "So while we're on, I've made the edit and I'm sending it to Marnie, who'll put it out."

"Just read it aloud please one more time," said Cynthia.

"'I did a disservice not only to the movie and its crew and to Sparta Studios, but to my fans and to myself.'"

"Perfect."

"And just to be clear, this goes out now during the call," said Marnie. "Then we'd appreciate at least half an hour's lag before you guys put out the statement from Sparta."

"Understood," answered Cynthia.

"So now let's turn to next steps," said Marci. "You'll have noticed we referred to 'extenuating circumstances' in Peter's statement."

"We did notice that," said Cynthia. "We're of course all curious as to what those were."

"Well, there were any number of factors at play, and what we'd like to do on this call is to set them out, discuss each one, and then choose which makes or make the most sense."

"Toward what end specifically?"

"To let people know, Cynthia," said Marci. "Get them out there. Obviously not through Peter, but it doesn't mean *we* can't through some means. Mitigation is the point. Turning sentiment. Yes, he screwed up, he's admitted that, but he's taking it from all sides. It's a public shaming. I don't think anyone on this call believes his behavior warrants that or that it's good for anyone involved. I mean, isn't that why we're having the Zoom in the first place? My husband is an extraordinary man who has gone through a lot. Yes, he's treated well, paid extremely well, and he can be difficult, but he's also given himself completely to this production. I don't think I've ever seen an actor work harder, between the training, the time with the other actors, his involvement with every aspect of production, and, of course, the playing the part itself day in and day out. No one else may be willing to say this, but I'm incredibly proud of him, and I think he needs all of our support, especially with this statement he's willing to put out."

"No one's arguing that. Obviously Sparta is as interested in whatever can help move us through this situation as you are, so long as none of what you're going to list puts Sparta or the production in a bad light."

"Why don't we just let Marci go down the items," said Marnie.

It suddenly struck Marci that Max Kaiser had yet to say a word other than a perfunctory "Hello all" at the introductions stage.

"How are you, Max?" she took a moment to ask. "It seems like hours since we last spoke."

"I'm well, Marci. Just listening, which is what's best when others are handling matters better than you can. We're all eager to solve this, so please proceed."

"Okay," she said. "So I'm going to go through these in no particular order, and they reflect not only what I've observed but Jeremy and Charisse as well, who, by the way, have been amazing."

"They're both extraordinary," confirmed Max. "They're on set right now I take it?"

"Yes," said Marci. "So the first is fatigue. Other than weekends, my husband has not had more than five hours' sleep a night since production started. Instead he gets between four and five, and this with him called every day usually for twelve to fourteen hours when you account for hair and makeup, plus his morning meetings with the director. Add another hour and a half for portal-to-portal travel, plus winding down time at night and up early each morning to train, and you get it. The guy is run ragged, and that tends to impact a person's emotional stability. You can be vulnerable to outbursts."

"Got it," said Cynthia.

"Next," said Marci, "Peter cares too much. This is a guy invested in this film to a fault. He engages thoroughly not just with every actor but with every crew member as well. He watches each take, checks in on every setup before it's shot, and even had a hand in the schedule. Everyone says actors should stay in their lane and just act, but that's not Peter. On this particular day he felt the scene was losing its focus and he snapped. He regrets it, but his intentions had to do with doing the best work possible. No one cares more than Peter."

"Okay," said Cynthia, manifestly uncertain as to the merits of item two. "What's next?"

"Peter was in prison. No, he was never raped, nor did he engage in any sexual activity with a male partner, but he witnessed a great deal of it, often nonconsensual, and anyone who's seen what Peter saw is bound to have sensitivities around issues of intimacy. This was no exception, and while he respects the job of intimacy coordinator and the need for it on a modern set, the oversensitivity to what to Peter was a manifestly chaste scene, especially when the coordinator seemed to imply he, Peter, might act as some sort of aggressor to his female costar, caused him to react in the extreme. This is the last fact about himself he'd like to share, given how it might impact his career, but Peter would be the first to point out that no one goes through incarceration at a maximum-security facility without it changing him in ways that are permanent and can surface when one would least expect. He was triggered."

"Oooh. Not sure about that last word," said Cynthia.

"'Triggered'?"

"I just don't think the public is going to buy it from a white cis male."

"Well, the public can go fuck itself. My husband was triggered."

"It's just a word, Marci, we can change it."

"I'm going to agree with Cynthia here," said Marnie. "Let's lose any mention of 'triggering.'"

"Fine," said Marci. "Next, Peter has been in horrible pain due to the physical nature of this role. For a normal actor, drugs could be prescribed, but Peter is militant about his addiction and takes no prescribed painkillers of any kind."

"I like this one," said Cynthia. "A lot."

"His physician has begged him to use the mildest opioid or even over-the-counter anti-inflammatories, but he refuses, taking only aspirin, and that rarely, as it acts as a blood thinner, exacerbating other problems he has."

"Is all that true?"

"It's true enough to be true."

"Meaning?"

"Yes, it's fucking true, Cynthia. What, you want me to go into the fact that aspirin makes his hemorrhoids bleed? Can I sometimes get him to take a few Motrin? Yes, but it's a pitched battle, or I have to offer sex. I mean, fucking hell. The interrogation over every single item!"

"It's not in any of our interests to get caught in a lie or it makes this all worse."

"So, what, are you now going to ask if he was really never fucked up the ass in prison?"

"I don't recall asking it when it was brought up, does anyone else?"

"Let's dial it back, everyone," said Max. "We're all frayed."

"I think I've been nothing but civil," said Marci.

"I'm sorry," said Cynthia. "I could be more careful with my words and tone. It's only in the spirit of getting it all right."

"I promise you my husband has been in pain and that he is extremely militant in how he chooses to manage it, which isn't even to mention the amount of caffeine he takes in, which itself could be another cause of all this."

"I believe you," said Cynthia.

"So those are the four items. I'd like to promote all of them, but I'm open to discussion."

"Well," said Cynthia, "I think the strongest two are the no painkillers and little sleep, maybe caffeine, and I'd like to stay away from what he did and didn't experience in prison."

"You don't like that he cares too much?" asked Marci.

"There's the implication with that one," said Cynthia, "that everyone who wasn't yelling at the crew didn't care enough."

"He wasn't yelling at the crew," said Marci.

"So giving the speech to the crew with a raised voice that has everyone on the internet attacking him for it."

"And why not his time in prison so long as we don't say he was triggered, which he obviously was?"

"I think you're opening yourself up to a lot of memes with that one. Plus, you don't want people wondering if he's telling the truth about was he or wasn't he."

"He wasn't!"

"Sparta would rather not be in the business of discussing sex in prison, which isn't even to mention Grand."

"Fine," said Marci, "so the two. Exhaustion and pain, possibly caffeine."

"Let's nix caffeine," said Max. "It feels like a grasp, even if it might be true. And who doesn't like their coffee?"

He chooses that on which to opine? thought Marci.

"Agreed. So whose shop?" asked Marnie. "From our end, we'd rather Sparta handle, so Marci and Peter don't seem to be secretly making excuses for him when, in the second speech and the statement, he expressly said he wasn't going to do that."

"Exactly," said Marci.

"So, you'd like for Sparta to put both out, but *as* Sparta?"

"If you guys are willing."

"And by the way, everyone," said Brad Klein, "*Deadline* has just come out with Peter's statement."

"I'm seeing that," said Cynthia. Everyone paused to read the article. "They published it in full, which is good. And it's good you gave it to Scott. I take it you'd already prepped him, Marnie?"

"This was all Brad," she answered. "And yes, he had Scott prepped so the article was ready to go and shot him the revision while we were on the Zoom."

"Good choice and well done, Brad. You're on mute, Brad."

"Sorry! Was someone talking to me?"

"We were saying good job."

"Sorry. Thanks."

"Scott's generally good to us too," Cynthia said, "especially when you give him the exclusive. Yeah"—she paused to peruse the article once more—"and it's generally neutral. Just the facts without any snark. This is great, and the addition about Sparta really does the trick. Well done, Marci."

"Thanks."

"So, we'll put out ours. And you said you wanted us to wait how long?"

"I think given the way this one was presented it might be stronger to go with yours right now," said Marnie, "so long as Marci agrees. Especially with the support of Peter contained in the Sparta statement, I think it'll be stronger."

"Read me the Sparta statement again," said Marci.

"'Sparta regrets yesterday's outburst on the set of *Major Machina*. While we stand behind our star Peter Compton in his personal apology to the film's cast and crew, his words and much of his behavior in the incident run counter to the beliefs of our company. Sparta remains devoted to gender equity in every aspect of what it does, from its products to its work environment.'"

"Could you add 'as well as the statement released this morning' to 'in his personal apology to the film's cast and crew'? Might be stronger," said Marci.

"Sherry?" Cynthia asked the attorney.

"I don't see why not," she answered, "so long as it's okay with Max."

"Fine by me," answered the studio head.

"Okay. Let's put it out. We've already placed it with *Variety*, so I'll just need to send her those edits."

"Sibyl?"

"Yeah, Sibyl."

"Great," said Marnie.

"Jillian?"

"Got it. Done," said a woman in her early thirties with a blond pageboy bob from her laptop in the Sparta conference room.

"Okay, so that brings us back to who gets these two items out and how," said Cynthia. "I do take your point, Marci, about Sparta projecting solidarity, but with these situations I've always found it best to be coming from a third party so that sympathy isn't seeming to be coerced by self-interest. Our putting it out would be clumsy, not to mention that the two topics—Peter's pain and his lack of sleep leading to him being excitable—are really not Sparta's business to share. It's too personal and also makes us seem callous."

"That's a fair point," said Marnie. "It needs to be from anonymous sources, and more than one person, to confirm the reality—preferably three or four, then a lot of comments agreeing."

"I'm not so sure we want our set to seem like an information sieve," said Max. "Can we be a little careful here?"

"Sure," said Marci. "So two people. Can Sparta set up the accounts?"

"We can absolutely take care of that," said another of the young publicists in the conference room, this one a brunette with glasses who had earlier introduced herself as responsible for tech. Marci didn't understand its precise relevance at the time, but now understood that at least part of her remit involved initiating dummy accounts in support of the Sparta mission. LED circles reflected in the lenses inside her frames, explaining why all the Sparta publicists were so well lit.

"Okay, so these should come out over the next day or so," Marci advised, "and obviously crew members."

"Understood," said the brunette with glasses. "Any preference on gender?"

"If I have a choice, I'd say both should be women," said Marci, "given all that went on. It would be nice to see that kind of support. If there are three, make one of them a guy."

"But just about the lack of sleep and the untreated physical pain," said Sherry. "Nothing else. And especially nothing about the intimacy coordinator."

"Anything sent out needs to be vetted by Sherry, Max, Marci, Marnie, and me," said Cynthia.

"Of course."

"Okay," said Cynthia. "We have a plan, everyone knows what to do. I think we should also commend Marci and . . ."

And whom? Marci wondered, staring at the screen as Cynthia simply stopped speaking.

"Cynthia?" she asked.

"Just hang on," answered the publicist. "Is everyone seeing this? Click on the Peter Compton alert. Now."

Marci abhorred Google Alerts. They were an all-or-nothing proposition. Were she to engage with every topic that strove for her attention, each day would be consumed sorting through a tangle of half-truths, innuendo, and trivia. As if to prove it, the entire Sparta publicity staff now gawked below their cameras and into their screens with a common expression of focused incredulity. Peter's team seemed to be doing the same.

"Anyone want to tell me what's going on?" Marci asked.

"Oh shit," she heard Samantha say quietly beside her. Marci looked to find her own assistant slack-jawed, right hand to mouth as she gazed into her phone, earbuds snug in both ears.

"Marci, what the fuck just went down on your set?" asked Cynthia.

"I'm sorry?"

"Did your husband hit you in front of the entire *Major Machina* crew?"

"He didn't hit me. I mean, he did, but he was raising his hand while I was moving toward him to comfort him."

"A video has been posted. I'm watching it right now, and if that's not him hitting you, I don't know what is . . ."

TWENTY

It was like watching cars traverse an intersection, one with the right of way, the other accelerating, oblivious to the sign meant to halt it. Had he been nearer, he would have taken her arm firmly and said, "He'll be fine. Give him a moment." And she would have listened, because while what had occurred the day before had made something of a sideshow of the set he was to be commandeering, the director's status had never been higher than it had suddenly become. Beginning with their confab the preceding morning, followed by the self-immolation of her husband that vindicated all Joel had been feeling and saying about the man, the position of leader that should have been his all along was ineluctably becoming just that. Marci had her husband to handle, Javier Benavidez was too distracted by his seemingly bottomless reservoir of animus toward everything Sparta, Declan Morris was mired in an accounting discrepancy that had him mostly off set, and Jeremy and Charisse preferred, in the alleged spirit of the nation's forty-fourth president, "to lead from behind." It was Joel's moment. "You managed Peter Compton and Javier Benavidez on the *Major Machina* shoot?" the industry would enthuse. "You were there when Peter Compton had his meltdown? And you not only got through it, you made a really great movie? You can do anything!"

He also sensed that, in spite of his own reservoir of discontent, in spite of all the drama, *Major Machina* might just be his strongest film. Forget his jealousy toward Jordan Levinson and his auteur cohort, his animus toward Peter Compton (now transformed into sympathy), he had somehow found the balance between real authorship and commerciality he'd always sought. Until now his films fell toward one pole or the other: too subjective to attract wide appeal, or widely appealing but derided by peers as cynically commercial. While he understood that much would be determined in postproduction, he also considered himself a stronger editor than shooter in a process far less vulnerable to the moods and whims of on-set collaborators. During the edit, particularly his ten weeks for the benignly autocratic "director's cut," he would enjoy complete say with a team beholden only to him, whether Peter Compton was in the room or not.

When Peter's hand caught his wife's jaw, the director's incipient optimism might easily have disintegrated, but Marci Levy proved herself once again to be as poised as she was beautiful. In fact, more so, because in rising to exhort the crew to get on with their day, and in kissing her husband publicly, Joel understood that her appeal derived more from her mind and soul than any physical attribute. Had I met this woman instead of Annie at the Avalon Hotel, I'd have done whatever it took.

"Well," said Javier as the medic followed her to the stage door, "I guess it's finally back to you and me."

"How the hell does she do it?"

"Trust me, I was intending to quit last night until she worked me over at dinner. Listen, I'm sorry how all this has gone. I actually like you, if you can believe it. Probably more than anyone on this set."

"I appreciate that, Javier."

"And we've shot some interesting stuff. Some of it even because of that asshole," he added, pointing to where Peter stood in a shroud of utter bafflement by his chair. "The guy is smart, and he's dedicated. I'll give him that."

"Well, before we start rehearsing, if you remember back from preproduction—"

"A hundred and fifty years ago. Before Lincoln, right?"

Joel laughed. "Just after. Reconstruction."

"In Mexico we had that prick Díaz. I would have been a lot better off here."

"We talked about staging it under the grates so Paul Kramer can step into toplight."

"Jesus, I can't believe we're shooting his introduction scene today."

"I'll walk him and the cast through it, but are you still good with that?"

"Absolutely. It's pre-rigged."

"That was gutsy," said Joel, cognizant of the number of times Peter had completely upended his and Javier's planned staging, resulting in hours of grip and electrical work undone.

"There's no other way for him to enter the room."

The two men hugged, the first time they'd done so in months, and Joel stepped onto the set.

"James," he called to the AD, who he remembered had stood just behind Peter the day before during both speeches and had likewise appeared in each online video, once over the actor's left shoulder, the other time several feet wide of his right, "could you call the actors over, please? Actually, Peter first."

"Copy that."

He sat on the corner of the desk in the center of Paul Kramer's underground lab. An array of mechanical augmentations rested on surfaces throughout the enclosure, where in the scene two government emissaries would appear to share suspicions of an amphibious alien creature posing a threat to world peace. The suicidal physicist and superhero would enter through a chessboard of sunlit squares projected through grates in the ceiling. Joel lifted a beautifully crafted bionic hand from the desk, estimating the prop had probably taken weeks to design, build, and paint. He looked around to discover a surfeit of such objects, their number easily twice what was required, given that few would ever appear in focus. I honestly can't fathom the extent of capital, creativity, and labor that went into this room alone, he mused. The money for just the furniture, inspired by the choice he and Kate, the Scandinavian production designer, had made to go with a midcentury industrial feel, could feed, shelter, and clothe a family of four for a year. Securing it had involved a container being shipped from a warehouse in Bremen to a port in New Jersey, where it was unloaded, then trucked overland across seven states at a steep cost Declan and the accountants at Sparta had of course defrayed with the help of Georgia taxpayers. Better to admire and not question.

"Hey there. Quite a last twenty-four hours," said Peter as he approached. "You look deep in thought. Trying to make sense of everything? You don't want to be me right now. That's what I would take from it and leave it at that."

"How are you, Peter? I know you didn't mean to hit Marci."

"That should go without saying, but thanks. It still doesn't make me not a complete asshole."

"We've had our differences, but you don't deserve any of what has happened."

"I watched the videos. I like myself a lot more when I'm playing a character than when I'm me, I've decided."

"But still."

"Look, Joel, you can't expect to have what I have without a lot of people out there very eager to see you fail. It's part of my job to know that, and even in a situation where it's a locked-down set with all the security we have, in this day and age when I speak in front of a group of people I have to assume there's some jerk with a cell phone filming it, or the sound guy's gonna record it and put it out, so it's ultimately on me. It's like this morning. Why couldn't I just keep quiet? I just accidentally clocked my wife because of my inability to keep my fucking mouth shut."

"Why couldn't you?"

"Keep my mouth shut? I'm an actor."

"Shall I get your scene partners in here and we can rehearse?"

"Yeah. And thanks, Joel."

"Thank you, Peter. Twelve days. We're gonna finish this film and it's going to be great."

"You really think so?"

"Are we going to win awards? Nudge the future of the medium in a different direction? I guess not. But it's gonna be a fantastic Sparta film, which is saying something."

"Then I'm the luckiest man alive."

Unable to locate the tone—ironic? honest? rueful?—Joel didn't know how to respond. Perhaps the actor himself didn't know what he meant, the sentiment delivered with such forlorn ambiguity. Not only the events of the preceding day shared the world over, but effectively striking his wife followed by her public kiss. Now he would film his hero's introduction in that character's eponymous film. A breath of wind and the guy would topple.

The actors playing the two government emissaries had been cast out of New York. Both seemed in awe of Peter, one manifesting this with obsequiousness, the other with subtle defiance.

"Why would we slink around the edges of the room like we're afraid?" asked the latter of the two after Joel had introduced the staging. "We're government guys. Technically he works for us."

"Okay," answered Joel, "tell me what you'd like to do."

"Can I show you?"

"Sure." He remembered the actor to be a recent graduate of Yale Drama School.

"So, like, we come in, and what I see is this central desk with the terminal. I'm going to check it out before Paul Kramer arrives, so instead of us waiting for him all afraid, he's the one interrupting us."

"But remember that Paul Kramer has no respect for his government handlers, and if you've read the comics—"

"I've done my research."

"So good. You know that Paul Kramer can be pretty lethal, especially with his augmentations. You don't know who's going to show up, in other words. Is it the cooperative Paul Kramer or the angry, deceptive, and vengeful one who puts mankind ahead of the government? If you're a good agent, you're careful."

"What do you think?" he asked his scene partner.

"I just want to know what Peter thinks. I mean, it's his scene, not ours."

"I don't know about that," said the Yale actor.

"Dude, we get killed ten minutes into the movie."

"Yeah, but we don't know that now. I mean, by that logic, we wouldn't even come here. We're innocent of that knowledge."

"What?"

"It means you don't go into a scene knowing how it's gonna turn out. You play the moment and status you're in."

"Which is precisely what I'm asking you to do," said Joel. "You've never been here before. This guy is dangerous, unpredictable. You go into the middle of the room, you're exposed."

"True, but—"

"Guys," said Peter, "he's the director. Not you, not me. He knows what he wants. Trust him."

Joel had rarely experienced such simply articulated support from a star, and this from the same one who'd spent the preceding two months undermining him. He blocked the scene quickly, with the two supporting actors skirting the lab and Paul Kramer stepping into the square of light dominating the room's center. It was the entrance he and Javier had imagined in their first storyboard meeting. The dialogue felt almost superfluous.

"Jesus," said Jeremy at the monitor. "We could almost wrap the film now."

"Don't say that," Joel responded. "All these interstitial scenes we have left will make or break us. I'm obsessed with transitions. And we've got everything at the UN."

"I'm just saying, you've now done all the toughest scenes in terms of the technical stuff and the emotional stuff. Plus, Peter's eating out of your hand, which he should have been doing all along given the results you've been delivering."

"You could have told him that earlier."

"You guys are geniuses!" exclaimed Peter from the DIT monitor.

"See?" said Jeremy.

"It's the best entrance in a film I think I've ever had. The staging, the lighting, it's all there. And I didn't fuck it up with my acting."

"I'm glad you're happy," said Joel.

"I'm happy, I'm relieved, I'm grateful. But now I'm going to go prostrate myself at my wife's feet. You guys need a few to turn the camera around, right? We're on them now."

"We're on them, Peter. Go see Marci, and we'll let you know when we're ready."

James stepped over. "Uh, Peter, now would also be a good time to get scanned, because after this it's a costume change and we're on the same set."

"Seriously?"

"Sorry, man. But I want to get both scenes in before lunch."

TWENTY-ONE

What do you give a person who has everything? That's Marci. Not just with gifts on holidays, thought Peter as he walked to the scanning trailer. There's honestly nothing I can say to her, nothing I can do, no extent of contrition, no ground low enough to scrape with my penitent self, that will account for the distance between her decency and my present embodiment of its opposite. She's impeccable in every comparative way: smarter, more disciplined, more attractive physically and spiritually, more complete and integral. Where do I best her? Fame? Earning power? Artistic talent? Sure, but what does any of that have to do with my actual self? Marci might be my priestess, but in this case, the priestess should supplant the object of her devotion, for in what such hierarchy does the clergy so regularly earn the contrition of the deity?

He stepped onto the square black pedestal and faced forward, away from the door through which he'd entered. The hexagon of several hundred cameras stood arrayed surrounding him on grids that stretched from floor to ceiling. A corresponding battery of flashes lay primed.

"Can someone please tell me why we have to do this every scene? I mean, I know everyone's just doing their job, but how many scans do you have of me in this exact suit?"

"Fair point, Peter," answered the technician, a tallish Asian man named Tyler. "But it's been policy since I started with Sparta."

"And when was that?"

"Before they started with these trailers. I'd have to walk around you guys like an idiot for twenty minutes snapping away, you despising me the whole time. Now it's just stand there, tolerate a bit of strobing, and you're off."

"But why so many times?"

"Subtle changes in the makeup, the hair, the clothing. It just covers all bases. Trust me, it's worth it. Bend your arms now."

Peter rotated his palms to face forward and hinged them slightly at the elbows in a gesture suggesting either enticement or supplication. He then waited for the series of flashes that accompanied hundreds of clicks as each camera captured his image from incrementally divergent angles. Within seconds it was over.

"Hang on, let me just check . . ." said Tyler as he perused images on a series of monitors at two consoles behind a curtain. "And . . . we're good."

"See you in a few hours for yet more of this essential ridiculousness."

"You got it."

He stepped back into the midmorning light and walked to his car, where George would drive him two hundred yards to base camp.

I didn't mean to strike her. Let's start with that. Yes, I promised not to speak, to let Jeremy handle it, but seeing all those faces left me no choice. Not to have addressed them would have been downright dismissive of their fealty. Emotion has always unsettled Marci, which, if I can say it, might be her sole fault. Yes, early on she would sometimes cry from the magnitude of our love, and not just after sex but at other moments—driving on the PCH to Mendocino for the weekend, sitting in first class our first time to Europe, watching the sunset in our private pool at the villa in Turks and Caicos—but for years now it's been all business, the feelings unquestionably there, but little time for showing them, much less enjoying them. It's like she became programmed with a single mission: the success of Compton/Levy. In support of that she has her maddening discipline, the whole apparatus cohering in a wellness of mind and body that has no equal. In fact, she no longer admitted distinction between mind and body. "Mind is body," she would insist. He could sleep in, skip a workout, but she could not, an orthodoxy, Peter had learned, that she shared with Joel Slavkin's wife, who apparently could never miss a run.

"I've met that barracuda, and I hope it's the only way in which we're similar. Women just have to work harder," she responded when he reported the similarity. "I know this seems strange to you, but we live inside a reality constantly under threat from the needs and agendas of men. You can scoff and roll your eyes, but it's true. You don't know how many classes I skipped at Penn to stay in with a boyfriend who gave me those puppy eyes. All it took was a few Bs and a guy's feigned concern to be done with that. I don't care if you're a man or a woman, you don't sleep in on life if you want to live that life to its fullest. Sorry for the bromide, but it's just a fact, and if you and Joel want your accomplished wives and are man enough to stand beside us, then don't complain when we get up for a workout or an early meeting when we say that's what we're going to do."

The fact that she was right didn't make it any easier to live with, or live up to for that matter. What, after all, had their experience in Atlanta been before his crack-up in front of the crew? Here they were with him playing the title role in a film she was helping to produce for the most successful franchise in the history of film, and all she could think about was how to capitalize on it; not one moment of actual relish or respite, just, What's next? And when he dared reside in any sense of accomplishment, she was the first to discourage.

"Sure, Peter, if your goal is to be on billboards and make eight figures, congratulations, but the guy I married saw this as an art form. These movies are fine, but let's not forget that what they really do is give you the power to play any role with any director you want. We can do *The Waste Land* now. *Lord Jim*, *The Raft of the Medusa*. Or we can discover the next Jordan Levinson." And of course the infuriating beauty of Marci was that when they went on and did a Faulkner film or one based on Géricault and he dared expose contentment, she'd harangue him with the need to do a studio film with a $20 million payday: "Otherwise, how are we going to be able to do another of these art films you insist on needing to do?"

Fifteen seconds. If she'd just waited one-quarter of one single minute, I'd have brushed aside my tears, caught my breath, and finished the speech. And with cell phones compulsorily dropped now with security at the door, there was no danger of its dissemination—a pity, actually, because what I'd said and how I'd said it, even with emotion overtaking me to the extent it had, was unimpeachable. Its viral spread would have been a boon. But she'd had to step forward, not only inhibiting the completion of what the crew was clearly eager to hear but humiliating me, Major Machina, Paul Kramer, Peter Compton, as some recklessly flouncing marionette controlled by the real brains of the outfit, the brilliant Marci Levy. As for the actual strike, she bounded into it, because that's how Marci assayed any challenge: head-on, without doubt or self-restraint. What did she expect was going to happen? I communicate with my entire body. She must have seen I wasn't in control of myself, already waving my hands like a moron as my love for the crew consumed me, which, to put a point on it, was a good thing! Why did she need to truncate it? To get on with the day? Fifteen seconds!

Of course then, as usual, the nonpareil Marci, who'd inflicted the moment on the two of them, rose to exonerate him with her public kiss—on the lips, yes, but as if he were a child—then whisper in his ear the words he'd remember to his death: "I'm going to go to my trailer now to meet with the publicists to clean up this mess you keep making worse. If I see you before they've shot your side of this scene, I swear to God I'm leaving you. As a wife. As a business partner. As a friend. Everything. You'll never speak to me again. Now do the fucking job you've been paid to do."

He stepped from the car in which a strangely taciturn George had driven him from the scanning trailer. The scene was going well. At least he could report that, he thought as he traversed the parquet of what had come to be known as "Compton Square." But rather than the restrainedly confident Marci he'd come to know, with whom he intended soon to have children, next to whom he hoped to be buried in Brentwood, perhaps Malibu, Santa Barbara, or, who knew, the South of France should they retire in Europe as was sometimes fantasized, he encountered, upon entering her trailer, a version of his wife wholly unfamiliar, seemingly defeated, head in hands on the faux leather sofa that took up the entirety of the longest pop-out.

"Marci? Honey?" he asked.

"Please, Peter, just give me a minute. Don't speak." She turned to a stultified Samantha: "Could you give us a moment?"

"Sure."

"And post up at the stairs. Bring a table over and just follow online traffic. Don't let anyone near the door. I don't care who it is. Not Jeremy, Charisse, Joel, Declan. No one. Guard it with your life until you see me."

"Got it. Hi, Peter," Samantha murmured as she passed him and descended the stairs.

"Shut the door," Marci then ordered without looking up.

"What's going on?" he asked after doing so. "Are they shutting the movie down? Am I fired?"

"Some asshole got his or her phone past security or didn't volunteer it—I mean, what were they thinking? That they didn't need to search people? Seriously, if someone wanted to bring their phone in, especially after—"

"Wait, are you saying—?"

She passed over her laptop that lay beside her on the couch. "Press the space bar."

He did and saw what he knew he would: the act of him striking his wife, though from the angle it was shot it looked nothing but intentional.

"You'll notice there's none of your speech, just the moment where you belted me."

"I didn't belt you!"

"Peter, you did. You didn't intend to, but you did."

"What are people saying about me now?"

"Is that really your question?"

"What else—?"

"How about asking if I'm all right? Physically? Emotionally? In any conceivable way? You come in here, you see me on the sofa in this state, you learn why, and you want to know what people are saying about you. You. Not me. Not even us. You."

"Are you all right?"

"No, I'm not all right. My jaw feels like it's completely out of its socket. I want to fucking cry . . ." And she began to. "Goddamn it!" He went to her. "Just keep away. I can't cry, because we've got to figure this out, which is now my life, figuring shit out for us for you to then go and fuck it all up and I have to start all over again. I do my best, Peter, I really do."

"I know you do. Marci, I'm sorry."

"But you're not sorry. Those are the words you say, but then you just, I hate to use the word, but relapse into the same behavior. Over and over and over. And why? Because ultimately everything has to be about Peter Compton. Of course you weren't going to let only Jeremy speak for the production like we agreed. It had to be you. Do you understand how pathetic and completely exhausting that is?"

"I do."

"But you don't."

"It's my head I have to live inside of, Marci."

"You see! There it is! You've turned the attention back to yourself. Now we're talking about you."

"You're the one taking my inventory."

"Oh God. And now the subtle allusion to your disease. I'm listing your shortcomings and that becomes the focus, not the fact that you nearly dislocated my jaw in front of an entire crew and it's now on the internet where we're the poster couple for an abusive marriage. Not even that Jeremy and Charisse and Declan are out there shutting us down for the day while Sparta decides what to do and Grand goes into full-on panic. No, it's that I'm 'taking your inventory.'"

He looked once more at the computer where the video, posted nearly an hour ago, already boasted more than three hundred thousand views. What did that calculate to per second? Per minute it was five thousand. How could such virality even be possible? Was he setting records? He pushed the space bar and watched once more, adding to the tally. There he was, a self-absorbed and unmanageable aggressor, smacking an innocent and well-meaning spouse.

"I'm sorry, Marci," he said. "Just please know I'm sorry. Everything you said is right."

He was already moving toward the door.

"What are you doing?"

"I'm sorry, sorry, sorry. More than you could ever know."

"Peter, don't leave this trailer. Do not!"

But he was already gone.

SUPERHERO

TWENTY-TWO

George Simms had been driving Peter in Atlanta for five years and was loyal to the extent that, in taking any job, he'd inform the coordinator he'd work "rain or shine, in sickness or health, 24-7-365." He adored the actor not just because he tipped handsomely, or took keen interest in the driver's NFL career, or had paid for the lawyer to get George's brother out of Rice Street, but because Peter had vanquished his own ruin with such an absence of self-pity.

George too had beaten addiction. After eight years as a linebacker in the NFL, he'd become accustomed to painkillers and the benefits they offered, especially when taken absent the torment for which they'd been prescribed. In the years following retirement his drug was Percocet, but then he learned from other retired players that OxyContin had no acetaminophen crowding out the stronger oxycodone. The purer opioid also lasted twelve hours, whereas Percocet tapered after only five. He'd also been instructed to crush the new tablets before use, snorting the powder instead of swallowing it, to intensify the high. When one added alcohol, life slowed down in beautifully lucid ways.

His wife walked out on him with their two daughters six months after his retirement. This no longer troubled him while high. Nor did what he would do with his life long term. A general euphoria furnished a happiness so immediate and convincing he could trust it would never abate. Until it did. But there were always more pills to crush and snort, more booze and pot with which to pair them. He loved the club scene in Atlanta, where he'd ended his career as a reserve player once the four surgeries on his right knee limited his use to packages suited more for straight ahead A- or B-gap run plays that didn't require much lateral movement, and only then when the younger starters needed to be spelled. He'd retired just after salaries for players started to rise beyond the relative pittance paid when he'd started his career, and thanks to a decent money manager he had $2 million in the bank and owned his Atlanta condominium outright. His wife took the home and half the money, and though he had to pay her $3,000 in child support a month, that didn't seem much of a dent in the million he had left over.

But the drug was expensive, and when high he felt generous while out with others. He picked up tabs, bought rounds for the entire bar, routinely ending nights $5,000 lighter, waking in the morning swearing he'd stop, but by the afternoon in search of his next high. And the women: beautiful beyond words, of all colors and persuasions. He liked the black ones the most for their righteous rage and accompanying strength, often revenge fucking him for some man who'd done them wrong one too many times. Plus, with the white women he felt fetishized; with his own he felt known. But regardless of color, they wanted things, and he couldn't help but oblige. He bought their drinks, their meals, and their drugs, but also their clothing and jewelry. He paid rents, student loans; he repaired two roofs. For one he purchased a car she then sold for the drugs on which she overdosed and died.

And still he kept using, knowing the end to be near. He stopped going to clubs, instead retreating to the basement of the home he was renting in Decatur with his bottle and his pills where he'd listen full blast to the Bud Powell records his father had bequeathed him, hoping blissfully to die. What, after all, could the years ahead offer that would touch what he'd had? Two Georgia state championships in high school where he was named a top recruit nationally. Trips on private jets to Norman, Baton Rouge, Lincoln, Ann Arbor, College Station. The four years at Auburn where he couldn't walk ten feet without reverent greetings from students he didn't know. Playing with Bo Jackson. Hanging in the athletic dorm with Charles Barkley. Drafted in the third round by the Chargers. The camaraderie of that locker room, especially the years they made the playoffs. The sheer speed of the game that called on both instinct and intellect in fractions of seconds to pick up the tiniest tells from tendencies he'd learn studying film week after week: what this tailback did before he was handed the ball, where this quarterback looked when the call was a bubble screen, how this tight end twitched before a pick play—all in a crucible of mayhem and violence greater than any drug concocted by man or nature. Even the pain had its beauty because it connoted a life lived to the extreme of physical possibility, not to mention the tantalizing reward of the narcotics prescribed to treat it. Yes, he could feel his body deteriorating, but he'd have a lifetime for recuperation.

His daughters were born on a Sunday in San Diego while he was away versus division rival Seattle in a game that would determine their postseason. The owner flew him home on the team jet hours after the win, and he was whisked by limousine with police escort to San Diego General on what he still considered the best day of his life.

After San Diego, two years in Philadelphia, four in the Canadian Football League playing for the Argonauts, and then his final two years mostly on the bench in Atlanta, where he'd been picked up on waivers. When he was cut during camp of the third year, he knew he was done; there'd be no other team. He'd been shot up with Percocet that morning and could still barely make it to his car. He swallowed two codeines with a shot of gin for the drive home, where he would inform his soon-to-be ex-wife of his forced retirement.

He woke from his last high with the nudge of a soft-toed Rowan boot on the foot of an Atlanta patrolman in the Avondale MARTA station. He'd been homeless for two weeks.

"Wait, are you George Simms?" the officer asked.

"In all my glory," the former linebacker responded.

"Shit. I've got your rookie card. San Diego. Then you was with Minnesota."

"Philadelphia."

"Philadelphia, right. You made the Pro Bowl with them."

"My best year."

"What you doin' sleepin' on a train platform?"

"Seemed as good a place as any."

The policeman's name was Marcus Brady, and a dozen years later George would serve as best man at Marcus's wedding to his third wife. But on that morning he drove George to a treatment center and halfway house on Trinity Avenue, where he insisted George be given a bed. As painful, humiliating, and devastatingly hopeless as the months ensuing were, with the help of never going a week without a meeting, George had been clean now for nineteen years with but a few stumbles early on.

Not until their second job together did he share any of this with Peter. It deepened a bond that already felt meaningful to each.

"Jesus, George, you had it worse than I did."

"Never went to prison."

"But homeless. Shit. How the fuck did you end up a Teamster?"

"That's the thing about the Program. We help each other out. Why I recommend it to anyone and everyone. Met a guy who set me up. Lucky for me I never had a record, never lost my license. A couple traffic stops here and there, but that's it, and somehow, thank the Lord, never while I was impaired. Got my CDL Class A on a HOPE Grant, and this guy put me to work."

"You can drive an eighteen-wheeler?"

"Started out on those. Camera, wardrobe, grip, and electric. But didn't much like the sitting around once the trucks were parked. Got my mind wandering too much, so I moved over to cast, much more my speed. And anyway, most of these guys don't want to deal with y'all."

"I don't even want to deal with me half the time."

During the season they'd sometimes watch football together if the actor was in Atlanta. Peter would even text him from Los Angeles or other locations during the late-afternoon game.

"Do you still like it?" he once asked.

"Yeah," George answered, "but it ain't the same sport."

"You mean in terms of strategy?"

"Mostly all the new rules. They couldn't chop-block you, and you could get flagged for roughing the passer or a horse collar or a blindside, but we used to take people out, Peter. That was the job. You remember a few years back when Sean Payton got in all that trouble for bounties in the New Orleans locker room? We had that shit every week, as in money in the pot. And targeting? I get it, but man, we used to need for receivers or whoever had the ball to know they'd been hit. And some of the blocks I took from tight ends. Forget that shit. I got my bell rung. I watch these guys pull up on a hit and wonder sometimes what game it is I'm watching."

"You think you have CTE?"

"I guess we'll see. Maybe all the drugs I took killed it."

"At least some good would have come from them."

"Oh, I don't know. I had some good times. I bet we both did."

"I guess that's true."

"Some weekends I don't even know if now is better, other than I've got a roof over my head and I'm still alive, which has got to mean something."

"You don't mean that."

"I guess I don't."

George had seen the video of Peter striking his wife well before Peter and probably not long after Marci. A Teamster named Burt, white and in his fifties from Valdosta who'd fought in Desert Storm as a nineteen-year-old and spoke with one of the most pronounced drawls George had ever heard, appeared at the window of the Cayenne.

"You better start lookin' for yo' next gig, George."

"Oh yeah?" He couldn't help but like Burt, though the vet did make a point to assure him he didn't see skin color, having been in the military around, as he unartfully put it, "blacks and Mexicans and Puerto Ricans every bit as brave as the whitest motherfuckers in the unit." When he said it initially it didn't trouble George, even though introduced incoherently in a conversation about Hemi engines, but by the fifth time it felt like a man struggling with persisting issues.

"Your guy just put a wallop on his wife in front of the crew."

"How you know that?"

"One of the fellers showed it to me."

George waited for Burt to leave, then punched Peter's name into his phone and, after a Geico ad, was one of the viewers between seventy-five and seventy-six thousand. "No matter what it looks like," he said aloud to the empty car, "Peter would not strike his wife, or any woman for that matter." Knowing from his daughters how meaning accrued to videos based on number of viewings, he did not revisit it. Nor did he read any of the surfeit of posts that had begun to accumulate.

After about thirty minutes, Peter appeared from the stage door and walked to the scanning trailer, suggesting that in all likelihood they were turning the camera around.

"George, take me to the village square," he then announced as he bounded into the car's back seat. "I need to let my wife know things are looking up. This is going to be a great scene."

Do I tell him? George asked himself. How to describe having just watched a video seen now by easily a hundred thousand of him decking his wife in a manner that would only be perceived as intentional?

"Why the dour face?" the actor inquired. "Don't tell me you heard what happened. It was a fluke thing and we're past it."

"I'm just in my own head, Peter."

"Well, I'm trying to get out of mine, which I'm sure you understand."

"That I do, and I'm happy things are better."

During the forty-minute drive to work four hours prior he'd done much to calm the star, going so far as to reveal, which he'd done with no one, the affair with his former wife's sister that had broken up his marriage, one he'd carried on during the month the sister had moved into their home to help with the twins when they were born. How he'd tried to kill himself when his wife left him over it months after being dropped by the Falcons.

"A man can come back from anything," George had said.

⚡

When Peter emerged from Marci's trailer, he stepped across a corner of the parquet to his own redoubt, from which he emerged carrying his wallet and phone. He marched purposefully to the back passenger-side door of the Cayenne and got in.

"Back to the stage?" George asked.

"Off the lot."

"Where we goin'?"

"Atlanta."

"The house?"

"Midtown. The Four Seasons."

"You don't want to change back into your own clothes?"

Peter glanced down. He'd traded his effects jacket for the unaugmented one, completing a pin-striped suit with a cream shirt and a loosely worn fifties tie, his top button undone. He wore thin, round wire frames and had a light stubble to connote late hours of research under a full head of mussed hair. The visage alone could be the film's poster. He removed the eyewear.

"I think I look great. Let's go."

"I'm gonna guess this is not what the producers have in mind."

"They will not be requiring my services for the remainder of the day, which you obviously know because of the sad face I encountered when I got in the car on the way from the scan, so just cut the shit and get us out of here."

"Maybe let me just go let your wife know."

"You go talk to my wife, I swear you and I will never work together again. I'm the reason you're on this show. Now if you want to quit, that's your prerogative and I'll respect it, but your choices are that or you drive me to the Four Seasons."

"May I ask why the Four Seasons?"

"A place to stay while I think things through."

"Why don't you come to my place?"

"Just take me to the goddamn hotel. Jesus, George. What? You think I'm gonna hole up with hookers and blow in the center of midtown where every asshole can see me? I mean, seriously, I'm not going to throw it all away."

The two locked eyes in the rearview. George levered the car into drive and drove twenty yards to where Peter's chef's trailer completed a forty-five-degree angle, and he turned right, passing the gym and makeup trailers before turning left toward the exit. Shawna and Justine, two of the base camp ADs, offered the last faces he saw, confused and slightly anguished as the actor and his driver departed the lot, not a quarter of the shooting day finished.

He checked his watch on I-85 heading northeast when they hit Union City. It was twenty-five minutes to eleven, and if traffic didn't intervene and he stayed on the interstate, he would reach midtown by a quarter after. Peter spent the entire drive scrolling his phone. Near the 285 junction George checked his own device. Marci had left half a dozen texts, each more emphatic than the last, the final two in all caps. "I've gt hm," he wrote. "Wants 4 Ssns." "HTL?" she responded. "Won't tk hm thr," he texted. Traffic began to move. He restored the phone to its holster.

"Were you just texting with my wife?" Peter asked.

"I was."

"Did you tell her where we were going?"

"I did not," he responded, grateful for how the question was phrased.

"Is that the truth, George?"

"I swear on the life of my daughters."

"No need for that, but I will take your phone."

"Whatever you say." George locked it and handed it over his shoulder.

"I'll give it back when you drop me, then you can text her whatever you want."

"Meaning you won't be getting a room?"

"What's that supposed to mean?"

"Otherwise, what difference does it make?"

The actor didn't answer. He simply pocketed the device then went back to reading from his own.

They turned down Trinity Avenue just after eleven.

"You want to tell me why we're going this way? Do you even remember where the Four Seasons is? Fourteenth Street."

"Makin' a stop along the way."

"Are you fucking kidding me?"

The asymmetric redbrick building stood just off Peachtree Street Southwest with access on either side to parking in the back.

"What is this place?" asked Peter. "And how long are you gonna be?"

Before shutting off the engine, George summoned the child lock icon on the flat screen and punched it, all doors but his responding with an unmistakable thunk.

Peter tried his door to confirm what had just occurred.

"You think I'm gonna run away? I don't even know where we are."

George pointed. "That right there is the treatment center where I spent six months getting clean."

"Oh, fuck you, George."

"Let's just call this a preemptive strike."

"Look, I don't know what you think you're doing, but you've read this situation entirely wrong. My wife just told me she basically doesn't want to see me again."

"I don't believe that for a second."

"It's fucking true. And not because I hit her, which was an accident, by the way."

"I know that."

"Though you wouldn't from what's being said on the internet. Yesterday was bad. Now you'd think I was Ted Bundy."

"I don't read that shit. Never have."

"I need to be at the Four Seasons to cool off. There's a room on the fifth floor that holds special significance because Marci and I stayed there on my first job here after I was clean. That's why I don't care if you text her where you drop me off; she'll figure it out anyway. I just want time to check in and get myself sorted out. I know her. She'll call me, which she's done ten times already."

"I thought you just told me she doesn't want to see you again."

"That doesn't mean she's not worried about me. I mean, come on, George, you're really starting to piss me off. Do you have any idea what just happened to me means?"

"That's exactly why we're here."

"Fine. Take me home then."

"And what? You call an Uber and they take you to the Four Seasons to meet whoever you called to meet you there?"

"You think I'm still keyed into dealers in Atlanta? Anyone I knew here is probably in jail, dead, or sober and raising a fucking family in some other state."

"Let's go inside, Peter."

"What do you need me to do? Swear on my life? I don't have daughters."

"I need you to go inside."

"Listen to me. I want to sit by myself in a room, away from everyone—you, Declan, Joel, the crew, and especially my wife—where I can think. You don't believe me, take me to a different hotel. The Loews. The InterContinental. The goddamn Clermont for all I care."

"Do you know how many interventions I've done?"

"I honestly don't care."

"I've heard every explanation, I've heard every excuse, I've heard every lie. I even know when a motherfucker is lying to himself."

"I am as far from relapsing as you are."

"You don't know what I am and can't pretend to."

"Which I can say back at you."

"Unfortunately, I've got the keys."

"Okay, so what do we do?"

"I told you, we go inside."

"George, do you have any clue what that could do to me?"

"That's exactly why."

"No, George, to my already completely murdered career. Where some junkie inside there decides to take a picture on his phone, and then it gets out I've checked myself into a rehab facility in downtown Atlanta. Which isn't even to mention it suggests I've been using, which violates every clause in my contract and could cost me tens of millions of dollars, and no, that's not an exaggeration."

"Nobody's gonna do that in there, Peter, which, by the way, we're in the back and these windows are tinted. Nobody knows we're here. And I can vouch for these people. I go to meetings here, which if anything makes you look responsible."

Peter stared down at the car's floor, twisting the toe of his black wing tip into the ply. The scene was becoming ludicrous, especially with the actor in costume. I'm putting Paul Kramer in treatment, George thought. Paul Kramer, who, in the comic, never overcomes his addictions.

"All right, fine, I'll go in," Peter finally said.

Knowing better than to trust him not to flee, George exited the car without disabling the lock, stepped around to the back passenger-side door, and used the remote before pulling the latch and allowing Peter to exit. He took him firmly by the arm.

"Jesus, you think I'm gonna try to outrun an NFL linebacker?"

"You're in better shape than just about anyone I know. The guy we're about to see is named Gerrold Potter. Reverend Gerrold Potter. When I met him he had just been ordained and was part-time here. Now he runs the joint. He was twenty-five when he changed my life. Fifteen years younger'n me, if you can believe that, so just a bit younger'n you. I texted him, so he's expecting us."

"Praise Jesus."

"Not much Jesus talk from the reverend, but if you want he can pull a switch and go hog wild with some testimony."

"No thanks."

"Mostly he'll talk about living life. Practical shit more than spiritual shit."

"How long are we gonna be here?"

"Like they say in the program. A day at a time."

"I was meaning how many minutes, George."

"I've only thought this through getting you in the door. Then we'll see."

Where they entered, a makeshift reception booth stood just to the right. Behind its bulletproof Plexiglas sat Aythelle, unimaginably slender and in her mid-sixties, a thick pair of red plastic frames attached to a chrome chain that hung past her ears then looped behind her neck. She'd been at the facility for nearly as long as the reverend but seemed not to have aged. If anything, she'd grown younger in appearance by the year.

"I heard you was coming by," she said with a wry smile. "It's been a while."

"Movie hours."

"Well, we always like to see us some George." She buzzed them in.

"This a facility or a prison?" asked Peter.

"Folks can leave whenever they want. They're careful about who gets in."

The place had scarcely changed since George was deposited there nearly twenty years prior. The walls were painted dark brown two-thirds up toward the eight-foot ceiling of the ground floor. A light mustard made up the final third under mineral fiber ceiling tiles of faded white that George helped install a decade and a half before. None of the original furniture had been disposed of, though some new pieces had accumulated over the years, including a Naugahyde reading chair where a Hispanic man of about forty whom George had never seen sat doing a Sudoku puzzle in a book advertising itself as "Intermediate." He looked up silently with sad, retiring eyes, then returned to his work, neither interested in nor troubled by the appearance of a former NFL linebacker and his costumed charge. Books of disparate categories lined three rows of long shelves sagging between metal brackets that spanned twenty feet of wall space. There were textbooks, novels, histories, expatriated encyclopedia volumes of random letters, similarly marooned law books, and at least a dozen Bibles interspersed, the collection defying any organization that might once have been imposed.

"His office is just over here," said George, stepping to a plywood door awaiting its first coat of paint. It had replaced one kicked in months before by a twenty-five-year-old client sanctioned with extra kitchen duty for not having cleaned the lint from the laundry room dryer.

"Enter," said Gerrold when George knocked, though the door stood ajar. He realized that he probably should have prepared Peter for the man's size, which had increased easily by 130 pounds in fifteen years. When George met him he'd been clean for three, his drugs of choice having been crack and heroin, which he'd do in succession for the euphoric contradiction of the push and pull, at once hyped and blissfully inert. As Gerrold told it, by the age of twenty-two, he'd lost much of his body mass and a commensurate number of teeth.

"Then I replaced drugs with food," he liked to say, "and let me tell you, I prefer it that way, and so does my doctor when I give her the options. Of course she'll say there's other options, but not any that I can see. I liked drugs, but I *love* food."

He rose to shake George's hand, his office chair rising a good three inches.

"George Simms, as I live and breathe! How's the movies?"

"I can't complain."

"Well, that's good. That's good. You look great."

"I saw you six weeks ago."

"A lot can happen in a month and a half."

"That it can."

"So, who's this here?"

"My friend Peter Compton."

"Welcome to our humble facility, Peter." The two men shook hands, Gerrold's engulfing the actor's as if it were that of a young boy. "Sit you down on that sofa."

Peter did, while George remained standing.

"So tell me why you're here, Peter?" Gerrold said.

"Honestly, George locked me in the car and gave me no choice."

"Hah! Well, George has his ways of persuasion. So now that you're here, why don't you tell me about yourself."

"If you don't mind, I'm gonna use the facilities and leave you two to it," said George.

"You know where they're at," said Gerrold.

"And, Peter, do yourself a favor," said George, "don't hold back. On anything, no matter what you feel or want to say. The more truth you give this man, the better."

"That's enough, George," said Gerrold. "You go on like you said and leave us two to chat."

"He's got to give me my phone first."

"We're not where we're headed yet."

"I'm not gonna tell a soul where we're at, Peter. You have my word."

The actor reached into his pocket and handed it over. "It hasn't stopped buzzing. My wife, no doubt."

The ground-floor bathroom seemed occupied by the Sudoku intermediate, as his chair was now vacant and the door to the commode shut. George descended to the basement, which served as a meeting area and sometimes stage for performances, presentations, lectures, and classes. The walls were brick and painted white. About thirty blue folding chairs stood in loose semicircular rows, suggesting there'd been a gathering that morning or the night before that included both residents and staff.

One thing was certain: Peter would use again, and that very day, if George didn't do all he could to prevent it. The actor's resolve in the rearview had provided all he needed to know. In his own relapses during the early years, he too had let the disappointment of others convince him it simply wasn't worth the effort to remain clean. He also understood the impulse for self-destructive revenge against those who actually cared.

One moment at a time, he said to himself as he released a halting stream of vitamin-infused piss into the bowl of the basement lavatory. Is it really worth it to pay for these daily supplements if all I do is send them through my one remaining kidney (he'd lost the other after an unpenalized spear block from a Bears tight end) and into the city sewers? And yet other than his knees, he'd not felt healthier since retirement, jogging two miles on days off and, when out of work, a regimen of twelve miles a week, along with free weights before he went to bed. Why did it take me until sixty to figure all this shit out? he wondered with a chuckle as he washed his hands. There's so much I would change, but the tragedy is I wouldn't know what I know if I hadn't gone through what I did, so here I am with maybe fifteen years left, and all that stupidity to thank for the wisdom. At least I'll have done some good for Peter. An hour with the reverend will either wise him up or scare him straight. And if he believes I actually think he's gonna stay here the night, all the better. I go upstairs, we do what we need to do, then I take him home to Marci. I'll even stay over if they want, because Lord knows, it might not be today or tomorrow or next week, but the man will thank me.

Shit! Marci! He opened his phone with the code of his daughters' birthday and saw at least a dozen unanswered texts. "I've still got him," he wrote. "I'll deliver him home unless you tell me otherwise."

"OMG," came the response, "I have been so worried. I said bad things to him. THANK YOU THANK YOU THANK YOU for being there. THANK YOU." Then, "Can you spk?"

He looked to the stairs beckoning toward the ground floor, then counted the bars on the device, which had also automatically joined the building Wi-Fi. He sat in one of the blue chairs in the front row and scrolled to Marci's name.

"Thank you so much, George," she said without a hello. "Where are you?"

"I'd rather not say, but it's a good place. Best place he could be."

"Well, that sounds weird."

"I promise you it's not, but it's not my place to tell you, it's his, which hopefully he'll do tonight."

"I'm his wife."

"I know that."

"Okay . . ." She furnished a pause he did not interrupt. "Fine. But not the Four Seasons?"

"No. Though he did say something about a room on the fifth floor."

"Yeah, well, that's bullshit."

"I figured as much. Said you didn't want to see him."

"I'm furious with him, but of course I want to see him. I want to help him through this. We all do, but he keeps making that impossible. We were so close this morning. Did you see the latest video?"

"Unfortunately."

"Does it look to you like—?"

"He's hitting you on purpose?"

"He wasn't. He didn't. It was—I walked into it. He was using his hands like he does. But you can edit anything to look like anything. And on your fucking phone. You can go frame by frame, so whoever put it out cut everything before and everything after, and then I think manipulated it."

"I'm sorry, Marci."

"I hate this time we live in. People are so vindictive and stupid and bored."

It's also the time of superhero movies, George thought without voicing the sentiment. He couldn't name a film he'd liked since *Pulp Fiction*.

"How long are you going to be wherever it is you are?" she asked.

"There's the off, off, off chance we'll stay the night, which . . . you'll just have to trust me."

"I do."

"But I'm fairly positive just a few hours. He might want to eat after, and then I'll carry him home. You gonna be there?"

"I will if that's where you're headed. We decided to keep shooting. There's the rest of the scene, which we can get with the double from behind, and after that inserts and pickups we needed anyway. My guess is we'll do that tomorrow too, and then we have the weekend, so it'll be fine while we do more damage control. I'm already putting out a statement from me, plus we have an entire crew ready to say it was an accident. I mean, this is so stupid. Why did he have to give another damn speech?"

"We've just got to love him for who he is, Marci."

"Well said, obviously."

"I better get back to him."

He hung up and thought of his daughters, who had decided to love him for who *he* was. How else to account for them even speaking to him after he squandered money he could have set aside for their educations, their children, their mother; after the missed child support payments blown on drugs, on impulsive generosity to hangers-on and sycophants, most of whom he barely knew, instead of helping them.

Their names were Shaylene and Charlotte. He found their group chat and FaceTimed. Charlotte picked up first, her phone lodged in a cupholder while she drove.

"Hey, Daddy. Bored at work? Peter's in his trailer?"

"Something like that. Just missing my little girls."

Shaylene punched in from the hospital in Waycross where she was a nurse.

"Both of y'all?" she chirped. "Doesn't anyone have a job?"

"I'm on lunch, girl," said Charlotte. "And not only that, meeting a client, so I get to expense it." She was an interior designer in Atlanta. Both had attended Vanderbilt and graduated with 4.0s. He'd love to take credit, but that rested entirely with their mother and her second husband, a lawyer from Athens who'd graduated from Tulane, then Yale Law School, before settling in Atlanta, where he represented a host of corporate concerns, including the Tyler Perry empire.

"Where are you, Daddy?" asked Charlotte. "I don't see a car ceiling."

"Stopped off to visit the reverend."

"Everything all right?"

"Never been better," he responded. Little reinforced the tenets of recovery than aiding a fellow addict in peril.

"All right," answered Charlotte. "You coming to the city this weekend like you promised?" she then asked her sister.

"I'll see you Saturday night."

"Where you want to go?"

"Take me to that place in Inman Park where you texted those pictures from."

"I'll get us a resie. Bye, Daddy. I love you guys."

"I love you too," he answered.

That's why I pay it forward, he said to himself as he climbed the stairs. I helped create two sisters who love each other like they do, and each making the world a better place. Coming out of the stairwell and looking diagonally across the main room to where the Sudoku player had resumed his meditative concentration, George could see the door to Gerrold's office, now open. Didn't they want privacy?

He found the reverend alone at his desk.

"Where you been?"

"On the phone with my daughters. Where's Peter?"

"He left. I went lookin' for you to tell you."

"You didn't stop him?"

"You know the rules. Nobody here unless they want to be. Ain't no point otherwise. This ain't a lockup."

"But, Gerrold, you know what he's gonna go do."

"And if he does, that's what he needs to do to get where he needs to get. You understand that better than anyone."

"He say where he was headed?"

"Not to me."

"How long ago was this?"

"You been down there awhile. Thought you was maybe building us a new bathroom."

He wanted to strangle the man for his affable humor in the face of such jeopardy, but he recognized it was precisely this deeply caring indifference that had attached him to the reverend in the first place.

He rushed through the back entrance to the parking lot with a quick wave to Aythelle, unlocked the Cayenne with the remote, and threw himself behind the wheel, cursing aloud as he started the car's virtually silent engine and toggled it into reverse.

He circled the block pointlessly, then in fifteen minutes was at the Four Seasons, where Vincent, the head doorman on the day shift, let him park along the inside curb parallel to Fourteenth Street. At nightfall he finally left, rarely having taken his eyes from the door, relieving himself in an emptied Fiji bottle Peter had left during the morning drive that seemed like months before.

On the hour he called Marci, reporting each time that the actor had yet to appear.

TWENTY-THREE

Peter Compton had been spirited off the studio lot by his driver. The Teamster had had his own issues with substances and determined that he, more than the three producers on set (one of them the actor's wife), the director, the AD, and the licensed medic, was the person most qualified to treat a movie star vulnerable to relapse. The place to which he'd taken one of the most recognizable stars in the world, a man worth well into nine figures? Max had looked it up online, and the only white people he saw were volunteers carrying boxes of clothing into a resale shop and two recovering junkies in their fifties, both of whom were probably dead by now from the look of them. Everyone else was black and impoverished beyond imagining, and serviced by a decidedly all-black staff. Perfectly fine for its clients, many of whom projected the radiance of the reformed, but what on earth did any of it have to do with Peter Compton? Would it provoke guilt? Terror? Revulsion? Did this idiot Teamster expect the movie star would spend nights there? The actor had given the experiment ten minutes, escaping while his self-appointed chaperone made phone calls in the basement.

Max was now well past feeling vindicated for his initial objections to casting the star; after all, he too had been caught up in the optics of a recovering addict playing a superhero likewise afflicted. Instead he found himself deeply concerned on two levels. The first, and this surprised him, was personal. Over the months, he'd actually grown to like Peter Compton as well as his wife. The woman was a monster, but one you absolutely wanted on your side. She pursued success for her husband with such dogged certainty one wondered what he possibly could have done to deserve it. He was her Leonardo, her Daisy Miller, her Aslan. But inside the partnership she made herself just as essential as her husband, an understanding Peter Compton seemed not only to accept but embrace. And who could blame him? Take away Marci Levy, and the guy was an actor. With her he was an industry. That he had struck her publicly, no matter its inadvertence, felt strangely inevitable; there was simply too much power between the two for combustion not to occur.

She would be fine regardless. But what of Peter Compton should he relapse? And what would be the nature of his descent should that be where he was headed? Imagining this instilled nothing short of dread: Was the actor in a hotel room somewhere? In someone's home? Was he even in Atlanta? Why had he contacted no one, not even his wife? So far as Max knew, it had been over a decade and a half since he had last used. How would he even go about it? He must have bought in Atlanta before, given the surfeit of films shooting there already sixteen years ago. But how would he achieve the privacy necessary to escape further public humiliation? Or did he want such exposure as perverse revenge against all the online ridicule? And none of this was even to mention issues of safety, given what was happening to users nationwide, including more than a couple of movie stars who'd died from overdoses in the preceding decade, two of them Oscar winners with the resources to buy the safest drugs imaginable.

What was it about America and its ever-increasing need for novel substances, most recently synthetic variants manufactured on the other side of the world?

At Oberlin he'd decried the hypocrisy of corporations doing business in China. One of the first images of political bravery he'd known was that of the lone protester standing before the tank in Tiananmen Square. As a comic book–obsessed twelve-year-old, he'd rejoiced at such heroics, cutting the image from *The Inquirer* and affixing it to the front of his locker to the bewilderment of his peers. He'd also cried when the students were violently removed from the plaza by Li Peng.

"Fucking hell, Max, what did you expect?" explained his father. "If a bunch of students occupied the Mall in Washington for weeks on end, eventually the president, any president, would call in the National Guard and have them dispersed. A society needs to function."

"I'll never be so cynical," he'd vowed.

"Don't use words you don't know."

"Thinking only about yourself."

"Maybe he has been reading, even if it's just the Sparta handbook," remarked his mother.

What a difference running a corporation made. China allowed thirty-four films from the United States to show in its theaters per annum, and the year before it had stopped including Sparta titles. Two factors were at play, the first of which was Max's mandate that not only women and minorities take title roles, but that gender and sexual orientation issues be more candidly expressed. He considered this especially important given the export of the films. Redress of inequities in America might inspire similar reckonings worldwide.

Chinese censors did not agree, requiring excisions around LGBTQ+ issues Max had to accept if the films were to be available to their audience. The final film in the *Retribution Force* trilogy had made more than $1.5 billion worldwide, nearly $700 million of that coming from China. With such numbers, how could he refuse? Why not take the resulting profits for yet greater promotion of a social justice agenda? he then reasoned.

Max had also, in the spirit of expanding not only the ethnic makeup of the SCG but diversity behind the camera as well, advanced to the production stage the first exclusively Asian superhero movie, titled *Youxia: The Tale of the Quiet Circle*, based on the *Youxia Wandering Warrior* series introduced by Sparta Comics in 1972. The film was to be directed by recent Oscar nominee Janet Yi, a Chinese American whose maternal grandparents had immigrated to work on the railroads nearly a hundred years before the Cultural Revolution, meaning little chance of problematic lineage. A search of her father's family likewise yielded no problematic ties to Hong Kong, Taiwan, or the legacy of Chiang Kai-shek. In terms of casting, Max and Janet found the male and female leads from China and South Korea, respectively, with supporting actors of Japanese, Taiwanese, Vietnamese, and East Indian descent. The movie would also feature a compendium of fighting styles, reflecting not only an embrace of various martial arts traditions but a reemergent popularity of hand-to-hand combat.

All proceeded uneventfully into postproduction, when Janet, in an interview with *The Guardian*, referred to the "country" of Taiwan. What made the ensuing Chinese outrage especially maddening was that the director had intended neutrality. Her full answer read, "I'm a filmmaker, not a political figure, so I'm not going to comment on any dispute between China and Taiwan. I want both countries to resolve any disputes peacefully."

"Janet," Max said to her on the phone three days later, when Chinese demands for recantation had only intensified, "you've got to apologize."

"Are you asking me to say Taiwan is not a country? Do you think it isn't?"

"I'm not going to answer that."

"Why, you think the CCP has hacked into the Sparta phone lines? Or even worse, Grand's?"

"I thought you weren't political."

"I don't speak out politically, but how could I not be political? I think the Chinese Communist Party is oppressing the Uighurs, I think they're reneging on the deal they made with Britain over the future of Hong Kong, and I think Taiwan is a country. I think to live in China under Communist rule is to be lied to and oppressed constantly and relentlessly. I'm not going to say any of that publicly, just like I won't tell people in interviews how much I hate Trump. I'm a storyteller, not an activist. But I'm also not going to apologize for accidentally stating a fact."

"You've got to say something if you want any chance of *Youxia* playing in the country of your ethnic origin, which I have to imagine you do."

The resulting statement—"I regret involving myself in the ongoing issue between the people of China and the people of Taiwan"—was heralded as abject apology in both the *People's* and *Guangming Dailies*.

⚡

Shunting thoughts of global statics opened the way for a second and equally pressing concern, which had to do neither with Peter nor Asia, but instead how to keep shooting without the film's star. For the remainder of the first day, when it wouldn't have been appropriate to have the actor on set anyway, they'd worked with the double from behind, then used the afternoon for a series of inserts. But on the subsequent day all work involved Peter, as did the shoot's final two weeks. A day of photography on *Major Machina* cost roughly $200,000, little of it recoupable beyond the rebate. It wasn't as if they could send equipment back to the rental houses or refuse to pay staff, location fees, and crew. Moreover, should they take the day off, it would effectively double costs, since they'd then have to add days to make up for those missed.

Yes, it could be reasoned that on a $160 million film, what was another $400,000? But Max had learned from Boaz that a disposition toward budgets always reflected a larger paradigm. Ten- to hundred-thousand-dollar increments made for increases that could become quite dramatic once those in control began meeting them with routine indifference.

"What I need to know, and the answer absolutely cannot be 'nothing' or 'very little,' is what can be shot tomorrow," he asked on a Zoom with Declan, Jeremy, Charisse, Joel Slavkin, and the first AD at 7:00 p.m. LA time, 10:00 p.m. in Atlanta, on the night Peter had disappeared. "I want everyone working tomorrow so that we're not wasting the day and we're not adding a day."

"As James will tell you," answered Joel, "we were instructed, because Peter was the one actor we had for run of picture, and most all the others were on weeklies, that we needed to prioritize getting the other actors in and out. Peter is our entire day. Other than day players, he's the only actor called."

"You honestly have no scenes without Peter you can move up and shoot?"

"There's the sentry scene at the aquarium where they're holding Jellyfish," offered the AD.

"But that's a night scene, and we're on a light split," answered Declan. "I was even going to argue that that be shot in LA at a later date, which would be cheaper even with the tax credit. It's basically a cutaway."

"Shoot it," said Max. "Make it a day scene if you have to, or day for night."

"I'll see if I can get the location. It was supposed to be next Friday."

"Get it."

"Yes, sir. But you're asking for a full day, and figuring in travel and set dressing, which, since it's something of a turnkey location for a night shoot if we go to a full split, doesn't involve a huge amount of work—I think some signage they might already have put up—we still have half a day with all the equipment at the stage, which, thanks to the schedule change we made by starting at the culvert, is where we're meant to wrap the whole show. I mean, almost all of our remaining days are at the stage, even the UN set."

"What about the double?"

"We can shoot him from behind. He's a piece of work."

"Who?"

"The double. But it's interstitial stuff on a half dozen sets on two different stages. Hallway scenes where he goes from one place to another talking with this person or that. We'd shoot the guy from the back in one scene and then, what, jump to the next with a re-dress and a re-light, and then have to do that all over again with Peter from the front and shoot the other half of each scene next week? It's hard to imagine accomplishing that without adding the extra day you don't want. You're really doubling the time for each scene."

"It doesn't sound like we have any choice," said Max, "except that you don't get that extra day. We're not going over."

"I'm sorry, Max," said Joel, "but that puts me in a very difficult position."

"Because?"

"Declan calls them 'hallway scenes,' but I don't consider any scene less important than any other. Now of course you'll point out that when Major Machina takes down Jellyfish, it's far more significant than when Paul Kramer visits some expert at Walter Reade, but not to me, because if the smaller scene doesn't read as credible because the lighting is off on the reverse or the day player gives a shitty performance or it's clear we're shooting over a double, that's what goes viral online, not the big set piece. And who gets blamed? The director."

"That just means you've got to be all the more vigilant about how you shoot this stuff, and with all due respect, I'm getting tired of everyone on this movie complaining about how hard it is for them, especially people making seven and eight figures where I'm writing the checks." He didn't want to speak these words, and in the tone he did, but his frustration over the last several days presented no option.

"Understood," said the director.

"And by the way, I know 'fix it in post' is now considered a joke, people say it so much, but there's a reason people do say it. And we have reshoots scheduled in five months anyway, so let's be real here. Anything that doesn't match, we take care of later, and if you get a bad performance, we re-voice. Jeremy and Charisse, you guys make sure this all happens. Get with James and Joel and Javier and figure it out."

"May I ask a question?" It was the AD, whom Max had met for the first time a half an hour before on the Zoom.

"Tell us what's on your mind, James," he said, "and by the way, you've done a great job from what I hear, especially considering some of the scheduling changes."

"I appreciate your saying so, but it's honestly been everyone. So, this is gonna sound a bit weird, and please forgive me, because I actually really like Peter. I know he hasn't been easy, especially with Joel, and that has pissed me off at times, but he's been good to my department and always on time. He's also truly irreplaceable and works his ass off, so don't take what I'm about to suggest the wrong way."

"Go on."

"Well . . . and again, I know this is a whole thing, especially with it being an issue during the strike two years ago, but we do have scans of every actor we've taken every day of the shoot, including, of course, Peter. You guys make it mandatory. Every new scene, every new wardrobe or makeup change. Plus we shoot balls and color cards on every set. And you have reshoots planned that ostensibly would involve Peter."

"I see where you're headed."

"Casting did a great job with the double, whom, if I'm not mistaken, Peter had to approve. I remember that because we had to wait to put his name on the call sheet. And the guy is a great match, even if he's a bit into himself. I mean, he even kind of moves like Peter. Half the time I walk on set and, especially from behind, I don't know who's who."

"Joel?" asked Max.

"You're asking me if I'm willing to shoot the double from the front, and we plaster Peter's face on in post from a performance he'll deliver later? What do you think I'm going to say to that?"

"You're going to say, 'Max, I'll discuss it with the VFX team and see what exactly is possible with technology that's evolving by the minute,' and we'll see because what the hell else are we going to do with half a day that's costing Sparta thousands of dollars a minute?"

"Understood."

"Jeremy and Charisse, get Joel together with the VFX guys, see what everyone says, and report back to me."

"Will do."

⚡

That had been the day before. It was now halfway through Friday, with no sign of Peter Compton. But the shoot was moving forward with two scenes of Paul Kramer's double rushing down corridors—one at an aquarium, the other at Stanford University.

"Please don't make me shoot him saying the lines," the director had said to Jeremy. "It's not fair to me and it's not fair to Peter. I'm a director of actual human beings interacting with one another. Otherwise, get an animator in here."

"Suddenly the guy has balls," Jeremy said to Max. "What do you want me to do?"

"Lose the dialogue. I don't want to read in the trades that there's a scene with lines in one of our movies where the actual actor wasn't on set. That's all we need, and it sounds like the kind of thing Joel wouldn't be able to keep his mouth shut about. He's never directing a movie with us again, I don't care how good the dailies have been. None of this has been worth it."

"You're blaming Joel for Peter?"

"What is it I always hear? It's a director's medium? Well, then directors get to be credited when things don't work."

"I feel like I should take some of the blame too."

"We all should, Jeremy. For hiring Peter; bringing on his enabling wife, who in spite of herself can't control him; picking Joel, Javier, all of it. Movies are chemistry. All the ingredients have to be right and measured in ways that don't combust. Let's just get this one finished."

"What a selfish bastard."

"Yeah, well, addiction is a nasty disease."

"I'm sorry, Max, but I don't have a lot of sympathy for a guy getting paid in two days what I'll make working for over a year."

⚡

He punched on to the Zoom to behold the same bank of faces he'd seen the day before when the video had dropped of Peter striking his wife.

"How are you, Marci?" he asked the square that bore only the letters of her name.

"I'm all right. I hope you guys won't mind I'm going to do this on audio. I'm not exactly in a state to be seen."

"Whatever you need," he answered, "though everyone on this call loves and admires you, and that's true in whatever state you are. I, for one, would love to look you in the eyes and let you know that, but I guess you can see me and that's enough."

"We all echo what Max said," offered Cynthia. Public relations mystified Max, if only because he couldn't imagine a person actually desiring a career in it, and yet some of the shrewdest people he knew, most of them women, absolutely thrived in the vocation. Their work had more than paid for the price of Sparta having an in-house team.

"So look, everyone," said Marci from her name, "I've written a personal statement that Marnie will read. We were up half the night crafting it, and you should all thank her for throwing out my first draft, which was pretty angry."

"No one could blame you, sweetie," said Cynthia.

"Thanks, Cynthia. So if it's all right with everyone, Marnie?"

"Okay," said Marnie Applebaum, the closest iteration Max had encountered of Woody Allen's line from *Deconstructing Harry* "Jewish with a vengeance." This included rabbis on four continents and a number of Israeli presidents. "First of all," she continued, "let's all give it up to Marci for putting out a statement at all after what's been written online about her and Peter, not to mention the insidious inferences characterizing her as a victim or an enabler, neither of which she is." Max blanched somewhat at the word "enabler," having himself used it to describe Marci on his earlier call.

"We agree," said Cynthia. "And thank you, Marci."

"Please just read it, Marnie, so we can put it out," Marci urged.

"Fine. It's not long. We cut it down considerably. 'Yesterday my husband, Peter Compton, accidentally struck me as I attempted to help him in an emotionally fraught moment addressing the crew on the set of *Major Machina*. Setting aside that this video never should have been shot or shared, what it does not show are the seconds just before when Peter was stating his gratitude to the crew for standing behind him and our film as we complete it. Peter did not intend to strike me. He did so with a gesturing hand, which would be abundantly clear had the clearly hostile person who shot and shared this video not edited it out. My husband loves me and is filled with remorse for this accident. I not only accept that, but I love him more than ever in this difficult time. The rest is between us. Our intention is to finish this extraordinary film together standing side by side, so that Sparta can share it with audiences in America and around the world. In the words of Paul Kramer, 'It's time we finish this.'"

"I love it," said Cynthia. "You guys couldn't honestly have done better. It's confident but not angry. It's positive. There's a bit of a soft underbelly with the 'stand by my husband' part, but the way you state it is all about your strength. Hillary could have taken a page out of your book."

"I don't know about that," answered Marci.

"I'm serious. Max, I think this is great."

"Anybody else want to comment?" asked Max. "Go ahead, Jillian."

"I'm just not sure about the quote from Paul Kramer at the end. There was that article in *Vanity Fair* last year about our movies making too many references to themselves. Plus, it isn't out yet. I guess it could be seen as a teaser, but people aren't going to know what it means."

"I actually think Jillian is right," said Marci. "When I wrote it I thought it would be a nod to what we're all working on, which should be our focus, but now it does feel a little too cute."

"Cynthia?" asked Max.

"Agreed. Let's cut it."

"So I end with 'so that Sparta can share it with audiences in America and around the world'?"

"Perfect."

"Good," said Max.

"And you guys are putting this one out?" asked Cynthia.

"Absolutely," said Marnie. "I'm sending it over to Scott right now."

"Marci," asked Max, "how can we help you?"

"Well, you've got security dealing with the police, which is great, otherwise I wouldn't have been able to report him missing yet in terms of the time span. He's not at any of the nicer hotels, at least under his own name or where anyone on staff recognized him. If he uses his credit card we're going to know about it. He's turned off his location on his phone, which how he did that without an assistant I couldn't tell you."

“He’s going to surface.”

“This is the longest we’ve gone without speaking since our first date.”

“And when he comes back it will be the longest you’ll ever go.”

“After I punch his lights out? We’ll see.”

TWENTY-FOUR

"Let me tell you a little about myself, Peter," the reverend said when George excused himself. "I don't sit in this office as an expert or some kind of guru or judge. I'm a guy who's maybe been where you've been who can listen to you describe where you want to be and maybe help you get there and stay there. That's it."

"Okay."

"So why don't we start with that. What is it you want right now?"

"What do I want?"

"Why are you sitting in my office?"

"George called it an intervention."

"You don't seem like you've been using."

"I haven't been."

"Do you intend to?"

"Absolutely."

"How long have you been sober?"

"Sixteen years."

"That's a pretty serious investment to throw away."

"I've already thrown it away."

"And how's that?"

"You don't go on the internet?"

"I guess not where I'd know what you're referring to."

"Do you know who I am?"

"You look familiar. I'm guessing if I went to movies, which I don't, I'd know your name."

"You would."

"You must be very successful. You'd throw all that away too?"

"Looks like it."

"Then what are you doing in this office?"

"What?"

"If you're gonna use you're gonna use. I'm interested in cats who don't want to use."

"You're telling me to leave?"

"Quite the opposite. I'd like you to stay. I'd like that more than just about anything in my life right now."

"Then maybe I'm not understanding."

"I want you to not want to use, but that's up to you."

"So I can walk out of here right now?"

"This ain't a jail."

Peter rose.

"I do think you owe George the respect of waiting till he comes back, though. That's what a man would do, especially when someone put himself out for you the way George did."

"I'll wait for him in the main room."

"Suit yourself. And leave the door open. That's how I like it. The door here is always open."

"It wasn't when we got here."

"It was, actually. Open a crack. Just enough to see if a person's ready to open it wider. And it'll still be open when you are."

"I'll keep that in mind."

He found the restroom empty, its door ajar, with a waft of recent use.

"Did you see the guy I came in with?" he asked the Sudoku player.

"Nope," responded the man without looking up.

I think I've found the one place in America where I can actually be anonymous, he said to himself. That alone would be reason enough to stay.

He stepped to the front door and made his way into the harsh daylight. His first challenge was removing himself as far from the halfway house as he could and as quickly as he could. He had his phone, its location tracker disabled, and on it his Uber and Lyft accounts. But since Marci had access to both, it would be too easy for her to find him simply by summoning up the most recent fares. As he walked west on Trinity, he wished he'd taken the time to change more of his clothes. It wasn't that the outfit was garish in a way that might call attention; in fact it conformed to the muted palette Joel Slavkin and his designers had chosen for the civilian world of the film. It was more the old-world cut and out-of-season fabric that made him conspicuous in ways that might inhibit transparency. And yet, because the movie was the first in a franchise, from which no images had been published, it did act as a kind of disguise. In furtherance of this he checked his breast pocket and found the Paul Kramer wire frames, donning them as he turned right to walk north on Forsyth. Up ahead he saw Marietta Street and realized he was a block from Woodruff Park. He walked to the intersection of Peachtree and Edgewood and entered the plaza.

Two drunks and a junkie languished at the base of the *Phoenix* statue. Peter gazed up at the bare-breasted woman being lifted by the mythological bird, a representation of Atlanta rising after Sherman set her afire.

"You from the future or the past?" asked one of the drunks, one of whom was black and the other white. It was the black one.

"Pardon?"

"You sure as shit ain't from right now."

Peter wondered if the query was inspired by his suit and eyewear or the vagrant's deeper understanding of his liminal state. "What does it look like?" he chose to ask.

"Depends on what you fixin' to do."

"I guess I'm about to order a cab."

"Cab to nowhere," said the man with a vague gesture in a tone suggesting the poetic.

"Something like that," said Peter.

"I was in quite a fix myself. Had a situation yesterday in Alpharetta. You been there?"

"Can't say I have."

"Place is like in a movie. Like a family movie. Or you seen that Jim Carrey picture?"

"*Pet Detective*?"

"The fuck is a pet detective?"

"*Ace Ventura*? Jim Carrey plays a guy who solves crimes related to pets."

"Not no motherfuckin' pet detective. In this picture everybody was in a movie but him. Well, they was all in the movie, but this was a movie inside the movie."

"*The Truman Show*."

"That was the name of the picture. Only he weren't no president, just a normal guy."

"I saw it."

"Right before he come out his house, folks'd get in place and he'd appear and they'd start moving. Whole thing is televised and the whole country tuned in to watch."

"Right."

"Well, Alpharetta's like that. Like the set of that show that he don't know it's a set. All perfect. They got shops up there, a town square, grocery store, restaurants, place to get coffee. Several places to get coffee. Apartments. You wouldn't never have to leave, is what I'm sayin'. And clean. Ain't never seen anything like it."

"Sounds amazing."

"Do it, though? I mean, I thought so at first."

"How'd you end up there?"

"Don't remember," he said, as if he'd yet to consider this feature of the story. "But I was surely there, which seems lately to be more important. Know what I'm saying?"

"I guess I don't."

"Used to be it was the gettin' there or the where to get. Now it's the bein'."

"So what happened?"

"The fuck you mean?"

"In where was it you said? Alphaville? That's a movie too, by the way."

"Alpharetta. Right. I rolled up in the town square–type area. Had me a forty. Couple, three forties, matter of fact. Decided to spend the whole day there. They got kids runnin' around, families, games, live music. Thought to myself I ain't ever gonna quit this place. I'm tellin' you, like heaven. American heaven. And the food. Folks leavin' whole plates full. Didn't even have to dig through the trash."

"Is that what you do to eat?"

"Not when I can avoid it. Got to playin' a game with these kids. Boys. Two of 'em. And the both of 'em darker'n me. Where you throw a little bag of beans into a hole. And I swear to you, havin' the time of my life. Like I was a little boy again myself. Apropos of my question earlier: in a way I was in the past."

"I see."

"And this man, and I'm gonna just take a swing here and say it was these youngsters' father, he come to wanna shoo me along like he's the sheriff of Alpharetta Square. And that situation, I'm here to tell you, it went from mother-fuckin' bliss to some kind of not-bliss and faster'n you can sneeze, because let me tell you, Jack, I'm a small piece of leather, but I'm well put together."

"You two got in a fight?"

"Somethin' like that. Turns out the man was higher'n I was. The both of us thrown in jail. They asked if I wanted to press charges seein' as how he threw the first punch. There was witnesses. I said, 'What does that involve?' They said, 'Well, you gotta come to the courthouse in a couple weeks.' I said, 'Come back up here? Never want to set foot in this place again in my life.' And now here I am under this bitch bein' carried away half naked by a bird."

"That's quite a story."

"And what's yours?"

Peter thought. "I guess I'm a superhero. Can't you tell?"

"Then you done answered my question."

"How's that?"

"You in the goddamn past!" After which the drunk wouldn't stop laughing, repeating his conclusion over and over as if doing so were essential not only for Peter's benefit but for the vagrant beside him, the incarnation of Atlanta being pulled aloft, and every passerby tracing an ellipse in avoidance of this raving man addressing a bespectacled figure dressed in the garb of another time. "You in the goddamn past! You in the goddamn past!" he kept saying, his voice growing hoarse from such voluble glee.

On the edge of the park Peter managed the unlikely feat of hailing a cab in Atlanta.

"You were just driving around looking for a fare?" he asked.

"On my way home, you want to know the truth of it," said the heavyset man who looked to be in his fifties. "I own this albatross."

"This cab?"

"This cab."

"Lucky me."

"Thank Uber."

"How's that?"

"Gotta make my payments. Fourteen-hour days and any hire I can get."

He saw the silver Cayenne, George at the wheel, parked in front of the Four Seasons from half a block away. "Keep driving," he told the cabbie.

"You got it. So what's your next project?"

"I'm not him."

"Who are you then?"

"Somebody who looks like him."

"You sound like him too."

"Yeah, well . . ."

"You mind if I get a picture?" the man asked at the hotel's loading dock, where Peter realized he should have requested to be left in the first place.

"I told you I'm not him."

"I could tell people you were him."

"It would be a lie," he said, paying in cash and doubling the fee with his tip.

He hadn't seen Raymond since the last time he'd stayed at the hotel, for the photo shoot with Marci and Giovanni at Arrabbiata's chef's table.

"Shit, Peter," said the sandy-haired dealer who'd worked the day shift as a bellman since well before Peter became clean. Back then Raymond had been in his twenties. In his late thirties now, the occupational look wasn't so flattering, though he had somehow escaped suspicion from his employer. Or perhaps his popularity among certain repeat guests the hotel would rather not lose made him something of a commodity. He was also one of only three whites among the greeting staff. "That's quite the getup," he said. "If you're trying to blend in you might just go with jeans and a sweatshirt. Maybe a Braves cap."

"So you got my text?"

"I'm standing here, ain't I? You sure about this, Peter?"

"I can control myself."

"Actually, you can't. You never could."

"Are we gonna figure this out or what?"

"Up to you, I guess."

"That's exactly right." He opened his wallet and peeled off five of the seven one-hundred-dollar bills folded there as per diem since he'd flown in for a costume fitting three months prior.

"So it's the same drill, but a different location. Go up to Crescent, make a right, then walk to Eleventh. You're gonna see a place called Manny's. Ask for Demetrius and say Raymond is good."

"I can't walk there."

"Why not?"

"I can't go a block anywhere anymore, especially in midtown."

"Lemme buzz the stand, tell 'em I'm gonna cut loose for a bit."

He made the call, and they descended to the lowest level, where Raymond parked his Challenger, bright orange with a black racing stripe and tinted windows.

"I really don't think this vehicle says loudly enough what you really do."

"Fuck, man, I just couldn't resist it. Especially when me and my wife are always drivin' up to Savannah."

"You're married now?"

"To the most beautiful woman you've ever seen. And guess what else? She's four months pregnant, and when that baby's born, I'm out of here. Got my GED last year and on to the next chapter."

"You're gonna stop?"

"I'm open to the notion."

"Good for you."

Manny's revealed itself to be a hookah bar. When they entered, a track by a rapper named Young Dolph played so loudly in the nearly empty establishment that the floor shook. Two women, perhaps prostitutes, perhaps not, sat languidly at the bar with drinks before them that looked to be of the tropical variety, pink with ice, umbrellas, and straws. One of them sucked on a hookah, blowing a fragrant, colorless mist out toward the dance area, where a single couple danced in half-paced synchrony with the pounding beat. Peter checked his watch. It was four in the afternoon. Perhaps the place had just opened for the day.

"He in the back?" Raymond shouted toward the two women.

"He sure is, honey," one of them answered. "Ain't you gonna come say hi?"

"Don't start what you ain't gonna finish," he admonished with a grin.

"Oh, I won't."

"And ain't you heard I'm married?"

"I heard."

Both women were big and fit and in their early thirties and wore stretch tops that dipped low enough that Peter had to look away for fear of not being able to. One had an exposed midriff that pooched slightly from how she sat. Thick hair sprung a good six inches from her head in every direction and fell densely across broad shoulders. Her lips were painted a rich shade of burgundy.

"You who I think you are?" she asked.

"I'm not sure," he answered.

"What are you wearing those glasses for?"

"You want me to take them off?"

"Them clothes is wack," said the other woman.

"I like them. They're different, and you pull them off," said the original speaker.

"I like your clothes."

"He want to see if he could fit inside 'em," said the other woman.

"Be quiet, Dawn."

"He wouldn't know what to do with you."

"You're a great actor," she said, ignoring her friend. "I saw the movie you did where you played the bank robber with the girl who didn't know."

"*Honeymoon Heist*."

"You did all those voices."

"I'd always wanted to play a character like that."

"So you gonna join us or what?"

"Give us some time Bella, we gotta see Demetrius," said Raymond.

She pointed at Peter. "Bring this one back when you're done."

They left Bella and her friend and made their way past the two dancers.

"Tell me about her," said Peter.

"By the time she's done with you, you'll have spent a lot more than you just gave me."

"She's a hooker?"

"Doesn't need to be, but that don't mean she can't make a man part with his money and whatever else she wants."

"Seems like there's a little more to her than that."

"I wasn't being negative."

They entered a long hallway leading to a door at the back. The air was loud with pot. Because he'd been clean for so long and was who he was, he mostly encountered the smell when passing through it on the street or perhaps at a party from a distance. Few ever smoked in front of him, but even the faintest whiff had its impact. At fourteen he was getting high daily, often upon waking. He wondered how much more powerful his brain would be had he abstained even by half. "I'd be the smartest man alive," he once told Marci. What he didn't admit was that he meant it. Would it all be over with Marci if he did what he was about to do? If he then emerged from the room to canoodle with Bella on the barstool? What of it? My wife has no idea what it's like to be me or, even worse, be me married to her. I have all the attention and recognition, but she enjoys the benefits without pressure or deficit. She hasn't been stripped of all privacy. She's not forced to look a certain way, be a certain way, play parts she doesn't want to play, and, what's more, be owned by a public to the extent you don't even know who you are anymore.

Tonight he would act not for others but for him. And when he emerged from wherever it was he was headed, he could worry once more about who and what he needed to be. That was the beauty of partaking with measured abandon. One started with sating the simplest hunger, and if done in the right proportions gradually, pleasure unfolded until one had no sense of time, place, doubt, trepidation, conscience, responsibility. He could even forget he'd augmented his reality, so thorough was the condition inside of it. In this way experiences could actually become more real, not the opposite: the perfect contradiction. In all his years of being clean, interacting with this dichotomy was what he missed most. Marci couldn't begin to understand the challenges of his existence without substances.

And what about berating him as she had? Had she not learned, from over a decade with him, that the very worst condition you could create was to make an addict feel cornered, morally and otherwise? When you offered no chance at dignity, he had to spite you by spiting himself. An addict would always prove you right if you exhibited no faith in him.

So pungent was the smoke that Peter expected billows of it as the door opened. Instead he entered a space of cool light from an energy-saving bulb that coiled nakedly from the ceiling where a fixture might once have diffused it. The walls were wood paneled and mostly unadorned, save for a whiteboard with a calendar drawn in blues, reds, and greens that stretched along one of the short sides of the rectangular space. A large African American man, most likely Demetrius, reclined in a swivel chair behind a desk, the soles of black high-tops facing Peter and Raymond as they entered. Two other men, one black and one white, sat across from him. The white guy, who looked to be in his early fifties with ruddy skin, short-cropped hair, and a ball cap worn backward and slightly askew, drew from a blunt he then passed to his neighbor. To Peter's right, on the side of the room opposite Demetrius and his guests, sat another man, black with a bouncer's build, at a wall of security monitors, presumably from cameras fixed at a dozen or so spots both inside and outside the establishment.

"My man Raymond, as I live and breathe," said Demetrius. "Why you ain't over at the castle droppin' the bridge across the moat?"

"Took an hour off."

"And you brought a movie star, or does he just look like a movie star?"

"You'll have to ask him."

"*Major Machina*. I about nutted when I read you were playin' Paul Kramer. Great piece of casting. You see this here," he said to the two men sitting before him, "he's even dressed like him."

"Sup?" said the white guy from under his cap, his informality not so gracefully matched with his late age.

"Hey, man," said the gentleman sitting next to him, who looked to be about thirty, his dark skin clear and dewy like that of an infant. He was heavy and contentedly inert, raising a thick hand languidly to shake Peter's. With the other he offered the blunt. "You want some of this?"

It was that simple, that easy. Peter coaxed with his hand after he'd shaken that of his new acquaintance and took the cheroot. He paused to behold it while everyone observed. Were they aware what this would mean? Of course each was. His life was everyone's.

"You can step back," said Raymond.

"Why would he want to do that?" asked Demetrius. "The couple days this man has had?"

"Yeah," said Peter, "why would I want to do that?" He put the blunt to his lips and drew—not as the man sharing it had done, in a casual manner as if enjoying one of a dozen cigarettes from a pack that came from a carton on hand, but as he'd learned to when weed was illicit and precious. He pulled the smoke deeply into his lungs and held it there for as long as his body would allow, willing himself not to exhale.

"Motherfucker's goin' old-school," said Demetrius. "Get you another, just so I can peep that technique one more time."

Peter did. His body warmed with a familiar and sympathetic bliss, no longer at odds with itself. Yes, a brief sadness presented, mourning so many years of rectitude, but the haze of goodwill rendered such concerns nugatory. Why, his whole body seemed to ask, had he been so stupidly abstemious when the rewards for not being so were this profound? Moreover, he'd proven now that not only could he stop, but he could do so for an extended period—the last one comprising a good 30 percent of his life. Tomorrow, or perhaps the day after, he would commit once more to the monotony of restraint. Tonight needed to count.

"You cryin', man?" asked the white guy in the cap. "Motherfucker's cryin'! What you cryin' for, dude?"

"I just missed this," said Peter, knowing this described something more akin to its opposite, but too confused and startled by how quickly things were happening. As unlike him as this was, he simply couldn't summon the suitable words.

TWENTY-FIVE

When he first learned photography, his sister emphasized two essentials: that the viewer always felt Javier's relationship with his subject 1) spatially and 2) attitudinally, even if the latter meant neutrality. It was about sharing not only *what* he had seen but *how* he had seen it.

"Don't ever cheat," she emphasized. "What and how you see in the camera is what the viewer has to encounter."

"But my eye and the lens don't see in black and white or with a lot of grain."

"Exactly, *mijo*. But you have to remember the second part of what I said, which is just as important, if not more so. The *how*. Once your object is seen, it becomes subject. Both you and the object understand that."

"Not if I'm shooting a door or a chair or a tree."

"Even then."

"No."

"There was this physicist in Germany who figured out that anything observed changes as a result. He fucking proved it. It's called the 'observer effect,' and he used it to develop a theory that can be applied to everything: the uncertainty principle. It's based on the fact that you can't observe a thing or system without having an effect on it. And if that's true with molecules, it's fucking true with people and things that are made up of molecules. Just by being there in front of it, you change a door or a chair."

"I just don't believe you."

"It was scientifically proven. A thing becomes a thing observed. You form a relationship with it. And that takes into account everything you plan in terms of sharing what has become its subjectivity. It's going to be in black and white?

You're pushing the film for more grain? You're going to use a contrast filter when you print it? Fine. When you look through the lens, see your subject in black and white, grainy, high contrast, whatever. And guess what? Half the time you won't take the picture because you'll decide that while it might be interesting, the light and positioning and contrast are wrong for black and white no matter what you do or where you stand. Let the subject communicate with you in that way. Let it change from your having observed it, whether it's a person or not. You're rolling your eyes, you little monster, but you're going to learn I'm right. This isn't mumbo jumbo. And if you think in these terms instead of resisting it, imagine how great you'll be when it's a person you're shooting, because you're not going to deny this is the case with people when a camera is pointed at them. They absolutely change."

"Of course, but that feels different."

"It's all about the truth of subjectivity, because objectivity, which is supposed to mean truth, actually has no truth because it doesn't exist."

"Why not?"

"I just explained it, *mijo*. Once we see a thing, it's no longer what it was."

"So then nothing is true."

"But a photograph, for its fraction of a second, gets pretty fucking close. If you do it honestly, it presents *your* truth: how you saw and interpreted a thing. And the beauty of it is that while it's that close to being true, it's now a record of that truth only in that moment, because the thing was changing already when you captured it. That's the tradition you're working in. So don't fuck around and use it to tell lies."

"How would I do that?"

"By sharing moments that aren't really yours. Your relationship with your work always has to be about trying to be as pure in your dialogue with your subject as possible."

"Of course."

"You say that, but it's not so easy."

"Like when a person tells me how to photograph them?"

"Well, that's tricky, because it's its own kind of truth. Maybe you agree and you capture that commonality in an expression of contentment or even self-satisfaction on your part and theirs, or you disagree and the frustration shows up. But you might take a picture of a building, and instead of relating to it in a way that's yours, you get into the mind of your viewer and you think, What do they want to see? instead of, What do I, as the photographer, *actually* see?"

Taking portraits of dinner guests at Avenida Ámsterdam, he began truly to understand how important a gift his sister had yet again given him, because his best images captured his subjects not only as they truly and naturally were, but in a conspicuous relation to him and his camera. Subjectivity, in other words, was not only confessed but foregrounded, both by Javier and the person being photographed.

When he started shooting films, he wondered how this would apply. Movies, after all, weren't ultimately orchestrated by him but by the director, and the more formal relationship in terms of subjectivity occurred between that person and the actors or objects or vistas being photographed, not Javier. This also happened at twenty-four frames a second. Thus, a series of photographed truths conspired to connote a lived and breathed experience rather than a single moment of one. Music and foley and sound design would then be added, in addition to dialogue. The director would then shape it all with an editor and postproduction sound mixer. How could he apply what he'd learned taking pictures of luminaries at his parents' dinner table or prostitutes and hustlers in Zona Rosa to shooting characters in movies where so many others imposed as much subjectivity as he?

"Look at it as refraction," his sister offered. "Remember that you can do things a director can't or, if he was once a DP, he doesn't want to do anymore, so you take his subjectivity into account and make that part of the conversation. In other words, it's no longer just you and the subject; it's you and the subject and the director's point of view all in conversation, and suddenly you're as essential as ever. After all, remove you and there's no image."

"But what if the director and I don't speak the same language aesthetically?"

"Then don't work with him! And your language always has to be the truth of the dialogue with the director, the truth of the relationship with your subjects, and the truth of your experience, even if that experience involves challenges. Once things start to seem fabricated in a way that strays from that, fight it with everything you can. And I'm not talking about unreality. Some of the best films you'll ever shoot will tell stories that could never happen and in places that don't exist. Things from fantasy or nightmares. It's when you're not allowed to tell the truth with your camera within the reality you've agreed on that you need to pack your things and go home."

Looking back over his career, his best work involved varied iterations of what his sister had so clearly advised. And far from feeling subordinated by these directors, he felt embraced, cherishing their keen sense of how the story being told could be seen. Moreover, when he saw the finished versions, it was as if he'd truly had a hand in making them. Not only do I see the film we shot, he could say to himself, but I see a collective truth. We all were there with a common sense of what we'd captured, even when the process itself was sometimes difficult.

It therefore didn't surprise him that the moment Peter Compton struck his wife, a restlessness began to inflect the shooting, springing from Marci Levy's almost provocative insistence that work commence. The film's heretofore unmanageable star had just smacked his wife in the jaw, and within half an hour there he was, rehearsing with Joel Slavkin and dutifully taking the director's side when one of the day players objected to the staging.

Javier checked the false color on his monitor to gauge the toplight. "Bump the fresnels in the grates ten percent," he told his gaffer.

"They're pretty hot as it is."

"Just do it."

It was the right choice. The sheer outrageousness of what had happened, the crew now on edge, along with the actor's restless shame, supplied a harshly perfect ambiguity: the stuff of which great performances were made. It called for stronger highlights and deeper shadow. Peter Compton had never seemed so interesting, his close-up downright dangerous. It's too bad, thought Javier, that if he was going to strike the poor woman, he didn't do it on the first day so it could have inflected the entire performance. He'd win a fucking Oscar. The day before the actor had been wounding others. Now he had wounded himself. As confounding as it was, Javier wanted suddenly to be nowhere else but standing there to capture it.

But with the star's sudden disappearance, the film, as happened too frequently to count, lurched from the unexpectedly magical to the worst kind of cynicism. They spent the remainder of the day shooting from behind the idiot double onto two-day players. Told of the new video Javier refused to watch, he then returned to his apartment in Cabbagetown fully expecting to resume shooting with a chastened Peter the following morning.

Instead he and Joel were called to the producers' trailer an hour before call, Marci noticeably absent.

"Are we waiting for her?" he asked, knowing how she tended to dominate such confabs, even when speaking less than anyone.

"She's at home."

"With Peter?"

"This isn't public knowledge."

"Okay."

"No one knows where Peter is."

Javier looked to Declan and Joel, who sat low on a faux leather sofa along the door side of the interior. Why do the people who do the least amount of work tend to get the most capacious on-set accommodations? he wondered. Of course, what would he do with a big trailer? He didn't stop working during lunch, instead going over shots with Joel, augmenting the schedule with James, or reviewing plots or pre-rigs with his team.

"Which is why we're here," said Declan, who looked to have gone without sleep for days. "I'll let Jeremy explain."

"The mandate has come down that we need to keep shooting. Max is not interested in extending the schedule."

There was a knock at the door.

"Great," said Charisse. "That's Anton and Nazak."

"It's like a convention," said Javier, not adding that it would now comprise a majority of his least favorite people on set, with Declan already present. Anton and Nazak supervised visual effects, and Javier had taken to calling them the "*Sí* Twins." Though of dissimilar size and build, they rarely appeared apart, and no matter the question, they always answered in the affirmative, and since this was a Sparta movie on which every department had a strict budget except for visual effects, they could justify such persistent can-do optimism knowing their resources to be unlimited. "Can we fix her hair so it matches the master shot?" "Yes." "Can we paint in the cloudy sky from yesterday and eliminate all the shadows?" "Yes." "Can we remove the plane? The trees? The helicopter? The grip who walked into the shot? All the signs? All the buildings?" "Absolutely, *yes*!"

He also found himself and his department unfathomably vulnerable to their demands, especially when it came to lighting. As but one example, he'd entered a set originally to have been shot at the Hoover Dam in which Jellyfish summoned hydroelectric power for his third act showdown with Major Machina. The promise of the location had been one of the reasons he'd signed on to do the movie, not only for the massive scale of the place but for its lore as a Hitchcock backdrop in *Saboteur*. Instead, on the biggest stage in Atlanta, they hung an enormous green curtain awash in light from a battery of LEDs where the dam would be filled in months later by artists on other continents. Not only did this limit his ability to shape light on his characters or to expose in the way he'd like, but it subordinated him to a department that as an occupational rule demystified every aspect of storytelling to the practicalities of the ones and zeros that represented their solution to any problem.

In no time at all such people had come to dominate effects-driven films. Not only did nearly every shot on *Major Machina* (including some close-ups) need to be approved by VFX, but a version without actors had to be delivered, regardless of any anticipated need. Additionally he had to film some idiot standing there on an otherwise empty set with a mirrored ball and a color board. These requirements snatched easily an hour from each day, a fact never accounted for by the director and AD when they scheduled, meaning effectively less time for Javier and his team to light, build track, balance the Steadicam, rehearse camera moves, and meet whatever other exigencies presented themselves.

"Hey, guys!" said Anton. "What did we miss?"

He grinned at the room, then dipped his head to the straw poking from his coffee beverage. Of course he's one of these *jodidos* who adulterates his espresso with milk and flavoring, thought Javier. Anton had attended CalArts and at thirty-five owned his own company. He stood just over five feet six with sandy hair and thick brows. A vintage plaid blazer opened to a black T-shirt with the Tasmanian Devil emerging from his dervish, daring anyone to mistake him for management.

Nazak, the daughter of parents who'd escaped the Islamic Revolution in Iran, was probably in her early forties. She had a pristine dark complexion and big eyes. Lean, tall, and less voluble, she was the smarter and harder working of the two. He was meant to bring the charm, she most everything else.

"Have a seat," said Jeremy, gesturing to two remaining chairs at the trailer's dining table. "We were just about to bring Javier up to speed."

"Great," said Anton.

"Please do," said Javier. "It must have to do with the work today, which obviously can't go on without Peter."

"I want to remind you that what I told you earlier stays in this trailer," said Jeremy. "Anton and Nazak and obviously Joel know, but let's not be so free in assuming that about anyone else."

"We don't have Peter. All of today's scenes are with Peter."

"I was getting to that."

"Is that why these two are here? Are they part of your solution?"

"That's exactly right."

"I'm going to say again that every scene left in the movie involves Peter. They might not be big scenes, but he speaks to people, and I need to shoot the actor from the front—a remaining standard in this industry when people are addressing others on film—to give the director what he needs. Unless, of course, Joel has agreed to cover everything from behind with the double."

"I haven't," said Joel.

"You guys are not going to be limited in terms of what you can shoot or from where," said Jeremy.

"In what reality could that be true?"

"We're going to film the double."

"From the front?"

"That's right."

"Saying the lines?"

"Yes."

Javier turned to Anton. "And you motherfuckers told him and Joel you can make it all work in the *pinche* computer?"

"As a stopgap, yes," said Anton. "Between the scans of Peter we've taken every day and all the footage, it'll actually be quite easy, particularly if you guys shoot scenes where he has the least amount of dialogue. Obviously Peter will eventually need to come onto a stage in LA for half a day, you re-create the lighting for the tighter coverage, you shoot the master however you like, he says all the lines, we do a composite from that and the scans we've been doing, record the voice, and there you go."

"I'm not shooting anything."

"Oh boy," said Jeremy.

"And you don't need me to. This asshole is going to be making the image, not me or any of my guys."

"That's ridiculous, Javier. We're talking about face replacement—not even that, compositing—in a few shots," said Jeremy.

"What you call compositing is so huge for me and so clearly small for you it makes me want to scream. You all realize, because I know Declan went complaining to you about it, that we are carrying three lens packages on this movie. Panavision C Series anamorphics. Each set is tuned for the part of the story we're telling. One for Jellyfish, one for Paul Kramer when he's in the civilian world, and then the Major Machina look. Even when you let us have all this, you guys were rolling your eyes because Anton here and probably everyone in post were telling you it could all be done in the DI. And you know what, and this will surprise you when I say it, they were mostly right. But in the end all of you are wrong."

"Why's that?" asked Anton, aggressively amused.

"Because a movie still lives and dies based on what happens on set. When I watch rehearsals, especially in close-ups, I'm watching performance and making changes based on what I see to accentuate choices an actor is making or little particulars in the staging. It's why I operate the camera myself in close-ups. When Peter or Ron or Jennifer or any of the actors makes a move—a simple nod, headshake, or look down or to the side—I can react; the camera can be there with them guiding the viewer. It's a dance. And an actor is a dancer. Not a fucking double who's only there because he's the same height and has the same hair color. And not this *pinche* digital compositor." He gestured to Anton.

"You know what, buddy?" said Anton. "I'm this movie's best bet right now. Without me and Nazak, we wouldn't even be in this trailer."

"Okay, let's all just cool down," said Jeremy. "Nobody in here should be questioning the value of what each of us contributes. We've frankly had enough of that this week. I think you've made your case, Javier, as to why shooting with the double can never replace shooting with the actual actor, and no one disagrees. But we don't have Peter. And let's not lose sight of the fact that his absence could mean any number of things. Putting what Marci must be going through aside, he's the center of our film—no disrespect to Joel—"

"None taken."

"And we all love Peter. I mean, the guy was right about one thing he said: he has committed himself to this part. Our job is to keep this film moving, not just for us but for him, while he figures out how to come back to us."

"By shooting with the double? Is that a joke?" asked Javier.

"I honestly don't know how else to proceed."

"I told you. By not shooting."

"Not an option."

"So it's about money."

"Also shooting schedule and release schedule and that no one person's travails should shut down production and have all of us twiddling our thumbs. Sparta is a team. We're all part of that team, including you, no one more important than another."

It astonished Javier how adroit Americans were at contorting sententia to their favor, even when the actual enforcement of a notion meant pursuing the very opposite of the advertised moral. How could Jeremy, not two breaths from having elevated Peter to the position of being the "center" of the film, suddenly be construing everyone to be equally responsible for doing his or her part? In Mexico a producer would at least have said, "I don't give a fuck what you think, you're shooting this because that's what you're being paid to do, otherwise go back to shooting christenings and bat mitzvahs." And this wasn't even to mention the ludicrousness of a producer working for the most cynically capitalist of studios adducing collectivism to drive home a point.

Was Javier supposed to quit? To moot the possibility yet again and not follow through would render him nothing but a shrill impotent. And what of production should he walk off? The operator would take over? His gaffer? Neither of whom had any sense of the finesse the job actually required both aesthetically and personally, given the maelstrom of demands on a nine-figure budget. He couldn't let it happen unless he was willing to pull his name from the film, which in spite of it all he wasn't interested in doing. It haunted him that the movie contained some of the best work he'd ever done at this scale.

"Okay," he said. "I'll shoot with the double."

"That's all we're asking," said Jeremy. "Everyone here knows this is untenable for more than a day."

"Oh, to be clear, I'm not doing this bullshit next week."

"We're dealing with the third video getting out," said Jeremy. "Charisse and I have already written our statement that striking Marci was accidental. You have my word: Monday, Peter is back."

TWENTY-SIX

Cody Dillard always knew he was an actor. It was the subject of much frustration as a forty-five-year-old that he hadn't pursued these impulses decades sooner. Evidence was there: popularity among his cadre of high school pals as the cutup, always ready with imitations of the geometry teacher with the cleft palate or the superannuated principal. His mother even told him more than once, "Cody, I swear, you should be on a stage." He did try out for high school plays but never landed a speaking role. Those, he learned, were reserved for the more conventionally handsome. Besides, he had more interest in drinking and smoking weed. This led to a year of community college from which he dropped out to work for a friend's family's home security company. That job lasted just over fifteen years into his mid-thirties, when he was fired by the friend's uncle who'd taken over the concern and was less patient with Cody's habit of hitting on customers.

"Did it ever occur to you that they hit on me?"

"It absolutely most certainly did not," said the uncle.

"Most of the women who come in here are single, a lot of 'em divorced, which is why they need the security system. What am I supposed to do if they purr? Just ignore it?"

"I'm your employer, not your pimp. And this is a store, not a club."

"Your brother liked me."

"And his annual numbers reflected his taste in the human species. That's why I'm here now and he's in Florida chartering out his fishing boat, the only asset he has left."

Cody couldn't dispute the uncle's disapproval. Once he'd discovered how much donning the compulsory stretch-knit polo shirt with the company logo that was two sizes too small did to expose his chest and guns, he began to exercise militantly. The results, coupled with his easy expertise regarding equipment options, made him an especially appealing purveyor. A willingness to bemoan how his devotion to the safety of others inhibited a social life also proved impactful.

"I'm in this business," he would say, "because I grew up with a single mom where I was the only protection she had."

On some weekends in the year before his firing, he'd be with one customer on a Friday night, another Saturday afternoon, and a third Saturday night and into Sunday. He gobbled more Viagra than anyone under forty he knew.

The job market being what it was, he wasn't out of work for long. He moved to a RadioShack in Edgewood and within two years was its manager. That's when an undeniably handsome young man named Rick Scanlon entered the store on a Tuesday in May to ask for a job.

"It says here you're an actor," Cody remarked.

"That's right."

"So is that like in theater?"

"Movies."

"In Atlanta?"

"More movies shoot here now than LA. I mean, that might not actually be true, but it might as well be, you compare the populations."

"I see the yellow location signs all around with the arrows, but I just figured it was small stuff. Is that the kind of movies you do?"

"First of all, it's big films. TV too. And yes. I went to school for it up at SCAD in Savannah."

"School for what?"

"Acting."

"Then what do you need this job for?"

"I didn't say I get paid a lot. Mostly right now I just work a day here and there, still trying to break in, which is why I was hoping for a job with you."

The deal they made was simple, the clearest of quid pro quos. Rick would be hired, even though his "real job" could mean truancy on any given day should a film or television show need him. In return, he would not only get Cody a meeting with his agent, but the agent would have to agree to represent Cody.

"That's no problem because she handles background artists too. Just looking at you, I know you'll do great. You'll have more opportunities for that than you got time for as a manager at RadioShack, that I can guarantee."

"What's 'background'? Like an extra?"

"That's exactly what it is."

"I want to be an actor."

"My first four jobs were as a background artist, and then a director noticed me and gave me two lines. That's the way you've got to think about this. Be there when your name is called and impress, impress, impress."

Cody signed with the agent and began booking work, though mostly on weekends and after hours when he was available. There were two commercials, one for a local automotive dealership and the other for a cable company. In neither did he have words, but his look and build pleased the respective clients, whose hands he went out of his way to shake. The two others were in crowd scenes for Sparta movies, which for the preceding five years had been shooting more and more in Atlanta because of the tax credit.

"Guess what I just got," he announced to Rick, who'd by then been working at the store for nearly a year.

"What?"

Cody produced the SAG card he'd received the preceding day.

"You're part of the brotherhood!"

"I know."

"Seriously. You're a fuckin' actor now. Same as anyone who walks on that set. You've got the same rights, the same protections, the same vote, the same everything."

⚡

He entered a period of his life in which all seemed to go his way. As the manager of his location, he could shuffle the schedule as he wished so long as doing so didn't negatively impact the bottom line. He therefore hired workers who were flexible with their hours, along with others willing to fill in as needed. This assured that his missing a few days or even a week didn't meaningfully disturb operations. It did involve firing Rick, who was just as unreliable as Cody, but Rick had served his purpose and had also begun to resent Cody, especially when the two would read for the same parts.

When the call came to meet with the line producer to be Peter Compton's stand-in for a Sparta film, it didn't surprise Cody in the least. Yes, he was of identical size and build, and more than a few had even mentioned a resemblance, but something else was at play. The director and producers, and perhaps Peter Compton himself, had surely looked at his reel (by this time, counting the two commercials and half a dozen background appearances, it was a good minute and a half) and seen something. They were grooming him as a backup to one of the industry's biggest stars to play speaking roles. And not only that, should he continue to impress, these parts would only increase in size and number. Why else would he have been selected from among the hundreds available for such a post? Additionally, he was informed that on those days Peter Compton wasn't working, he'd be called to stand in for others "as needed." He would make $1,200 a week for fourteen weeks, less than what he'd clear logging hours at the store, but, as with other bookings, he could make up for that by pocketing the five-dollar-an-hour difference between his managerial wages and what he would pay those he'd bring in to spell him. This was justified since he'd be checking in remotely throughout the day as well as monitoring the video feed on his laptop at background holding.

"Wait," asked Rick derisively on the phone, "you think you're some kind of 'star in training' because you're a fuckin' double? All you're gonna do is stand there when they light. It's the worst fuckin' job on set."

"The producer said they were lucky to have me. He even took me out and showed me his car."

"You'll see."

In spite of Rick's envious pessimism, Cody relished the job. Though never given the full script, he studied each scene assiduously, always ready to do whatever was demanded of him. Sometimes this involved observing Peter during the crew rehearsal and then aping this while the camera department lit the scene and the art department dressed the set. On other days, when Peter was running behind, they would actually stage the scene with Cody, after which he would show Peter where and how he was to move and stand. In such instances, even though he was told exactly what to do by Joel, James, or Javier, he couldn't ignore the magnitude of his contribution. Anyone visiting the set would see him, Cody Dillard, establishing a version of how the scene would be staged and performed.

On the night after Peter struck his wife, he received a call from Declan Morris. In it he was informed that the following day he would be playing the film's lead role opposite other actors and that he would be saying the lines on camera, including in close-ups. He should therefore memorize pages being sent forthwith. Resisting the impulse to call Rick and gloat, he instead rang his agent. When she didn't pick up, he texted.

"What's the emergency, Cody? It's nine thirty."

"Uh, I think you're gonna want to know that tomorrow I'm playing the role of Major Machina in the movie."

"How's that?"

"As in Peter has done a kind of patty melt, if you haven't been reading about it online."

"I saw."

"So while they figure out what to do, I'm stepping in."

"Not possible."

"From the way it was explained, it's a whole digital thing where I do the part while he takes a day to settle down, and then they replace my face with his later. But the thing is, I'm basically playing the role. I mean, how I move, how I say the lines, is gonna be how the scenes are filmed. Shit's happening, Rhonda."

"Slow down, Cody. Just make sure you know your lines and *don't, please* don't, walk onto the set tomorrow morning like you're suddenly number one on the call sheet. In the meantime I'm going to call production and get you a bump."

His pay went from $240 for the day to $350, less than he expected but still considerable. He was also allowed to eat both breakfast and lunch in the main tent where cast and crew dined, rather than in the overcrowded hovel reserved for background. He would even sit with the three other actors working that day rather than in background holding. All this arranged by Rhonda.

But the real frisson came in performing the role, this in spite of undisguised hostility from scene partners no longer afforded the thrill of working opposite Peter. He couldn't blame them. And how were they to know Cody was a card-carrying member of their union? Yet still, it rankled him.

"I'm not sure what's going on," he said to Joel, "but I'm tryin' to do my work here for you as best I know how, and I'm not getting much back from my scene partners."

"What is it you feel you need that they aren't providing?"

"Well, like Robert didn't even look at me during his off-camera lines."

"When the camera was on you?"

"Yeah."

"Well, luckily you won't have that experience again, because we've shot it."

After his close-up, which was shot four times—twice for performance and twice from a botched camera move pushing in on his face—he began to rehearse a conversation with his franchise owner, informing him the time had come to devote himself full-time to film. He had over $18,000 in the bank, which would take care of food and rent for three months. Rhonda had shared several days before that she had no fewer than three auditions lined up for him the week after wrap. With Sparta alone, a television series based on *Jugular* was to begin shooting the following month, along with the much-anticipated *Dagger* origin story soon after.

"You're doing a good job," Declan Morris said at lunch.

Surprised to have been addressed by a man who'd scarcely appeared on set that day, he asked whether the producer might share this assessment with Sparta.

"Who at Sparta?"

"You know, some of the higher-ups."

"Unless you want to speak with Max Kaiser, you don't get higher up than me, which is something I wish a few more people around here understood."

"I didn't mean—"

"Don't worry about it. I'll let them know, though I'm not sure what good it'll do you right now. You might do better to stay as far away from me as possible."

Before he could protest this unlikely fit of self-deprecation from the man with the coolest car he'd ever seen, the producer was gone.

At wrap, when the scene was finished, James the AD stood beside the camera for a frequent ritual, given the size of the movie's cast, and spoke to the crew.

"Everyone, that is a picture wrap on three of our actors today." He announced the names of Cody's scene partners to tepid applause. But he then continued: "And let's also hear it for Cody Dillard, who stepped in as our Paul Kramer and did such a fantastic job!" This time the approbation was nothing short of thunderous.

TWENTY-SEVEN

In the two days since Peter's disappearance, Marci had slept maybe five hours, and these only from a combination of Ambien and Far Niente Chardonnay that could deliver a few hours between updates. Not even the doorman at the Four Seasons who'd helped furnish drugs three hours after Peter had fled the halfway house knew where her husband was, nor did the woman with whom he'd spent a debauched night putting his dick in whatever orifice she chose to offer up. Peter Compton. Some "face of America."

"We can only lean on the local authorities so much, and that's because I have friends in the department," the head of Sparta security told her. "There's a whole thing about not committing more resources to the well-to-do and the connected than to regular citizens, and there's a lot of missing people in Atlanta. Plus, they figure we have our own assets, which we do. You've just got to be patient."

"My husband could be in some alley right now gorked out of his mind, and you're asking me to be patient?"

"No one we or the police have spoken to describes Peter as any more than intoxicated. Either he's going to turn up or we're going to find him."

That had been Friday afternoon, and the trail, such as it was, had gone cold.

It began to occur to Marci that her husband could be dead. "I just know it. I feel it."

"Listen to me, Marci," her mother responded over FaceTime from Southampton, "that's an imaginary horrible, and you do nothing for yourself by indulging it. I'm not saying he isn't perhaps in a bad place right now, because trust me, if you hadn't talked me down I was prepared to buy a gun and take a plane and kill the bastard myself after what he did to you—"

"Mom, it was an accident."

"If you're going to flail your arms, don't flail them near my daughter."

"I should have let him keep speaking."

"Don't blame yourself. We always do that."

"Who's we?"

"Women."

"Really, Mom?"

"It's what you were doing."

"Maybe I was," she admitted.

"Look, I get it. You know how your father and I felt about your marrying this guy. We were scared shitless. Who could blame us? But the one thing that was clear was that he loved our daughter. And our daughter loved him. And from when you could walk, you always wanted adventure, strolling right out into the surf in Mallorca, making your father, God bless the man, take you on the Scrambler at Coney Island. Moving to LA to work in entertainment when you could have done anything with that education you got—business school, law school, investment banking . . ."

"Kill me."

"You wanted the ride, and now you're on it. Big highs and big lows."

"Thanks, Mom, this is really helpful."

"To tell the truth, we all envy you, which you know. But it's the Scrambler all over again and you're strapped in. Make no mistake, Peter loves you too much to throw it all away and do something truly stupid. Twelve hours from now you'll both be on your way to figuring this all out. I promise."

"You don't know addicts."

"I know human beings, and last I heard, addicts are still in the species."

Her mother's words, as always, had brought comfort, but it was now Saturday morning, and those twelve hours had elapsed. Where was he? What was he doing? Did he even think for a moment of her or the hundreds of others his actions were impacting? The thousands of others? The tens of millions, should one count the fans?

“It’s like living with this other person inside me,” he once explained, “and we’re in a death struggle for control over my body and what it wants and needs. This other person will do whatever it takes to win. He also not only hates me, he has no respect for me. He’s like the most rebellious teenager you can imagine relating to a hapless parent. The me who wants not to succumb to partaking is square, out of touch, a killjoy, doesn’t understand. I’m a conformist, boring, uncreative, get good grades but never get laid, have no friends, a desk job guy. This, as opposed to the teenager, who’s brilliant, sexy, sneaking out on weekends when he’s grounded, taking the family car and totaling it but living to tell the story, and everyone wants to be him. He’ll be the guy on the talk show with the audience howling. And he gets in conversations with the square guy, and he says, ‘Come on, what are we going to do with our time here on earth? Are we gonna be like all these other idiots and play by the rules, or are we gonna really live? Plus, you know you want this shit as badly as I do.’ Now sometimes this conversation goes on and on, and sometimes it’s very short, but always, from when I took my first toke on the beach in Malibu when I was twelve, the addict won. And the more he won, the more I hated him and the more I hated myself, because I began to *know* he’d always win, so the conversations weren’t even conversations, they were just tyrannical demands, and the me that was me, and right now *is* me, was simply no longer there. And that was not so interesting anymore for the addict part of me, because he had become this sadist who had to look at himself in the mirror every day and see exactly who he was and what he was doing to me. But remember, he’s an addict, so all he can do is keep doing it, which is why the endgame ultimately for the addict is abstinence or the overdose, because all he knows how to do is keep hold of his power at all costs. He now owns the body completely and he can’t let go. To hand back control and ask for forgiveness just isn’t an option. He has to keep beating me into the ground. Even in his morass of self-hatred he’s relentless, grinding me down as if to say I deserve it for allowing him to vanquish me. He hates me even more now in fact for having let him do it, because if somehow I’d just put up a better fight, he wouldn’t be the awful, disgusting, and utterly toxic being he knows he is.”

"But, Peter," she asked, tears welling not only in empathy for the man she loved but for the descriptive power with which he was able to expose the awful reality of his condition, "how does anyone overcome that? How did you?"

"Well," he said, laughing, "certainly not on my own. That judge at my sentencing hearing who wouldn't let me talk my way out of it was a start. I'm not sure he gave much of a shit about *me* per se, as much as he did about making the system just a tad more fair by treating me like he'd treat anyone else, which is what he should have done and two other judges didn't. Then there was prison, which, make no mistake, you can get drugs in prison, but by that time they were out of my system—which was its own kind of absolute hell—and it was clear to me if I used there I might not die of an overdose but wouldn't be alert and savvy enough to stay alive. Either I'd be on the stuff or wasting most of my energy making sure I could get more. Plus, getting my career back became a mission. I needed to get back at the world. That encouraged me to wake up every day, both there and when I got out, and do to the addict what he had done to me: not just keep him down but utterly destroy him."

"Wow."

"And, of course, I met you. The only chance an addict has is having something to live for. In this case not only a romantic partner, but the absolute best friend I've ever had. I get something that's better than any drug, because even when we fight, when I'm pissed at you or you're not talking to me, my feelings for you are still there. Or if it doesn't feel like it, I'll do whatever it takes to get them back."

"Isn't that another kind of addiction?"

"I'd prefer it to the alternative."

The painful cogency of his description aside, he had little inhibition sharing the reality of his former self (along with some of his more lurid excursions under the influence) in company or even on talk shows, and not without what she would have to call pride. He even advertised enjoyment of such abandon to the extent she actually resented it. She had played completely by the rules—no cocaine, no pills, no hallucinogens, not even speed or an unprescribed sedative—with a 4.0 in high school and a degree cum laude from an elite college. How could she now be considered subordinate to a person with such an irresponsible and sybaritic past?

At dinner parties, forget it. Who wanted to hear about her all-nighter for a paper on the use of the olfactory in *The Guermantes Way* or why reading *Critique of Pure Reason* had altered how she thought about God, when Peter was there to recount waking in bed with two strippers in Mojave without his clothes or wallet, needing to find his way back to Studio City for a 9:00 a.m. call? Even his time in Corcoran and the relapses leading to it, normally evidence of weakness and shame, had outrageous currency. And Peter being Peter, he spent it lavishly, unfolding story after story while listeners, Marci included, marveled at his having come through it all with such charm, such a raconteur's spirit. She'd seen him at least two dozen times hold entire rooms in Malibu, Brentwood, Beverly Hills, and Bel Air utterly spellbound while he recounted lockup and the characters he'd met there. Men wanted to be him. Women (and some men) wanted to fuck him. Peter always won.

And try as she did, she could not imagine how, when he did return, this time would differ. Yes, his shame and her wrath would evince passions and extremes neither had ever levied against each other, but these too would be managed. Heroically the Comptons would, to paraphrase Faulkner, not only endure but prevail. But at what cost to Marci Levy? It would be she, not he, who managed the rebuilding of all he'd destroyed. They'd finish the film, either before or after his rehab at some $5,000-a-night redoubt in the desert where he'd be fawned over and coddled while she dealt with Sparta and the agents and the manager and the publicists. He would even be saved a day's work for his weekend bender, needing only to waltz onto a stage in LA to shoot some scenes in close-up since production and VFX had covered for his absence with the double.

And who would pay the overages? Not Peter, but Sparta.

Her husband was like the banks in 2008: too big to fail. With his demise would go a Sparta franchise, which simply could not be. It wasn't just that it threatened the loss of too much money already spent, but multiples yet to be made.

TWENTY-EIGHT

"I CAN'T BELIEVE I'm partying with this motherfucker!" the white man said. He seemed forty but was probably in his late twenties, and they called him Freddie B. He'd driven in from Athens because he liked to be in the city on weekends, where he was welcome in the clubs, could hear the latest trap music, and be among his "people." "If I could change anything it would be my skin color. I'd be black as coal," he announced.

"No, you wouldn't," said Bella, who hadn't left Peter's side since he'd emerged from Demetrius's office at Manny's. They were at a house party in Douglasville where Bella had driven them in her Mustang, Peter in front beside her, Raymond and Bella's friend Athena in the back. "You got no idea what it is to be black in this country. You just keep walkin' around in that white skin and be the lucky man you are."

Peter liked Bella. They'd made out in her car outside the club while they waited for Raymond and her friend. He couldn't believe the softness of her lips, how she tasted the inside of his mouth with her tender, agile tongue. He was still high from the pot he'd been hitting at intervals for the past four hours. He'd avoided drinking at the bar. He'd also not partaken of any of the cocaine now riding his hip. He'd promised the better half of himself that the violation of every principle he'd learned to hold dear would last only one night. After this he'd return to sobriety, a feat he'd accomplish without reporting to a facility, as doing so would attract even more opprobrium than what he was already experiencing. He therefore needed this one evening to progress slowly so he could enjoy each transgressive moment. He liked how life had begun to decelerate.

Bella was playing with his dick from the outside of his pants, and he knew that without the barrier of clothing she would bring pleasures of a sort he hadn't experienced of late. If he were going to cheat on Marci, this was the way to do it.

When Raymond and Athena appeared, they set out on the forty-five-minute drive to a single-story house packed with guests, most of them black. A bright red bulb illuminated a room thick with music and smoke beneath a fan at full tilt at the center of the eight-foot ceiling. Trap music shook the main room to the joists.

People wouldn't stop saying hello, though he allowed no pictures. Yes, word could get out, but security at the party was tight, something about a vendetta against the house's owner, and guests were admonished not to text about the unlikely presence of the movie star in their midst. Something told Peter such rules would be followed more here than on the Sparta set. Sweaty from dancing, he and Bella had moved to the back porch, where they joined Raymond, Athena, Freddie B, and others looking out on a freshly mowed lawn fenced on all sides with chain link. The upper body of a mastiff stretched from a doghouse in the penumbra of light thrown from the party.

"Hot take: you've actually got no idea what it is to be poor and white," Freddie B said to Bella, unwilling to concede his interest in switching races.

"I been poor and black. Trust me, it's worse."

"You guys got the best music, the best bodies, the best looks. I mean, what white chick gets to go around lookin' like you, Bella. That fuckin' hair."

"Don't talk about a black woman's hair."

"I'm serious."

"Me too."

"I mean, you're fuckin' real. You got humanity, and what is it where you can get back up?"

"Resilience?" she asked.

"Fuckin' resilience. You were fucking wronged by us."

"Ain't nobody wronged me."

"I mean as a people. And you still fuckin' got up and not only survived that shit, but you're our heroes now. In sports, in the arts, you even got a fuckin' president before women did. I mean, seriously, there's no one I'd want to be who's white."

"Who you want to be, Freddie B, and I can tell you why you wouldn't want to be him."

"Michael Jordan, Saquon Barkley, Kobe—"

"Kobe's dead, you wack motherfucker."

"Before he was dead."

"To where you take a white woman to your room and she say you raped her and there's nothin' you can do about it but pay her two million dollars to go away?"

"Fine, maybe Kobe was a bad example, but take away the situation at the hotel and it's pretty sweet. I mean, I wouldn't want to die in a helicopter crash, but that weren't because he was black. And by the way, if I was Kobe, I wouldn't've took her up to my room in the first place."

"Which is my point. You're wanting to be black, but that means anything you do, you got to think, How's this gonna look if it goes bad? Because if that happens, everybody, including a lot of black folks, is gonna see the situation and assume I did what the white folks say I did."

"Michael Jordan managed it."

"For one Michael Jordan you got twenty million other black men who can't do what he could in whatever it is they choose to do. Nobody fuckin' could, white or black. But maybe because they want to or think they can, they don't take care of the other shit, like school and practicing whatever it is they *can* do, the way Michael Jordan practiced his jumper. Then it's too late, so they got to hustle in a white man's world and shit goes south fast. Plus they never learned the good habits it takes to live life right."

"The best things in this country come from—"

"That ain't even true, and I'm black."

"Music, for one. Rap, jazz, the blues. Even rock music. Everyone says it."

"You want to be a rap artist?"

"You kiddin' me? Be up there onstage. Make dope records. Get me some tail whenever I want. Hittin' the runtz. But I sure as shit wouldn't want to be a white one. Fuckin' Eminem, Action Bronson. Those dudes, that's poser shit."

"Bubba Sparxxx is pretty badass," said a white twenty-something who'd been listening in.

"Don't even talk to me about that tattooed goober honky motherfucker. If you're white, don't rap, don't play blues, don't even play jazz," decreed Freddie B.

"I don't know about a world without Bill Evans," said Peter, "or Chet Baker or Benny Goodman or Joe Pass."

"Look, I know you're a movie star and all that, but I don't know a single person you just said, which basically proves my point."

"What point is that, Freddie B, that you're fuckin' ignorant?" asked Bella.

"Why is it the white dude right now that's arguing that black people are basically baller?" wondered Freddie B, undaunted.

"Because that ain't what you said. You said you want to *be* black."

"You don't like bein' black, Bella?"

"I was born black, so it's who and what I am. In this body, with this face and this brain. Maybe all brains are the same, but I tend to doubt it, so I'm gonna say I got a beautiful and complicated black brain, just like Peter here's got him a white brain. Neither one better than the other, but his suits him and mine suits me, and by me I mean my whole being, which includes my black body, so yeah, for who and what I am, I want to be just the color I am."

"That was amazing," offered Peter.

"Lookit, Freddie," she continued. "Love my people all you want, but when you say you want to be black, it frankly insults me, because it shows you have no understanding of what a black person goes through on a daily basis, and that makes me think you don't respect me."

"I'm fuckin' in love with you, Bella."

"You want to fuck me, but you are not in love with me."

"How do you know what's inside my head?"

"Call it my black intuition. Did it ever occur to you that that black music you like so much, including the hip-hop, comes from a level of anger and disappointment you can't even imagine? And I'm gonna go ahead and say *ever* imagine?"

"That's why I admire it."

"Let's talk about something else before I belt you upside the head."

"Fine." Freddie B turned to Peter. "So what the hell are you doing here?" He produced a pack of Marlboro Reds, offering one. Peter took it, and Raymond raised a Zippo he flicked open in a practiced manner and sparked.

"I'm just here with Bella," Peter answered on the exhale.

"I always thought I could be an actor."

"A black actor?" asked Bella.

"Now wouldn't that be somethin'. Put me in the movies!"

"I'd like to do porn," said Raymond.

"No, you wouldn't," said Peter.

"You got some experience?" Raymond queried.

"I've met guys who have, and I've done my share of love scenes. In fact, that's what got me in trouble a few days ago. Or was it yesterday?"

"I seen that on the internet," said Freddie B.

"I'm sure you did."

"What I want to know," Freddie B then asked, "is don't people have better things to do than be on the internet all day reading about movie stars?"

"How'd you know what I did?"

"Because it came up on my feed. You couldn't avoid it."

"Can we change the subject?" asked Raymond.

"You're the one brought it up," said Freddie B.

"All I said is I want to be in a porn movie."

Peter watched as the mastiff rose. He was chained to a stake or clamp of some sort inside the dwelling. He yawned and stretched, exposing a pair of intact testicles, then disappeared through the entrance, none of him any longer in sight.

"But seriously," said Freddie B, "what is it about y'all?"

"I don't understand the question," responded Peter.

"I mean, like, here you are, and all right, you're handsome and obviously pretty smart and whatever, dressed kinda weird. But I've wanted to fuck Bella since the first time I seen her. I mean before I even heard her speak, I knew, and then when I got to know her, forget it. Far as I'm concerned she's the hottest woman in all Atlanta. And here you are, in half a night and she's on your arm. From the look of you, you gotta wake up every day and brush your teeth and put on clothes. I got a job and you got a job . . ."

"What's your job?" asked Peter.

"Do what Raymond here does, but without the bellboy cover."

"You ever think that might have something to do with the level of female you're able to attract?" asked Bella.

"Aw, bullshit. What's the difference between any of it except somebody decides one job is legal and another ain't? And look here, one day gettin' caught with more'n five ounces of weed would get you locked up, and I mean in prison, not jail, and the next you got dispensaries sellin' it by the half pound payin' taxes to fix the roads. Full-on legal like a restaurant or a filling station. Me? It was never wrong to smoke weed any more than drinkin' a beer. The beer's worse, because I ain't never heard of nobody beatin' his wife high on weed like the way my stepdad used to go after my mom when he was drunk, or my uncle beatin' on his wife, forget it. And the rest of it? Somebody wants to take pills or shoot up, that's their business, long as they don't hurt nobody else."

"Except you do that and you *do* hurt yourself. And the people around you," said Bella. "I ain't no preacher, but let's be real."

"Bullshit, Bella. Who do I hurt? I bring joy, just like Peter here."

"Until Peter gets hooked like he did and gets thrown in prison."

"Talkin' about his acting."

"Or you hurt yourself and those who love you. And damn, there's a reason a lot of that shit is still illegal. People abuse it. I never wake up happy the day after I drink too much. Why mostly all I do anymore is smoke weed."

"Well, good for you. But what business is it of mine that folks do what they want? And if it ain't me it's somebody else gonna provide it. This is America. And I'll tell you somethin' else. It's all part of the economy. My dollars are as good as anyone else's, and when I go to see one of Peter's movies, nobody asks me how I earned the fifteen dollars to get in the door and the twenty for the popcorn and Coke, which what's that all about, Peter? Chargin' me twelve dollars for a bag of popcorn's got too much fake butter on it?"

"How the theater makes its money."

"And I'm the one doin' somethin' illegal?" he asked Bella.

"People don't want to pay that much, they don't have to buy it," she retorted.

"Well, the same's true with what I sell. This whole damned country is corrupt if I am. We don't hardly produce nothin' anymore that makes us better. And yes, I do include myself in this. Mostly we just amuse ourselves, whether it's drugs or alcohol or video games, music, sports. What else? Food. There's parts of Texas I've drove through you can't hardly breathe from the smell of the slaughterhouses. We're slaughtering cows and pigs and chickens and shitting them out so we can work a forty-hour week to sit in front of a screen and watch Peter here. Used to be our heroes were men on the moon, war heroes, athletes. Politicians even. Fuckin' Abraham Lincoln. What's his name? Roosevelt. Now it's Peter, or, worse, celebrities on the internet."

"That was quite a speech," said Peter. "I could listen to you and Bella all night."

"So go on, tell me the difference between me'n what I do and what Peter and the folks who make movies do."

"You watch a movie, you don't end up dead on the street."

"You can't blame me for someone else's addiction any more than you can blame Peter for folks bein' addicted to their televisions spendin' five hours every night starin' at a screen."

"That's a fuckin' stretch."

"Look," said Peter, "Freddie B's not entirely wrong. Back to your original question, I can't tell you why people love celebrities. In fact, it's easier to explain why we like drugs, because it's physiological. Endorphins and receptors and dopamine and how painful life can be, not to mention genetic predisposition. In ancient Greece the athletes and poets were venerated, wreathed with laurels and honored by the masses. It's where the word comes from, actually—well, the Latin, not the Greek. *Celebritas*, meaning 'honored.'"

"How the fuck you know all this?"

"Well, first of all, for obvious reasons the phenomenon interests me, and second, you might have heard I had about two and a half years there with a lot of time on my hands."

"He's fuckin' read a lot of books," said Bella.

"But you're right, about how contorted it all is, because celebrity went from being honored to just being famous, and there's a difference. Movies, TV, and radio had a lot to do with it because they suddenly allowed for a person like me to be everywhere without having to *go* everywhere, and that conferred a huge amount of power. I could be recognized in places I'd never been, and not just from a picture of me, as in a photograph, or even my voice on a record or the radio, but eventually a moving, speaking version of me on a screen. But even better than that, because as sound got better and color entered the picture, pun intended, it was this hyper version of me fourteen feet tall, bigger and louder and better than life, and so intimate you could hear my every breath and whisper. Plus it's in the dark, so I'm not even like a human anymore but some weirdly divine vision. Our brains weren't ready to handle that, in a strange way, and so it overwhelmed the culture like—absolutely—a drug. To be a celebrity isn't to be honored anymore, it's how many people know you as something greater than your actual self. It's the biggest deception there is, and somehow we're ravenous for it, like you with black people. And now with the internet, forget it. No, it's not in the dark, but you can see shit on your computer screen, and I'm not talking about the hideous videos of me from the last few days, which is a whole other story, but you can see shit now nobody should ever see, from beheadings to porn, bestiality, little girls taking their clothes off in their rooms for money, crackpot mass killers and their manifestos, deepfakes with AI. And it seems like all people do anymore is sit there and devour it all."

"When you can speak like he just did, and he's been smoking all night," said Bella to Freddie B, "come see me."

"He basically just agreed with me!"

"Not quite," said Peter.

"Let's dance some more," said Bella.

"I've pushed my luck with that. Too many people in there, and I'm not ready to go back to my life yet."

"I'll be right back then." She returned minutes later and took his hand, leading him to the back of the house, where she produced a key that opened a locked door.

"Where'd you get that?"

"This is my cousin's house. This is her room."

It was lit with Christmas lights of red, green, and gold and smelled faintly of incense, the remains of which Bella found in a burner on a long yellow dresser strewn with jewelry. She lit it before moving to sheer curtains on either side of a low picture window facing the trees of a neighboring house. She closed them. With the music beating from the other room, the walls throbbing from the heavy bass, they undressed each other. In all his experience he'd never encountered a body like hers, thick and strong, but also timeless somehow in its beauty. She lay back, and he snorted the coke he'd been saving from her breasts. It fired into his brain just the way he remembered, every sense alerted to what manifold pleasures lay in store. He took a bump on his finger and touched her with it before moving inside her. The sheets were silk and warm with their bodies, and Peter lost himself in an intensity of sensation he'd been missing for more than a decade. Whatever the consequences, he thought, they will have been worth it for what and how I'm feeling right now. I could honestly perish and be fine with that, but I'll do whatever it takes to make this last as long as possible, and when it's over, I'll do whatever it takes to get it back. I'm going to pursue and never stop. This is just too good.

When they'd finished he lay by her side while she spoke to his dick. "Can you do that again?" she asked.

"It may take a minute. Or forty."

"We can wait."

"What do you do?" he asked.

"As in when I'm not hangin' out where we met?"

"Something like that."

"I tend bar at a restaurant in Buckhead. I also paint."

"Paint?"

"Went to school for it."

"No shit. Where?"

"San Francisco."

"Is that where you grew up?"

"I sound like I grew up in San Francisco? Was raised in a house about a mile from here."

"Why'd you come back?"

"I found out this is the best place I know how to be."

"I guess in a weird way that's true for me too, I just never thought about it that way."

"Why not?"

"I essentially grew up where I live right now. Different part of LA, but not really. And I still own the house where we went weekends in Malibu. As crazy as my life is, it's like it was preordained way back then. Other than prison and on location and some years in New York, I've never lived outside of a fifteen-mile radius. How did that happen?"

"You get in your life, and before you know it that's what it came to."

"What do you paint?"

"People."

"People you know?"

"I prefer people I don't. No preconceived notions."

"So models?"

"Not those either. People I see. Maybe even for a second. Then I try to remember them and paint that. When I started, I did the opposite. Painted the people close to me and obsessed over every detail, but I found the more I looked the less it was me seeing. Other shit got in the way. When I have to recall it's more about me somehow, since we all remember things in ways that are just us."

"Are you gonna remember this?"

"Are you?"

"Like it's the last thing I ever did."

"What'd you say that for?"

"I don't know," he answered, kissing her. "I might have said it in a movie. In fact, I'm pretty sure I did."

She laughed and swatted him playfully, and as she did the red and blue lights of a police cruiser rotated through the curtains. Almost simultaneously came banging at the door to the room in which they lay. Bella gathered the sheet to answer it, while Peter rose frantically to pull on his underwear and pants, his penis still tingling from the cocaine.

"What's the problem?" he heard her ask.

"Police is here to shut down the party," Freddie B answered. She twisted the knob and the door pushed open. He entered somewhat frantically with Raymond, Athena close behind.

Bella began to laugh. "What the fuck is everyone getting so excited for? Nobody's gonna take anybody in. They ain't got a warrant. It's a damn noise complaint."

"I can't be seen here," said Peter. "I'm totally fucked if I get taken in."

"Just stay in this room. I been through this a hundred times."

The music shut off to a chorus of disappointment, followed by raised voices encouraging compliant and orderly departure.

"Folks are gonna leave and that'll be that," Bella said as she reached for her dress. "Freddie B and Raymond, you know you aren't gettin' a look at this, so just turn your asses around."

They did so.

"You guys have a good time in here?" asked Freddie B, gazing forlornly at the bed denuded of its top sheet.

"Until you showed up," she answered.

Peter was coming down quickly. The sudden company, the absence of music, the steady flow of bodies moving past the bubble lights casting a succession of blinking shadows on the wall—each had their effect. He lowered himself to the bed, his head in his hands, the likely consequences descending like an acrid mist. Where was he? No longer in Atlanta, he was fairly certain. Douglasville, someone had said. Where was that even? Had he been in the car for an hour? Two? He'd just slept with another woman for the first time in his marriage, and there she stood: ravishing, smart, astonishingly wise in her way, but, painting aside, a prostitute for all he knew, sitting in an Atlanta hookah bar in the middle of the afternoon dressed as she was and with a late-model Mustang. No, likely not a prostitute, but just what she said she was. Yet still. He beheld Freddie B and Raymond, two cracker drug dealers. Raymond he'd known for years, but Freddie B didn't come off well in any company, particularly when one considered how residency in Athens implied selling to college kids. If I don't extricate myself from this situation I'm going to end up in jail. This isn't self-destruction, it's idiocy. My marriage is probably finished, but I can't go back to prison.

"I need to get out of here," he announced to the air.

"Just give it a few, Peter. You go out there now, it's gonna go south for you quick," responded Bella.

"She's right," said Raymond.

"How do you know somebody out there hasn't said something already? Even for their own gain. For leniency."

"I keep saying this is just to break up the party," said Bella.

"People are looking for me. No one knows where I am. The studio . . ." He pondered the consequences of being found in this condition. It wasn't the place—in fact, being at a mostly black party might even recommend him—but the drugs, the philandering. He'd taken the goodwill of the industry, his fans, the world, and he'd shat on it. And Marci. She must be apoplectic with worry, let alone how she'd feel upon learning of his actions. "You have to get me out of here."

"Easy, Peter. You're just coming down," said Raymond. "Freddie B, get him a glass of water from the sink." He pointed to an en suite bathroom Peter hadn't noticed. If he had he'd be barricaded within instead of sitting meekly on the bed. "We'll wait this out, then we get you back to Atlanta like none of this ever even happened."

"But it did happen."

"Or we take you somewhere where you can sleep it off, or you sleep it off here. Everything's gonna be fine. Like the old days."

"Ray's right. Act like it never happened," said Freddie B. "I mean, my guess is you ain't gonna forget what you did with Bella in here . . ."

"Shut your damn mouth," she said.

"I'm just sayin'. But this was what it was. A stop on the road of life." No one seemed eager to amend such unalloyed wisdom. Instead they listened as the sounds of voices, the slamming of car doors, and the starting of engines persisted.

Bella sat beside him on the bed. "Wish it hadn't ended this way."

"You got any more coke?" Peter asked Raymond. He needed a boost, just until he could be alone.

"You don't want more of that," Bella said. "That's the last thing you need."

"I need something," he said. "Just to get me through the next few hours, or I'm gonna really lose my shit."

"I shouldn'ta let you do it in the first place, but we just got carried away. That was on the both of us."

"Just a little more."

"I ain't got none," said Freddie B. "That party was crazy. Fuckin' cleaned me out. Almost want to move back here."

"What about you, Raymond?"

"I don't carry. You know that. And I wouldn't give you more anyway. Bella's right."

"Why you're still a doorman," said Freddie B.

"Why I ain't in prison too."

"You see any bars around me?"

"Not yet."

"You idiots want to take this outside?" asked Bella.

"I'm fine right here," said Freddie B. "Besides, maybe I got somethin' else can help."

"What's that?" asked Peter.

"You wantin' to ease yourself down, there's nothin' better than Percocet."

"My driver used to do that drug," said Peter.

"Your driver? George?" asked Raymond.

"Never mind," said Peter with no absence of shame. "But you have some?"

"Peter, you don't know where he got his pills," said Bella.

"What's that supposed to mean?" asked Freddie B, his voice raised.

"Means I don't trust your country ass and never have. I want no part of this." She took up the earrings she'd removed and put them in her purse. "Where's my shoes at?"

"On the floor where you couldn't take 'em off fast enough with the rest of your clothes."

"Come on, Peter, I'll drive you back to Atlanta," she said, moving to the curtains and pulling them aside. "The police are gone."

"Can I get a couple of those pills?" Peter asked Freddie B.

"You come out to my truck you can."

"You go out to his truck you can ride with him," said Bella.

"It's just to help me come down," he said.

"I don't want some shit in my car I don't know how to deal with. You want to come down before you get back to Atlanta, come to my place and do it the right way."

"Let me just stop by his truck, then we do that."

"I said what I had to say."

"I'll drive you back to Atlanta," said Freddie B. "Drop you wherever you want to go."

"I'd drive you, but I ain't got my car," said Raymond fecklessly.

"Come on, Bella," said Peter.

"I said what I had to say."

Peter stared up at her from the bed. In spite of the fact she'd bedded a married man and done drugs with him, she seemed preternaturally decent. He'd carry what she said about painting from memory with him always, perhaps even apply it to his acting. A quick inventory confirmed Freddie B to be her opposite: shifty, close-set eyes, peeling skin, prematurely receding hair, stained, crooked teeth, and a stubborn smile that showed around the mouth but in neither cheeks nor eyes, advertising an insincerity palpable to the point of off-putting. His very being seemed to insist: Trust me, and you will perish.

"You'll drop me anywhere in Atlanta I say to go?" he asked.

"You pay for the gas, I'll drop you anywhere in this country. The whole wide world."

"'The Universe; the Mind of God,'" said Peter.

"What?"

"Nothing. It's from a play."

"Well? What's it gonna be?"

TWENTY-NINE

“Sometimes the dealer doesn’t even know what he’s selling.”

“But one pill?”

“One, two,” answered the doctor. “It could have been three. We’re talking about measures equal to ten to twelve grains of salt that can cause hypoxia. I’m not sure this brings you any comfort, Ms. Compton, but what’s important for you to understand is that your husband wasn’t intending what happened.”

Within twenty minutes of taking one or more pills he believed to be Percocet, Peter’s respiratory system had shut down, depriving his brain, the defining feature of his being—more than the face that had adorned the sides of buildings, billboards, and buses worldwide, more than his voice, his legs, the feet on which he trod the ground—of oxygen. Effectively he’d suffocated without understanding how or why in a Ford F-50 Lariat pickup truck driving ninety-two miles an hour on I-20 (photographic records from highway cameras established the speed) from Douglasville to Atlanta, after which he was deposited in brush off a two-lane backroad bisecting a place called Deer Lick Park by the terrified driver who’d given him the drugs. In all likelihood he had undergone a seizure in the passenger seat, after which he became inert. Again, based on camera footage twenty minutes on either side of the event, he’d possibly been abandoned while still alive, but after ten minutes his brain had ceased to function. This had been early Friday morning. He wasn’t found until Saturday, when an amateur photographer drove out from his home fifteen miles away to capture the phenomenon of circling vultures from directly below where their carrion lay. Marci could only imagine the man’s surprise to find Peter Compton, who’d finally been reported missing not five hours before, lying there in the garb of his character, his barely recognizable face directed at the sky, as was described by the suddenly renowned shutterbug.

Marci's pain, and it was beyond anything she'd imagined possible for the human body to endure, had consumed her without respite since learning of her husband's fate. It came in what felt like lethal shocks, one after another, that moved through her body to the extent she had no control of them. She would collapse in spasms, as if learning the news from some different perspective each time. Given all they shared, these seemed endless, like an infinity of geometric points. Then there was the simple imagining of what her husband had gone through. The pain of it, the loneliness, the anger he must still have been feeling toward her, the shame.

Her mother, who'd flown down with her father and sister from New York, insisted on a sedative administered by injection. She'd slept for nine hours, after which she woke, not knowing where she was and why she'd been asleep in the middle of the afternoon. Or was it morning? Wasn't she making a film? She lay motionless and bewildered, intuitively discouraged to call out. Atlanta, she said to herself. Peter and I are shooting. I just dreamed Peter was dead. I dreamed my mother was here. My father. There were police. She rose in a nightgown she vaguely remembered having donned with someone's help. And doctors. But surely that was part of the dream. Why am I not on set? With each increment, silent interrogation gave way to dread, causing her finally to open the door, where her parents and Samantha sat speaking with the head of Sparta security and a man she didn't know. He wore a navy oxford suit and a crisp button-down shirt of pastel yellow with no tie.

"You've been asleep," her mother said simply. "Samantha brought you some food."

Details from the preceding day began to surface. First learning the news from Jeremy, who received the call while in her house. The refusal to allow her to see her husband's body. The phone ringing constantly. The police coming in and out. Joel Slavkin visiting, and later Javier and Charisse. Her pain. Shrieking at everyone to leave. More pain. The arrival of her parents, her mother taking over. Her berserk rage. More pain.

"I'm okay, Mom," she said quietly as Esther Levy embraced her and wouldn't let go.

"I know you are, dear. I know you are."

Jesus, Marci thought, it's as if she's happy to be needed in this way. It's even weirdly cruel. Was she there when I saw the body? What happened, and what am I imagining? And so what if a part of her lives for this? She remains one of the most capable people I know. It's going to cost me for the rest of my life, but that bill is already so overwhelming without this on the tally, what difference does it really make?

It was then she learned the details of Peter's final moments: leaving a house party in Douglasville with a twenty-something criminal he'd met not four hours prior. Taking Percocet laced with fentanyl purveyed by that criminal. That he'd been removed from the truck and left to perish. All this information provided by Sparta security, who'd learned it from the police, as well as the doctor who'd been hired to be on call around the clock by her mother and who, not without awareness of its morbid coherence, had her on prescription sedatives to help her assimilate that her husband had perished from an overdose of drugs he'd ingested by trusting another blindly.

Within two days all she wanted was to leave Atlanta. She despised the place, from the city itself and the towns surrounding it to the very house in which she and Peter had spent their final hours strategizing against an onslaught of opprobrium. She couldn't enter the kitchen in which she'd persuaded him to publish the statement apologizing. The text that, had he simply resisted the need to address the crew that final time, might have sufficed. Besides, Samantha needed something to do, so why not have her drive for coffee and takeout, not to mention the white wine Marci and her mother drank together prodigiously each night once the sun began to set, this against soft admonitions from the doctor.

"With the Ativan I don't recommend it, but nor can I say honestly you can't. Just limit it as best you can." Last name Adelman, he was in his early sixties with thick silvering hair, tanned skin, and the body of someone who golfed regularly—neither overweight nor especially fit, but moving with an ease in space that connoted some form of outdoor activity. Her mother had a knack for finding Jews of a particular sort when it came to professionals. Be they in medicine, law, or finance, they had to project success in the WASP milieu without actually being WASPs.

"This way you get the best of both worlds," she once explained when confronted. "It's why I love the Hamptons."

Max Kaiser appeared unexpectedly on the third day.

"I'm at the Four Seasons," he said on the phone. "I'd love to come by, but can certainly understand if you'd rather I didn't."

What was she to say? "Max, you're precisely the last person I want to see. I simultaneously despise you for putting my husband in this spotlight where your security team couldn't do the basic job of protecting him from exposure and myself for being part of the process that upended your film. All this while I mourn my husband. And you show up in Atlanta asking after you've already landed if you can come by? Are you fucking joking?"

"Sure, Max, it means a lot to me that you flew down. Come over."

To his credit, Sparta had hired a security detail of a half dozen around-the-clock guards to keep paparazzi and onlookers beyond forty feet from the property gates. He'd also arranged for the Grand Studios jet to fly both her and the body back to Los Angeles three mornings hence when both forensics and the Fulton County morgue had completed their work. Peter's death had been ruled a homicide, though given her husband's intelligence she couldn't shake the suspicion of suicide. How could he not have known, given his keen interest in the news, that to take any controlled pill not purchased at a licensed pharmacy was effectively to play a very poor-odds game of Russian roulette?

"Marci, I can't pretend to know what you're going through right now," Max said with solemn empathy. He'd left his Phillies cap with his driver and wore a dark crewneck sweater over his customary unadorned tee. The man was perhaps the most deservedly charmed person she knew, relentless in every respect, including decency. She'd heard rumors of a bad childhood with an alcoholic father.

Why then did she so resent him? What vexed her most, she supposed, was his projection of utter contentment. It didn't matter the situation, setback, victory, or challenge, you got the same guy: a person who understood he'd reached the summit and would remain there until he chose to vacate it. Difficult upbringing or no, he was, to put a simplistic, contemporary spin on it, the very epitome of white male privilege. No, he couldn't be blamed for who and what he was, but a woman or a person of color could never have achieved what he had, and should they have, by some circumstance that would have had to involve divine intervention, they wouldn't have enjoyed the latitude to sustain it for any meaningful period. A woman would long before have been displaced for being wrathful, picayune, bitchy. A person of color as paranoid, token, incapable. While still powerful, Sparta was also in gradual decline. Was this Max's fault? No. Would any other person have been removed at the outset of this descent? Absolutely. But Max wore the brand's flagging status with an ease that made one simply want to smack him.

"I want you to know," he continued, "that whatever you need right now, whatever we can do, the studio is there for you."

"I appreciate that, Max."

"You've been told about the plane and getting the body back. We've also arranged for the funeral home to meet you at the airport. We'll stock the refrigerator at your house—we got a list from your assistant—and anything else you need. Truly. I met your parents and sister. They're spectacular people. Your mother is incredible. You're very lucky to have them here."

"I appreciate that, Max. All of it. What's going to happen with the movie?"

"Honestly, Marci, no one is concerned with that right now. Nor should they be. This kind of tragedy serves to remind us what's really important."

The idea that Max wasn't thinking about his $160 million investment in a billion-dollar franchise was frankly risible. Knowing the studio as she did, meetings had already taken place, and writers would soon be hired to triage scenes so that what Peter was to have said could be uttered by others. And should that not suffice, would they recast and reshoot? Who would now play Paul Kramer? This could no longer be solved with the idiot double.

"We're a family," he continued warmly. "You and Peter were a part of that family. You still are. You've lost a husband, a partner, a best friend. I've lost a brother and collaborator. I can't tell you how excited I was to keep working on this character with him, and not because of the movies to come but because

I admired him so much." This she actually believed. "What he'd been through, how he'd turned setbacks to his advantage. I mean, truly, he was as smart a person as I've known. The sheer bandwidth. Which just goes to show what a powerful disease addiction really is. It doesn't discriminate, because if a person of Peter's intellect and spirit and talent and decency can succumb to it, any of us can."

"Yes," she said inanely. Why doesn't he just stop speaking? If I have to hear more of these platitudes I'm going to go find—what was his name?—Freddie B and take half a dozen of his fentanyl myself.

"That's what I think made your husband one of the greatest actors of our time. True artists live the tragedy of being human, with all its pain and perplexity, in ways we'll never comprehend. And sometimes the cost is just too much."

"He was a fucking drug addict, Max."

"I know, Marci, but why? I think he needed narcotics, kind of like Paul Kramer, if you'll allow it, because he just saw and understood more than the rest of us."

"Yeah, I'm just not there yet."

"Nor should you be. I mean, my God."

"And please don't say he was like Paul Kramer again, especially publicly. I really don't want that out there. Peter was an actor, not a comic book superhero."

"There are no superheroes. I wish there were. Sorry, but a superhero would have sunk the ship carrying the drugs, destroyed the lab in Mexico or the cartels getting them across the border. The American dealers selling them."

"And the people like my husband buying and using them?"

"Fair enough. That's the downside of why the movies are so popular. We need solutions that just aren't there in the real world. In front of the camera your husband was embodying that as well as any actor we've ever hired. He was an extraordinary human being."

Unable to resist, Marci pictured Peter in whatever bedroom to which the woman he'd met at a hookah bar took him, banging away, high on coke. What a human being indeed. Statues should be erected. Museums. Memorials on every continent.

"Yeah," she said, "with all due respect, I don't think the world is going to see it that way, and I'm not sure I do either. Quite frankly, I'm furious with him right now."

"Of course you are."

"You think you understand what I'm saying, Max, but you don't. Yes, I'm angry and wounded in a way that will never go away that he disposed of everything he and I had for a single night that got him killed. But it's more than that. He took all that he represented, everything you just described, and let it be pitched in a ditch in the woods off a rural backroad."

"He didn't know what he was taking."

"Let's put that aside. He knew what he was *doing*. Just think for a moment what Peter meant to people. And I'm not just talking about the ones who watched the TV show or *Honeymoon Heist* or any of the other fifty movies he did or who were wetting themselves over the prospect of him in *Major Machina*."

"Which they'll see."

"Okay. I don't know how you accomplish that, and when I asked you earlier you didn't want to discuss it."

"I can tell you people will see the character he was filming. Sparta owes everyone that."

"Please stop it, Max, because right now you're making me want to strangle you. But I want to make the point I was making more."

"Make it, Marci, please."

"My husband was not only given a second chance—one could argue third and fourth chances—he was actually rewarded for his transgressions. The redemption narrative of his life was something almost absurd. It seduced all of us, me. Hell, I married the guy. What an idiot I was."

"That was a lot of pressure to have put on you and your husband."

"Did we turn down the planes, the drivers, the eight-figure paychecks, the notoriety beyond what exceeds what everyone but maybe a hundred people on the planet enjoy? Peter's death was in every newspaper in the world. The fucking Chinese Communist newspapers published obits. Let's not go into the irony of that given the origin of the drug. On their front pages. North Korea even, which practically denies the existence of American stars. Bangladesh, Eritrea, Malaysia. I don't know why, but I've searched them out. It's become a kind of morbid game. Every country in Europe. That he fucking overdosed. He didn't just have a responsibility to me and to completing this film, to

Sparta—and fuck the notion that you owe Peter anything—he had a responsibility to the world to keep up the end of the bargain he made with them. He had everything. And you can't tell me he earned it or even deserved it, because if he did, then this is one fucked-up world."

"Marci, what does any of us deserve?"

"Oh, I don't know, I can only talk about me. For my husband not to have OD'd and died?"

"Sure. What I said was stupid."

"For any of us, including me, not to say something stupid right now is next to impossible. Just don't try and make a saint out of Peter."

"Sadly, Marci, there's going to be a lot of that. It's what happens to the greats. To the people who knew them they were flawed, but the public never wants to see it that way. Peter had his fame because he could make us think we could be smarter, funnier, more appealing, more heroic. Or the opposite: more evil, ugly, fragile, tragic, whatever, depending on the part. Artists, and especially actors, are like priests."

"Oh God."

"You may not want to hear it right now—"

"You remember when the terrorists attacked us on 9/11 and a certain segment of people, most of them educated and thoughtful, I think Mario Cuomo was one of them, said, 'I just want to know why they hate us.'"

"I do."

"Well, what you just said is why everyone hates Hollywood. Actors are not fucking priests."

"I only mean it insofar as storytellers. Don't call it religion if that doesn't work for you. Your husband was touched by something that made him riveting. I don't care what he did on one weekend night. It's hard to be what he was and still be what he also was: a human being."

⚡

She flew to Los Angeles with the body three days later attended by the same crew that had flown her out. At her request George drove her, Samantha, and Jay Lynne to the airport. For the entire ride the driver wept.

"I did everything I could."

"I know you did, George."

"But in the stupidest way. I thought I was gonna be some kind of big hero. Took him off campus when I should have just sat behind the wheel outside the trailer and refused to go anywhere. Thought so much of myself that I was gonna have the answer, then didn't even have the wisdom not to let him out of my sight."

"None of us was going to stop him."

"I didn't give anybody but me the chance."

"*He* didn't. And maybe you were the one person among all of us who tried the hardest."

"I would've done anything for your husband."

"I know you would have."

"When he got my brother out of Rice Street—not only paid for the lawyer but found the best one around—I knew. He didn't just enjoy his good fortune, he shared it. Saved my brother's life for a time."

"I didn't know about that."

"My little brother. Who loved Peter, by the way. When he was nineteen, got caught on a weapons charge but had a couple ounces of weed on him at the time, so it compounded. Stupid motherfucker. This was a half brother by a different mother."

"Was?"

"He was killed two years ago in Oakland City. Not a bad kid, just stubborn and wrongheaded. I mentioned his situation to Peter in the car on the way to set one day—this was on *The Executioner*. The one where he killed bad guys with hand tools."

"A movie he never should have done."

"He could tell I was upset, just because I didn't think it was fair, not to mention the fact if he got sent upriver to the pen he wouldn't last there. Get himself killed in a fight for sure. And it's not like the weapons possession had a damn thing to do with him having weed on him."

"Peter did a lot for other people when he had a mind to."

"He listened about my brother and that was it. I don't even know how much he paid, but it was easily in the thousands, and I never heard a word about it, and he wouldn't take my money. I said to my brother, 'You know who got you out of the mess you got yourself into? Peter Compton.' He couldn't believe it. I told him, 'You better,' because Peter was as good a man as you'll ever meet."

Opening her laptop on the plane, she couldn't escape exegeses on his death. The country was obsessed. Her own statement, succinct to the point of minimalist poetry, discouraged no one from inferring not only how she might be feeling but how she *should* feel. "I thank all who've expressed sympathy and ask only for respect and privacy while I, along with our family, mourn" seemed to inspire the opposite of its desired response.

"I'm just thinking of Marci Levy," expatiated one female solon on CNN. "The poor woman absolutely deserves our empathy and support. But eventually she's going to have to say something. As she mourns, so does America. Peter Compton wasn't just her husband, he was an American redemption story. He belonged to all of us."

It became clear the nation would feast on Peter's demise in the manner of scavengers on the savanna. After the lion (though females had caught the quarry) and the lionesses and cubs, then would come the vultures and hyenas, then the jackals, the rodents, the ants, until there was only bone. But with her husband's remains it was happening all at once in frenetic disregard to any discernible ecosystem. Moreover, the tragedy was being construed to mean far more than issues proximate to the victim but instead to the very concept of twenty-first-century America. There were disquisitions on the nature and pressures of fame, the relationship between movie stars and the culture, even the male id, whatever that meant, in the context of a man identified with a disease that did not discriminate by gender. Beyond these were broader examinations involving the chasm between those who played superheroes and their actual characters and, of course, on the very concept of the modern tragic hero. Peter was Charles Foster Kane, Jay Gatsby, Marilyn Monroe, Kurt Cobain, even John F. Kennedy by one moronic reckoning.

There were entire segments devoted to the opioid epidemic and fentanyl in particular. How it was a metaphor writ large for the decline of the entire American experiment. We were killing ourselves with capitalism's inherent corruptions, with our hedonism, our lassitude, our intolerance for pain of any sort, and, of course, the favorite of the Right, our porous border. Movies, chirped one self-satisfied academic on NPR, had become a religion every bit the "opiate for the masses" Marx had described. While an entire generation was dying from an infiltration of drugs they didn't even know they were taking, we were distracting ourselves with frivolous narratives starring the likes of Peter Compton, himself such an addict.

Nothing that was written or said was entirely untrue, but the exploitation of Peter's death seemed opportunistic to the point of nauseating. And the hypocrisy struck her as almost absurd, given the fact that those decrying the infiltration of screens and the pursuit of fame upon our lives were appearing on screens themselves doing little more than seeking the very notoriety they derided.

Finally came the outcry of fans demanding that Sparta provide the world with the *Major Machina* film the studio had promised. Especially infuriating was the ubiquity of the word used by Max Kaiser: the studio "owed" the world, as well as Peter Compton himself, the performance the star had sacrificed his life to give. What else, proceeded the logic, but the demands of playing such a role could have toppled the reformed Peter Compton? Not only were there the physical and emotional rigors connected with finding the human truth inside one of the Sparta canon's most flawed superheroes, there was the devastating spiritual affinity as well. Peter had succumbed to his addiction because he'd given himself to a fictional kindred. One blogger compared him to Jesus.

Looking back at the threads, she discovered it hadn't been an hour after the revelation of the overdose when the first such pronouncements appeared, after which it had become the rallying cry for a movement: *Major Machina* must be released, with no one but Peter Compton in the role.

In their online responses, Sparta had been brilliantly coy, first insisting it inappropriate even to discuss the future of the movie when its star had just died. Peter's family, the company, and, dare they say, America itself needed first to mourn. Then there was a day of being "honestly moved" by the fervency to honor the work of such a great artist by ensuring his final performance not be lost. And at last the revelation, on the morning after her return to Los Angeles, that Sparta would indeed do all it could to complete the film with Peter as its star.

THIRTY

Jordan Levinson called Joel the day after an informal memorial at Marci Compton's house to honor the one-week anniversary of the star's overdose.

"I saw you there," he said. "I wanted to say hi, but it was so packed by the time I arrived."

"No worries. Pretty crazy night."

"How are you?"

"I'm okay, considering."

"Did you have any inkling? I mean, had he been using already?"

"I have no way of knowing."

"Annie said it was a sort of up-and-down relationship between you and him, which is why I wondered. I mean, I can't imagine anyone not getting along with you."

"What exactly did she tell you?" Joel had still not gotten over her taking Jordan on as a client. Now it appeared she was sharing marital confidences. What good did it do for anyone to know he'd had issues with Peter Compton, regardless if the star was dead?

"She said you handled him beautifully."

"He was difficult, but it was always about the work. In a sense the guy couldn't help himself. He had an extremely restless mind. Certain people, they can't just sit there and be with themselves. But was he using? I don't think so. Yeah, he kind of cracked up, but that was about other things. I mean, frankly, I didn't really blame him for the first outburst. We're just getting so far from the creative process anymore with all these monitors and facilitators. He was having a tough morning, and it was just bad timing all around. I probably should have seen the situation coming. Between you and me, I sort of blame myself. I could have just told the woman to step back and we'd call her if she was needed."

"You can't blame yourself for him going off like that."

"The director is supposed to run the set."

"The AD is supposed to run the set."

"I'm not blaming James. When you take a job and there's a cast member already in place, you're agreeing to the responsibility of handling him. That was a tacit part of my contract with Sparta. Not only did I know what I was getting into, I sought it. I went to his house in fucking Brentwood with a look book and kissed the ring. Both his and Marci's."

"What's she like?"

"She didn't deserve this."

"I've met her a couple of times. Sexy too."

"Yeah, well, it's a complete package. Not that she doesn't work it, but if I were her I'd work it too. Gorgeous, a brain like that, savvy like you wouldn't believe. Always knows just what to say. I could go on and on."

"I won't tell Annie."

"I wouldn't know what to do with Marci Levy. It's like she's not even human."

"So again, how are you doing?"

"The weirdest thing is that I miss the guy, something I never imagined I would say. There were days when I never wanted to see him again in my life. I wanted to quit. It was Marci who talked me down. And fucking Javier Benavidez, he actually did quit a few times, Peter drove him so crazy. It was completely dysfunctional. But at the same time the work, once the camera was on and all our energy was going into that, was incredible. Peter brought everyone's level up. People are so complicated. Man, did I really just say that?"

"It's true."

"We were making a really good film for what it was, and I have to credit Peter as much as me or Javier or the writers—all eight of them—"

"Eight writers?"

"It's a fucking Sparta movie, Jordan. Half of Peter's ideas were wrongheaded and costly, but the other half were often amazing. Yeah, he took all the oxygen in the room. I've never met someone so adroit at taking attention. But usually there was no one or nothing else more interesting than him and what he was saying or doing."

"Fucking actors."

"This was more than that. Like I said, in terms of the performance, the guy was rarely late, always knew his lines, where he was in the story, what he wanted, what was in the way of it, everything. Sure, there was the whole thing with the energy crystals on set and burning the sage and the five trailers. Plus the guy following him with the suitcase of vitamins."

"You just said a lot there."

"The trailers?"

"The other shit."

"He had a whole ritual with the set and making the energy right. I don't want to get into it."

"And the vitamins?"

"There's a guy he always had with him who monitored his health. He worked in concert with the chef. It was all about chemical and karmic balances or something. But this was also a guy—Peter, I mean—who was keeping his addiction in check, working out for an hour or two a day on waking in addition to the time on set, where he was arriving early for hair and makeup and him and me meeting each morning to go over the day."

"That would have driven me crazy."

"Yes, it was a power play, but it held me accountable in a way that made the movie better. And the weird thing is that on the morning of his crack-up, I finally felt like he and I were turning it around. I stopped seeing him as this person looking over my shoulder but instead as a collaborator. For a day or two anyway. I don't know why I was so threatened."

"People threaten us, Joel."

"You mean humans threaten other humans?"

"No, humans threaten directors! That's why we need to assert our power. The guy was trying to run your set."

"In the end a person like Peter doesn't happen without the rest of us being complicit. He had everyone's attention because we were giving it to him. Take the audience away and the guy was nothing. And that goes for what happened to him too, what he did to himself, however you want to put it. I'm not saying we killed him, but we're all a part of what killed him."

"I'm not a part of it."

"We did coke when we were at AFI."

"What does that have to do with anything? And I don't do it anymore."

"Me neither, but we did. And Annie and I get high four or five times a year."

"That's legal now."

"Americans do drugs, and that includes, or in your case *included*—maybe you're some kind of ascetic now—us. No, I didn't kill Peter, nor did you, but as Americans contributing to that appetite, we had a tiny little hand in it, just like we—you indirectly as a part of the industry and I directly as his director—had a hand in making him as famous as he was, writ small and writ large. His tragedy is all of our tragedy."

"I don't buy a word of that."

"It doesn't make it any less true because you don't want to acknowledge it."

"Jesus, Joel, I called to see how you were doing, and you're jumping down my throat."

"Sorry. You're right. I appreciate it. I kind of just want to pack it in for a bit if you want the truth."

"That's understandable."

"Maybe write again finally. Obviously I've got to wait and see what Sparta has planned."

"You mean in terms of the film?"

"Business affairs called my agent and reminded him I'm still under contract. I figured as much, but when my agent asked what that meant, he was told, 'Everything it's meant to mean.' That is a quote. It's of course a little weird, since my contract stipulated that I was directing the film with Peter in the lead."

"What's left to shoot?"

"Hallway scenes, but all of them have dialogue. And then four pages where he gives a speech at the UN."

"So basically that's going to be cut."

"If they want to make the movie as scripted with Peter as the star like they're now promising. Of course they do have all those writers."

Jordan laughed. "How are you doing emotionally?"

"Crying a lot, which frankly surprises me." It suddenly occurred to him that Annie must have told Jordan this as well, which is perhaps why he had called.

"Why does it surprise you?"

"Because I'm not even sure why. I mean, is it for Peter Compton? Ultimately I barely knew the guy. Is it because my movie was shut down ten days before wrap? A movie I've been working on day in and day out for well over a year? Sure, there's that. Back in film school I had such specific hopes for myself, very few of which came true. When I used to describe the life I wanted, it was basically what you now have."

"Going around hat in hand to get your movies made?"

"You write a script and it gets financed. And it's always your script."

"My next project is a miniseries for a streamer, which I never expected I'd do, and somehow I've convinced myself it's tantamount to what an indie feature was back in the early 2000s. And my guess is that you got more to make *Major Machina* than I'll ever have to make anything."

"Somewhere I just got off course. Seduced by just enough adulation and encouragement from people to do what was easier or most comfortable and, of course, most remunerative."

"What people?"

"Agents, lawyers, studio heads, everyone telling me how good I was and offering me movies I didn't believe in, didn't care about, giving me more and more resources, more and more days. It was a fucking honey trap. A really amazing one, because, I mean, Jesus, I'm still getting to direct, but I've just been slowly rotting on the inside. And no longer really in control. The only person who ever really understood it was Annie. The night I got offered *Major Machina* she knew. I had to get a fucking therapy dog."

"Every dog is a therapy dog."

"The fact is, I hate the damned animal."

"Maybe that means you're getting better."

"Maybe I've been so upset because Peter's death, and I don't think this is too much of a stretch even though it sounds like one, marks the end of something, and not just for me."

"Certainly for him. Sorry. I couldn't help myself."

"I would often look around the set in Atlanta and remember when we made *Crop Circles* with a camera operator, a focus puller, one G&E, Nathan operating the boom with a portable Nagra on his hip, the production designer doubling on script, one AD, the actors, and the two of us, stealing locations, shooting on the highway without ITC. And I'd marvel at the fact that both movies, *Major Machina* and *Crop Circles*, were still stories told by way of moving picture and sound. Pretty amazing. But then I figured out that what we did back then and what I do now don't have a thing to do with each other anymore. Sure, when Javier Benavidez and I could get in a room by ourselves we could reference Gordon Willis and Fritz Lang and Christian Matras, but then, of course, once we started implementing our ideas they went through this grinder of executives and producers and marketers saying this was looking too dark, and did we really want so much saturation (not even really knowing what the word meant, mind you)? Or the one dope who kept talking to us about too much cyan in the camera test, so we keep turning down the blues on the LUT in the monitor just to appease him—"

"He was actually at the monitor?"

"There were six people from the studio at the camera test, Jordan. But I keep turning down the blues, and he screams, 'You're not changing it at all! You think I'm an idiot?!' And suddenly I realize he thinks cyan is cayenne!"

"Red?"

"Yes, red!"

"That's got to go into your memoirs."

"I don't want to write a damn memoir. I want to make movies, and it's not what I'm doing anymore. Very few people are. And I think that's why I've been so emotional, which, of course, boo-hoo, poor me."

"People are making movies all the time. You can buy a camera now for two thousand dollars with a cinema-grade sensor. You can get a sound package for next to nothing that picks up better than microphones from the eighties. Buy some cheap LED lights that can change temperature, you go make a movie."

"I mentioned Christian Matras a minute ago. You think anyone other than Jean Renoir and a few department heads were looking at his dailies when they shot *La Grande Illusion*, or if they were, that they were giving notes? Or that people were weighing in on Stroheim's hair or the cut of his uniform, or can't you make Dita Parlo prettier? Because that's the world I live in now, and when I succumb to it, you know what happens? A guy like Peter Compton, whose father was an actor and who came up like us, looks at that and he says, accurately, that I'm no more than a traffic cop, and that if the movie's going to have any integrity at all beyond what moves the stock price, he's got to take over, and that's what he did, God bless the dead asshole. By pushing Javier and me the way he did, he was basically screaming, 'Be better!' over and over, until we paid attention."

"I doubt you'd be saying any of this if he were still alive."

"Does that ultimately matter if it's true and I didn't realize it at the time? That almost makes it worse in a way. And like I said, right when all the shit happened is when I'd figured out how to deal with him. And if I'm even partially right, what does it ultimately say?"

"You tell me."

"Peter wasn't just railing against an intimacy coordinator. Shit changed during his time in prison. I was at the Academy Governors Awards dinner about eight years ago, and they gave an award to an actress for her work on gender and pay equity, and she got up in front of a room full of the most powerful people in Hollywood, and she said that producers and studio heads should have the lines counted in scripts that characters spoke, and that if it wasn't at least fifty-fifty man and woman, the screenplay should be rectified to make it equal or don't make the movie. I thought to myself, Does that apply when women have more lines in a script than men? Should we not make *Little Women*? Now look, I get it. There have been issues with our industry that needed to be addressed—still need to be addressed. But with this kind of self-defeating stupidity? What about period war movies that are mostly combat and bunker scenes? Movies in prisons with male inmates. Gangster movies. None of those anymore? We're going to put line counting ahead of telling compelling stories? And you know what that room of so-called storytellers did?"

"They applauded."

"A standing fucking ovation! I looked around, and these virtue-signaling idiots couldn't get to their feet fast enough. I thought to myself, Everyone is either a moron or a coward, and I don't know which is worse."

"Did you stand and applaud?"

"Fuck no! And do you think I got some harsh looks? No! Not even from women, which answered my question about stupidity versus cowardice. I probably spent as much time with HR on sexual harassment policy training and DEI training on *Major Machina* as I did with my production designer. You think I'm exaggerating? A whole weekend seminar for each. And why? Is it because Max Kaiser and the people underneath him are all true believers? I'm sure they are, to a degree, just like I am, in spite of the biases I admittedly have, that we all have. Fair enough. But no, it's because they're fucking terrified. So between that and the constant oversight to protect the brand or the hundred-million-dollar-plus investment, no one has room just to make a film, not if you want to do one of any scope with the money that costs. Even wokeness has become corporatized. And I have to admit, by playing the game, I've bought into it."

"I don't think that's why Peter Compton took fentanyl."

"To look at what happened to him and not see it as a reflection of our culture is to me a kind of blindness, not unlike walking down the street in downtown LA and seeing the homeless and not understanding you're part of the society that's not only allowing that to happen but perpetrating it in certain ways. We're not living in a dictatorship."

"Neither of us killed Peter Compton. Nor did what you call the 'culture.' Not even Peter Compton killed Peter Compton."

"Yeah, go ahead and keep telling yourself that."

THIRTY-ONE

"That's not the question to ask."

"Then what is?"

"Would he have wanted for the film to get finished in the manner you set out to make it?"

"Obviously, yes. As scripted, with minimal compromise, and him performing the role."

"Then you have your answer," said Melanie Kaiser.

How many such conversations had he had with her over the years as moral ambiguity kept stubborn pace with the market cap of Sparta. She would always tell it straight, and if she were to object to a decision or line of thinking, Max could trust such instincts as he would his own.

The way it had been explained to him was simple, though the sheer technological feat of it, not to mention the computing power involved, seemed anything but. Using Peter Compton's double, a manager at a local RadioShack if it was to be believed, *Major Machina* could be completed as scripted. The moonlighting retailer would perform the lines and all the movements associated with the various interstitial scenes, most of which took place in corridors, in stairwells, outside of rooms, and on sidewalks. He would also do the same for the final set piece that culminated in Paul Kramer's speech to the UN General Assembly. Visual effects would then transform this into something virtually indistinguishable from a Peter Compton performance. "Don't get scared, we're not *creating* Peter here, we're filling him in, furnishing a generated image." This would be matched with the sound of him saying lines he'd never recorded.

"Can you please explain how this isn't going to look and sound ridiculous?" asked Max. "I know this kind of thing can be done so it's real enough on phone screens and computers, even TVs, but we're talking big screens in multiplexes with amazing sound, which isn't even to mention IMAX. Every time something is digitally rendered, even in our own movies, I can tell."

"Trust me, you won't know Peter wasn't playing the scenes," said Anton.

"Again, think IMAX. The speech at the UN alone is two pages, with plenty more dialogue on either side of it. And Joel is going to want to go in close. We *want* Joel to go in close. Paul Kramer basically exposes the whole theme of the franchise in that speech."

"We could almost shoot the entire movie over again with the double at this point and you wouldn't know the difference. It's all about our database."

"The footage we have of him? You're calling that a database?"

"We've scanned Peter every day in every look. If there's something specific in the clothing, the makeup, the wrinkles around his eyes even, we have a reference for it with low ISO, so maximum information on the sensor. Then there's every scene we've filmed from all angles, but especially the close-ups with enough of his dialogue to give us not only every possible thing the guy did with his mouth as this character when forming pretty much every possible vowel and consonant, but we have the sound images as well on the boom and the lavs. And with the two stems, a postproduction mixer can put the guy in any room on Earth with a trackball and mix board screen alone. All of it already digitized. That double you guys found in Atlanta is no Daniel Day-Lewis, but he looks the part size-wise and moves serviceably well. But even those little issues we can correct in terms of how he stands and walks if it comes down to it. Again, we have the data."

"I've seen demonstrations and read about the technology. I was on the negotiating committee with SAG during the strikes and heard all the fears. But at the end of the day you still don't have Peter."

"We can generate any conceivable creative choice, visually or sonically, you want, and with so much nuance you won't know it isn't him down to every hair and pore. The power of this software is truly unbelievable. As strange as it is to say, and I know this terrifies everyone and for obvious reasons, but by about a month into the shoot, you no longer needed Peter Compton."

"Please don't say that."

"I guess that's why they tend to keep me locked away with the computers or on set behind the monitor. I love telling the truth."

"Actors, especially ones like Peter Compton, do things a computer would never come up with."

"Yeah . . ."

"What's that supposed to mean?"

"For starters, the computer is able to discern patterns we don't know are there. We forget most of what we experience and see, so what feels like unpredictable or erratic behavior actually isn't. And that aside, mostly the reverse is true, and people familiar to us are pretty predictable. Haven't you ever said to yourself you know what your wife is going to say before she even says it, and not only that, but exactly how she'll say it?"

"Sometimes."

"Well, imagine a computer that has all the data of almost an entire performance, and in a really granular way, in every situation, and it doesn't forget anything. Once there's enough information, nearly everything is predictable. It's incredible how simple we actually are and how pattern oriented. And if you want to really get into it, I'd wager the *illusion* of being mysterious and unpredictable has been essential for us as a species, because we'd destroy each other if it weren't the case. We need to be off-balance as a kind of deterrence. But a computer could have figured out five years ago that Peter was going to relapse and give some pretty surprising odds on where and how and with what tainted drug. You think I'm joking? I'm not. So what do you do with that?"

"Other than be scared out of my mind?"

"My vote is that we use the technology for the good."

"By not needing the actor for his own performance?"

"When did I say we didn't need the actor? We need Peter more than Peter needed Peter."

"How can you say that?"

"He certainly doesn't need himself anymore. Sorry to put it that way. And how are we even doing what I'm describing to you without Peter? He's the key to it all."

"Joel Slavkin is going to say to me that he requires a real actor there to direct. I can already hear him: 'How am I supposed to shape a scene when the performance is being handed to me by AI?'"

"First of all, you just proved my earlier point."

"Yeah, I already know what Joel is going to say. Answer my question."

"He needs to think about it like when he works with us on the VFX. He gives notes, and we make the changes. And by the way, it may take a bit longer to see the results, but he won't get any argument. He asks, and the performance is delivered. It's like he gets the best of Peter without any of the bickering and eye-rolling and one-upmanship everyone saw on set every day. Forgive me, but true. And the same goes for you, by the way. If Sparta needs changes in the performance, all you do is ask. Same with reshoots. You guys want to *add* scenes with Peter, we make those happen. Change a reading or performance or line in any other scene, done."

"I'm not sure whether I want to thank you or put a gun in my mouth."

"I'd advocate for the former, particularly since what I'm describing is an incontrovertible reality. We can either use it to our advantage or decide it's the end of mankind. Forget movies. Yes, it's essential we be wary of it, but we also need to welcome it, bring it into the insane beauty of what it is to be human and what our species has accomplished since we crawled out of the sea. What? Are you going to trade in your iPhone, a computer in the palm of your hand a hundred thousand times more powerful than the one NASA used to send us to the moon, because kids incur psychological damage from social media or people get in car wrecks while texting? A device that can communicate via satellite, with a tiny battery and without wires, with someone in Japan or China with instantaneous translation in real time? Of course not. Every technological revolution has brought a certain amount of peril. Maybe we're on our way to extinguishing ourselves, but we haven't done it yet, and I'd rather believe in what's possible than what's potentially devastating."

"Well, by your reckoning, the computers have already figured out where it's all headed anyway."

"If they haven't they will. And, Max, forgive me, but what choice do you have? Are you gonna recast the film? Rewrite it?"

"We're certainly not going to recast."

"And if you rewrite and don't go this route, are you going to have no scenes with Paul Kramer or Major Machina in them where he has lines? And even then, by the way, if you show his face in scenes he's not in, it's CGI anyway."

"I'm aware."

"Which countless films have already done, so honestly, what's the big deal?"

"Before I bring this up to Marci, whose blessing we're going to need from a publicity point of view, I need to see a test."

"It's in the works."

The following week Max, Jeremy, Charisse, Javier Benavidez, a decidedly glum Joel Slavkin, and three of the writers met in the Grand screening room with Anton and Nazak and the rest of the visual effects team, along with the head of Gateway AI, the company Anton had enlisted to handle the test.

"Whatever you show me has to be projected large. No monitors," Max had insisted.

"A good monitor is going to be more unforgiving than a projected image."

"Then I'll look at that after, but I want to see what an audience in Dubuque would see, or Seattle or New York or LA, in a theater."

What he beheld chilled him as nothing ever had. Peter Compton himself seemed to address the camera from a bench in Atlanta in front of the Federal Reserve building on Tenth and Peachtree. It was magical, astonishing, and morbid beyond words.

"Hey, Max," he said as pedestrians (presumably real) passed by. "It's me, Peter, sitting in front of what I understand to be one of your favorite examples of Beaux-Arts architecture in the country. The unmistakable influence of Paul Cret."

"Who the fuck told him that?" he exclaimed, before realizing he was speaking about a deceased person. "I mean, how did you guys know that?"

No one answered as the person who seemed to be Peter continued.

"I'm actually sorry you can't be here with me, but, of course, I know you have to be in Los Angeles lording over your countless minions. Anyway, here's to hoping we can finish this film. No, I'm not talking to you from the grave, but I am, in a sense, speaking from my heart. Call it my . . . uh . . . Platonic heart out there in a digitized world of forms. Or if you'd rather resort to some other way of thinking, call it a truth that's a lie, like most truths. We've all put too much work into *Major Machina* to squander it because of what happened to me. And I'm sorry about what happened. I truly am. Sorry about what I did to myself and to all of you. If I could go back and change it all, I would." To Max's further astonishment, the image of Peter began to cry, wiping away what seemed actual tears. "I would. I swear to you, Max. But I promise you that if you let us, we'll finish this film beautifully. Trust Joel, Javier, Jeremy, Charisse, of course Marci, and above all yourself to bring this home."

The clip ended to stunned silence.

"Excuse me," said Joel Slavkin, who sat to Max's left. He rose and left the room. Max then looked to his right, where Javier Benavidez stared stoically forward. All others present turned to await Max's verdict.

"I don't even know what to say," he said.

Devoid of artifice of any kind other than the familiar ones of projection and sound, he'd effectively just seen Peter Compton. It was his body, his face, his eyes, his mouth, his voice. But more important, peculiarities of the studio head's relationship with the now deceased star suffused every nuance—not just the lines uttered, replete with offhandedly peppered references to schools of thought to impress an Oberlin graduate, but in tones simultaneously apologetic and wryly ostentatious. Both their wariness of each other and their mutual respect were there, along with the tearful remorse combining sincerity and manipulation, all specifically informed by the betrayal of the actor's overdose and its impact on Sparta and Max. It wasn't just Peter; it was Peter for an audience of one.

Too startled to address the VFX or AI teams who'd accomplished the feat, Max turned instead to Zach Golden, one of the writers.

"You wrote that for him? Or for it—the double or whatever?"

"Not exactly," said Zach.

"It was written by the computer," said the head of Gateway AI, whose name was Charlie Loeb. He was squat of build with a freckled face that widened steadily from the chin into a massive bald pate.

"How did it know about my obsession with the Federal Reserve building?"

"You probably talked about it in an interview," answered Charlie.

"Maybe ten years ago."

"We ordered the program to write a monologue for Peter Compton to deliver to you, in his style, in support of finishing the film as scripted. Remember, the software has access to everything you've ever said or done that might have appeared online. We asked it to choose a spot in Atlanta. We asked it to charm you, also to reach you emotionally. Then we gave what came back to the writers, and they polished it a bit."

"Saying 'a bit' is even generous to us. I think we changed three or four words," said Zach.

"It was like he was saying it all unrehearsed. I'm going to keep saying 'he' because it's the easiest way to describe it," said Max.

"We understand," said Anton, grinning. "Believe me . . ."

"I mean, he even stuttered a few times," continued Max. "He was also searching for words—barely—but as much as Peter ever did. And the crying."

"The idea was," said Anton, "to task the platform with more than what we're going to be asking of it, just to prove to you that this can work, which is why we not only had it create the performance with an emotional range, but the actual text. The hope was that it'd bring more of the actual 'Peter' to the party than we even need. We'll be able to let the program kind of improvise around the lines, which of course is what Peter did, as Joel will tell you. Where is Joel?"

"He stepped out," said Charisse.

"Anyway, it was about allowing the computer to write the speech and then even do one better by improvising. That's how you get the searching for words in the moment."

"And Jesus, the reference to Plato. And Paul Cret."

"You know how Peter was."

"Of course, but the rhythm of his voice, the 'uh' right before. Peter always would throw in the 'uh' before dropping the intellectual ordnance, just to make it seem casual even though he knew exactly what he was doing."

"The computer has more of Peter to draw on than anyone on Earth. Everyone combined, truthfully. A process that isn't humanly possible."

"Okay, so then what?"

"We took the speech," said Anton, "hired a local crew—Javier and Joel were in LA—got the double, dressed him in some clothes from Peter's rack, and had him perform the speech. And when I say perform, I directed, and I'm not a director. My instructions were that he had to memorize it, which let's just say he sort of did. Then I said, 'Just speak the speech and don't worry about anything but facing the camera and saying what's written.' That took a while to tone down, because of course he thinks he's now playing the part. But finally we got him to just say the words. Then we had the computer generate a version of Peter's face doing it based on inputs of every bit of footage we have of him in every scene—"

"This I knew."

"Plus the thousands upon thousands of photo scans from the on-set booth."

"Yes."

"*And* all the footage of him from every movie and interview and red carpet appearance that's on the web. Put that all together with the generated text, and you have a disembodied face saying the words. CGI sutures it together with the double, corrects for what seems at all jagged or contrived, and we have what you just saw, which, I want to say, can actually be even better."

"I'm just speechless."

"Our workflow on the film would basically be what I just described, except that not a word of the script needs to be changed—unless, of course, you want the platform to 'Peterfy' it."

"'Peterfy'?"

"The way Peter would always change the syntax or the vocabulary to make Paul Kramer sound smarter," said Zach. "It used to piss me off, because of course the implication was that he was a better writer than the writers, and naturally I was terrified he was right."

"So in other words, the computer would start generating the performance before the double would?"

"You're going to want that," said Anton, "and so is Joel. This double has a fucking agent."

"Declan told me."

"Where is Declan, by the way? We were psyched to show him this," said Anton.

"Declan is no longer on the film," said Max in a way that foreclosed further questioning. The line producer's admission, under relentless pressure, that he'd purchased a six-figure automobile with $30,000 of rebate money (along with putting a car dealer's children in the film) brought to mind Henry V's line to Lord Scroop: it was "like another fall of man." Max had trusted few in the company's infrastructure more than Declan Morris, to the extent that when the man was on a film he barely glanced at cost reports. Yet in a single act of chicanery he'd endangered Sparta's entire presence in Georgia. And for what?

"I can't explain it, Max," he had said fecklessly over Zoom, tears streaking his face.

"Just try, Declan. Please."

"I had to have it."

"A car?"

"It could say things about me I was never able to. Like it could be my turn to get noticed for something other than the fucking budget and schedule."

"You certainly succeeded."

"I'll pay the money back. I'll do whatever you ask. Just please don't make this public. It's not just my career. Obviously that's over, but my family."

"Trust me, there's no upside to this getting out. Sparta is covering the overage with what we might have paid you. We don't want the paper trail of a reimbursement, as weird as that sounds. Nor is the Georgia Film Office eager for anyone to know. The last thing they want is the legislature coming after the rebate program. Enjoy the stupid car."

"Obviously I'm selling it."

"Declan, nothing is obvious to me anymore." The poor man was done in the industry, no matter how many titles he'd brought in on budget, no matter how many decades he'd given to his trade. If he'd been so unhappy as to have squandered it all with such a self-destructive impulse, perhaps it was for the best. There was even suspicion he'd been the one to have released at least one of the videos, but that inquest had been terminated by Max within a month of wrapping in Georgia. What difference did it make anymore?

"But yeah, you're right in terms of workflow," said Charlie Loeb. "The software helps generate the lines and begins building Peter's performance. The double says them as they've been rewritten in the manner of Peter, which we do recommend, and then the software and the compositors go to work."

"And when Joel wants changes?"

"Exactly. I mean, what, do I speak to the computer?"

Max turned to Joel, whose return had escaped his notice. The director's tone suggested that coaxing his participation in any iteration of what was being proposed would require persuasion.

"Well," answered Anton, "I would suggest you give the notes to Nazak or me, and we'll speak with the team at Gateway, but yes, effectively your adjustments would go to the AI and be accomplished. You want it funnier, angrier, faster, slower, we make it happen."

"That's not the way I speak to actors. This isn't a diaper commercial."

"Sorry, Joel, tell us how you speak to actors," said Anton.

"Not in terms of results, which is insulting."

"You don't have to worry about insulting the computer. But if that's a concern, you can speak to us or to it however you'd like, and it'll give you whatever you want. And the more you interact with it, the better it gets at giving you what works particular to how you're asking. It learns from you. In other words, Max, because it was your question, any changes can be made from notes Joel might have, from altering a line, a line reading, to whatever. We can have Paul Kramer drunk on the moon if you want."

"Very helpful," said Joel. "Really constructive."

"Lines are one thing," said Max, uninterested in conflict. "What if Joel wants a reverse shot while someone else is speaking. I mean, if this double isn't an actor, we're not going to be relying on him to help represent how Paul Kramer would take what's being said to him."

"The computer can not only decipher the meaning of words and combinations of words as they're spoken, it can interpret tone. It's also got more than enough data on how not only Paul Kramer reacts in every conceivable scenario, since we've fed it every close-up take in every scene where half the time he's listening to a scene partner, but we've got the entire internet database of Peter Compton listening to people as well. It's the same paradigm. And again, Joel still directs the performance."

"Jesus," said Max. "Is this even legal?"

"We've actually begun to delve into that," said Jeremy, the first time he'd spoken. "First of all, if Marci signs off, it's really not going to be an issue. But even if she were to object—"

"If she objects, it's a nonstarter," said Max. "I think I've already made that clear."

"You have, but say she did. We own every frame of footage we have of Peter to exploit as we wish. He doesn't have cutting rights on the film. That rests with Sparta. We paid the guy fifteen million dollars for the shoot. As long as we meet that obligation, even though technically he didn't meet his end because he didn't finish the film as described in the contract, we're good. Obviously he's not getting his five million for publicity."

"Yes, but—and I'm ignoring my feelings here, which, as I said, no Marci approval, we don't move forward—but just looking at the spirit of the contract as opposed to the letter of it, couldn't Marci say that exploitation of his image was for the purpose of creating the motion picture?"

"What else are we proposing, if not that?"

"We're using filmed versions of Peter to teach the computer to *be* Peter so that we no longer need Peter."

"Peter gave us no choice, Max."

"I'm not sure how that makes a difference. And by the way, he didn't intentionally kill himself."

"He did take drugs, which was a violation of his contract."

"True . . ."

"Which even further divests us of any obligation to go looking for the spirit as opposed to the letter of the contract."

Everyone waited while Max thought. They made it seem like the simplest of steps. Taking it would be to traverse a canyon.

"I need to speak with Marci."

THIRTY-TWO

"**The only person** who can stop this is you," said Joel Slavkin on the phone. "Max said as much. If you object, they aren't going to do it."

"What do *you* want?"

"Ultimately that doesn't matter, Marci."

"But what do you think?"

"Well, first I think about you."

"Forget about me."

"That's difficult."

Jesus, thought Marci, for once could a man speak to me without an undercurrent of longing?

"Take me out of the picture," she said.

"After you I think about Peter, who, yes, would have told the studio to go fuck themselves, because after all they created the situation that sent him spiraling out of control."

"Yeah, not so sure about that."

"Three times security failed to stop people from filming him."

"I can't deny that."

"So a part of him would have wanted the studio to suffer for that. But he also would want the movie to be finished with him and not someone else playing the part, meaning the best movie possible. Also, I think he would have been weirdly intrigued by the concept of AI creating a performance and that he'd be the first actor to have it done. I mean on a strictly intellectual basis. His misgivings about the capacities of AI aside, I remember him talking to me one day about the *Times* article where the bot freaked out on the writer."

“Yeah, he was obsessed.”

“And it was interesting why. How the brain was essentially no different. First of all, it’s electrical. Secondly, it recognizes patterns and exploits that recognition to pursue a kind of ‘simulacrum’—his word, because it struck me at the time—of reality to pursue what it wants, the super-objective of which is self-perpetuation, which is what everyone most fears will happen with computers at our expense. As usual with Peter, he had me arguing with him inside of my head all day.”

“That was my husband.”

“But then at the same time, he always said computers could never do what humans do.”

“You still haven’t answered my question.”

“I don’t want to direct a stand-in. It’s not what I signed up for. And especially not going from there to giving notes to a computer once removed by talking to Anton and Nazak, two of the most infuriating people I’ve ever met. And then there’s the sheer callousness of it all. Yeah, Max is going to talk to you about doing this for Peter, but Sparta is the big winner here. You can already see the “Dedicated to Peter Compton” at the end of the film before any other credit, including mine, and of course I’ll agree to that gladly, but all of this has only made the film more valuable to them. It’s fucking sick.”

“All correct.”

“But I mean it, Marci. If they go this route, which de facto means you agreed to it, I’ll be there, and I’ll do as good a job as possible.”

“What about Javier?”

“I’ll try to persuade him. I’ve actually grown to love the guy. Kind of like I was just beginning to appreciate your husband. Javier might be one of the last true purists. I don’t know what he thinks about me right now, but that’s all right.”

“What do you mean?”

“He left the screening room without talking to anyone.”

“And Jeremy and Charisse?”

“They want to move forward.”

“Of course.”

“And Max listens to them.”

"Should I watch the test?"

"Absolutely not."

Max Kaiser buzzed from the gate at a minute past ten the following morning. He'd been parked just outside it for fifteen minutes, texting in full view of the security camera.

"Let's sit in the kitchen," she said. "Samantha got pastries from Amandine, and she can make you an espresso if you want."

"That would be wonderful."

"How do you take it?"

"A latte would be great. Hello, Samantha," he said to her assistant, who donned a colorful vintage sundress in response to Marci finally banning the darker, muted hues that had proliferated in the month since Peter's death.

She guided Max to the Angelo Mangiarotti dining table she'd purchased the week they'd closed on the house and before the kitchen was renovated. She loved how the white marble bounced the light that came in from the windows that faced southeast toward West Hollywood.

"This is a great room," he said. "I'd never want to leave it."

"Sometimes I stay in mornings, instead of going into the office, and sit here with my laptop and the phone."

"I love those tiles."

She turned to the long backsplash of green-on-white four-inch glass squares on the wall separating the kitchen from the great room.

"Yeah, my sister found that tile maker in Binghamton. It's all from recycled materials, and no one like another. They remind me of home."

"How are you, Marci?"

"A bit crazed trying to organize this memorial I feel obligated to have. Ideally it would have been the get-together at the house, but obviously that's not what I signed up for when I married the guy."

"Not to mention the fact that you were, to say the least, instrumental in not only the rehabilitation of his career, but it soaring beyond what I'm sure either of you imagined possible."

"Peter was already doing pretty well when he was sent upriver."

"Not what he is now."

"That's an interesting use of the present tense."

"Not intended. Despite why I'm here, I'm aware he's no longer with us."

"Good to know."

Samantha delivered the latte in a black mug, the surface of froth painted with the shape of a frond.

"Jesus, Samantha, were you a barista before you landed the job with Marci?"

"In college to help me through."

"And where was that?"

"Wesleyan."

"What is it about that place? So many people in film."

"As it's been explained to me," said Marci, "there was this one professor. A woman named, what was it, Basinger?"

"Yes," said Samantha.

"Though Sam was Russian lit."

"My wife and I met in a Russian lit class."

"Novels that aren't afraid to be big," said the assistant.

"Twentieth century, though."

"So Bulgakov, Zamyatin, Bely, Solzhenitsyn, Pasternak, Grossman?"

"Wow," said Max. "You really know your stuff."

"Not really," she said in a way that was only half sincere.

"So," said Marci, "you're here to tell me why we need to finish *Major Machina* with Peter in the lead and how that's going to be accomplished."

"Let me be clear, Marci. Regardless of what you decide, this is bigger than the movie or Sparta."

"Then why does it have to be my decision?"

"Because we're not doing this without your blessing."

"Fine. I'll make it easy. I'm not going to speak out against the film if you AI my husband."

"You'd have every right, but it wouldn't come to that."

"Of course I'd have every right. I can say what I want unless it's libelous, which even then I can say, because neither you nor Grand is going to like the look of suing the grieving wife."

"Unfortunately we need more than your silence. Your public neutrality, in other words, means we don't move forward."

"You want me to show up on set every day while the double says the lines? Work with Joel and Nazak and fucking Anton to make sure the computer-generated avatar of Peter is just spot-on? I mean, what are you saying, Max? This isn't like you."

"You don't have to show up on set, you don't have to watch any footage. You don't even ever have to watch the movie."

"So, what, then?"

"First off, to say to me it's truly okay with you that we do this. That you support it."

"So that, what? You don't feel guilty at night?"

"There's that, yes. You're looking at me like you don't believe me, but please, give me a little more credit."

"You're misreading my expression."

"What were you thinking then just now when you contorted your face in total contempt?"

"That my husband would find this entire conversation ridiculous, and that at the same time he would have predicted it almost to the word."

"I'm sure that's true."

"Because let's just be clear what you're proposing. Just over four weeks since he died, before there's even been a public memorial, you're sitting at my kitchen table wanting my blessing for the most cynical thing you could propose so your investment doesn't suffer."

"Marci—"

"No, you're going to listen."

"Should your assistant maybe go into another room?"

"I want her to hear this. After all, it's her brave new world even more than it is yours and mine. No matter what you say to yourself, you're here not because you cared about my husband or care about me or my feelings, but because you guys are fucked. You can finish the movie without doing what you propose, but you're missing key scenes, so you'll have to rewrite. A couple hundred thousand bucks, no big deal. But you do that, you're under the scrutiny of the fans, who'll skewer you for it regardless. The critics too. Lots of: 'It's manifestly clear the film suffers from cheap-fix revisions to account for the tragic absence of its lead actor for lynchpin scenes.' Plus, they'll pummel you for choosing to contort the plot so you can profit off a dead guy suffering from addiction who didn't know the drug he was taking. Yes, you'll say you did it to honor Peter, but no one will buy it. Your second choice is to reshoot with another actor, which will cost you easily forty million dollars. And then every fan and every critic will say, 'Yeah, it was fine, but imagine the film with Peter Compton.' Then there's the third and wildly preferable way to go. You get my public support for your computerized necromancy, where the wife comes out and says some version of 'This is what Peter would have wanted. Sparta honors him by completing this film as he would have hoped for,' and you have everything. You release the movie where no one knows which scenes were AI and which weren't, which is its own boost to sales, because every fan and film buff and bored idiot will want to go and wager on which was which, and of course Sparta will 'never tell' out of respect for Peter, stoking interest even more. Plus you get all the publicity of being the first film ever to do something like this, which even if it's 'bad' publicity, you know what they say about publicity. Ultimately my husband's death, even though it means he's not around to promote—unless you get AI to do that too—will be a net gain for you guys, and a huge one. You'll maybe even allude to Paul Kramer's death in the teaser after the credits in a way that makes the die-hard fans cry, and it's the movie event no one can miss."

"Wow, Marci."

"Yeah. Wow."

"Regardless of how you construe it, and much of what you say is accurate in its way, no one is out to get you here, or Peter."

"I didn't say you were."

"And just because the way forward I'm advocating is what's best for Sparta doesn't mean it isn't best for your husband and his memory. It's not a zero-sum game. I mean, do you really want to have no Peter and no film?"

"Now you see why he runs the most successful franchise in the world," Marci said to Sam. "The guy is shameless."

"If I didn't feel this was the right way to go, for everyone, I wouldn't be here. My God, Marci, I feel like an asshole right now, and I really shouldn't."

"Aren't you doing reshoots in four months anyway? Why not let everyone take a beat? A lot of what you're getting from me has to do with your haste."

"Unfortunately this is about more than just reshoots. If we're starting from scratch, which is a real possibility, or even if we're doing some sort of hybrid that includes Peter and a new Major Machina who isn't Paul Kramer, we need to know now and get the writers writing. Are we using some of our sets? Scrapping them all? Is it a page one rewrite? Or . . . can we finish what we started? Everything is on hold. Is that fine? Yes, we can handle it. But unfortunately it's a state of abeyance that can't go on forever, especially, I'm sorry, but in what's now a publicly held company by virtue of Grand that, for better or worse, is a lot bigger than you or me. But that aside, yes, you're Peter's widow, but you're also a producer on this film. You understand better than anyone that decisions need to be made."

"I see."

"And you don't have to agree, but the way I see it, and again, this is just me, finishing the film is its own form of closure. I'm not saying it needs to be that for you. In fact none of us can even begin to imagine what you're going through. But if I didn't feel this was the best way to honor your husband, I wouldn't be here."

"Kind of checkmated, Sam, don't you think?" Marci asked.

"I think you do what you feel is best," her assistant answered.

"She's right," said Max.

Marci stared into the depths of the marble tabletop, quarried in southern Italy half a century ago, sculpted, machined, and honed at the Battaglia foundry she'd insisted she and Peter visit four years prior when in Milan, and where of course they were given a private tour by the owner himself. Peter had adduced references to traditions in stone dating back to ancient Athens to the designer's astonished delight.

She couldn't look anywhere and not encounter memories of him and their time together. She could tear down the house and build another, she could decamp to another city, state, country, continent, and it would be the same, because whatever physical manifestation of their union—whether object, place, structure, or environment—she might replace, associations would still present. This would be true especially in the abstract. Emotions, thoughts, and ideas were no longer hers alone. What new experience could she approach without asking herself what might he have thought or done, how might he have responded? It brought no comfort to understand that had she been the one to die, the same condition would be afflicting him, perhaps even more profoundly. She had after all been the "Virgil to his Dante" (his way of describing it) in navigating a world that had changed so profoundly during his years away. In fact, the suspicion he'd be having it worse only deepened her despair.

The preceding four weeks had been simply awful, beginning with the event at her house the Sunday following his death. About forty people had shown up initially, including Max and Joel; Peter's agents, lawyer, and accountant; Peter's assistant, Jay Lynne; Samantha; a peppering of Peter's actor pals; some friends from high school, three out of four of whom had been sober for over a decade; and Peter's brother, who flew out from Chicago, where he had an oncology practice (how that happened from the insanity of an actor father and borderline schizophrenic poet mother, Marci never quite understood). In the spirit of Peter's professed indifference, she did serve alcohol and even let folks light up outside. She couldn't honestly be sure coke or pills hadn't been consumed, though she discovered evidence of neither.

Everyone gave speeches, more in praise than in mourning. It astounded her how accurate many of them were, as well as coherent in their totality. The man the lawyer described scarcely differed from that of the recovering heroin addict who'd known Peter mostly in his teens, suggesting more than anything that Peter had been consistently and indiscriminately who he was no matter the person or nature of the relationship. In this way the event took more the form of a wake, though the deceased wasn't laid out on a table, and she anticipated folks would depart before sundown, having arrived by 2:00 p.m. per the selective invitation.

But no one would leave, and the number of guests (none arriving past 5:00 p.m. invited by Marci) only swelled. Paparazzi had appeared outside the gate starting at 1:00 p.m. Anticipating this, she'd hired guards to keep them twenty feet from the entrance, but by 11:00 p.m. the number of photographers had increased, and Marci missed two speeches to negotiate overtime with the security detail.

"Where did all these guests come from?" she asked Jay Lynne.

"Word got out."

"From here?"

"People have been texting and posting."

It all seemed of a piece, everyone wanting his or her say, the continual buzzing from the gate as new mourners arrived, which meant more lachrymose encomia, each variously moving, poignant, tragic, ridiculous, the whole of it made possible by advances in technology that rendered everything accessible, immediate, but also ephemeral, not to mention symptomatic of the appetite that had helped drive her husband to his death. Her home had become that night's place to be, each person outdoing the last to assert the necessity of their presence with tales more outrageous than the last (and each sadly credible, given the life her husband had led). But within days some other astonishment would eclipse this one for real-time obsession until it trended and waned. I couldn't conjure a more lucid image of our present, she said to herself, looking out over easily several billion dollars of earning power and notoriety between the producers, stars, directors, publicists, lawyers, agents, executives, and studio heads who'd breached her gates to tweet or Instagram, TikTok or text, that they were present.

An Academy Award nominee for Best Supporting Actor some seven years prior told what she considered the story of the evening, one she'd never heard, which surprised her since Peter held little back regarding his time before prison, including his dissolute youth in and around the family beach house where by his teens he was spending most of his time. The eulogist was clearly drunk but a distance from incoherence—in that sweet spot where inhibition had vanished and an almost poetic lucidity overtook. It was what Marci referred to as alcohol's magic hour, which, like the film term that described the thirty minutes of perfectly soft light when the sun has set but it isn't yet dark, lasted for a short time between when a drinker's obnoxiousness had settled and incoherence had yet to fell him.

"So Peter and I were doing this film," he began. "It was an indie that was actually pretty good but didn't end up going anywhere. I think they paid Peter a million, and the rest of us were getting Schedule F—fifty-five grand or something. But as a consolation prize for the pay inequity, since it was a so-called ensemble comedy, he convinced the producers to have us all stay at his beach house for the weekend to rehearse with the director. Of course this being Peter back in the day, before Sparta even existed, before streaming, when movies like that one were actually getting financed for theaters, we were serious about work and serious about play. We'd rehearse in the mornings in front of the surf, and the director would draw out the sets in the sand, I kid you not, and block out the staging. And there we all were, barefoot in our shorts, playing our parts. Absolutely idyllic. There were pastries from a bakery in Malibu in the morning, coffee, a Pavoni should you want espresso, fresh juices, the works. He brought in a cook to make us lunch and dinner. In the afternoons we drank, played poker, smoked a lot of weed; some of the guys had guitars, some other stuff I'd rather not mention. But me and Peter decided to take a walk on the beach with a big fat joint. And I've got to tell you this was early on in my career. I'd auditioned for my part, and here I was with fuckin' Peter Compton, already then one of the coolest actors on the planet, and we were strolling the beach in Malibu with a cheroot. I definitely wasn't in Missouri anymore, which is where I'm from. The sun was nearly down over the Pacific, the light was almost rose gold the way it gets out in Carbon Canyon, our shadows to our right but slightly ahead as if they were leading the way, the buzz fucking perfect. So we're walking and we approach this sort of Craftsman house built in the seventies, and Peter says, 'You see that house? When I was sixteen my best friend lived there, and I was fucking his mother. She was in her late thirties and gorgeous.' I just keep walking, of course, because how does a person respond to that? And Peter being Peter, this was only the beginning of the story. 'So then,' he says, 'it's Christmas, and we've been at it for about four months, usually in the afternoons when my friend had soccer practice and the dad was down at work in Century City where he sold junk bonds or something. And I've been invited by my friend, who has no idea what's going on, to open gifts, and as usual my parents were God knows where, even on Christmas. Anyway, everyone is there unwrapping, and it comes around to the dad, and the wife hands him this box about a foot long and eight inches wide that's passed along through me and it's got some heft to it, clearly something solid in there, no rattling of any kind. And the dad starts unwrapping, and he's saying, "Absolutely. Yes. Thank you," to the wife before he's even opened it, so you can tell he's told her what he wanted to celebrate the birth of one Jesus Christ. What is it? A fucking gun. A .38, to be precise, the kind policemen carried back then.' Now this was Malibu in the late eighties, so Peter's thinking this has got to be one of the weirdest families he's ever seen, and while he's thinking this, the dad has taken the pistol from the box, and he's raised it and swiveled it over to point directly at Peter's head, and he says to Peter, 'You have a gun to be able to say to people, "Don't fuck with what's mine." You get me, Peter? Don't fuck with what's mine.' 'Jesus,' I said to Peter, 'what did the wife do? What did your friend do?' And Peter said, 'The wife was silent, my friend kind of mildly troubled by it. He said, "Dad, what are you doing?" or something like that, and the dad says—this I'll never forget—he says, "I'm teaching your friend Peter here a life lesson, but for right now, this second."' And all the while he's still aiming the pistol at Peter. Then he says, 'Have you learned it, Peter?' And Peter says, 'Yes, sir, I have.' 'And the wife still doesn't say anything?' I ask, and Peter says, 'Not a word.' 'So what did you do after that?' I asked Peter. We were now directly in front of the house, and he stops and we're both staring at it, and he says, after one of those perfect Peter pauses, 'We kept fucking. For about another two months until she got bored with it and moved on to God knows who or what.'"

Only Peter, thought Marci when the story had concluded, could elicit such a tale as a part of his obsequies, let alone provide the biography to inspire its telling.

"Why, among all the possible experiences I had with this incredible person, would I choose to reveal that one a week after his death?" asked the actor to the spellbound room. "I'll tell you. To me it contains all of Peter. There was the time and setting itself, strolling a beach at sunset in Malibu in perfect light smoking a joint. There's the willingness of a huge star to hang with a character actor who was completely unknown and just casually share such a personal and frightening story. And then the amazingly carefree nature of its ending. That he'd kept on with the woman at peril to his life until she was bored, and Peter telling it in a way that made clear he took none of it personally, including having a gun aimed at his head. And then you put that in the context of a crazily charmed life with so many crack-ups and missteps along the way. There was so much rejoicing and hardship, the former well fought for, the latter almost all self-inflicted, and in his Peter way, with so much intelligence and generosity inside of a person who just wanted to keep enjoying himself, even when a gun had been put to his head. We all got to walk with him on that beach, some of us actually, others metaphorically, each of us, especially him, probably knowing this was how it would end."

What a crock of shit, she thought, standing there as most in the room, including her, *actually* laughed and cried, a true instance of the mawkish and overused oxymoron one rarely experienced. Because of course the asshole had also been right, for what better story to illustrate her deceased husband? He'd basically never changed from that sixteen-year-old boy, a bullet chambered to enter his skull, but unwilling to forgo pleasures to which he should never have been exposed. And what of the story's unspoken tangential realities? How his actions affected others. What of his friend, whose family his behavior was threatening? What of the mom, in whose self-destruction he was participating? What of the husband, clearly not an exemplary human, but whom the boy was making a cuckold all the same? And Peter himself and the betrayal of his own future, risking his life for the tawdry offerings of a bored Malibu housewife. What of him?

At 3:00 a.m., having instructed the security detail to admit no others, she finally spoke, introducing her improvised eulogy with the coercive assurance hers would be the last.

"My God, look at all of you. I don't think our house has ever been so full. But the way the evening evolved, I think my husband would have loved. I mean, what, when we started out there were maybe three dozen of us? But people just couldn't stay away, wending your ways from all over Los Angeles—from the ocean, downtown, Los Feliz, Beverly Hills, the Valley, Santa Monica, Manhattan Beach, the Palisades. Leland and Jane are here from Ojai. Some folks from Santa Barbara. All to tell stories and empty my bar. Peter always did like a party, even when he couldn't partake. I've never met a person as riddled with—maybe afflicted with would be a better word—so many opposites. He couldn't have been more simple. Give him a great role and he was happy. But oh, what went into the roles. The hours and hours of research. For Paul Kramer, I'm not exaggerating: by the time we'd begun shooting it was like I was living with Niels Bohr or Oppenheimer. He could explain, and I'm telling you this not because I knew, but because he'd assimilated it enough to teach it in a way I could understand, how an atom was constructed of electrons and quarks. And electrons surround the nucleus and each electron has a charge, and how a neutron is shot at the nucleus and causes fission, and how with uranium and plutonium excess neutrons are released, creating a chain reaction, and that's what creates the explosion. And of course I'm just parroting him right now and don't really know what I'm saying, but Peter actually understood it. He made sure of it, repeating it over and over, because Peter had this thing about being a fraud, which I guess came from wanting to be believable as an actor, so if he learned a thing, he really learned it, and as we all know, pity the person who would challenge him on a topic and not be ready to bring it. So yeah, really simple to make him happy. Give him a role, and he just learns the lines and puts on the clothes. The thing is, I just can't imagine what it was like to *be* Peter, and that's what makes me almost as sad as how much I'm going to miss him. To live with that mind and that thirst and that drive and that yearning to understand everything he took on. Opposites. His was also simultaneously the happiest and most tormented soul I'll ever know, because he just took everything in so thoroughly. I would think, How does he carry that brain inside his head with all the mostly self-taught learning and passion riding inside of it? And all that love. Because as crazy as he might have driven you, he loved all of you, and that can only happen inside a person who loved life as much as Peter did. Directors and producers and sometimes other actors would come to me and they'd say, 'Marci, does the guy ever stop? Does he ever relent? Why is he like this?' Joel, you remember."

She took in the director who sat with a mug of coffee at the end of the long sectional that anchored the living room. People crowded behind him. Beyond them, the sliding doors open, stood at least a dozen others on the very section of patio where just over a year ago the director had appeared with his look book to argue about whether Paul Kramer would carry a phone. The poor man had been one of the first to arrive. Why was he still here?

"Joel, as many of you know, was the last person to direct my husband. But my answer when people would ask this was always the same: 'He doesn't ever let up because he can't do anything half-heartedly.' My husband was an addict, and in the end need won out. In a terrible way it had to. And no, I'm not romanticizing. I hated the addiction." She was weeping now and knew it wouldn't stop until it had wrung itself out. "I hated it more than I think any of you—and I'm sorry, but any of you except perhaps some of his fellow addicts or alcoholics—could understand, because it was everywhere, and it was maddening, and because of course that meant I loved it as well. What choice did I have? The addiction is partly what made him learn the roles the way he did, read as many books as he did, make all the movies he made, keep the friendships he had, love me the way he did. Yes, I could talk about my parents, my sister, but no one I've ever met loved the way Peter loved. And again, contradictions. Somehow tender but also desperate. Sensitive but also unforgiving in the most infuriating ways. Frightening but never dangerous. Always too much and never enough. 'Why can't we be like normal couples?' I would ask, feeling so pathetically silly for the sentiment, and of course he knew enough to answer only with an incredulous look. And yet, fame aside, never, not once, did I feel from Peter like his subordinate or somehow less than he. Because of course this too was the magic of Peter. Yeah, he needed all the attention he pretty much always merited and always, I mean *always*, got. We wanted to hear what he had to say because he did so in a way that made us feel appreciated for our interest, a necessary recipient in a true partnership—that in a weird way we were more important as listeners than he was as a speaker. That he needed us. Which of course he did. In fact, I've never felt so needed by anyone. I've never felt as appreciated for being smart, wise, keen, loving. He made me feel like more of a woman in all the best ways than anyone I'll ever know. And let me tell you something, I love being a woman, meaning he valued most about me what I value most about me. And here's another Peter contradiction: because he did that, because I knew him as deeply and necessarily as I did, I'll now *somehow*—I can't tell you exactly how in this moment, but *somehow*—be able to live without him for his having taught me so beautifully how to live *with* him. And there you have it. All at once I feel deeply, deeply, deeply betrayed, hurt, cheated, and enraged by him being taken from me and of course having a hand in it—because let's not lie, he did what he did—but like I want to strangle God if there is a God, or maybe go back to the first cell division that started life or the fucking Big Bang and just stop the chain of events that brought me to this level of pain. And at the same time nothing means more to me than that I got to be with this infuriating guy for some of his best years of being alive. I used to say this thing to myself that always embarrassed me, because it was of course hard to think it without seeming to lose myself. And what it was was that 'Peter is life.' I didn't say '*my* life,' I said 'life.' And that's actually and tragically of a piece with everything that happened to him as well. Life is joyous, unfair, demeaning, unforgiving, beautiful, and, in the end, probably a lot more painful than not. It's one of the biggest stars in the world falling off the wagon while playing a superhero and not knowing he was popping something lethal in an effort to make the pain and fear he was feeling subside. It's a guy who threw it all selfishly away, and that includes every one of you and me as well—he threw us away along with himself—because the dependency his body developed from the first toke he took at twelve years old finally overcame one of the most powerful brains you'll ever come across. I see Max Kaiser standing over there."

The room grew even more still. Many of those gathered loathed Sparta. Would she now excoriate the SCG? Would she go so far as to inculpate the studio in his death?

"I often asked myself how Sparta movies got so popular. It's hardly an original question, Peter and I talked about it all the time. I mean, half the characters in capes, leotards, masks. Many of the storylines either so ridiculous or convoluted you truly want to question how the same species could take such an interest in them and also produce a Picasso, a Proust, a Joyce, a Galileo. In the movie he died on, Peter was playing an irradiated half machine saving humanity from a jellyfish. And the world was panting to see it! Well, I'm gonna let the room in on a little secret: Peter and I had grown to love this movie. Why? Bear with me. The notion of God in the traditional sense might largely be dead, at least in the Western world, but *mythology* has never left us. Do people believe in Sparta characters in the way the Romans and Greeks believed in their deities? Of course not. But you want to know what a superhero movie is? It's the need to simplify the mess we make of life into paradigms that allow us for a few hours to pretend that there are actual principals out there at work that can inflict structure on all the chaos and amorality and violence arrayed against us by a universe we'll never understand. Yes—forgive me, Max—superhero movies have terrible dialogue and ridiculous storylines, but we need the respite they offer, even those of you who deride them. And do you know who taught me this? Peter, of course. Once he'd signed on, he was all in. There was the research on physics I already talked about, but also watching every movie and television show Sparta had ever made, and reading every single *Major Machina* comic, re-

reading Joseph Campbell and extolling his brilliance, and talking about Sparta as a shared world myth. And this after deriding me for making the same point when I was trying to persuade him to do the movie! I honestly started wondering if Max was having some serum put in the coffee my husband drank all day. 'It's right in front of us, Marci,' he said. It was the end of our first day of production, and we'd gone over because, yes, Peter had forced a scheduling change that upended everything. I was frankly furious with him. And he said, 'We can either take this seriously and embrace that we're part of an ongoing story being told to the whole planet, or we can cash our big checks and laugh about it. We'd better earn this honor.' You know the rest. Nine weeks after saying that my husband suffocated to death in the passenger seat of a pickup truck with no idea what was happening to him or why. And so goes the sad fragility of being human where perhaps the more passionate you are, the more uncontrollably brilliant, the more deeply feeling, the more beautifully and painfully flawed, the more extreme in every sense, the more impossible it is to keep on living. But the story is always the same: those that love get left behind. Here we are, Peter," she said after a pause. "Still your audience, but waiting for words that aren't going to come. We'll be waiting for the rest of our lives, thankful we got to hear any at all."

A silence ensued, as if the assembled expected spectral affirmation from the deceased, some sign of encouragement to get on with it, his memory now very much a part of them as all the movies he'd done. She could tell Max Kaiser wanted to speak, but not only did she wish to be last in her own home, she needed for her words to conclude all that was said. For once the head of Sparta would have to cede status.

"And with that," she said, "I'm going to ask that you all do me the favor of bringing your plates and glasses to the kitchen. It's been a long day and night, and extraordinary that all of you showed up, but I need time on my own, if only to absorb and reflect on all that was said. I hope you all will do the same. And please drive safely."

People obeyed wordlessly with the exception of Max, who assured that her words not only had honored her husband beautifully but also clarified why Peter's work was so important to the art of cinema. It was, he insisted, one of the most compelling eulogies he'd ever heard. Joel Slavkin and some others wanted to help clean up, but she insisted that between Sam and Jay Lynne, she had it covered.

When the assistants too had departed, she sat on the sofa and beheld the dawn reflecting off a low haze west of downtown. The sky blended from pastel violet to pastel pink, accented by a few clouds brightening to orange over the Pacific. It was already 9:00 a.m. in New York. Other than a few crumbs Sam had missed with the Dustbuster and the odd coaster and napkin, little evidence remained of the crowd she'd at last dispersed.

She realized only then that she was experiencing her first minutes alone since Peter went missing, the struggle to convince the two assistants to leave—they'd been alternating nights in one of the guest rooms—nearly as exhausting as convincing Esther Levy to return to New York from Atlanta rather than accompany her to Los Angeles.

She wandered to her bedroom with a glass of the Marcassin Chardonnay Peter's lawyer had brought that she'd stowed in the bottom drawer of the fridge. At least she'd now be able to booze it up freely in her own home. Perhaps I'll become an alcoholic, she thought as she touched the icon on the wall console to lower the blackout curtains in their bedroom, then swallowed an Ambien with her wine. She lay in bed, pulling the sheets that had been changed by the housekeeper the previous afternoon to just below her shoulders. They were a cream paisley, and she'd ordered them online from Atlanta before her and Peter's return, wondering at the time whether he'd notice, reminding herself not to take it personally when he didn't.

"What's it like," she'd often asked, "to know everything is done for you? That there's always juice in the fridge, granola in the cupboard; that housekeepers will be here daily on an organized schedule so that everything is clean and in its place; that light bulbs are always replaced; that every lamp, gadget, and appliance always works?"

"It's great," he would answer simply.

What had she expected? And after all, was her life so difficult having to supervise the arranging of it all? It wasn't she doing the legwork but others, and usually not at her behest but that of Samantha or Jay Lynne, two women in their twenties commanding others twice their age. I caused that, she would think, when watching Sam instruct the Mexican housekeeper which glasses to wash by hand or that the cushions needed vacuuming, or telling the fifty-year-old Venezuelan plumber which toilet needed snaking. So who is really worse, Peter in his obliviousness, or me using our little white girl minions to lord it over the older and mostly immigrant proletariat? Which of course made her resent Peter all the more for his aloofness from such unseemly hierarchies. At least that complication would be gone from her life.

She awoke in near darkness six hours later, grateful, once she navigated the morning ritual of remembering she was a widow in Los Angeles, that she'd unplugged the house phone and had switched her own to silent. She reached to the console next to the bed and raised the curtains to afternoon sunlight. A spider made its way across the ceiling twelve feet above her, and she theorized tritely that it was somehow Peter, or a sign from Peter, or a sign from God about moving forward even though she was upside down.

She listened for noises downstairs and heard what she concluded to be Sam emptying a dishwasher or perhaps rinsing a glass in the sink. It was just before two, so it could be the housekeeper. How would she keep all this up? Her own income had increased to well more than necessary to sustain a satisfactory lifestyle, but how much of that remuneration depended on her association with Peter. The brand was more his than hers, and much of her responsibility to it involved keeping her husband focused and under control, a reality rarely spoken but surely understood by any who hired them as a team. Would she even produce anymore? If so, under her and Peter's banner, her own, or someone else's? Would anyone even bother to send her scripts? Should she leave Los Angeles? The country?

She rose, showered, and stepped into a dress she'd bought in Paris for their anniversary three years prior and walked barefoot downstairs, where both Jay Lynne and Samantha sat with the remains of what appeared to be Greek salads next to half-filled glasses of cold-pressed grapefruit juice.

"Interesting night," she offered.

"That's an understatement," answered Jay Lynne. "He probably would have loved it."

"I think so," said Marci. "Though other people doing all the talking, even if it was all about him."

"I liked what Joel Slavkin had to say. It was so honest."

"Joel is an honest guy."

"You do know he's in love with you," said Samantha.

"He thinks he is. Total spaniel. Peter had grown to appreciate him at the end. They probably would have worked together again, which would have been great for Peter. I mean, to have someone like Joel on his side, but not in a way where Peter was taking things over, which is where Joel was headed by finally standing up for himself."

"God, Peter hated his dog, though."

"Right," said Jay Lynne, "the therapy dog."

"I might need one of those," said Marci. "Our Bouvier doesn't quite qualify."

"It can be arranged," said Samantha.

"I'm aware. Anything can be arranged." The participle reminded her of her responsibility for the funeral/memorial that would occur weeks hence and how it would essentially entail a far shorter and more formalized version of what had transpired the night before, that in fact the real event had now happened and what was to come would be more for public show. What she didn't want was delay, to have the prospect of it hanging over her. Per his wishes, Peter would be cremated, his ashes to be kept or dispersed as Marci wished, such diversion of responsibility a consequence of his resolute and terrified vitality. The writing of their wills had been forced on him by Marci and the money managers, his answers more aggressive with each passing minute. "My fucking ashes are Marci's. She can stir them into her coffee for all I care. Shake them on a steak and eat them," was how he'd put it. "Just don't spread them on the beach in Malibu" had been his only stipulation, as if to do so would even have entered her mind. She now wondered if the prohibition had something to do with his indiscretion with a friend's mom when he was sixteen.

⸸

She kept her remarks at the public funeral short, mostly centered around a section from William Carlos Williams's "Asphodel, That Greeny Flower," which the poet had written for his wife, a work Peter had admired for the ferocity of its love in the form of confession. She read:

There is something
something urgent
I have to say to you
and you alone
but it must wait
while I drink in
the joy of your approach,
perhaps for the last time.
And so
with fear in my heart
I drag it out
and keep on talking
for I dare not stop.
Listen while I talk on
against time.
It will not be
for long.

The memorial was packed, with a crowd standing in the back at the TCL Chinese, where she'd had to hire a valet service and where reporters from all over the world stood before cameras to speak the babel of the planet. The agency provided flowers—easily $20,000 worth. Her parents catered a breakfast, having arranged it all from New York before flying in the day before. Marci put them up at the Four Seasons on Doheny.

The ceremony involved no procession to a graveyard or cemetery. Attendees handed in their tickets at the stands outside and drove their astonishing cars off into a day in Los Angeles like any other. The frisson of having been at a movie star's funeral would now feature in their lives, at least for a time. The last person with whom she spoke, of all people, was Javier Benavidez, who had come alone, invited also to the preservice breakfast, which he'd skipped.

"I was hoping I'd see you," he said. "I won't take any of your time."

"You can take all of it you'd like. I was grateful you were at the house a few weeks ago but sad we didn't speak."

"I figured you had your hands plenty full."

"You're one of the people I actually think needed to be here today. For Peter's sake."

"Why do you say that?"

"You never believed it, but Peter respected the hell out of you."

"I don't think I was entirely fair to him. He drove me crazy, like he did everyone, but I didn't understand how much pain he was in."

"None of us did."

"It's so easy to get caught up in your own absolutes. There's a reason I haven't won an Oscar since my first and only one. I was too busy being angry to use the system to get what I wanted."

"Every argument Peter and I had professionally was some form of that dichotomy. What I finally said to him was that movies, especially how they're made, are a microcosm of the country. That's what always strikes me about how people hate Hollywood. Sure the stars and directors and producers moralize and go way left of center in terms of our politics, but to a degree that's all just noise. It's the product and how it's all made that's important. Peter and I took a trip down the Amazon in Peru and stopped at a native village, and Peter's picture was on an old man's T-shirt. Now sure, who knows how it got there. Some donation from who knows what NGO from clothing bins God knows where. But still, can you imagine? 'What does it mean?' I asked Peter. 'That what we do matters in ways we might not even want' was his answer. And you're probably thinking, Sure, but, like you said, it was basically random, and anyway only a few of these villagers knew who the hell Peter was. And, of course, there you're wrong. He was mobbed, and not just because they made the connection between the image on the shirt and this guy, but because they actually did know who he was. There were televisions there, more than a few phones. And what had reached them? Big-budget American movies. Of course right now I'm wondering, just as Peter said, whether I want that responsibility, which I neither asked for nor deserve."

"Except that that fame is why Peter and you were paid what you were."

"Like I said. America."

"I take your point."

"Maybe the only solace—or perhaps it's worse—is that it's a system, no one singularly to blame. What's scary is that an example like Peter suggests otherwise, and his death, particularly the manner of it, does no one any favors."

"Maybe it calls attention to some things."

"There's no glory in dying the way he did. Trust me, I saw the body."

"I don't envy you that."

"It'll make mourning him easier."

"I'd think the opposite."

"I'm not going to go into the details, but let's just say when I think of mortality, I'll remember Peter at the morgue. Ridiculous that I was finally summoned to verify it was him. I mean seriously. 'You really need me to identify the body?' I asked. They were not amused. But of course they did, because he was barely recognizable. What death, at least that sort of death, does to a person. Bloated, blue, bug bites all over his face. It will forever remind me I was married to a human being. Sometimes I lost sight of that. By the way, and I don't mean this in a self-aggrandizing way even though it'll sound like I do, but so did he."

"So did he what?"

"Lose sight of that with me. We worshipped each other, which is fine to a degree, until one of you ends up the way he did. If I didn't have his mortality shoved in my face the way it was, I might be in the nuthouse. So what are you going to do now?"

"Heading to Mexico for a week."

"I thought you generally avoided that."

"My sister is very sick."

"I remember you mentioning her. Are you guys close?"

"There's no one closer to me on the planet. My wife maybe, but Lucia has the advantage of my knowing her since the day I was born and teaching me about nearly everything I value. I wouldn't be here without her."

"She raised you?"

"She made sure I didn't waste my life."

"Wow."

"She's also the reason I came to America, although she gets higher marks in that story than I do. She loves her country in ways I never could. There should be plazas named after her. But instead she'll die in relative obscurity. Meanwhile, look at me."

"Are you being fair to yourself?"

"What you said the other night about Peter was beautiful, especially about him giving a shit the way he did. The way we filmed the double saying the lines when he was missing. It's not my world any longer. Or Peter's or yours, for that matter. Let that *jodido* Anton run the show."

"When will you be back?"

"Well, certainly ten days from now."

"Why's that?"

"Something about a test they want me to see."

"Having to do with *Major Machina*? I hadn't heard anything about that."

"I'm sure they figured you have other concerns right now."

"Do you know what it is?"

"I have my suspicions, but I'd rather not say."

Her parents returned home the following day, her mother furious for being shooed back east, her father doing his best to mollify. What Marci did know as she dropped them curbside was that she would stay in Los Angeles no matter what.

"These are not your people," her mother said as they drove south on the 405.

"And who are my people, Mom?"

"The kind you grew up with, went to college with."

"Half of them came out here. It was like a mass exodus from Penn."

"Not the right half. Everything fancy, everyone living in their bubbles of self-importance."

"Is the Upper East Side any different?"

"On the Upper East Side I walk. I run into people. I talk about things. I didn't have a single conversation out here in the last three days other than with your father where people weren't talking about movies and television. And everyone just wanting to go on about themselves. I wasn't asked a single question about me. Or if I was, trust me, the conversation veered away from the humdrum life of the old lady pretty quickly and it was back on to them."

"That truly astonishes me, Mom."

"At least you haven't lost your gift for irony."

⚡

She resolved to face her widowhood in the most direct and un-cosseted way possible. It wasn't that she didn't wish to burden others with her pain, but more that she found others a burden. At least with her mother she could rely on the permanence of family (especially hers) in which one could say anything and survive it, the relationship perhaps even deepening for the honesty with which they could speak to each other. With friends in Los Angeles she could never divine how a remark or potential offense might ramify, or who might hear of it to her disadvantage, which was of course always the case in an industry town. She stopped answering the phone and emails, leaving the former to Jay Lynne and the latter to Samantha, requiring they report only the most pressing, meaning startlingly very few. Opportunism would too easily disguise itself as empathy, which included visits as well.

"You can't accept that people want to comfort you?" asked Samantha.

"Nobody's going to come through that door who doesn't want something. I'm fine with that, but not while I'm grieving."

"Can't you take in that people care about how you're coping?"

"Let them do it from afar where I don't have to put on makeup and stock the fridge and have snacks and put on acceptable clothes. Just having to answer 'How are you doing?' or being expected to reminisce or commiserate on someone else's terms. And why? So they can say, 'I was at the Comptons' and saw Marci,' which then means others expect an audience with the grieving wife, so more and more people come. I learned that lesson with the impromptu memorial. They'll sit here and tell me how they can't imagine what I must be going through, how Peter and I have meant more to them than anyone, how they admired us so much as a couple, how right now I need to think only about myself, how they'll get groceries, fill my car with gas, bring food over, sleep over. Then a year from now it'll be: Will I read this script? Will I call this actor? Will I bring this into the studio? Will I produce their movie? Will I make an introduction to Max Kaiser or Joel Slavkin? With every visit will come a hundred chits."

"Jesus, Marci."

"Yeah? Too much? Cynical? Misanthropic? Realistic. It's the species, but specifically our industry subgroup. You've got this combination of a basically infantile need for adulation with only so much room on the stage, and a system that ensures only the absolutely obsessed and most cutthroat survive. And yes, I include myself. We're all the same, it's just that the best of us know how to mask the ugliness with charm and civility. So sorry, right now there will be no transactions within these walls."

The solitude allowed for a meditation on grief that exposed her to herself in ways she'd never expected, most surprising being how much her attraction to Peter had derived from a need to save him and that failing to do so, and maybe even having participated in his demise, would be a lasting affliction. This thesis presented in such an incontrovertible way that she understood quickly it wouldn't ever be debunked but instead would serve as a kind of operating principle.

What did that sound like when refined to its essence? That her deepest experience of life's greatest reward, the love of another that transcended the self, had failed, and it had done so because the hope that one could love truly in that way was life's most beautiful and essential lie. You could love another person, yes, but neither that nor its reciprocation had sway over deeper frailties that would always prevail. Nor were such frailties specific to Peter. Her own impulses constituted deep inadequacies. Everyone spoke, both before Peter's death and after, about how perfectly they fit together, like Aristophanes described in his exegesis on love. A mate exists for each of us, the ancient had insisted, who makes up the completion of a circle with whom we match perfectly, each of us broken, looking to be made whole. The goal in life was to find your unique counterpart. She and Peter had conceivably done so, but indifferent forces had intervened to inflict on that mended shape the lesson we all must learn: that all hope, by definition, is transitory. Did this make love futile? Perhaps. But it also made it necessary. Her love for Peter had enabled all that now seemed good and rendered insignificant most everything that wasn't. In a sense, she finally determined, he'd afflicted her with his own disease: she'd become addicted to another person. The rest of her life would be its own enforced recovery.

⚡

What then to do when Max Kaiser sat before her proposing not only that she permit the fabrication of a performance Peter never gave, but that she publicly support it. Within the metaphor of treatment, would the computer-generated version constitute for her and his fans a kind of methadone? The need for her approval also somewhat baffled her, since the language in the contract explicitly allowed for what the studio proposed—Sparta owned all footage of Peter as well as all stills of Peter. His (or now her) only power pertained to publicity stills and bloopers.

"You say Peter would have wanted this, Max, but I'm just not sure that's true. Set aside that this is an issue that threatens the profession to which he devoted his life, which is, of course, why actors struck over it and will probably strike again. What Peter most prided in himself was spontaneity. 'If an audience doesn't know what I might say or do next, I've done my job,' he would tell me. And in achieving that he tried to keep everyone off-balance, which included all of us watching him—producers, director, scene partner, whatever—and that while always hitting his marks and getting the lines right. It's what made him one of the greats."

"I've made the same point myself."

"So would he really like himself—or footage of him inside a character anyway, which is a whole other thing because ultimately that too is artifice—to be fed into a program that'll give the illusion of the real thing when it's a deliberately generated version? It's the opposite of everything he stood for. And what will that ultimately mean for those who come after him when the form can just hoover up data and create a seemingly indistinguishable facsimile?"

"You're overthinking it."

"A term Peter and I always hated."

"Hear me out. Ultimately it goes back to what everyone, most of all Peter, invested in this movie and whether we're going to dispose of that when we don't need to. I brought along an email he wrote me at the end of the second week of shooting. And by the way, I had it printed out when I got it, not for the purpose of bringing it to you today."

He reached into the breast pocket of the black blazer he wore over a gray T-shirt tucked into his ironed Levi's 511 jeans. The sheet he handed her was folded twice over into thirds and had enough wear to suggest the veracity of its stated provenance. She opened it and read aloud.

"'Dear Max, I just wanted to thank you for trusting me with this role and for trusting Marci and me to make this film with you.' I'll give my husband this," she said, "he always included me in that way. Always." She wiped a tear and read on. "'It's so easy to dismiss what's popular as a severely degraded version of what's best. In fact, it can be argued too easily sometimes that what's popular represents the worst of us. Look at some of the presidents we've elected. But this experience instructs a different point of view.' I still can't believe my husband never went to formal college."

"I thought it after nearly every interaction."

"'I don't pretend to be Gielgud or that we're making *The Godfather* or *Citizen Kane*, but we do have a chance here to enrich expectation in a way that asks more of what we do. If we don't do that, in fact, it's criminal (and I know something about criminality).' Hardy har har. Typical Peter."

"But funny."

"Yeah, well, standard repertoire. 'This is just to say that you have all of me. We're going to do everything we can down here to make something special. With love and gratitude, Peter.'"

She handed back the paper, which Max refolded and restored to his pocket without offering that she keep it, a gesture she'd have rebuffed.

"So Peter wanted the movie to be good."

"As you've said yourself, he saw the quality of the film as his responsibility, the shirking of which he labeled, albeit with a joke, 'criminal.' The best way forward here is to finish *Major Machina* as well as we can with Peter in the lead as it was written. I've truly thought this through. We all have. There was even a version we discussed whereby we'd have Paul Kramer be killed off-screen, completely obviating any need to generate a version of him but still including what we'd shot, but that felt wrong, using the film to imitate the tragedy of losing the actor. And would you want that?"

"I'm not sure it's any worse."

"Marci, Peter's memory belongs to you more than anyone. There's obviously his brother, though from what I gather he distanced himself from the crazy artists. Both his parents are dead, he has no children. But the grieving for him, like his legacy, doesn't just belong to you. Or to Sparta, or to the other filmmakers and producers who put him in their stories. People want to experience what he did with this role. Millions upon millions do. I'll even go so far as to say it's part of the deal he made by pursuing the life he did. Why do you think we have standard behavioral clauses in our contracts, or, in Peter's case, the abstinence clause he broke?"

"That sounds like a threat."

"I already told you that without your blessing we're not going ahead with this. My point is Peter bought in. He took publicity fees and appeared on talk shows and dressed and acted a certain way in public. He was neither a bad boy nor a recluse when he got out of prison. You guys tended to his image in a way that was noticeable, which is in part what gave me the confidence to hire him."

"I'm inordinately grateful."

"I'm sorry. That was insensitive. But whatever the circumstances of his death, he understood as much as any actor his relationship with the public."

"My husband no longer flew commercial. You do know that?"

"Jesus, I can barely fly commercial from the people who recognize me and corner me. And that's me."

"Let's hope this conversation isn't being bugged."

"Just as your husband felt it was his responsibility to make this film in the right way, it's our responsibility to finish it in the right way. You can call it morbid or wrong, but it's what we should do. It's what's best for the film, you, Peter, Sparta, and, of course, the crew who've put so much of themselves into it."

To her left Samantha stared at the macchiato she'd made for herself during the initial stages of the sit-down. When they'd first met four years prior, they'd discussed *Anna Karenina* for nearly the entire meeting, with the young woman actually diagramming the novel's structure on a napkin in a manner that Marci had never forgotten.

"Ultimately the book anchors itself to the marriage between Oblonsky and Dolly," she explained.

"Not Anna and Vronsky?"

"That's the story you follow, obviously, and Anna's the title character, but without Dolly and Oblonsky the novel loses its bearings, not to mention its cultural ballast. You've got three relationships: Levin and Kitty, Anna and Vronsky, with Anna's marriage to Karenin occupying space within that, and then Dolly and Oblonsky. Dolly and Oblonsky's is the only one that actually works, as imperfect as it is, because it's the one that balances the practical with the emotional. It's not unrealistic, in other words. This is a novel whose first sentence is about what? Families. And families, at least back then, started with marriage."

In addition to knowing then and there that this woman's script coverage would be as good as any in Los Angeles, Marci needed to watch such a mind develop into that of the producer she knew Sam could become.

It also caused her to think about marriage in a new way. As elevated as they were in terms of status, her relationship with Peter was exquisitely practical. That one exchange with a potential employee just a few months beyond twenty-two had done more to explain her love for Peter than any therapist, of which there'd been many.

"Okay, Sam," she said. "As the representative here of Gen Z, with AI and, of course, a thousand Sparta movies in your future—whatever movies are going to even be thirty years from now when Max and I are out of the game—what do you make of all this?"

"How am I supposed to answer that? I also don't think it's fair of you to ask, given you two sitting here and the context of the question."

"There'll be no judgment, recrimination, or resentment. In fact, if you're honest, all you'll get from me is gratitude, because frankly I'm at a loss."

"Well," she answered carefully, "then I need to know a bit more what it is you're asking."

"In my shoes, what would you do?"

"But I'm not in your shoes. I'm twenty-six. I have a boyfriend, not a husband. Yes, he and I live together, but in no way that resembles what you and Peter had. He's not even in the business."

"What does your husband do?" asked Max.

"He works for Raytheon," said Marci.

"Wow."

"An engineer," Samantha added.

"I guess a pretty good one," said Max.

"Peter loved him," said Marci. "When they were over for dinner all he wanted to do was talk to Noah."

"I can imagine."

"He was a huge resource for Peter in preparing for *Major Machina*," said Sam.

"True," confirmed Marci. "Peter even broke protocol and let him read the script, which accounted for a lot of the revisions Peter advocated for."

"To everyone's benefit, I'm sure," said Max.

"Sam, I want to know what you'd do in my situation," Marci insisted once more.

"I'd let Sparta finish the movie with an AI version of Peter."

"Wow. So certain. Why?"

"It's funny we're mentioning Noah, because he and I have talked a lot about these new technologies, and his point is that even if there were some kind of worldwide ban it would ultimately fail, because someone somewhere is going to continue developing what's already been accomplished, even if it's some Sparta-like psychotic genius bent on destruction. And then the only manner of deterrent will be an embrace of the same tactics to defeat it, which means engagement with the technology in a way that's more advanced. So regardless it gets more powerful. If what Sparta did works in the way everyone at the screening describes it did, the studios are going to exploit that. It's the story of mankind. Noah was pretty harsh when the writers and actors struck over AI. He said that instead of being threatened by what it would do to writers' rooms and actor performances, writers and actors should be placing premiums on being able to do things AI can't. It's like robots in factories. Ultimately you can't stop certain efficiencies. Instead you focus on what makes what you do unduplicable."

"And how does my husband do that exactly? Or how do I do that with his ashy remains?"

"This is why I didn't want to answer the question."

"You're right. I said I'd accept what you had to say without recrimination."

"Obviously Peter can't deliver a performance anymore, which is tragic for you especially. I get why you'd fight any attempt to let Sparta or the world off the hook by allowing the creation of some version of him to help with their loss. For you an AI version of him is almost worse. You want to say, 'Fuck all of you. You should feel even half the loss I'm feeling.'"

"You're a very perceptive person," said Marci, realizing the young woman had touched precisely the source of her umbrage, the specifics of which Marci herself hadn't yet really understood. And how, as the person from whom the most had been taken, could Sparta and the rest of the world be arrayed in such absurd rectitude against her pain?

"I'm not meaning to score points in that regard," said Samantha. "I'm just trying to say I have a sense of where you're coming from even though I can't begin to claim I know what you're feeling. Obviously Peter can no longer personally combat the proliferation of AI, and perhaps in this case you can. But to what end? You're not going to slow its development. None of us is. As for movies, haven't you always told me they're always changing?"

"I'm not sure Max here cares much about the future of movies."

"I don't think that's fair, Marci," he said.

"For what it's worth," said Samantha, "I don't think computers can ever best what an actual actor can do, nor will audiences be interested in anything other than the genuine article."

"Besides, Marci, for eighty-five percent of the film we have Peter. Do you really want for us to throw that all away when there's a solution that actually centers him in every respect?"

The sheer crush of it was becoming unbearable. Would she really force Sparta to reshoot with another actor? And would this ultimately be what Peter wanted—for his performance never to be seen? This was a man, after all, who'd effectively immolated himself in front of a crew of three hundred because he couldn't stand that another might have the last word before a captive group.

"All right," she said, "I'm going to go along with this. And, to be clear, I'll endorse it. I'll come to the premiere, I'll thank Sparta for all it does."

He's truly dead now, she thought. What better proof than his digital resurrection?

"Thank you, Marci. I think you've made the right decision. Not just for Sparta and moviegoers, but for Peter and, I dare say, in the long run, for you."

"Max, you and I both know there really wasn't a choice. It was made, given where we are, the moment Peter accepted the part."

And so it was with life: our births the start of our deaths, as they'd always been. But our deaths were now a new kind of birth, an immortality of sorts, no longer fixed or fading, but always there, always possible, always a poignant version of what they were.

THIRTY-THREE

"So, Joel, we're here at one of the most iconic movie theaters in Los Angeles, probably in America, the TCL Chinese, where just over a year ago Peter Compton's memorial took place. It's the red carpet, journalists from everywhere, complete excitement, but still the tragedy of Peter Compton's death looming. How do you address that at a moment like this?"

"Yeah, I guess I try to think about Peter being here with us all, experiencing the outpouring of interest and support and anticipation for what he did with this amazing character. We need to look at this not just as the premiere of *Major Machina* but as a celebration of Peter and his talent."

"What was it that made Peter Compton so great?"

"Oh my God, where do I begin? I'd say more than his talent, it was the amount of himself he put into each part. He took nothing for granted, especially not his stardom. If you asked Peter, he would say he was an actor and that's all he'd ever been, and that never changed even with all the notoriety, both good and bad. The set was a sacred place for him. I mean, he actually said a blessing for each location with a ritual. He wanted everything to be pure. With Peter it was always about making a great film, and thanks to the support of Sparta and, of course, the amazing Marci Levy, we've been able to do that. What people are going to see tonight is because of Peter more than anyone."

"You mention Marci Levy. Can you talk about what she brought to this project and what it's like to be here with her on a night like this after what happened to her husband?"

"Well, for starters Marci, along with Jeremy Davidoff and Charisse Thorn produced this movie, and when I say that I mean without her it wouldn't be what it is, and that involvement continued after Peter's death. No Marci and we wouldn't be here. At least not with this movie."

"Can you talk a little bit about that?"

"Just that when Peter died, Marci didn't retreat into her grief, which of course would have been understandable. It's what I wanted to do, frankly. Most of us in fact. It was Marci who said, in no uncertain terms, we need to finish this film with Peter as Major Machina and *for* Peter, and that's what we did. There was nothing more important to her."

"And how do you feel right now? After all that's happened, to be finally here, all the work done, the first public audience to see the completed film?"

"You know, I grew up in Indiana. My first movie, a sci-fi I did with some friends in the eighth grade, we made in a field near my house after I convinced my dad to let me use the lawnmower so we could create alien markings."

"Did he make you mow your own lawn as payment?"

"Of course he did! But he let me use the mower, and then later I turned that four-minute short from when I was thirteen on video into my first full-length feature that I did after film school with Jordan Levinson—"

"I've heard of him!"

"Hasn't everyone?"

"In fact he's here tonight."

"Indeed he is. We both are. My first premiere, though, well before Jordan, was in my parents' living room with sheets on the windows and all my friends and the parents of the other kids who worked on the movie watching a videotape, and ultimately it was every bit as exciting as this right here. This is the greatest life for myself I could have imagined."

"A Sparta movie!"

"That's right."

"And what about Peter Compton before the end? I mean before everything that happened. Was his the life he imagined for himself."

"It's complicated, obviously. No one does this casually, or if they do, they're not going to last long. Wow. This is suddenly getting very serious for a press line. But my sense of Peter was . . . my sense of Peter . . . Yeah . . . We had this dinner early on down in Atlanta. This was before we started shooting. Some of the best food I've ever tasted. And we had an argument about the schedule that seemed very important then but of course is meaningless now. But what I realized that night was that, sure, we become adults, and we can even work on a huge scale where the stakes seem enormous, but basically it's like my premiere in middle school. I think this was especially true for Peter. Like everyone who does this, he could be a bit childish, and I want to be very careful here because I include myself. What I mean is that probably the most creative parts of myself, all of us—leaving aside that you have to manage those parts in a very grown-up way—are those that are the most naive and innocent. And that applies to audiences too. I mean think about it. When we're watching a movie we're ten years old again, spellbound in the dark, aren't we?"

"I guess we are."

"And the best films are made by people who are uninhibited like children. That was Peter. What happened to him was tragic, but a part of him was still a kid in some really great ways. And what's amazing about a night like tonight is that we get to see the best aspects of that. What's of course weird is that someday this movie, with all the special effects and even everything that's been accomplished and written about in terms of completing the project without Peter—"

"The use of AI."

"Yes. All that will seem quaint and old-fashioned years from now with whatever comes next. Anyway, I see that Marci is right behind me."

"Indeed she is!"

"Hi, Marci."

"Joel! Oh my God! You do realize you've just interviewed one of the best directors alive."

"Oh God, Marci, please."

"If his answers to our questions are any indication, I believe you."

"Did you see the movie?"

"No, I missed the screening this morning, but there's one tomorrow."

"Well, Joel really nailed it."

"That's incredibly kind of you. And it's Marci who nailed it. Without her support and, above all, wisdom, I never would have been able to direct this film."

"Joel, we really need to move on to your next—"

"Sorry. They're calling me away. And you're going to want to talk to Marci anyway. She's amazing."

"That's what I hear."

"I'll see you in there."

"Great. We're in the same row. I asked for that. Annie came, right?"

"Of course."

"So, Marci Levy. First of all, I love your dress."

"Oh! Thanks! My assistant, Samantha Blake—well, not my assistant anymore, actually. My partner—excuse me—*producing* partner. So Samantha's friend, and I promised I would say the name if I got asked, and you asked. Her friend Mako Yashiri designed this, and all the work is done here in LA at a resuscitated dress factory downtown with ethically sourced material, and it's not only beautiful, it is one of the most comfortable pieces I've ever worn."

"Amazing."

"I'm sorry. I'm a little hyped tonight. You just said you liked the dress and I—"

"No, it's fine. Who can blame you? So, Marci Levy, first of all, what's it like to be here, after all you put into this film, which you produced—"

"Not just me. Jeremy and Charisse and Max Kaiser and frankly all of the amazing team at Sparta."

"Of course. But what's it like for you right now, to be here, on this night, with this film?"

"Well, obviously it's mixed, because I wish Peter were with us. We used to do these press lines together, which is something he insisted on even though he was really the one everyone wanted to talk to."

"Is that really true?"

"Of course! Peter was incredible. But he was also the star. People don't see films for who produced them. And by the way, that's a good thing!"

"Why is that a good thing?"

"Oh God! We go to movies to see the characters and the story and the direction. The whole point is to hide all the work that went into it."

"What would you say to him if he were here right now?"

"Wow . . ."

"I'm sorry, if you don't—"

"No, I do. Just give me a . . . It's funny, because obviously I knew there'd be questions like that, and I was thinking about Peter all day, which of course I was, that never stops, but in a very specific way. He had an interesting attitude toward premieres because he grew up around them with his dad, who was an actor."

"Yes."

"And, no offense, but it was always easy to dismiss all this as kind of meaningless because it has so little to do with what we do. Making movies is messy, with, for most of us, fourteen- to sixteen-hour days where you're getting up—see this is why you don't want to be talking to the producer—"

"Please go on."

"Working over breakfast, working on the drive to set once there were cell phones, working all day and after wrap. Same with the crew when you count load in and load out. Often you're shooting at night and sleeping days, or you're on splits where you go in at three in the afternoon and leave at four or five in the morning. Life-and-death arguments about lines, and blocking, and wardrobe, and keeping on schedule, and do we really need this shot, and the boom's in the shot, and every other thing you can imagine. We love it or we wouldn't do it. You *have* to love it, but it's the opposite of all this."

"Meaning this is all bullshit?"

"Of course not!"

"Then maybe I'm not understanding."

"Peter actually loved premieres. He said we needed them, and of course, as you know, he was amazing on the press line. Did you ever interview him?"

"A few times."

"So you know. This was when he was at his best. It was like he needed the premiere for some sort of closure. 'Sure,' he would say, 'nothing could be further from the grind of production than the red carpet, but this is the celebration of the illusion, and what better way to do it than to estrange ourselves from any reminder of how hard it all was to get here? I think his only regret was that the crew wasn't celebrated along with the actors. Sort of the opposite of what I've been saying about producers!"

"Your husband loved the crew?"

"Oh my God, are you kidding me? I mean obviously he could have issues with certain people, the whole world learned that, but I promise you there was no actor I ever encountered who had more respect for what crew members did."

"Do you think he would be proud of this film?"

"Every aspect of it. The incredible story we're telling that does the Sparta Comic Galaxy proud, the special effects, the editing, the costumes, oh my God, the production design, the photography. Javier Benavidez couldn't be here tonight, but his cinematography is like nothing you've ever seen in a film like this. He manages to give his own signature look to what could have been like so many of these other films, which, nothing against them, but Javier just insisted we push the possibilities for this genre further, like something out of Bosch or Goya. The guys is incredible. A true intellectual."

"Beautiful."

"And then, of course, the acting. Ron, Jennifer, Victor, Rodney, Evie. All of them led by my husband, who put as much into this role as any he ever played."

"I heard he practically built a nuclear bomb in your basement."

"Hah! That got a little blown out of proportion."

"Not even a model?"

"Not that I know of. Suddenly I feel like we're in a Monty Python sketch."

"Perhaps it's my British accent."

"Perhaps."

"And finally, can you just talk about the challenges of finishing this film, which hadn't been fully shot, without your husband?"

"Yeah . . . well . . . obviously that was a decision we all had to make—as to whether we were going to move forward and how. But with me there was never any doubt. And to be clear, Sparta consulted me. They weren't going to finish Peter's performance without my blessing, which I was frankly more than eager to give. I wanted this for Peter."

"Is it what Peter would have wanted?"

"Well, of course . . . I mean, for his incarnation of Paul Kramer to have been honored in the way this film does?"

"Which, to be clear, is virtually unprecedented in movie history, where a performance was in part created by a computer."

"You can't look at it that way."

"Because?"

"The performance is Peter. The voice you hear, every word of it, is Peter. What the computer did was to assemble part of that—visual and sound images of my husband, my actual husband—into the rendering up on the screen in a few of the scenes. I look at it this way: it's never really Peter or any actor you're seeing up there anyway, but a two-dimensional representation of the performer captured by a digital sensor with all sorts of effects added with picture and sound. You can say that's still compiled from the actual Peter giving a performance, but I would say the computer did the same thing. There's not a frame up there that didn't originate with the actor. Any performance is ultimately a nuanced compilation, and what's amazing is that I defy anyone to watch this movie and identify one moment that doesn't come off as truly Peter's performance of Paul Kramer and Major Machina."

"Did you help in the editorial process?"

"I'm not sure what you mean. We all did."

"In terms of looking at the performance generated by the computer—"

"Again, you're misrepresenting what this really is. It's Peter's performance."

"What I mean is that in looking at your husband's performance, which must have been pretty startling, did you ever say, 'No, I don't believe Peter would have made that choice,' or the opposite, 'That's exactly what Peter would have done.'"

"It was a lot more of the latter, I can tell you. And when it was the former, it was more wanting to push the character in another direction than not believing it was him. And if anything, it was a bit strange that of course you weren't giving notes to an editor or actor. I guess that's when I missed Peter the most, because I wasn't getting to see what he was so great at, which was making adjustments. I used to watch him in the monitor do three or four takes, one after the other, each completely different from the last. A computer can't surprise you that way. And of course a computer can't go home with you at the end of the night and talk about the day, and sleep beside you and wake up and do it all over again, and come to a premiere like this and stand next to you and say, 'We did that.'"

"Do you see this film as a fitting testimony to your husband?"

"It's about a flawed superhero who saves the planet. My husband, like all of us, was certainly flawed. He never saved the planet, but to me he was a superhero."

"And we're sure you were something of a superhero to him."

"Well . . ."

"Good luck with this film, Marci."

"Thanks."

"God, I can't believe I said that to her."

"What?"

"'I'm sure you were a superhero to him.' So fucking stupid. Okay, who else have we got?"

"Well, we've done Jennifer. There's Ron Huston, but it looks like he's still finishing with *Variety*."

"Do you guys want Max Kaiser?"

"Of course we do."

"Just give us a sec."

"Is he—? Right away? Should we wait?"

"Yeah, he's just finishing up."

"Great."

"Have you interviewed Max before?"

"No, this is my first Sparta premiere. A bit of a shit show for all the money this must've cost. I've never seen so much security."

"Yeah, it's always like this, but the whole Peter Compton of it all . . . Definitely the most people since before COVID."

"Here he is."

"Max Kaiser. Six minutes."

"Hi, guys."

"Max Kaiser, the genius behind Sparta."

"Sparta is the genius behind Sparta. The comic book company started almost a century ago. Ultimately that inspires everything we do."

"Let's talk about that. This is the first *Major Machina* film. Why *Major Machina*, and why now?"

"Great question. When we decide what films to make and how to make them, whether they're an origin film, the first in a franchise, or a sequel, we're always insisting on relevance to the now, so in the current moment looking at our polarized country and world, riddled with conflict, whether actual or ideological. Just to put a point on it."

"I think you pretty much summed it up."

"It then becomes about determining what in our library or in our evolving storylines relates to that. *Major Machina*, a title personally very important to me, also has as much present relevance as just about any property of ours

I could name, and most of all the fusing of—as the title suggests—man and technology to fight for the good. What could be more timely?"

"Interesting."

"*Major Machina*, in a hopefully very entertaining way, explores how we need to set aside our differences in that context and come together to face a common enemy."

"Jellyfish."

"Well, sure, Jellyfish—that's the entertainment component—but in the original comic we were facing the threat of total world destruction in the Cold War. Jellyfish can be seen as silly and weird, and easily ridiculed for the name, but he was actually the perfect villain because he could exist in water or on land—not quite the nuclear triad, but close—and he could transform, a menace that could be anywhere and disguise himself in any way. The comics were written by extremely smart—brilliant, really—but also extremely funny guys who knew they needed to satisfy the brains of nerdy kids back then—boys like me, frankly. With Jellyfish, the writers McNaughton and Davies, and this is documented, challenged themselves with making the most ridiculous villain they could imagine also terrifying to readers. I think they succeeded. And now we make these movies for everyone, regardless of age, race, or gender."

"You spoke about technology, but what, if any, are the statements this film is trying to make?"

"Well, Paul Kramer is a guy managing his own issues—alcoholism, feelings of inadequacy and hopelessness—in a very shaky world. He's got a government that wants to rein him in, but also a love of humanity that overmatches the misanthropy he also possesses. Most say he's the most complex of all the Sparta heroes. Our world needs a force like that to help us overcome our own existential flaws. The wealth divide not just in our country but globally, climate change, the refugee crisis, the growing divides between great nations—the United States, China, Russia—drug use on the rise, I mean, obviously, right? Tribalism. Racism. I could go on and on. And all of this in the face of technological advancements that are revolutionizing every sector of global societies even while all the problems I just mentioned only get worse. Now I know our movies aren't considered high-end fare, but we're still serious about what we put out. Hopefully *Major Machina* will do its tiny part with its huge audience."

"Let's talk about Peter Compton."

"Great."

"I've heard you say there wasn't any other actor who could have played this role."

"Correct."

"And why is that?"

"Well, getting right to it, Peter had all the complexity of the character. It's what made him so compelling as a performer. We've seen him be a detective, a lawyer, a Frenchman in *Marseilles Madness*. Plus he played de Gaulle. He did a Brit in that E. M. Forster movie—"

"*The Other Side of the Hedge*."

"Right."

"But I think in a weird way Paul Kramer, as outlandish as this sounds given the fact that we're talking about a guy who's half machine, was the closest to the actual Peter in terms of inner conflict of anyone the actor ever embodied. What people are going to see in there tonight, with all the extremes of one of these movies, the exaggeration, the superhuman strength, is an actor truly exposing himself. Laugh at me, turn it into a meme, do what you want, but it's true, even though this is a popcorn movie filled with special effects and a bunch of stuff that isn't, quote, unquote, 'real.' It's still at its heart depicting a guy overcoming challenges within and without. He just happens to be saving humanity while doing so. And hell, what's better than that?"

"If Peter Compton were here right now, what would you say to him?"

"Jeez. Uhm . . . 'Peter, first of all, thank you. Not just for this movie but for everything. This night is for you. It's also for your fans, who are out in force. I mean, look at this! Really out in force! And the press . . . It's a line like I've never seen, and they're all here because of you. I guess you could call it mourning in a way, but I'd rather see it as a celebration. You didn't deserve what happened to you, not the disease of addiction, not the way your vulnerability to it ended your life. This movie is no substitute for you or the roles you'll never play, but at least we can be here in an iconic venue to watch your incredible talent as you literally carry this film on your shoulders. Because with all the effects and the defying the laws of physics and the heightened reality, there's a beautiful soul to this film, and that soul is you.' Sorry, I got a little emotional."

"Not at all."

"Okay, I've got to pull him away."

"No worries. I wouldn't want to ask him another question after what he just said."

"Thank you. What was your name again?"

"Astrid."

"Thanks, Astrid."

"God, can you believe all this?"

"What?"

"Everyone. I mean seriously. Peter Compton was a good actor, but he was a fucking dope fiend who was married and screwing some other woman and doing coke after hitting his wife in front of the entire planet. What is it about Americans that they need to turn him into some sort of tragic figure to worship?"

"Are you serious?"

"Absolutely. Honestly, why, and I'm sorry, but why is he even still in this movie?"

"He didn't know he was taking the drugs."

"He didn't know what was in the *pills*. He fucking knew he was taking the drugs, Reggie. And now look at all this. All these people, and everything about *him*."

"You were asking the questions."

"Because I have to. What about the million actors out there who don't do drugs and don't go to prison and slap their wives and then cheat on them who'd give anything to have one one-hundredth of what Peter Compton got? Fifteen, twenty million dollars a picture and ferried everywhere on private jets and in black cars and put up at five-star hotels, everyone treating you like a god."

"Maybe all that had something to do with it."

"Oh, piss off."

"What?"

"He was a selfish prick, not some great man, certainly not deserving of any of this. A handsome (okay), narcissistic actor who took all that was given to him and took a big shit on it. By the way, to the manor born as well, because he was not only given his good looks, but his dad was a legend in the business, so a guy basically handed all of it—"

"He played small parts early on. And his life wasn't easy. Jesus, maximum-security prison. Divorced."

"Divorced because he was doing coke and cheating on his first wife. News flash: he did it again! And are you serious? He struggled because he was doing 'smaller parts' in movies in his late teens and early twenties? Actors spend their whole lives trying to get what you're calling 'small parts.' I guarantee you he was making six figures even then and probably paying a publicist. What are you going to say now? That he did television?"

"Why are you getting so worked up? The guy died. I think he got his."

"Did you see all those people with the Peter shirts? It's going to be like Che. Or James Dean. But at least James Dean died in a car accident. Now that was tragic. Or Lady Di. That was tragic. Someone who, okay, she was a royal, but the Windsors treated her terribly, and she did some good in the world. Peter Compton was a completely different order of human being."

"Are you sure you're in the right business?"

"Trust me, if I could be in Moscow or Lebanon or Beijing right now I would be. Look, it's already emptying out. They'll finish with the pictures, pretending they all love each other; they'll go in and watch the film, lie about how great it is, go to the party and get hammered. Maybe we'll read about a DUI in the paper tomorrow. Or worse. By tomorrow morning all this rubbish will be cleaned up like it never happened. And this being America, people will become obsessed with the next undeserving idiot, while you and I and most of the rest of humanity were never even noticed."

THIRTY-FOUR

Javier arrived at the hospital just past 10:00 a.m. It gave him guilty comfort to learn his sister had not regained consciousness since he'd been with her the night before. The nurse, who reminded him vaguely of their mother, had ushered him to the door as visiting hours had long expired. Lucia had been asleep for half an hour anyway. It was hard to imagine this frail woman, down to ninety-one pounds at five foot four, had been so ferociously uncompromising. She'd stared down corruption, injustice, rampant inequity, an entire governing apparatus that had done all it could to silence her. They'd had her beaten, violated, even jailed for a time, but she wouldn't stop making films.

When PRI was finally voted out in 2000, ending seventy-one years of what Mario Vargas Llosa had described as the "perfect dictatorship," she hoped she could make movies unmolested during two comparatively liberated decades at the end of her life. But the government by and large had been replaced by cartels and kidnappers, murderers of any entity that dared oppose them. Four years before, when her husband was shot and nearly killed gassing up his car five blocks from their house in Polanco, she decided she was finished calling out those whose interests had come to embrace the psychotic.

"I won against the government in the end, but these people are a different entity, *mijo*."

Her last three films, documentaries (mostly what she'd made for the past decade), dealt with indigenous people in the south and the despoliation of their land. She'd worked with local directors, mostly women, who knew the region, traveling with them and their tiny crews to remote settlements where they lived among those they filmed. The works were sensitive, intimate, but also expansive in a way that got him thinking not simply about the subjects themselves but about all humanity, and the slow erosion of simple decency among the so-called civilized. It also struck him that the focus of her work had returned exclusively to her ideals when young: the plight of those disenfranchised by progress and power. Considering her work in this way, he became more and more convinced he'd not only wasted her tutelage, he'd participated against it, the entire misadventure with Sparta the culmination of that.

"Remember that evening we had on the back patio together after Dad died?" he asked her in the hospital room two days before she passed.

"I do."

"It was probably one of the most perfect evenings of my life. The smell of the bougainvillea, Dad's Priorat. Your face, which I wanted to photograph then and there. Where the fuck did my life go?"

"Which life is that, Javier? The one where you've shot nearly four dozen films, won every award? Live in a nice house in Santa Monica with a white gardener just to make a point?"

"You know what I'm saying."

"I don't, actually. Other than your usual whining about having everything you ever wanted."

"Maybe what we want is exactly what we shouldn't get. Once it was to have a photography business and live in a big house in Roma. You got me off my ass and saved my soul doing it."

"What's this about not going to the premiere of your own movie?"

"There's frames in there I didn't shoot or even oversee."

"But most of them you did."

"It might as well be video games at this point."

"You worked with some amazing actors. And from what you said, what's his name? The director?"

"Joel Slavkin."

"Joel Slavkin was pretty good."

"In the end."

"So because of some AI to keep the dead actor's lead performance? People complained at one time about zoom lenses, and about color, about sound even. *The Third Man* was cutting edge in its time. Now it's a relic."

"Oh my God. *The Third Man*. What are you even saying? If that were shot today, which it wouldn't be, you'd paint in set extensions instead of finding the right location, because if you went to the actual place you might not get a tax credit. And the studio would tell you to stop tilting the camera and ease up on the shadows. The biggest pain in the ass on that film was Orson Welles. No surprise. The actor."

"I like Sparta movies."

"No, you don't."

"You think if I could have produced one of those blockbusters I wouldn't have? Why not let audiences have their fun?"

"What happened to my sister? The one who once told me the profit motive was the end of all art?"

"I never once said that cinema was meant solely or even primarily as art. That's what was always coming out of your mouth."

"Then what is cinema?"

"Sometimes it can be art, but at a certain point it can't be. Seriously, *mijo*, in what reality does an artist go to a patron and tell him he needs a hundred million dollars to do his work? And by the way, the Medicis interfered too, and all the others who kept the greats in food and clothing. Same with the galleries who drop artists all the time, and the record labels, and the people who send the message by not buying the work."

"You never compromised."

"When I made the film that pissed off PRI and started all the trouble, I was being an agitator. So was my director and most of the crew. It wasn't art, it was subversion, and we all paid dearly for that, which I'd gladly do again. In fact, I wish I were twenty-five again right now. Moving images are the most powerful tool in the world. I'm not sure that's a good thing, but it's true. But when you add sound and music, forget it. And with technology, it's a game changer, because within seconds what you share can be everywhere. And at least until AI it was difficult to lie."

"Exactly my point."

"Except that movies have always been lies. Even my documentaries, which tell only the side of a story I choose to tell."

"The difference is that there have always been limits to your fabrication."

"Good for documentaries, but I'm not sure that's anything but a hindrance in fiction. The more real a Sparta movie can make some idiot in a cape fly through the sky the better, don't you think? And why wouldn't you want to be a part of that?"

"We're leaving Los Angeles."

"Where are you moving?"

"Argentina. Maybe Mexico."

"You'd come back here?"

"We've just elected a Jewish woman who's not PRI to be our president. There's a national abortion law. Trust me, I know everything that's still wrong here; I've watched every film you've made. But it's a lot better than what's going on to the north. Alma can paint anywhere and ship to her gallery, which would love the idea of telling their rich clients how the artist lives in South or Central America. Nothing would make her happier than to go back to speaking Spanish all day."

"Jesus, Javier."

"Don't worry about me."

"It's not that I worry about you, it's that I can't believe it."

"More importantly, what are you going to do?"

"What everyone does, *mijo*. I'm going to die."

Not forty hours later, that's precisely what she did.

He walked from the hospital to the store in Cuauhtémoc that had been there since he was a child and, to his astonishment, still had a selection of film cameras. He chose the Nikon F2 over the Pentax K1000 in spite of his sentimental connection to the latter's manufacturer. Once he could afford to, he'd switched over to Nikon for the better glass, and the F2 had been his favorite. Standing at the counter before an indifferent clerk, he opened the back, switched the speed to bulb, and pushed the shutter. The curtain opened with a snap and remained so until he depressed his forefinger, the black fabric snapping closed. He inspected it for wear and could perceive only a small wrinkle, which neither surprised nor troubled him. He advanced the same dial to 1000 and watched the operation once more, deciding the spring was true. He doubled the speed to

2000, this time listening with his ear pressed to the housing. He removed the lens—a Nikkor 35mm f/1.2—unscrewed the skylight filter, and put his eye to the curve of its surface. Whoever had owned the camera had cared for it: not a single scratch. He blasted the air can the clerk presented across the exposed element and restored the filter. He unlatched the lens from the camera and found the back element to be just as pristine. He twisted the aperture ring and clicked the iris clockwise, resting at every stop. He did the same with the focus ring, feeling for glitches and finding none before replacing the lens to the bayonet mount.

"Qué cuesta?" he asked. "Y voy a necessitar filma también. Seis rollos."

"Qué tipa?"

"HP5 si tienes, por favor."

Once the bill had been tallied and he'd paid with his card, he opened a canister of the Ilford HP5, set the ASA to 1600, and opened the back of the camera once more. It had been easily ten years since he'd handled film, and the smell of the silver halide, cellulose, and polyester returned him immediately to a boyhood intrepid with promise. He unspooled two inches and wound the narrowed end onto the receiver to the right, then cranked forward twice with two presses of the shutter at a sixtieth of a second until the film was advancing. He hinged the film door closed, advanced the roll twice more, and stepped outside into the light.

ACKNOWLEDGMENTS

This novel would not be without the friendship and generosity of the DP and director Guillermo Navarro, not only as inspiration, but for research as well. I also depend on early readers to keep me disciplined and clear; in this case, Amanda Seyfried, Ari Aster, the producers Kyana Davidson and Debbie Liebling, the playwright Keith Reddin, my great and abiding friend Daniel Rothenberg, my high school pal J.B. Bird, the legendary publicist Mara Buxbaum, the novelist Will Chancellor, my attorney Steve Breimer, my manager Amy Guenther, and of course my wife of thirty-one years Lisa Benavides-Nelson, who supports unconditionally whatever I choose to do creatively. I also thank my editor and publisher Chris Heiser of Unnamed Press, as well as the agent Byrd Leavell who introduced me to him.